The Tower

The Tower

by Gill James

The Red Telephone

British Library Cataloguing in Publication Data

A Record of this Publication is available from the British Library

ISBN 978-1-907335-29-7

This edition published 2013 by *The Red Telephone*
Manchester, England

All Red Telephone books are published on paper derived from sustainable resources.

Contents

Isolated

Forgetting Rozia

Day 170 Louish's News

Well, that was fascinating!

Louish was as dramatic as ever.

First off, she greets me in a bright royal blue tunic covered in glittery sequins. It was an incredible outfit. It had great pleats in the body of it and the sleeves as well. Mind you, it really suited her. And her make-up! I mean, I'm wearing make-up all the time now, but I try to do it so that it doesn't show. But Louish! Long curly eyelashes. Thick eye-liner. Bright blue eye shadow that matched her tunic. A huge beauty spot. And lipstick so red it almost looked as if her lips were bleeding.

Then there was all her prodding and poking – trying to get things out of me. So much so that I ended up telling as much about Julien as I dared.

"Well, my dear," she said. "You're looking well. Any sign of any new romance?"

At that point, I felt my cheeks burning.

"Ah, I see there is," she said. "Well, do not fear anything from me, sweetie. If that nutcase of a grandson of mine can't appreciate what is right in front of him, what's offered to him on a plate, well then he's even more of a fool that I thought."

She stroked my hair and then gave me a huge hug. I don't know why exactly, but that set me off. I couldn't hold back the tears. Was I still sad about Kaleem? Was I pleased she accepted the idea of Julien?

Maybe she defined it herself in the end.

She sighed. "I'm sure he's a fine young man, whoever he is," she said. "But he'll take you away from our family I expect."

The lunch was superb, of course. Louish is always so cheerful and she tells such funny stories. But as we had coffee afterwards she became deadly serious.

"I want to arrange a meeting," she said. "A secret meeting.

Between you and Razjosh."

I couldn't begin to imagine what Razjosh might want with me.

"Oh?" I said.

"Yes, he wants to discuss the whole switch-off thing with you. Making sure it becomes permanent."

"Ah," I replied. I couldn't think that that was going to be easy. He had just had such a narrow escape from switch-off himself. "What does Elder Frazier think?"

"He's all for it, my dear. In fact, he'll be at the meeting too," she replied. "You will agree to it, won't you?"

How could I not? Louish is such a well-meaning person. I nodded.

"Great!" she said, and beamed.

The rest of the afternoon was lovely. We went for a walk together. She told me all about what she and the other elders' attachments get up to. Despite this rather heavy task she's landed me with, it always does me good being with her. I really can't believe she's a grandmother and that her grandson is grown up.

"End and delete," said Kaleem. That was definitely the last time he would read Rozia's glog. Now that his grandmother knew about the new man in her life perhaps she would stop nagging him about getting back together with Rozia.

Rozia. She was obviously happy with Julien. That had been the plan. Leave her. Allow her to find someone else. There was no place for romance in the life of a Peace Child. He'd even told her that he approved, even made it sound as if he didn't care.

Yet still she was producing her glog in Wordtext. She was doing that for him, he knew. He doubted whether Julien could read Wordtext. And every time now that he read her glog, he just hoped that she still wanted to be with him. But she was with Julien now. Just as he had planned. No point hoping it was otherwise. What was the point, then, of her writing this glog in Wordtext? Was she trying to torment him? There was certainly no point in him reading it anymore.

He sighed. What was there to look forward to now, though?

The door to the apartment swished open. Kaleem tensed, hoping there would be just one set of footsteps and no voices.

"I'll get some coffee on the go," he heard Marijam say. "Then I'll go and get Kaleem."

"Great stuff," he heard Nazaret reply.

He could do without this. The sooner he got his own apartment, the better. It had been good at first, finding out that he had a father who was still alive. He actually liked Nazaret, for goodness sake, but he just couldn't feel comfortable when he and Marijam were together. He wasn't sure why. Perhaps it was because he'd lived for all those years with just his mother. Perhaps it was because Nazaret had abandoned him and Marijam. Or did it come down to Rozia again? After all, Nazaret hadn't had any choice in being taken from Terrestra. He hadn't known that Marijam was pregnant. Perhaps you could you say that what he'd done to Rozia was worse? Leaving her when she was so ill? Or was he jealous because Nazaret and Marijam had carried on being in love over all those years of separation; neither of them had found another partner. And Rozia had found Julien. In just a few weeks.

Then, even if he could argue himself out of all of those points, he and Nazaret were always awkward around each other. He longed to have the same easy relationship with his father as he had with his mother.

"Hey, sweetie," called Marijam, bouncing into Kaleem's room. "Your father's got something really exciting to tell you. Will you come and join us?" Her eyes were shining and her cheeks were glowing pink.

It was so good to see her so happy and full of fun these days. She had always been so serious when they lived on Terrestra in the cave apartment.

"I'll be in in a minute," said Kaleem. It was so stupid how he always had to brace himself to be in the same room as Nazaret.

"I'll call you when the coffee's ready," said Marijam, beaming.

That was why he kept on staying with them. His mother was

so happy having both of her men under the same roof. And it wouldn't, after all, be forever. At some point he would have to go off on another Peace Child mission.

He supposed he ought to check again on how Project Acorn was going. The dataserve whirred into life before he as much as made a voice command. He ought to be used to how the dataserves here seemed to read your mind. He'd spent enough time on Zandra, but it was still disturbing, not least of all because he couldn't work out how they did it.

Movie clips of the Supercraft in London Harbour and Zandra Dock 1 started loading and a voiceover began reading off numbers. Kaleem frowned. He would prefer this in Figurescript as he could read it. It would be quicker and he could just look up what he needed to know. He opened his mouth ready to give the command. The screen flickered and suddenly rows and rows of figures appeared.

I wish it wouldn't, thought Kaleem. *But this is better.*

He'd hardly had time to think than when the screen changed again.

"Receive message from Don Edmundson?" asked the machine. A static picture of Edmundson, the coordinator of Project Acorn, appeared on the screen.

What now? thought Kaleem. He sighed. He'd better speak to him he supposed.

Edmundson immediately went live.

"Good morning, Kaleem," said Edmundson. He was frowning as usual. "I need to arrange a meet with you. I take it you have no objections?"

He doesn't give anything away, thought Kaleem, looking carefully at Edmundson's face for any clue about what he might be thinking or feeling. It was expressionless apart from the frown.

Always the same neutral face.

"There isn't a problem, is there?" asked Kaleem.

"Hope not," said Edmundson. "Three tomorrow afternoon, Gengis Hall 231?"

"Yes, of course," said Kaleem. There was no point prodding

Edmundson. If it was something he could have said by a dataserve link he would have said it. There must be a really good reason why he wanted them to meet in person. Kaleem dreaded what that might be.

"Good," said Edmundson and the screen snapped back to the Figurescript pages.

"Coffee's ready," shouted Marijam from the lounge.

It just gets worse, thought Kaleem.

Marijam was pouring the coffee herself as he walked into the lounge. Even though she and Nazaret had every modern convenience including the state of the art house droid, Marijam often preferred to do her own catering. She beamed at Kaleem.

"Hi, Kaleem," said Nazaret, a little stiffly "would you like to come and see this?"

What did he want now, Kaleem wondered. He sat on the comfisessel next to Nazaret, who was looking at a small portable dataserve on the coffee table in front of them.

A movie clip started up. It showed some woodland with trees and all sorts of grasses and flowers growing under them. Kaleem supposed it was from Terrestra, but did notice that most of the trees were very young.

"These are young oak trees on one of the new Zandrian plantations," said a voiceover.

"And those flowers are all native to Terrestra except that little one there," said Nazaret, pointing at the screen.

The screen zoomed in at once to a small flower Kaleem had never seen before. It had papery ivory petals with delicate thread-like streaks of very pale pink and blue woven through them.

"The Zandrian ice-bell," explained Nazaret. "And those there-" He pointed to what Kaleem recognised as bluebells. "Are native to Terrestra, but only one variety is appearing. This is the one which has white pollen. The stronger one, the one which grows so viciously that it tends to take over, is not appearing at all. Then there are all the usual fungi and mosses – everything that you would expect to find in Terrestran woodland."

"How?" asked Kaleem. He did not feel quite so uncomfortable

with Nazaret when they were talking about things like this.

"A bit of a mystery," replied Nazaret. "We would expect a few spores and seeds to get mixed up with acorns. But why the type one bluebell exclusively? It would be more understandable if it were the type two, the hardier one. And the ice-bell is a real mystery. It is not one of those plants whose seeds lie dormant until the soil is turned. There were plenty of those around before the deforestation disaster. Why is it precisely this one that has come back and not the others?"

Nazaret was beaming now. Kaleem wished he could feel as enthusiastic about his father's work.

"Even more exciting," Nazaret continued. "All of the plant life has adapted extremely well to the Zandrian clock and season rotation. At any one time plants at all stages of their cycle are present."

"Come on you two," said Marijam. "Drink up your coffee before it gets cold. And you should tell him your most exciting news."

"Aha!" said Nazaret, taking a sip of his coffee. "Guess who is going to head up the research into all of this?" The man's eyes were positively shining. He looked like a child with a new toy.

For a moment Kaleem felt content. He could be proud of his father taking on such an important job. He could be happy that he was so happy. He did like the man for goodness sake. That was never the problem. He wasn't really sure exactly what was.

"That's great," he said.

"Isn't it?" said Marijam. She got up out of her seat and made her way over to Nazaret. She put her arms round his shoulders and planted a brief kiss on his cheek.

But Nazaret pulled her face back to his and kissed her full on the lips. He lingered a little too long for Kaleem's liking.

Oh for goodness sake. Why shouldn't a man kiss his attachment? Even if it was your father kissing your mother? *Get a grip, Kennedy-Bagarin,* thought Kaleem. *It's not as if they're about to have sex.*

He gulped his coffee down.

"I'd better get on," he mumbled, getting up to leave the room.

"Don't work too hard," called Marijam, pulling herself away from Nazaret, who seemed reluctant to let her go.

Kaleem sighed to himself as he made his way out of the room. He wished he didn't have to be like this.

Zandra

Gengis Hall 231 was just like any other meet venue that Kaleem had been in – either here on Zandra or on Terrestra. Boring, but particularly so when your meet partner was running late. Kaleem stared at the holoscene which showed through the window. At least it was convincing. You really felt as if you were looking at a view through a window, just like you might on Terrestra. It was storied from a real place: one of the infant forests, complete with bluebells, ice-bells and all the rest, one of the very forests that his father was working on.

He gets everywhere, thought Kaleem. He wished Edmundson would hurry up. He needed to find out what he wanted. He was beginning to imagine all sorts.

The dataserve whirred into life. Edmundson's face appeared on the screen.

"Listen, Kennedy," he said. "I'm going to be another fifteen minutes at least. Load the stuff about acorn and vaccine exchange. You tell me what those statistics mean."

"Of course," said Kaleem.

Edmundson was still not giving anything away.

The screen blanked over before Edmundson said goodbye. In fact, Kaleem supposed, he probably hadn't said goodbye. Edmundson never wasted time on superfluous words. Before he even thought about what he'd been asked to do, the screen suddenly started showing the Supercraft at London Harbour and Zandra Dock 1. He was now watching similar scenes to the ones he'd seen yesterday. He didn't bother, though, asking for the Figurescript version of the statistics this time. He was fairly certain that Edmundson couldn't read Figurescript.

It was quite mesmerising listening to the robotic voiceover. "Day 116 3520, acorns imported 7500, vaccine exported 5679. Viability in package from day 116 3519 96%. Vaccine to date 97% effective. Forecast for new needs, Day 118 3520, 17,000 acorns, 18,644 doses of vaccine. Forecast for reciprocal needs met Day 220 3527…"

Goodness, if I ever can't sleep, thought Kaleem, *I'll load some of this stuff up.*

It struck him as he watched the split screen picture of London Harbour and Zandra Dock 1 that although Zandrian droids and Supercraft were not quite the same, there was more the same about them than different. The Supercraft were more or less the same shape and had the entrances in exactly the same places, the droids were the same height and walked in the normal slightly stiff manner and the metal containers being loaded at either end were exactly the same size, colour and shape, but the Zandrian ones had a green cross on them to show that they held medication and the Terrestrans had green hexagons to show that they contained plant life.

"Do you see what's missing?" a voice behind him asked.

Kaleem jumped.

He turned to face Don Edmundson. The man was even scarier in the flesh than he was usually on screen. There was absolutely no expression on his face at all.

Kaleem shook his head. He just couldn't think with Edmundson staring at him like that.

"Doesn't it strike you as odd that there are no people around?"

Kaleem looked back at the screen. Well, there were people, but only very few. Most of the work was being done by the droids.

"I mean, getting on and off the Supercraft," said Edmundson.

"Forecast daily rate for this lunar period," the robotic voiceover droned on.

"Fine, we know," said Edmundson, looking pointedly at the dataserve screen.

The screen went blank immediately and the serve itself gave a final bleep.

Edmundson nodded to Kaleem that he should sit down and took one of the not-so comfisessels himself.

"Everything is going according to plan," said Edmundson, "as far as acorns and vaccine are concerned. But another part of the bargain was a greater connection between the people of Zandra and Terrestra. I don't see it happening."

"What do you mean exactly?" asked Kaleem.

"I mean that we need people, Terrestrans, to come to Zandra now. And we need to get Zandrians on Terrestra."

Yes. Of course. Kaleem had known that all along. In fact that had even been his excuse for coming here. Or that was what he had told everyone including his parents and his grandparents: he was here on a Peace Child mission. He had to oversee the first visits to Zandra from Terrestrans and then increase the number of visitors from Terrestra to Zandra. There had been just a few – himself, his mother and the small team that had come across on the first mission to Zandra in search of the vaccine against the Starlight Racer disease. If he was honest, though, he had really come here to get away from Rozia and everything associated with her.

"Well? said Edmundson. "Do you have any concrete plans yet?"

"No," said Kaleem. "You can imagine how carefully we have to tread with Terrestrans."

"I don't have to imagine," replied Edmundson quickly. "It's all too obvious. It was part of the original agreement that an exchange of persons as well as materials would actually take place. You and your mother are hardly enough. And besides, that is not an exchange: there are no Zandrians on Terrestra."

Kaleem knew he was absolutely right. He would have to do something and soon. He would probably have to ask Razjosh for ideas.

"I suggest," Edmundson continued, "a person exchange. Six people go from here to Terrestra, and meet with six Terrestran delegates. They travel back to Zandra with our people. Not too much to ask is it, just for a start?"

No, it wasn't. But Kaleem knew he would be pushed to find six. Maybe Pierre and Stuart. Razjosh was too old really and probably wouldn't count as he'd been before. Rozia, he knew, would come like a shot. He daren't ask her, though. He wouldn't be able to cope with her being there. Not now that she was with Julien. Abel and Kevik – but they were too busy in the Z Zone. Saratina maybe? But how would they react to her here? No, he shouldn't think like that.

"Well?" asked Edmundson.

"It sounds reasonable," said Kaleem. Reasonable but almost impossible.

"Good," said Edmundson. "I'll get Emmerline to show you the ideas we'd had."

Kaleem shuddered. Edmundson's secretary droid was famous. It was always difficult to remember that she wasn't a real woman. She was so life-like and always carried so much authority. But of course, not being human she never tired.

The door swished open and in she came. Only the slightest jerkiness in her movements and the data that started streaming across the screen as she moved into the room gave away that she was a droid and not a sexy young woman. She moved her hips as she walked and her long straight blond hair flowed behind her as she moved. She was connecting directly with the dataserve, though. Soon images flickered and flashed making Kaleem blink. So, she was a droid after all.

"Data download is now complete," said Emmerline. The voice was astoundingly human. No way was she a droid. Why was Edmundson the only one to have something as sophisticated as this? She tossed her sleek hair back and smiled at Kaleem and Edmundson.

"Talk him through it," said Edmundson.

"Yes, certainly. A delegation of about six persons should go to Terrestra. Kaleem should help decide who. They should have a diplomatic tour, stay in a good hotel but also have direct contact with Normal Zoners and of at least one in the newly integrating Z Zone. They should have ample opportunity to sample Terrestran food…"

"What would you know about that?" whispered Kaleem. Droids didn't need food – well at least not the same sort that humans needed.

"It's a most important part of human life," said Emmerline, staring at him. The pupils on her artificial eyes widened as if she was trying to take more of him in.

Great elders, she was scary. The scariest female that Kaleem had ever met... not that she was really female, he reminded himself. She was just a machine.

"Essential, in fact," continued Emmerline. "Fundamental. And also extremely puzzling why food is so much better here on Zandra than on Terrestra where you have better raw materials."

Kaleem had to concede that one. And he had no idea how they did it either.

"Naturally, we would also like to learn more about your diastics systems," continued Emmerline. "My searches reveal the following academics may be able to give advice."

Movie clips of Terrestran scientists showed for a few seconds each on the screen.

And to think all you need is microchips and some good programming, thought Kaleem.

"We would also like to arrange a discussion between the delegates and a committee made up of heads of service and elders. And yourself of course." She flashed Kaleem another smile. She flicked her hair out of her eyes and her pupils grew even larger as if she were flirting with him.

For a few seconds Kaleem was almost convinced that she really was human and that it was just some trick of Edmundson's and a female friend of his. Edmundson seemed to be finding it all extremely amusing.

"Show him the timetable," he said to the droid. It was clear he could hardly keep his face straight.

A chart immediately appeared on the data screen.

"These show the timings," said Emmerline. "Red is for food discussion, blue for investigation of scientific matters, yellow for social activities and purple for further negotiation of the peace."

Now Kaleem wanted to giggle. This was just too much. It was much too precise.

Edmundson suddenly looked stern.

"Stand-by," he ordered Emmerline. "You see, she really is a droid."

"No, no," said Kaleem. "I just found it all too neat and tidy. You can't do things that quickly."

"Hmm," said Edmundson. "But it ought to be a lot more focused than you're making it." He turned back to the droid. "Continue," he commanded. "Show Terrestrans on Zandra."

A movie clip loaded on to the screen. Kaleem gasped. There were Pierre, Stuart, Saratina, Rozia, Sandi Depra and Ben Alki. They were here, on Zandra, looking at one of the oak plantations. Of course, why hadn't he thought of those two?

"It's all right," said Edmundson. "She can read your mind."

"But I never thought of Ben Alki or Sandi Depra," Kaleem murmured.

"Good, isn't she?" continued Edmundson. "She can even read your subconscious mind." He was grinning.

Here we go, thought Kaleem. *Another mission impossible.*

The droid whispered something to Edmundson. The executive's face went pale.

"Really?" He said. He turned to Kaleem. "I'd get home as soon as possible if I were you. You don't want to be caught here with me with what might be about to happen." What was he talking about?

"Go on, I mean it," said Edmundson, his face now red. "Skedaddle."

Kaleem could see that he meant business. He set off home.

Imagining a Tower

Enmerkar looked steadily at the stranger.

"What did the King say he wanted?"

"He says he wants to discuss a plan for a new building, something very big. Perhaps the biggest he has ever planned," the messenger replied.

The man's clothes were covered in dust. He had obviously been riding a long time. In this heat as well.

"You must be tired and thirsty," said Enmerkar. "May I offer you some refreshment?"

The messenger nodded and bowed slightly.

"Mariam," called Enmerkar.

His sister arrived. Her eyes met his, she smiled briefly, bowed to the messenger and then lowered her eyes. Even with her head covered and even though her diamond-like eyes were no longer showing, she was more beautiful than any woman Enmerkar had ever met. No, he didn't have any improper thoughts about her. She was his sister and you just did not think that way about your sister. But it did make it difficult for him to take a wife himself. His sister was setting a high standard. Besides, he had to look after her until he had found a husband for her and she was married. That was proving difficult.

Enmerkar smiled to himself, though, as he watched the man's eyes grew round. His sister always had this effect. No man between here and Babylon was able to resist her. Despite his tiredness, this man, Enmerkar could see, was aroused.

"Fetch some wine, some olives and some of our best cheese," commanded Enmerkar. "And wear a full veil when you return," he whispered.

"She is betrothed?" asked the stranger after Mariam had left them.

Enmerkar sighed. "No, she is far too fussy. Much too grand to elect a mere messenger from the king."

The man blushed.

Enmerkar regretted what he had said straight away. He was not superior to this man. Yes, he was a master builder, like their father had been. They were a well-respected family and were quite wealthy now but they were after all just workers, servants almost. Someone from the king's court would actually be a very good match indeed for Mariam.

"Do you have any idea what he actually wants?" asked Enmerkar as he watched the man eat and drink.

"No, just that it is a big project," replied the man. "A little crazy perhaps."

"And there is no other builder who can do it?" asked Enmerkar.

The man shook his head. "He asked for you."

Enmerkar sighed. "Well, I guess we should set off at sunrise tomorrow. But I warn you, I shall have to bring my sister."

King Nimrod slowly paced up and down as he talked. He waved his long arms every time he spoke.

"It will have to be the grandest building ever made. It must be glorious. It must speak to God!" He turned to look at Enmerkar. "You will have your chance, my friend," he said, "to show off your fine building skills. To use your little baked bricks. It will be your moment of glory."

Enmerkar shuddered inside. The type of building project Nimrod seemed to be talking about would take years. He only had a few skilled men who knew how to make the bricks and how to slime them together. Even training up others would take months. And he daren't use unskilled workers.

And Nimrod was being so vague about exactly what he did want.

"Is there really no other builder you can use?" asked Enmerkar. But he already knew the answer. He was, after all, the master builder.

Nimrod stopped pacing. "I will even accept your sister as a wife for my youngest son," he said. "Without a dowry." Then he laughed. "Though with what I propose to pay you for this project you could give a handsome dowry for a dozen sisters."

That would be something, Enmerkar supposed. Get Mariam off his hands. Surely she would not object to marrying a prince? Even if it was not one of the heirs to the royal title. In fact, Nimrod's youngest son, Joshua, was far pleasanter than the twins, Hunor and Magor. He'd even seen Mariam talking to him and laughing – without her face veil, the hussy – so perhaps already something was there. Perhaps this young man could make her happy.

He would have to accept this challenge. The building was going to be difficult. At least his sister would be settled and maybe he too would have time to seek out a wife. Maybe a fine one, here at the court. And with the sum Nimrod was prepared to pay, he would never have to think about money again.

"Very well," he said. "But only if I have full control over the design, the choice of materials, the choice of workers and the pace at which the work is completed."

"Indeed, my friend," replied Nimrod and embraced Enmerkar.

The king was a tall, muscular man and immensely strong. Enmerkar could barely breathe as Nimrod squeezed him.

"Now let us send for our young relatives and let them know the good news," said the king, finally letting Enmerkar go.

It was even hotter here at the palace than at home. Enmerkar was finding it difficult to think straight. He dreaded baking the bricks for such a project. Would it be easier to have them made at home and transported here? It would be cooler there. A little at least.

Home. Ah! This would be his home now. For years. Yes, years, not months.

There was one consolation. Mariam had accepted Joshua as a husband with only a little protest. "Oh, but why not Magor or Hunor? Think, brother, your sister as a queen!" In the end, though, she'd settled for Joshua. And he'd been right; they were falling in love. He'd even caught them lying together and had had to play the angry brother – though not too much so, because he was dealing with the king's son. Secretly, though, he was pleased.

So, a wedding had to be planned too. The sooner the better perhaps, if that couple were to carry on being so promiscuous. A prince's bride should not be with child when she marries. Planning a wedding anyway was a welcome distraction from planning this impossible tower. And there was something further that was also occupying his mind: the friendship he was enjoying with Naomi, the king's niece. Could it be… would she be the one? She didn't excite him, hardly aroused him even, but she was certainly pretty enough. Good company, in fact. He presumed love would grow…

But now he must get back to the tower. If he made it 5433 cubits, if he made it taper… then surely the bricks at the bottom wouldn't collapse. He wanted it to be a sort of Ziggurat, Nimrod had said, but much bigger than normal. Just how many bricks would that need? How much clay would he have to find and how many men would he need to fetch the clay, shape the bricks and then put them together? He had some calculations to do now. He must not be distracted by the thoughts of weddings and of women.

Soon he was absorbed again in his mathematics. The base was going to have to be huge so that the tower could taper and still be useful at the top. No one had been able to tell him – not even the sages Nimrod had asked in for advice – just how high he would have to make the tower so that it would touch the sky. But if Nimrod really wanted a true Ziggurat… well the spiral pathway up the tower would be so wide that he would be able to place small lodgings at the sides… maybe even small fields for the animals. And of course, people walking to the top or travelling by ass would need places to rest and take some refreshment. It wouldn't just be a tower. It would be a whole city.

The noise of someone clearing their throat broke his concentration.

"And so how is it going, my fine friend?" asked Baltuus.

Enmerkar recognized the man he had dined with the night before. He was one of the sages who knew a lot about mathematics.

Enmerkar sighed. "It is going to take a lot of clay, a lot of fire to bake the bricks and a lot of men. And no end of time." He looked down at the notes he had made. "Seventeen years. And only then if I can find enough good men to train and if their training works."

Baltuus shook his head. "Why must he build the tower so high? What does he hope to gain by it?"

"He wants to show what man can achieve," replied Enmerkar.

"But why not just build a fine city?" asked Baltuus. "Won't that do just as well, be more useful, and in fact much easier to build?"

"He wants to stretch it to Heaven, so that even Yahweh will have to admire how great man is," replied Enmerkar.

Baltuus shook his head, as he examined Enmerkar's calculations. "That will never work, my friend."

"The bricks won't hold, you mean?" asked Enmerkar.

"No, no, no, not that," replied Baltuus. "Your calculations are correct. I'm talking about trying to impress Yahweh. Look around you. Look at the mountains and the seas. And the trees and the beasts. Now that is an impressive creation. Your tower is nothing in comparison.

"Now if you said that you were building the tower so that you could talk more easily with Yahweh, that might be a different matter," said Baltuus.

"It would make him angry," answered Enmerkar. He could just picture Nimrod's answer to that.

Baltuus nodded his head and tapped Enmerkar's shoulder. "Take care, my friend," he said. "You are right. This tower will cause anger."

Despite the heat, Enmerkar shivered.

Contacting Terrestra

Kaleem's journey home was entirely uneventful. He could not understand why Edmundson had got so agitated… unless it was something to do with that strange droid. He dreaded to think what that might be.

Marijam was out when Kaleem got back. Nazaret, however, was not. He could do without this, he really could. Yes, it was totally illogical but it was there: he was uncomfortable around his father, even though he actually liked the man and this was the very same father he wondered about for years before he eventually met him, seventeen years after he'd been born.

Nazaret was working at the communal dataserve in the lounge. Why did he have to be there? Why wasn't he working in his office downstairs?

"Mum gone out?" asked Kaleem.

"Yes, she had a meet," replied Nazaret. "We may have something to celebrate later. Looks as if they have the credits for the artificial photosynthesis project. If that goes ahead, we'll have this planet looking like Terrestra in no time."

"Oh, good," mumbled Kaleem.

"Just give me a couple of secs – ah here it is," Nazaret looked up from the dataserve and grinned at Kaleem. "This is all in Wordtext and I'm so slow at it. I need the expert help of my one and only son."

Kaleem cringed. He looked at the screen. Oh, it was easy to read, and not all that important. It was just about the expected success rate of farmed acorns' ability to germinate and produce oak trees. Well, they knew that already and Nazaret had taken it much further.

"Thanks," said Nazaret, after Kaleem had finished. "And how was your meet?"

Now we're getting to it, thought Kaleem. *You're just being nosey.*

He told Nazaret all that Edmundson had said and all about Emmerline.

"Ah yes," said Nazaret. "The famous Emmerline. Now I really would like to meet that droid one day."

No you wouldn't, thought Kaleem. *She's a tart and you're a married man. Married to my mum, in fact.*

"But you already knew that, didn't you?" Nazaret continued. "Don't you think it would be better to get some new people here? That bunch is already committed enough, don't you think? It's other Terrestrans who need to be educated."

"It's not what Edmundson said," replied Kaleem. "Look, I'd better get on."

"Don't work too hard," Nazaret called as Kaleem made his way to his room.

I wish he wouldn't interfere, thought Kaleem. Yet he knew Nazaret was right.

As soon as he walked through the doorway into his room the dataserve switched itself on. The machine was loading up before Kaleem could even think what he wanted to do.

"Communicate with Terrestra?" asked his own younger voice. He really must get that voice changed. And he really must find out a bit more about how these machines did it.

"Yes," replied Kaleem. "Razjosh Elder, please."

Within seconds Razjosh's face was filling the screen. Just two years ago that would never have happened. Zandra would not have been able to communicate with Terrestra that easily. *We must be doing something right after all,* thought Kaleem.

"Ah, Kaleem," said Razjosh. "Good to hear from you. Can I be of any help?"

Kaleem explained about the meet with Don Edmundson, about Emmerline's suggestions and about Nazaret's reaction.

"So, I think he might be right," said Kaleem. "Shouldn't it be Terrestrans who've never been here before who come here? And ones that need educating. Those friends of mine don't so much."

"Or would you consider that it might be too much in one go for most people? It may even be quite a lot for these friends of yours, despite their openness," said Razjosh. Then he smiled. "Though I expect Mz Sandi Depra will cope admirably. As actually, I suspect, will Saratina." Razjosh suddenly looked serious. "But Rozia. Rozia Laurence. How will that be for you?"

Kaleem wished the elder hadn't mentioned that. He couldn't bring himself to think too much about it. It would be just too painful having her here if they couldn't be together.

"Is she well enough to travel? How is she? Have you heard from her?" Razjosh continued.

"Yes, yes, she's fine now," replied Kaleem. "Fully recovered."

The elder's eyes lit up. "You're in touch?"

If only, thought Kaleem. "Not really," he mumbled. "I've been watching her, though." That sounded terrible. He felt himself blush. He tried to work out what Razjosh made of that but the elder's face was like stone. He was completely unreadable.

"Take care with her," he said. "And take care of yourself."

"So you think I should ask that delegation to come then?" asked Kaleem, changing the subject.

"I do. I do indeed," replied Razjosh. "There is one thing, though."

"Oh?" said Kaleem.

"You really shouldn't be relying on me for advice," said Razjosh. "I shouldn't be here now and goodness knows what might happen at any time. I can't imagine I've got that much time left."

Kaleem's mouth went dry and his heart began to pound. "There's nothing wrong is there?" he asked.

"No, no, no. Nothing specific." said Razjosh. "But I am getting on bit."

That was a relief.

"You do have your father there. You can talk to him. And there is also your grandfather. But," Razjosh sighed, "a Peace Child really does need to be able to keep his own counsel."

Kaleem couldn't think what to say.

"Come," said Razjosh. "Not so glum. I'll always be delighted to hear your news. And I won't be beyond offering a snippet or two of my collected wisdom, now and then, for what it's worth. But you can do it, you know. On your own. So, take care, Kaleem. Good bye."

"Good bye," whispered Kaleem as the screen went blank.

Well, I'd better get on with it, he thought. The easiest would be Sandi Depra. Definitely. Sandi's face appeared on the screen within seconds of Kaleem calling her up.

"Hey, Funny Head," she called. "How's it going?"

"Good," said Kaleem. What was she calling him funny head for? Her own today hair was frizzy and blond with thin pink strips of straight hair that had been wired to stand upright.

"So how may I help?" she asked.

Kaleem told her about Edmundson's suggestion.

"You mean I get a second chance to come to Zandra?" she said. "After I missed out the first time. Mind you, the Supercraft trip was good. Even the scary bits."

"You did get to Zandra eventually," said Kaleem.

"Yeah, after all the fun was over," replied Sandi. "You'd done it all by then. And we were only there for such a short time. This time we'd really matter. Count me in!"

It was good to see Sandi so enthusiastic about the project. Mind you, she always was enthusiastic. About everything. She never seemed all that serious really. It was difficult to work out how she had become head of health.

"Well that's good," said Kaleem. "One down, five to go."

"Yeah, Rozia," said Sandi. "That's a tough one. Do you think she'll come."

"Oh yes!" said Kaleem. Rozia would always do what was right – no matter how much pain it caused her. He didn't think he could bear it though, the pain of being so near to her and not being able to be with her, knowing that she now belonged to someone else.

"Hey, come on Funny Head, cheer up," said Sandi. "You'll do it. You know you can."

"If you say so," said Kaleem. He just didn't know how and he wished somebody could tell him.

"Way to go! We're off to Zandra!" cried Sandi. "Woo-ooh!" She twirled round on the spot and then turned back to grin at Kaleem. "Keep me informed, Peace Child babe! Tata for now."

Kaleem wished she had stayed a bit longer. She did always manage to cheer him up. In fact, he was having some difficulty stopping himself from laughing. He would have to calm down before he moved on to the others.

The others were remarkably easy to talk to as well in the end. None of them hesitated. Saratina was really excited though it was impossible to tell what she was saying.

"Om zanna? Eelee? M iarateena? On oopooraf? Es! Es!"

Kaleem guessed by the way she was clapping her hands and jumping up and down that the answer was yes. The vigorous nodding of the head was a further clue.

"I take it that means 'yes'?" he asked.

The jumping, clapping and nodding became even more vigorous.

"Ank oo aleey!" she said. Then the screen went blank. Ah! So the Z Zone wasn't quite up to speed yet.

Pierre LaFontaine was at a meet so his communicator was on standby. Kaleem had to talk to his partner Stuart Davidson instead.

"I'm sure Pierre would love to come to Zandra," he said. "He often talks about how envious he was of you when he knew you were leaving Terrestra. And of how he envies you being involved in all of this diplomatic work."

He's envious? thought Kaleem. *I'd swap him any day. Well, apart from having Stuart Davidson as a partner.*

"Well, what about you?" asked Pierre.

"Yeah," replied Stuart. "Yeah, I'd like to come."

"You have changed!" said Kaleem. *A bit different from your dad,* he thought.

"Yeah, well, you know, my dad had got it wrong," said Stuart Davidson. "He really thought it was right and it was better for everybody on Terrestra if we didn't mix with other people."

I guess he did, thought Kaleem.

"Do you know the funny thing is," Stuart continued, "it was actually reading Wordtext and some of the stuff I then read that made me start thinking a bit differently?"

Kaleem laughed. "Well, I'm glad I thought that punishment up for you," he said.

"Oh, yes, it was a punishment all right," replied Stuart. "Bloomin' hard work. But I'm glad I can do it now."

Stuart confirmed that he and Pierre would come and they would get in touch again soon.

Ben Alki Mazrouth was also enthusiastic.

"About time I did something useful," he said. "I haven't really up until now."

"Well, what about when you helped to stop Razjosh's switch-off?" said Kaleem.

"Well, that was me and a few others," said Ben Alki.

"Yes, but we couldn't have done it without you," said Kaleem.

Ben Alki shrugged. "I'd really like to do this," he said. "Not just because it would be exciting, going to another planet. I'd like to work with you – for you, if you like, all the time. The projects I've done so far have been pretty meaningless."

Kaleem couldn't believe what he'd just heard. Somebody actually wanted to work with him.

So, everybody was in agreement then. They would all come on this mission and perhaps more importantly would happily receive visitors from Zandra.

There was just one more communication he needed to make now. Rozia. That one he was dreading.

How could he ask her to come here? How could he even talk to her? He couldn't be comfortable around her, that he knew. What would it be like for her?

He was suddenly hit by a wave of memories. How he'd first met her. How they went into the Z Zone together. How good she'd been with the Adulkis. Then the terrible scene when she'd fallen unconscious. All those weeks when she'd been in that coma. And finally when he'd had to leave her. He didn't want to.

Of course he didn't. But it had been the right thing to do.

He'd followed her Glog all those months. He knew how it was for her now. She was with Julien now. She loved this new man as much as she had once loved him. In a different way but just as much.

Kaleem could not imagine himself being with anybody else. That at least was something he had in common with Nazaret. Now that he had found the one, there could be no other woman for him.

Obviously different for her. But that's what he'd wanted, wasn't it? That she should be happy with someone else. Well, it was one thing knowing that this was right. It was another entirely feeling okay about it.

Whatever the rights and wrongs about it all, how was he going to face her? How was he going to do it?

But do it he must.

He called up her sign.

The dataserve screen flickered. Then it went black. In fact all the lights went out in the apartment. An alarm started sounding. The whole building started to shake. The doors on cupboards flew open and objects on shelves fell to the ground. There was a low rumble all the time. Kaleem found it hard to keep his balance.

"We have to get out," shouted Nazaret.

Landquake

"It's a landquake!" shouted Nazaret. "We have to get into the safebox! It's a landquake."

"What?" asked Kaleem. What was a safebox? What was a landquake for that matter?

"This way, quick," called Nazaret. He was passing a laser key over what Kaleem had never even realised was a door.

"It's not working. Come on, come on!" He kept passing the key over the panel. "We've only got a few seconds."

The whole building shook again.

"Stand in the doorway, at least," called Nazaret. "Quick. The big one will happen in a minute."

Kaleem did as he was asked.

Nazaret continued to fiddle with the laser key.

The building carried on shaking and rumbling. Kaleem had heard about earthquakes on Terrestra but although they used to do a lot of damage, they wouldn't do now because the buildings were made so well. And there had not been one for over a thousand years. Since all of that activity in the early twenty-first century it had been relatively quiet. Even then, though, the quakes had only lasted a few seconds.

"Thank goodness," called Nazaret as a door sprang open. "Come on. Get in. Quick."

As soon as they were in the box and Nazaret had sealed the door the shaking and juddering stopped.

"What's going on?" asked Kaleem.

"It's a landquake," said Nazaret. "It hasn't happened for nearly two thousand years."

"So, what is a landquake?" asked Kaleem. "Is it like an earthquake on Terrestra?"

"Same effect, different cause," said Nazaret. "It isn't something happening underneath the planet's crust, like on Terrestra. It just happens up on the surface. It's sort of rippling caused by sudden changes in temperature."

"What causes that?" asked Kaleem.

"Sun spot activity, massive storms…" Nazaret went pale. "By Zandra, I hope it's not all the new plantations that have done it."

"It wouldn't be, would it?" said Kaleem.

"Who knows?" said Nazaret with a shrug.

The safebox suddenly started to vibrate.

"What's happening?" asked Kaleem.

"We're almost down," said Nazaret. "The box is preparing to land."

"How does this work, then?" said Kaleem.

"The box has very strong shields, sensors and stabilisers," replied Nazaret. "It finds its way through the falling debris and finds a place to land where no building can fall on it."

"So do all buildings have safe quake boxes?" asked Kaleem.

"Yes, they have to, by law," said Nazaret.

"Nobody ever told me," said Kaleem. Huh! Look well if he'd been in the house on his own.

"Well, it's more of a superstition now really," said Nazaret. "We'd begun to think it was never going to happen again."

"Box landed," said an electronic voice. "Doors opening in twenty seconds"

"Oh well, here goes," said Nazaret. "Let's hope your mother got out okay."

Kaleem and Nazaret stepped outside the safebox. Their building looked quite damaged but not destroyed. *I suppose they must build everything to resist landquakes,* thought Kaleem. There were several other safeboxes on the ground. Already builder droids were clearing the rubble. People were milling around looking dazed but not hurt.

Kaleem suddenly remembered Edmundson's panic. Had he known about the landquake coming? Was that why he'd told him to get home quickly? What would have happened if it had started on the way home?

Nazaret's personal communicator buzzed.

"Darling, thank goodness you're okay," Kaleem heard Nazaret say. There was a pause while Marijam said something. "Yes,

yes, he's fine. He was in the apartment and came down in the safebox with me." Another pause. "Yes, yes, you're right. And I need to find out how the plantations are." He turned to Kaleem. "Let's go and find a public dataserve centre."

They didn't have to go far. They found a centre with only a small queue. Kaleem held his breath as his father called up the plantation centre.

Nazaret went pale again. "No!" he gasped. He slumped in his comfisessel. His hands were shaking. Kaleem thought he was going to pass out.

Kaleem looked over his father's shoulder at the screen. Two thirds of the plantations had been destroyed.

The Babel Book

She felt tired. So tired. But it was pleasant here, dozing in the early morning sun. It would be so hot later on and they would turn the air conditioning on and it would get too cold and it would be too noisy. Really, she should get up now. It was the best part of the day. She'd promised Melissa, her only grandchild, that she would use the crayons they'd brought her to do a little picture of a teddy bear's picnic. It was for her birthday party invitations. She should really get up and do it. But she felt so peaceful and comfortable today. All of her aches and pains seemed to have gone.

Memories seemed to be drifting along like bonfire smoke on a summer's day. She remembered the day Rob proposed to her when a sudden storm forced them to have a picnic they'd planned on the lounge floor instead of at Primrose Hill. And she remembered the wedding, of course, and two days before that finding out that the tumour had gone for good. She'd never had another seizure after that. The dreams had stopped as well. She remembered when the twins were born. The day the millionth copy of the Babel book was sold. Janey's wedding. Melissa's birth.

A cloud drifted across the sun. She remembered Rob dying in her arms. He couldn't help himself though he had saved so many others. The ambulance arrived too late.

Rob. Dear Rob. She missed him so much but she was so glad they had been together so long. He had always been a lovely, lovely man. She thought she heard him call her name.

"Rob, darling," she whispered.

A bright light was shining. It was calling her. She knew she had to go towards it. She knew she would never do the sketch of the teddy bear's picnic. A pity she wouldn't be able to say goodbye. But it was better like this really. Better for everyone. She allowed herself to be pulled towards the light. She felt peaceful. Yes, it was the right time to go.

"These are what granny wanted you to have," said Janey. "Do

you know what they are?"

Melissa looked at the large brown trunk on the lounge floor. "Are they granny's pictures?" she asked.

"Yes, that's right," said Janey. Melissa seemed to understand more than Janey would have ever thought possible in a five-year-old. Should she have let her go to the funeral? Surely not. Five was just a bit too young, wasn't it?

"Can I play with them?" asked Melissa.

"I don't think you should play with them, darling," said Janey. "They might get spoilt. We'll look at them together and then put them away safely. When you're older you can decide exactly what to do with them."

Janey started taking the pictures out one by one and showing them to her daughter. She was really glad that Davina had decided to pass on all these sketches and book illustrations to Melissa. It saved the arguments between her and Julian. He would have wanted to auction them all off, clear all of his debts. There was no need. Davina had left them both plenty of money. Janey would have preferred just to keep these lovely memories of her mother. Maybe get one or two framed.

The phone rang. Janey went to answer it.

"Mummy, Mummy," cried Melissa. "Can I carry on looking at Granny's pictures?"

"Yes, but be careful," said Janey. She could keep an eye on Melissa easily while she spoke on the phone. It wouldn't hurt to let the child carry on looking. She was always so obedient. She had been told to be careful, so she would be. Janey knew she could trust her.

"Hi, Janey, it's Julia," said the voice on the other end of the phone.

Janey was always glad to hear from her mother's best friend. "How are you?" she asked.

"I'm good, I'm good," replied Julia. "But listen, I know what Davina intended for Melissa. And I think she should have Timmy's book as well."

"Oh Julia, no," said Janey. "That was Timmy's book." She

remembered when she and Julian used to play with Timmy before he became so ill.

"But Janey," said Julia, "Melissa's collection will be incomplete without the Babel book. She must have it."

"But it's Timmy's. Surely you want to keep it?"

"Now, listen," Julia continued, "Timmy would have wanted her to have the book, if he'd ever grown old enough to know her. She must have it."

"You're sure?" said Janey.

"Absolutely," replied Julia.

"That's really kind of you," replied Janey. She was vaguely aware that Melissa was systematically taking out the contents of the box and laying them all over the floor.

"Look, I expect you're still very busy," Julia continued. "I'll let you get on.

"We are, but a break would be good," said Janey. "Why don't you come for tea on Saturday and you can bring the book with you then?"

"That would be lovely," said Julia.

"Mummy, look," said Melissa. "This is my favourite."

Janey looked at the picture. It was one of the illustrations for the Babel book. Janey was pretty sure that it was the one Davina had told her the story about. It was a crude version of the final spread. This was where Davina had first experimented with the silver, blue and gold tones, on the day when she had at last remembered something of the dream that had haunted her.

"And this is my second favourite," said Melissa pointing to a similar crude version of the cover of the book.

Strange, thought Janey, that Melissa was looking at pictures for the very book that she and Julia had just been talking about. Oh, perhaps Melissa had understood what she and Julia had been saying. Even so, it still made her feel uncomfortable. Especially given the history of that book.

"What did Julia want?" asked Melissa after Janey had ended the call.

"She wants to give you the book that goes with these pictures," said Janey.

"Why has she got the book?" asked Melissa.

"Because Granny gave it to her little boy," said Janey.

"Doesn't he still want it?" asked Melissa.

"Timmy died before he grew up," said Janey.

"Oh," said Melissa. "That's sad."

"Yes, it's sad," said Janey. "Very sad."

Melissa looked thoughtful for a moment. "Mummy," she said, "will the book have the voices like in the picture?"

"The voices?" asked Janey. Then she noticed that Melissa had also taken out some discs and a disc player. The recordings of her mother's hypnotherapy sessions. What were they doing there? Could Melissa have found out how to play them?

"Have you been playing with these?" asked Janey.

"No, Mummy," said Melisa.

"What do you mean about voices?" asked Janey.

"The people in the picture, look," replied Melissa. "All saying funny things. Mummy, I can't understand what they're saying."

Janey shivered. She remembered Davina saying she could almost hear the voices of the people running away from the falling tower. She'd never got it herself though she really did love all of her mother's work.

Melissa suddenly ran over to her and buried her head in Janey's lap. "Mummy, they're frightening me," she said, beginning to cry.

"Come on, let's go and play in the garden," said Janey. She gathered everything back up into the box. She would hide it away somewhere until Melissa was much older.

Outreach

Devastation

"The transport systems will all be down," said Nazaret. "It will be a while before Marijam will back with us."

"How long will it be before they get it all up and running again?" asked Kaleem. At least they knew that Marijam was fine. But Kaleem worried that she would become anxious. She had never been quite the same since she had had that very peculiar version of the Starlight Racer disease.

"It won't be a priority," said Nazaret. "The droids have got to make the buildings safe, build temporary accommodation and secure the life support systems first. The transporters will be a low priority. Besides, they don't want people moving around too much." He frowned and bit his knuckles. "I hope by Zandra she'll cope."

Kaleem suddenly felt sorry for him. He knew how he would have worried about Rozia. Sure, he was anxious about his mother too, but it still wasn't the same as if it had been Rozia. "My mum's stronger than you'd think," he said. "She'll be fine. And the minicompus seem to be working okay. We can keep in touch."

Nazaret smiled. "I know," he said. He rubbed Kaleem's arm. "We'll just have to be patient."

There was nothing they could do except wait.

"Will it take long for them to secure the buildings?" asked Kaleem. It looked to him as if they had almost finished.

Nazaret shrugged. "Hard to tell," he said. "It's sometimes more complicated than it looks." His personal communicator suddenly beeped. Kaleem could tell by the way his face lit up that it was Marijam. "Great," he heard Nazaret say. "Amazing! So see you soon." He grinned at Kaleem. "She's coming back on an executive emergency transporter. She's with some bigwig who needs to get near to the plantations. They're picking us up on the way. Our temporary accommodation is already sorted – right next to the plantations – or what's left of them."

But Nazaret was grinning. Kaleem was beginning to be impressed. The man's hard work of the last few weeks was shattered. Yet he was grinning. So, Marijam was more important to him than his work.

Then it hit him. This was great for Nazaret, but it was not going to happen to him. Probably ever again. What he'd had with Rozia had been so fantastic. It could never be the same with anyone else. And he wasn't allowed that because he was the Peace Child. Why did he have to be the Peace Child?

Ten minutes later the transporter arrived. Marijam stepped out. Her face was flushed with excitement. "Come on you two," she called. "There's no time to hang around."

Kaleem and Nazaret climbed into the transporter. It was one of the elegant ones reserved for Zandrian executives.

"How does it get its power if most of the power lines are shut off?" Kaleem whispered to Nazaret.

"They can always find a way for important people," said Nazaret. "You know how these things work."

Oh yes, he did, only too well and he hated it. It was embarrassing being treated like a VIP all the time. He felt so ordinary.

"Hold tight, everyone," said a navigator droid. "This will be a bumpy ride. We can't go on autopilot. We have to negotiate the debris on manual."

"How long until we get to the temporary accommodation?" asked Nazaret.

"We have to go slowly, sir," replied the droid. "Estimated journey time: two hours."

Normally it would have taken just forty minutes to reach the plantations.

"I should introduce you," said Marijam, blushing. "This is my attachment, Nazaret Bagarin, and our son, Kaleem Malkendy. Executive Raymond, Head of Emergency Planning."

"I'm so very pleased to meet you," said Executive Raymond, offering first Nazaret and then Kaleem the Zandrian handshake. "It was so fortunate that Marijam and I were in the same meet. We would have wanted to find you two anyway. This just made it quicker. I'd introduce you to my daughter, Ella, as well, but I daren't wake her."

He pointed vaguely towards what Kaleem had assumed had been a supply of blankets and covers. As he looked closer, he could see that it was a person sleeping. She was covered completely.

"She's been awake for over forty-eight hours," said Executive Raymond. "She and her team have been working to prevent the landquake. In the end they couldn't stop it completely. But they did manage to lessen its impact considerably. The big worry, though, was that the safe boxes might not work after all this time. It's technology that hasn't even been tested recently – landquakes haven't happened for so long."

So there had been some warning then. Kaleem guessed that Edmundson had known.

"Well, I'm so glad you two got out all right," said Marijam hugging Kaleem and Nazaret.

"And you," said Nazaret, kissing the top of Marijam's head. Kaleem shuddered.

"What about your… I mean, is Ella's mother your…" Nazaret mumbled.

"My attachment, Elvira, is safe on another planet at the moment, thank you," said Executive Raymond. "Though we've not been able to communicate with her yet. Unfortunately interplanetary communications aren't working at the moment. And yes, she is Ella's mother."

No one seemed to know what else to say. Kaleem resigned himself to looking out of the window. This journey reminded him a bit of travelling by Z Zone kartje. The Zandrian transporters did have a hover function, though normally they did not need to use them as they travelled mainly along pre-determined routes which went in a straight line. Actually, the ride was not as smooth as in a kartje. It was far clunkier. You couldn't make this type of transporter dance like you could a kartje. But the way it went up and down and from side to side was quite similar. He could see through the windows that the landquake had done a fair amount of damage to the buildings. It was mainly superficial, though. The structure of them seemed still quite firm. The droids were clearing up amazingly quickly and all of the safe boxes seemed to have worked well. There were no signs of any people who were badly injured, though some seemed to have cuts and bruises and some people looked quite dazed. Kaleem guessed it was the shock.

"Why do we have to go into temporary accommodation," he asked, "if they're repairing everything so quickly?"

"Because of the aftershocks," replied Raymond. "They can go on for over a month. They can be quite strong, and with buildings already weakened… Anyway, the droids are just making safe at the moment. All buildings will also have to be reinforced."

"So, what will the temporary accommodation be like?" asked Marijam.

Kaleem smiled to himself. Since he and his mother had been able to give up living on their cave apartment on Terrestra and Nazaret had installed them in a luxurious flat on Zandra she seemed unwilling to give up her comforts. He didn't blame her really. Her life since she left the Normal Zones on Terrestra until now that she had found Nazaret again had been really harsh.

"Oh, it will all be quite comfortable, even if the units are a little ugly," Raymond explained. "You'll be living in safe boxes that have full infrastructure. They're ideal for one person or for two attached people sharing. They'll be up and running by the time we get there."

It went quiet again in the transporter. Executive Raymond must still be worrying about his attachment and all of them even the droid seemed to want to keep quiet so that Ella could sleep. Kaleem also sensed a tension in Nazaret. Soon he would see at first hand the devastation that the quake had caused to the oak tree plantations. Marijam rubbed his arm, but Nazaret just stared ahead and frowned. Now that he knew she was fine he could worry about his trees.

At last the transporter stopped.

"Leave Mz Ella to sleep," Executive Raymond said to the

droid. “She’ll wake when she’s ready.”

Nazaret stared ahead as they were shown to their safe boxes. He seemed to be avoiding looking to the left and right where you could see nothing but fallen oak trees. Marijam seemed to be supporting him. Kaleem could not think what to say.

His safe box was a garish yellow inside. He supposed he’d eventually get used to the colour. Marijam and Nazaret had been shown to a pleasanter pale blue one. Executive Raymond had taken a neutral grey.

“I expect Ella will like that red one,” he’d said. He’d given Kaleem a strange look. The one he’d chosen for Ella was just a few metres away from Kaleem’s. “We can’t put you in with your parents,” he explained to Kaleem. “Units will only hold two adults and two small children. But we won’t force single people to share either.”

You don’t need to worry, thought Kaleem. *I’m not ready for anything like that yet.*

Once inside his own unit he had a good look round. Yes, it was quite comfortable. The space was a little small, but he had a fully functioning bathroom and Zandrian kitchen with food delivery drawer. The air control seemed to work well and there was a full dataserve system. He could even choose from a small range of holoscenes for an outside view. The real window anyway was tiny so this was a welcome addition. There was even a small wardrobe full of clean Zandrian tunics and underwear. The dataserve switched itself on and explained how the safe box unit worked, how food would be delivered, what he should do about laundry, how they would be kept informed about new developments and how they would know when it was safe to return to their real home. It would do, he guessed. Comfortable, but small.

The communicator buzzed.

“Visual,” he commanded.

It was Nazaret. “Will you come with me to take a look at the damage?” he asked.

He’d been dreading this. But he guessed he should give his

father some support.

"I'll be right out," he answered.

They walked in silence towards the main entrance to the plantations. Kaleem could not see a single oak tree still standing. One of the plantation workers joined them. He introduced himself as Tom Davis.

"Is it all like this?" asked Nazaret.

"It's worse here and around the other edges," replied Tom who Kaleem guessed was about the same age as himself. He seemed to know a lot about the work and he was amazingly calm.

Nazaret was looking very pale.

"Do we have any idea of how many trees are destroyed?" asked Nazaret.

"Well, it's difficult to tell how many have been destroyed exactly," said Tom, "because we think some of those that have fallen may be saved. But about seventy-five percent have been toppled."

"It'll depend on how healthy the roots are and whether they can be persuaded to take again," said Nazaret. "And on what the aftershocks do."

He bent down and looked at one of the fallen trees.

"Well, at least the acorns can be harvested from this one," said Nazaret to Tom. "But its roots will never work again."

"How can we decide?" asked Tom.

Nazaret looked up. "I'll need to instruct all the plantation workers on what to look for. We need to make some movie clips. And I'll need about ten workers to help me."

"I can get that arranged," said Tom. "It'll take me about an hour. Would you like some tea while you wait?"

Nazaret accepted. The tea did seem to do him some good. The colour gradually came back into his cheeks. "Will you stay and help?" he asked Kaleem. "It'll be quite hard physical work."

You obviously don't know what I got up to in the Z Zone, thought Kaleem. "I don't mind," he said.

An hour later, he, Nazaret, Tom and ten other plantation workers were moving tree trunks, sampling acorns, uncovering roots and it was all being filmed by droids.

"If they look like this," Nazaret said, pointing to one set of roots, "the tree is unsalvageable. Whereas these might take," he added, pointing to another. "And ones like these we should be able to replant."

Six hours later, they had filmed every condition of tree root and acorn that Nazaret wanted the workers to identify.

"How long will it take before we know the full extent of the damage, sir?" asked Tom.

"I think with everyone working full out – I include myself in that and I am sure Kaleem will join me too, maybe even Marijam, – it should take about three days," said Nazaret. "Then the real work will begin. But I think we'll call it a day now. Everybody needs to get some rest so that we can start bright and early tomorrow."

He and Kaleem walked together towards their safe boxes. The other workers were living in large communal ones a little further away in the other direction.

"You know," said Nazaret. "I think it would actually be easier to plough the lot in and start again. But I don't suppose Terrestra will be willing to increase the supply of acorns, do you?"

"I don't know," said Kaleem. But it was becoming clear to him that Donaldson had been right. They had to make the links between Zandra and Terrestra stronger. He would have to do something soon.

They arrived at Nazaret's safe box. "Will you come and dine with me and your mother?" he asked.

Kaleem shook his head. "I just want to eat quickly and get a good hot shower and then some sleep," he said.

Nazaret laughed. "I don't blame you," he said. He patted Kaleem's shoulder. "Get some rest," he said. "And thanks for your help today."

Kaleem nodded. Nazaret went into the blue box. Kaleem turned and made his way to his yellow home. He noticed that the doorway to the red box was open and light was streaming out.

"Ah, the Peace Child," said a voice in the dark.

The outside light snapped on. And there she was. Ella Raymond. Looking glorious in the artificial light.

Kaleem was sure he had never seen such a stunningly beautiful woman before.

Ella

"Peace Child boy?" cried Ella. "I can't believe I'm living right next to the famous Kaleem Malkendy Bagarin Kennedy."

She seemed to shimmer in the light. All Kaleem's feelings of tiredness were disappearing fast. She was wearing just a short blue tunic. Her bare legs were long and astonishingly graceful. She had beautiful sleek blond hair and blue eyes that shone like sapphires.

"Oh oops," she said, looking down at her legs. "I should be better dressed." She grabbed a shawl from inside the safe box wardrobe and tied it round her waist so that it formed a long skirt that now covered most of her legs. "Only I think there's something wrong with my air control. I cooked pasta – rather I called up pasta – and it's delivered too much and it's made the place too hot. You're not hungry are you?"

Kaleem realised that he was starving. He also realised that not only was this woman absolutely gorgeous but that she had a good sense of humour as well. But did he really want to get into this?

"I'm a bit mucky," he said.

"Well, go and have a shower first," she said. "I'm sure this will keep hot. For ages yet."

It wouldn't hurt, he supposed. It would even save him the bother of getting some food. She sounded as if she was going to be good company anyway. As he showered, he found himself whistling.

Watch it, he said to himself. Oh, what the heck. Even if she was an astoundingly beautiful girl, he was only going to eat pasta with her. He didn't have to get involved with her. And he didn't have to worry about being faithful to Rozia. There was no him and Rozia. There would never be him and anyone else. And he couldn't hurt Rozia because Rozia was now with Julien. It wouldn't hurt. No, it couldn't hurt.

When he returned to Ella's box twenty minutes later, she was fully clothed in a silky blue tunic with matching leggings. She had wound a scarf into her hair and scraped it up from her neck. Kaleem had a strong feeling that he would like to kiss the back of her neck.

Stop it, he told himself. *You haven't got time for that sort of thing.*

"There," she said, placing two bowls of piping hot pasta in a prawn sauce in front of him. "I told you the unit's gone bananas. There's enough here for a whole family."

She was right. But he was hungry. He managed to eat his entire portion and half of hers. He noticed she only played with her food. But she talked a lot and didn't seem to expect him to say much. That he found relaxing. She told him all about her work on land control and how normally it was deadly boring but that it had certainly been interesting in the last few days.

"More frega?" she said after he'd drained his first glass.

He was now beginning to feel extremely relaxed. Another glass would be good. He nodded. "Where did you manage to get something as good as this at a time like this?" he asked.

"Oh, it's very useful having my father around," she said. "He's always prepared for an emergency."

He didn't want to drink this too quickly. It just all felt too comfortable. He began to realise he was beginning to feel very cosy. This girl was so easy going and she was certainly very attractive. Better slow down. He went to put the frega glass down on the small table. He could hardly stretch his arm out. He tried to suppress a groan. He didn't quite manage it.

"You are going to be so stiff in the morning," Ella said. "You must let me give you a massage."

I don't know about in the morning, thought Kaleem. He knew that Ella was not going to take no for an answer. And anyway, it would be good to feel gentle hands all over his body. Maybe it might feel a bit too good. It could get embarrassing. On the other hand, the thought of this beautiful young woman touching his aching body was irresistible.

"Come on," she said. "Into the bedroom." She grabbed his hand and pulled him along. "And strip. Well, you can keep your underpants on if you insist. Now, I just need to get some bits and pieces from the bathroom. When I get back I expect to see you undressed, lying face down on the bed."

That he could manage. Goodness knows what would happen when she touched him though. He undressed quickly.

Then seconds later she was back and the massage began. Oh, it was good. Incredibly good. She certainly had a skilled touch. And it was a massage rather than anything else.

"Is this good for you?" she asked.

"It's wonderful," he murmured. "Don't stop."

"I won't," she said.

She was suddenly straddling his back, her knees either side of his buttocks. He gasped when he realised that she was also naked. She stroked the inside of his thigh.

"Don't," he murmured.

"It's all right," she whispered. "I won't let anything nasty happen to you."

It's not anything nasty I'm worried about, thought Kaleem. He was slipping out of control.

"Well, do you like this?" she said, stroking his back and unsettling him again. "And this," she said, as she slid her hand along his thigh, and kissed him lightly on the shoulder.

She was hard to resist. It had been quite a long time.

"Yes," he whispered.

His throat was dry. He thought fleetingly of Rozia and felt a tiny slither of guilt. But this was now and that episode was over.

He gave in. He turned to face her, pulling her to him and pressing his lips to hers. Soon there was nothing in the world except him and this beautiful girl, and the gentle touch of her and her perfume, and then his excitement, and hers, and her seeming to control both of them, and then a great crescendo and the tension of months falling away and all the time being nowhere but precisely where and when he was then.

He felt good afterwards. In a sort of athletic way, like he did after a good jogging outing, though, but not full of the tender feelings he had always had with Rozia. It had been good to be so lost in that one moment and to forget the problems after the landquake and the worry about the visit he had to arrange to Terrestra. He felt physically tired now, in a really pleasant way, and mentally energised. And it was so pleasant lying next to such a beautiful young woman.

"Was that okay?" asked Ella.

"Great," said Kaleem.

She patted his shoulder. "Good. We'll have to do that again sometime," she said, "but now I'm kicking you out." She slid out of bed and wrapped a scarf around her, covering most of her body.

Kaleem stood up as well and started getting dressed.

She turned her back on him and started brushing her hair, looking at herself in the mirror. There was something very graceful about the way she moved. Her bare shoulders were very enticing. He began to feel aroused again.

"Look," she said, turning to face him. "I want to keep this casual. No strings. Nor romance." She grinned. "But – as often as you like."

"Fine," said Kaleem. He blushed. It was fine, actually. He probably needed that. And by all the elders, it had been great.

"I learnt all of that when I was on Eros," she explained.

Eros, of course. How appropriate.

"Anyway, sleep well," she said as he left her safebox.

He would. He really felt very good about this. What she'd suggested really suited him.

"You too," he replied.

She blew him a kiss and then closed the door.

As he walked back to his own safebox, Kaleem suddenly wondered how easy it would be to get black Tulpen after a landquake.

Adulkis in the Park

Thoma passed the daisy chain he had been making to Kaleem.

"Thank you," said Kaleem. He bent down so that the Adulki could slip the fragile necklace over his head.

"Can we go to the tower?" asked the little man.

"Of course," said Kaleem. He stood up and brushed the grass from his Z Zone tunic. He didn't resist this time as Thoma slipped his hand into his. He suddenly felt easier around the Adulkis.

For once the Adulki walked quite slowly. Kaleem was grateful that he didn't gambol along as normal. Adulkis normally had no regard for their own safety.

The tower caught the late afternoon sunlight and looked as if it was made of gold. The other Adulkis got up off the grass and walked quite calmly over to Kaleem and Thoma as they got nearer to the tower.

As they got very close to it, the door opened. A young woman stepped outside. Kaleem's heart skipped a beat as he recognised her. Rozia!

She beckoned to them and smiled slowly at Kaleem. She smelt of the gentle perfume she always seemed to wear though he'd never seen her use it. He wanted to reach out and touch her.

"Welcome, Thoma! Welcome, Kaleem," she said, and turned to go into the tower. They followed her.

The other Adulkis filed in behind. "It's time to write," she said. She handed him the quill pen and pointed to the book, which seemed even bigger than ever before.

Kaleem took the quill and dipped it into the ink. He didn't know what he was going to write but he knew that as soon as the pen touched the page he would know exactly what to do. Not that he would have any chance, because before he really got started the tower would begin to crumble.

This time, it didn't though. It seemed as if time was suspended. His hand remained poised in the air. Rozia was staring at him.

Moods flitted though her eyes – pleasure, hope, concern, alarm and then horror.

He could not see the Adulkis but he could feel them looking at him and he knew that although he'd felt comfortable with them a short while before, there would now be that question in their eyes again. The question that he could never answer.

Thoma nudged him. "Kaleem, you've got to write," he said. "You've got to write. Kaleem. Come on. Kaleem. Kaleem, you've got to write." The Adulki was shaking him quite violently. "Kaleem! Kaleem!" he screeched.

Kaleem woke up. So, the dream had been different again. It had actually started off quite well. But then the usual not knowing and panic, and the feeling that he had let everybody down. Still, there had been a pleasant edge of something this time.

Rozia. He had dreamt of Rozia.

Not, not that. That would be a painful reminder.

He suddenly remembered Ella. He remembered the perfume of her and how good it had felt as her hands had explored his body.

How would that work out? He wasn't sure about having a relationship that was only about sex. But it seemed uncomplicated and could be fun. And he felt good physically.

"Kaleem! Kaleem!" he heard again.

He realised it was his father's voice. It was coming from the dataserve.

"Kaleem, get dressed quickly and come over to us."

Building a Tower

Enmerkar ached all over. And he was missing Naomi. She had been out visiting her nephew – their nephew. He had been born just two days before – a son for Mariam and Joshua. It had been a great relief when the princess became pregnant. She had given birth to a still born child a little less than nine months after her marriage and then had failed to conceive again for a long time. Enmerkar had worried that there were then problems between the two young people. Perhaps she was refusing to share her bed with her husband? He had heard that women could be like that sometimes after childbirth. She had had a long labour and a lot of pain only to produce a dead child. Enmerkar presumed that the pain and the still birth were punishments from Yahweh because Mariam and Joshua had lain together before they were married.

Now, though, two years on, all was well again. Mariam seemed to become even more beautiful as her pregnancy started. She and Joshua seemed more in love than ever. Enmerkar liked his brother-in-law. He knew he would take good care of Mariam. Perhaps the problems they'd seemed to have earlier were just because of the great sadness they'd felt at the loss of a child.

He'd been right about Naomi, too. Love had grown. They'd married just half a year after Mariam and Joshua. He loved her now. And just one gentle touch from her smooth hand was enough to arouse him. They made love frequently. He needed that so much as a contrast to the hard work and the worry involved in building the tower.

He wished she'd hurry home. He could, of course, take his bath now, but he longed for her help. It wouldn't be the same without her gentle touch. It would probably lead to love-making, then they would sit and eat on their pretty terrace, and the wine would relax him and make him want her again.

But in the meantime, he must look to his accounts and send out orders for more supplies and worry about how he could find all the materials and men he needed. Weary work, but it must be done. And best to do as much of it now as he could before she got back and he became distracted.

She did come back at last. Enmerkar was almost asleep, his head drooping over his scrolls.

Naomi burst into his study, her eyes shining.

"Oh, he is so grand, your little nephew," she said. "He has all of his toes and all of his fingers. And he has Mariam's eyes – no, maybe even your eyes. And he is handsome like his father and beautiful like his mother. And he looks at you as if he has the whole wisdom of the world in his heart. Oh, he is so lovely. You must meet him soon."

Enmerkar smiled. "I shall, very soon," he said. He pulled his wife into an embrace. His lips found hers and he kissed her hard, wanting her, wanting her oh, so much.

She returned his kiss, but then suddenly pulled away from him and turned her back to him.

"I'm sorry," said Enmerkar. "I'm filthy… but I didn't want to bathe… until…"

"It's not that," said Naomi, turning to face him. There were tears in her eyes. "It's just that I'm so…" She couldn't finish her sentence. The tears began to stream down her face.

Enmerkar took her back into his arms. He held her tightly and stroked her hair.

"It will happen for us, too," he said. Surely it would. Normally the problem was the opposite. Babies came all too easily. Not surprising, with how excited he felt now, just enjoying holding her so closely.

Then he remembered the conversation he'd had two years ago with the sage. Could Yahweh be angry with him for trying to build a tower to show off how great was man? Was this the cause of their childlessness? Suddenly, all his desire disappeared.

The last cartload of bricks arrived. It would take the men just two hours to use those up and then they would have to stop working. Oh, they wouldn't complain. They'd be only too pleased to finish early in this heat, especially as the king had agreed to pay them anyway, even if they were held up for a couple of weeks. But if the Westlands did not agree to supply more of the clay, the men would be off work for weeks and the progress of the tower seriously held up.

Enmerkar looked down at what he had achieved so far. It had taken almost the whole of the first year to get the foundations right. The king had tried to hurry him.

"No," Enmerkar had said when the king pressed. "We cannot start on the walls yet. "The walls and the roof will not hold unless the foundations are absolutely firm."

The king had been a bit cross at that but had then been delighted as the walls rapidly reached the height of one house in just a few days.

"Your little bricks are truly miraculous," said Nimrod.

Progress wasn't always so visible, though. Enmerkar insisted on finishing off the whole of the inside of the tower before he increased the height of the walls. This made it comfortable to work in as it grew – and gave them plenty of time to find more clay for the bricks as they went along. Now, though, the men were getting very skilled at laying the bricks. They always looked as if they were directly over the ones below, but Enmerkar had calculated exactly how much the sides need to taper and in turn how much each row of bricks needed to be offset. His men now knew how to calculate that fraction of a hair's breadth by sight. They worked quickly.

The tower now stood at the height of four houses. It was still very wide, and two carts could pass side by side with almost room for another in the middle on the spiral roadway making its way up the tower. Yes, the tower was getting thinner as it went up, but it still needed a lot of bricks.

Enmerkar ran his hand along the top of one of the openings. It was beautifully finished and smooth. He smiled to himself. He was allowed to be proud of his work, wasn't he? The king had been pleased so far. Maybe his continued good craftsmanship would appease the king if there was a delay in the work.

He turned to watch his men. They were going too quickly.

Much too quickly. But at least they weren't cutting down on the quality.

What was he going to tell the king?

Suddenly there seemed to be a lot of noise coming from the bottom of the tower. A fanfare sounded. Enmerkar recognised the king's call sign. A few moments later Nimrod's chariot rumbled into view.

"My friend, my friend," called the king, jumping down from his carriage and rushing to embrace Enmerkar. "It is settled, it is settled. The Westlands will supply us with as much clay as we need."

"But at what cost?" asked Enmerkar.

"Freedom to use the tower," replied the king.

Enmerkar's mouth went dry. That would mean far too many people wanting access to it. They would have to restrict how many people went up and down. Or perhaps they would have to charge a fee. That meant that the very men who had built the tower and their families would probably never have the chance to visit it. And people might think they were imposing restrictions because he had not made the tower strong enough.

"But what of your promise of free use of it to our own people?" asked Enmerkar.

"Oh, they will soon tire of it, these Westlanders," said Nimrod. "They will soon stop making the long journey to visit it." He waved his hand dismissively. "It will be more ours than theirs." He rubbed his hand together. "Now how long before we get to five houses?"

Enmerkar braced himself to give the news he must now deliver.

"I'm afraid we must give the men a little holiday," he said. "It will take at least four days for the clay to arrive. Then at least another week before the clay is moulded and dried, even using our ovens."

Nimrod's face fell. Enmerkar thought he was going to get angry.

"Once the bricks are ready we can work quickly," said Enmerkar. "And with a constant supply…"

A grin cracked across Nimrod's face. "Then we shall have a great party," he said, "for all who have worked on this project and their families. In what there is of the tower already. There shall be feasting and dancing. Singing and music-making. You and your lovely wife shall help me to arrange it. At once."

He climbed back into his carriage and gave the signal to depart. Then he paused. He turned to Enmerkar.

"We shall show Yahweh how well man matches His creation," he called.

Enmerkar found it hard to sleep that night. Naomi was sleeping peacefully and breathing gently. He had been tempted to wake her, to make love to her and hope that that would make him sleepy. But she looked so peaceful, he was too worried to be truly aroused and he knew that every coupling gave her the false hope that she might conceive a child. She was barren, he was certain, and it seemed that they were never going to be parents.

And yet that seemed the least of his worries. What did Nimrod think he was doing, saying that man could match Yahweh's creation? Wouldn't that make Yahweh angry? And would he succeed to build the tower as high as Nimrod wanted it? Would this stubborn, demanding king be satisfied with his work? Would the supply of materials be constant? Would the workers remain loyal? This project was killing him, of that he was certain. Perhaps it was his fault that he and Naomi were not parents. Could all the stress of this work be sapping his strength?

At last, though, he slept. Then came the strangest of dreams. It was some sort of grand ceremony – the opening of the tower, perhaps? – and he and all the others, dressed in their finest clothes of blue, gold and silver, were making their way up to the top. But there were some strange people there as well. Children with adult faces. A young man with golden hair in a strange robe and with cloth covering his legs so that you could see the shape of them. Stranger still, a woman in even more mysterious clothing, clothing that clung tightly to her and indecently showed her figure, sat at the side of the path. She seemed to be making a picture of the tower, but as if she was looking at it from the outside. Her eyes caught his. She seemed to recognise him. She started to say something.

Suddenly, though, the tower was shaking. He could see the woman's lips moving but couldn't hear the words she was saying. The rumbling and then the sound of bricks crashing to the ground was too loud. Then over that noise came the sound of people screaming and shouting words that Enmerkar could not understand.

Enmerkar woke with a start. Someone was shaking him.

"Come quickly," said Delilah, Naomi's young maid. "The mistress is ill."

Enmerkar's jumped out of bed. He could hear Naomi retching in the garden. His heart was beating violently. He couldn't bear her to be ill. He hurried out to her. Delilah followed.

"Fetch her some water and a washing cloth," Enmerkar commanded the maid.

Delilah set off obediently.

Enmerkar rushed to Naomi's side. "My love," he started.

But she looked up at him with shining eyes.

"I have not had my monthly bleeding for nine weeks now," she said. "And this is just the sickness that comes with a new life in the womb. And look…"

She lowered the top of her robe to reveal her breasts. They were large and full and her nipples were standing up pertly.

"Yes," she whispered. "We are to be parents."

He pulled her into an embrace and went to kiss her. She hesitated.

"I've been vomiting," she said. "Surely…"

But she didn't smell of vomit. He pulled her close again. She didn't taste of it either. If anything her kisses were even sweeter than normal. Her robe slipped further down.

They ignored Delilah's gasp and the sound of the water jug crashing to the floor and shattering.

Decisions

Kaleem showered as quickly as he could. Whatever Nazaret wanted, it was clearly really urgent. He expected the worst. Maybe the destruction was far worse than Nazaret had thought at first.

Kaleem selected a grey double ripon tunic. He guessed there would be a lot of physical work to do today. And he guessed it might be a bit mucky. He pulled on his leggings as quickly as possible. His hands were shaking. Goodness knows what they would find out there. But he was partly excited as well. As least he would be doing something useful and doing something with Nazaret. Maybe he'd feel less uncomfortable around the man if they were working together.

Something else tugged at his memory too. He was pleased about something and he couldn't work out exactly what. Then he remembered. Ella. Ella! That had been amazing. Perhaps there would be more of that. He certainly hoped so. He smiled to himself.

The door communicator buzzed then there was a loud thumping. Kaleem looked in the mirror at his hair. It was sticking out all over the place and looked like straw. He tried to smooth it down.

"Kaleem, come on! Move it!" he heard Nazaret call.

Kaleem gave up trying to control his hair. He hurried out to Nazaret.

Kaleem was shocked by his father's appearance. He looked even more unkempt than himself. Surely he hadn't had a busy night as well, had he? *Don't even go there,* he told himself. He guessed, though, his father had not slept well and good grooming was the last thing on any of their minds. And luxurious as these safe boxes were, they were not like permanent homes. There was a feeling of having to make do.

"They've made a thorough analysis of the damage," said Nazaret. "They're going to give us a full report. It's worse than we thought at first. I think we're going to need you."

A transporter was waiting for them. It was only a short ride to the plantation headquarters. Kaleem could not think what to say. Nazaret sat very still, staring at nothing in particular, his hands gripping his legs. Just how bad was this going to be, Kaleem wondered.

As soon as the transporter stopped, they were ushered quickly into the main meet room of the plantation headquarters. Kaleem recognised Tom from the day before. A dataserve screen was already showing the images of acres of toppled trees.

"Sorry to drag you in so early in the morning," said Tom, "but I thought you would want to know straight away. In fact ninety percent of the trees have fallen and only twenty-five percent of those have viable root systems."

"And we don't know whether those will actually retake," said Nazaret. He sighed and covered his face with his hands.

"Can't the droids raise the trees back up?" asked Kaleem. "Wouldn't the roots take again then?"

Tom shook his head. "Already dead, in most cases. Because of our rapid season changes and our poor soil the trees' root systems were always going to be fragile. The frost got most of them."

"Shouldn't the droids have got on to it sooner?" asked Kaleem.

"Well, there are only so many droids and most of them were used to check for any people hurt by the quake," replied Tom. "Then the next priority was getting people housed and getting the infrastructure reorganised. We were just allowed a few droids to initiate the damage investigation. All our droids have now been reassigned to us – just a few hours too late."

"I'm going to take a look," said Nazaret.

Kaleem went to follow him out of the door. Tom shook his head. "Give him a bit of time," he said. "I can show you some more of the pictures and a few ideas I've had."

Tom started calling up some files. "These are the plantations," he said, "as they were just before the quake. See? All down to your father. And yes, obviously because of your negotiations. But Nazaret has really pushed it. The trees have grown quickly and we've lost hardly any. Good acorn yield as well."

Kaleem had to agree with him. It was certainly impressive, what his father had achieved in less than two years. Acres and acres of trees, mainly healthy and bringing with them a great improvement in Zandra's atmosphere.

"This is the best," said Tom.

The next scene was the one that Nazaret had shown him the day before. The plants growing under the trees.

"That might save us," said Tom. "There are a few patches like that. And the ones I've seen are still healthy." He looked meaningfully at Tom. "Though I expect we'll also have to get some more acorns. One way or another."

"And what if it happens again?" asked Kaleem.

"Ah well," replied Tom. "Now there's a question."

Then Kaleem had a horrible thought. "You don't think it was planting the trees that caused the landquake in the first place, do you?"

Tom shrugged. "Who knows?" he said. "We'd have to get some information from the planets that have frequent landquakes – Patch 1, Melafile and Bratzia maybe and those that have earthquakes as well might be able to give us some useful information too… Plutino and of course Terrestra."

Right, thought Kaleem.

"Do you want to take a look outside?" asked Tom. "See it all for real?"

Kaleem nodded. It would be good to see the little plants up close.

It was almost the hottest part of the day. Kaleem was now regretting his double ripon tunic. It was making him sticky. But there was something good about working directly with the plants. He had taken the gloves that Tom had offered at first but after a while it became obvious that he could work better without them. Within the first hour he was used to it and actually enjoying the feel of soil between his fingers. He was getting faster and faster at picking up the damaged plants, measuring their roots, testing the soil, resetting the plants and dictating the data into his minicompu.

"I guess it will soon be too hot to do any more," said Tom. "But the measurements we've taken so far are indicating that ten percent of the ground where oaks have been planted has developed a rich enough subsoil to support natural and rapid growth of a vegetation cover similar to the ones on Terrestra and other natural planets."

"So can it get back to the way it was before the quake?" asked Kaleem.

"Not without increasing the number of acorns being imported," said Tom. "We don't have critical mass yet. But the good news is that everything your father has been trying to do is working."

"So, we're going to have to increase the amount we send?" asked Kaleem. That would not be easy. The ratio of acorns to vaccine had been carefully worked out. He didn't think his fellow Terrestrans would feel generous to enough to supply extra for nothing and there was only so much vaccine they could use – despite the end of switch-off and the integration of the Z Zone into the Normal Zones. And although most people on Zandra had accepted the Z Zoners now, most of them still wanted to be independent of other planets.

"Problem?" asked Tom.

Kaleem nodded. "Terrestra won't need as much vaccine as Zandra will need acorns."

"Yeah," said Tom. "And we don't like charity."

"Are we going to look at any more?" asked Tom. He didn't want to get into a debate about Terrestra's trading record.

"Nah!" said Tom. "It's getting too hot. We're going to go in and eat. We'll leave the rest to the droids."

"But I thought you said this work was too fine for droids?" said Kaleem.

"Kidding you," said Tom. "Wanted you to get your hands dirty. Take your mind off your old man. And let you know what makes him cheery."

"What?" spluttered Kaleem staring at his dirty tunic.

"Got you," said Tom, laughing. "The droids will do the whole lot in half the time we've been out there. But you had to see for yourself."

The makeshift canteen at the main plantation centre was crowded. All the plantation droids were now working with the plants and the specialist builder droids had still not come to check the permanent buildings. A temporary cafeteria had been set up by joining several safe-boxes together.

"It certainly makes you feel hungry, doesn't it?" said Tom. "Working out of doors and getting you hands dirty?"

Kaleem had to agree with him. His stomach was grumbling. He could smell roasted vegetables and rich sauces. *Not bad, considering,* he thought.

Tom sighed. "I don't suppose we'll get any meat today," he said.

They collected their food and managed to find somewhere to sit. It really wasn't easy with all these people. Kaleem found himself thinking about the Z Zone and wishing he was camping there in the open air. Safe-boxes made a pretty smart solution to the quake problem. They almost seemed to take the problem away before you'd even noticed you had a problem. Kaleem wasn't sure that that was really the best idea. Something was going through his mind about problems actually being good for you. It wasn't so good having everything so easy. Was that something he'd learnt from his time in the Z Zone?

"Not hungry then?" asked Tom. He had already finished half of his bowl of vegetable stew.

"What?" said Kaleem. "Oh, er, yes." He started eating. He was hungry and it did taste good, although on a normal day he would never have chosen this.

"I guess Nazaret's taken a trip around the whole plantation," said Tom.

"What do you think he's doing exactly?" asked Kaleem.

"Oh, he'll just be checking for himself. He always likes to see things with his own eyes," replied Tom. "Mind you," he added. He frowned. "I can't understand why he's not in here now. He can't still be out in the heat, can, he surely?"

Kaleem was worried now.

Tom shrugged. "Probably nothing to worry about," he said. "He's probably having a working lunch somewhere looking at a dataserve. Typical!"

Perhaps Tom was right. He called up Nazaret on his personal communicator. No luck. He went to all the indoor places he could think of until the heat died down, then he joined Tom outside again. Tom was no longer digging. He was now leaving all the heavy work to the droids. He just gave them their instructions. There was really nothing much for Kaleem to do.

"I wonder where he could be," Kaleem muttered almost to himself.

"He'll turn up. He always does," said Tom. "Before he got back with your mother he'd sometimes be away for days on end."

Kaleem guessed he could understand that. He was like that as well. Liked his own company. Wanted to see things for himself. And working with Tom this morning he'd really begun to understand why Nazaret was so keen on plants. But that might be the trouble. This landquake had really damaged a lot of Nazaret's work. Kaleem knew what that was like as well. He remembered how Kevik's activities in the Z Zone had almost totally undone what he'd tried to achieve.

Suddenly he felt sorry for his father.

"Why don't you go and look for him?" said Tom. "Take a droid. Then you can cover more ground."

The droid was becoming less effective. Kaleem suspected it needed a recharge. They were in the thick of the plantation now. He ought to put the droid on standby. The recharge centres this far in were still out of action. He'd be in trouble if a droid powered down completely and lots its memory banks. He could leave it here until all the energy outlets were reconnected correctly. When would that be? Soon, he hoped. Look at all the work they'd got to do here. All those fallen trees, now dead, their root systems ruined.

More worrying still was that there was not sign at all of Nazaret. It was getting dark and the frost would start soon. He shouldn't stay out in that, but could he give up his search for Nazaret? It was really puzzling. He'd been the entire length and breadth of the plantation. The droid had surveyed it too and its farsight was pretty smart. Not a sign.

His personal communicator buzzed. Could it be Nazaret? No. Tom.

"You'd better get back," he said. "We don't want to have to look for two…"

Go on, say it, thought Kaleem. *Two bodies.*

"We think he'll probably be all right," said Tom. "He usually knows what he's doing. We're sending you a mini-rapid-transporter."

Seconds later the transporter was there. Shortly after that it was gliding quietly and quickly towards the safe-box colony. Kaleem had to admit he was feeling tired. He'd love a bath… and then, for the first time since breakfast, he thought of Ella. Now there was an idea…

Kaleem smiled. What perfect timing. Just as he thought of Ella, the transporter arrived at the edge of the new oak plantations and started making its way through the older, more formal flower beds, and was now passing a bed of black Tulpen – bigger and in better condition than any he had seen before. Had seeing them made him think of Ella? Or had thinking of her made him notice the Tulpen?

Then he noticed something else. There was someone crouched down by one of the Tulpen beds. Could it be…? Yes, it was. What a relief! But why was he there?

Kaleem commanded the transporter to stop. He stepped out of the vehicle.

"What are you doing here?" he called to Nazaret. "You're going to freeze to death."

"No, no, I won't," said Nazaret. "I'm not stupid. I was on my way home. I wouldn't do that to your mother… or to you. And good that you've come by. We can ride back together."

"It's amazing, isn't it," he said as they gathered speed again, "that those of all plants should be the ones to survive? The ones that are so expensive because they're hard to cultivate. Their roots are fine." He sighed deeply and covered his face with his hands. Kaleem knew exactly what he must now do. He'd got to negotiate with Terrestra as soon as possible.

Nazaret remained silent for the twenty minute ride back to the safe-boxes. He kept his hands over his face. Only as they began to slow down did he take them down. He looked grey.

"Thank you for your help today," he said to Kaleem. "I'd invite you to eat with us, but I'm going straight to bed, I think."

"No problem," said Kaleem.

He watched as his father walked back towards his safe-box. He looked old and his back was stooped. Marijam waved from the door. Kaleem watched her face become full of concerns as Nazaret spoke to her. They were too far away for Kaleem to be able to hear what they were saying but he could guess at the gist of it. It wasn't Nazaret's fault that this had happened. He must take care of himself. Of course he would, for her sake, for Kaleem's sake… oh dear, then it would get embarrassing.

Kaleem turned away from them and gave his attention to the transporter. It was easy enough to send it back to central control. Yes, and now he knew exactly what he must do. He must get in contact with his friends from Terrestra again. But he was a little tired as well. It could wait until the morning. He made his way over to his safe-box.

Someone was sitting on the ground outside. "I guess you could do with another massage?" a voice said. Ella! "Only can we eat at your place this time? My kitchen unit's gone on strike."

Suddenly Kaleem's tiredness was gone. Yes, a *massage* would be good. He suddenly saw the big bed of black Tulpen and wished he'd thought to bring some.

Kaleem grinned. "A massage would be great, thanks," he said.

Terrestra Bound

It was cold in the safe-box they were using as an office on the temporary accommodation site. But it wasn't just the room temperature that made it seem cold. It was partly to do with Edmundson. He was listening for the third time to the audio files that Kaleem had loaded to the dataserve. He was frowning slightly and his eyes were squinting at the screen as he scrutinised the images that accompanied the suggestions. His arms were folded across his chest.

"Why exactly do you think it's a good idea for Zandrians to go to Terrestra first?" he asked. "Wouldn't it be better if the people we chose came here first? If they saw the damage for themselves wouldn't that make them want to help?"

No, it would not, thought Kaleem. He knew, though, that he was partly thinking that to avoid the whole Rozia question. "I know you Zandrians don't like to be thought of as charity cases," he said. "If we go to the Terrestrans we might be able to persuade them that we are people worth trading with." He had said "we" when referring to the Zandrians, and he had said it easily. How had that happened?

Edmundson continued to frown. He rolled his lips and scratched his nose. Kaleem found it impossible to get any impression of what he was thinking. He went to say something then hesitated.

Oh, come, on, man, thought Kaleem. *Yes or no. Get on with it!*

Edmundson drew a deep breath. "Well, I suppose you're right," he said. "As long as the Terrestrans come here as well afterwards. Who do you have in mind?"

The door suddenly swished open. A young woman sauntered in. Emmerline! She looked even less droid-like this time. There was no data streaming from her chest.

"So, gentlemen, is your meeting finished?" she asked.

"No, it's not, more's the pity," replied Edmundson. He smiled at the droid. He looked much more interested in her than he had in Kaleem's presentation.

Great elders, thought Kaleem. *He's flirting with her. Yuk!*

Emmerline turned to him. She raised her eyebrows and stared at him out of clear blue eyes. She ran her fingers through her long blond hair. Then she smiled. "So Kaleem, Terrestran Peace Child, what are you going to do about our devastated forests?"

Kaleem could see her chest going up and down, just like a human who was breathing. She was so convincing. And as she was a droid she had been made with perfect good looks. Edmundson was still staring at her.

"Well, Kaleem?" she asked again. She sidled up to him. She was a little shorter than him and looked up at him, her head to one side and almost touching his shoulder. She placed her arm around his waist. "What are we going to do about it all?" She sighed. "A big strong young man like you." She traced a finger down the front of his tunic.

"That'll do," said Edmundson. His eyes had narrowed again. "What do you want, Emmerline? I didn't send for you."

"Oh, I just wanted to see what my boys are up to," she replied. She shut her eyes and opened them again. A faint half smile spread across her face.

"Nothing, with you around," said Edmundson. "Now, get out of here."

"If you say so, big boy," she said, pinching Edmundson's cheeks. "Toodle pip, gentlemen." She sauntered slowly out of the room, her hips swaying.

"I'm sorry about that," said Edmundson. He blushed brightly. "I'm going to have to reprogramme her."

What had he been up to? Kaleem suddenly thought of Ella. Gosh! Were Edmundson and Emmerline…? Just using her as a… But what about him and Ella? That was all right, wasn't it? What they were doing? It was his turn to blush.

"Well," said Edmundson quickly. "Who do you think should go with you to Terrestra?"

“Charlek Smithin and Alistare Rogerin,” said Kaleem without hesitating.

“Smithin, the prison warder?” asked Edmundson. “Won’t he be a bit intimidating for your gentle Terrestrans?”

Kaleem found it hard to remember that Charlek was a prison guard. They’d been pretty good friends in the end and he had been with Kaleem when he’d found Nazaret.

“I don’t think he’ll be a problem,” replied Kaleem.

“Perhaps not,” said Edmundson. “But who’s this Alistare Rogerin?”

“Oh, he’s just a good friend of mine,” said Kaleem. “He’s in the number corps.” Kaleem realised that he had hardly, in fact, seen anything of either Charlek or Alistare since he’d been back on Zandra. He hoped they’d survived the landquake all right. He was doing it again, then. Just like on Terrestra. Ignoring his friends. Just like before he’d been so caught up with his problems he’d not made time for them and now he was calling on them to help. He was repeating the pattern he’d had with Pierre Lafontaine.

“Well, I’ve never heard of him, but number corps sounds good. And I’ve got a suggestion myself for two more,” said Edmundson.

“Oh?” said Kaleem.

“They are people you know. Tulla Watkins-Ransen and Petro Ransen,” replied Edmundson.

Kaleem gasped. They had been good friends too. And at one point Tulla had wanted to be a bit more and he would have liked to take her up on that but it hadn’t been practical. He thought about the black Tulpen she’d sent him. And she looked so much like Rozia.

Edmundson didn’t seem to notice his consternation. “Yes, they’re just back from interplanetary and so they could well be in the right diplomatic frame of mind,” he said. “I really think they should go with you.” He looked at Kaleem in such a way that Kaleem knew he could not refuse. “And then, maybe… a special friend? I’ve heard certain rumours about you and Ella Raymond…”

How on Zandra does he know about that? thought Kaleem.

"It's useful having a bit of female company, you know," said Edmundson. "It would do you good. We all need that occasionally."

Kaleem tried not to think about Edmundson and the droid. He blushed again anyway.

"You could do with one more, I think," said Edmundson. "Someone with a bit of psychological understanding. You know, somebody who understands what people are thinking. Know anyone?" Kaleem shook his head.

"Well, you'd better get your thinking cap on. Come up with something quick," said Edmundson.

"Fine, I guess," said Kaleem. He felt tired at just thinking about all the connections he was going to have to make and all the negotiations with Terrestrans and Zandrians – let alone the actual journey back to Terrestra.

"Good," said Edmundson. He grinned. "If I were you, I'd start with Ella." He nodded briefly to Kaleem and made his way to the door. "Emmerline, meet me at my safe-box," he said to his personal communicator.

Calver Toms

"I think it's exciting," said Ella. "I'm up for it anyway. Have you heard back from the others?"

Kaleem didn't know. The dataserve was on standby. His personal communicator was on silent. There may be messages waiting for him. He didn't want to move, though. It felt too good lying next to Ella. Besides, he was tired. She had really put him through his paces tonight.

"Come on, get to it," she said, tapping his bare leg.

"I don't think I can again," he said. He felt a little as if he'd overdone it on the hologym.

"I don't mean that," she said. "You've had enough fun for one evening. I mean check the dataserve and your communicator."

Kaleem blushed. He still didn't think he could move. But Ella pushed him gently out of the bed. And he found that his feet did work.

"Anyway, I need to go and see how that droid is getting on with repairing my kitchen. I can't keep sponging off you," said Ella. She was out of bed in seconds and soon after that was fully dressed and moving towards the door.

Kaleem called up his messages while he dressed. The first was from a Calver Toms. He did not know that name. He hesitated about opening the message but before he could make up his mind, the communicator buzzed again. "Calver Toms," said the dataserve voice. Kaleem hesitated again but before he could tell the dataserve to hold the message, or even decide whether or not to check this Calver Toms out, a face with penetrating black eyes and short black sleek hair appeared on the dataserve screen.

"You don't know me," said the stranger, "but I think you need me. Forgive me for taking control of your machine."

"Okay," called Ella. "I can see you're busy. I'll get going now." She kissed Kaleem lightly on the forehead and slipped out of the safe-box door.

"Ah, I see you had the lovely Ella with you," said Calver

Toms. He smiled. "I'm sure having her on the mission will be a great advantage."

Who was this guy? And how did he know so much?

"I'm sure she'll have much to offer as well as anything she can do you personally," said Calver. "She is valued."

Kaleem could see that he had messages from Charlek, Alistare and Tulla. Tulla! Gosh, she really did look like Rozia. Would he be able to cope with being with her? He'd have to get rid of this guy as quickly as possible.

"I think you'll find that they have all accepted to come along and one young lady in particular is extremely pleased," said Calver. "Not that you will need to worry. She is firmly attached to her partner."

I'm more worried about me, thought Kaleem.

"And of course, you will behave impeccably despite any feelings Tulla Watkins-Ransen may arouse," Calver continued.

What was it with this Calver Toms? He was just like the Zandrian dataserves. He seemed to be reading Kaleem's mind.

"There's nothing mystical about it," said Calver. "It's not magic or anything. I just read people well. And because I spend so much of my time looking at the programming of all of the dataserve systems, I really understand the logic they use and can apply it myself and to any situation." He paused again. He was grinning. "But go ahead. Check your messages."

Kaleem quickly commanded the messages open. Charlek, Alistare and Tulla were all enthusiastic about the project.

"Petro's incommunicado at a meet at the moment," said Tulla. "But I know it's exactly the sort of thing he'll want to do."

"She's right," Calver's voice said.

Kaleem was glad that this wasn't a live communication. He didn't know how he'd be able to talk to her directly. He couldn't even maintain eye contact with her on the screen.

Calver's face popped up in the corner of the dataserve. "You will get used to it," he said. "It will get easier."

Mighty Zandra, this was irritating as well.

"And you'll get used to this," said Calver. "My constantly

interrupting your messages. I promise I won't keep on doing it, once you're convinced."

"Convinced?" asked Kaleem.

Calver was now looking very serious. "Of why it's a good idea to have along someone like me who can read people."

"Can you predict the future?" asked Kaleem.

"Not exactly," said Calver. "I'm just pretty quick at working out how people are likely to behave. I don't have any funny dreams or visions or anything."

"Do you think you'll be as good with Terrestrans?" asked Kaleem.

"Well, we'll see, won't we?" said Calver. "But I can read you. Even the Terrestran bits."

"Ah!" said Kaleem. He could see that Calver was trying not to laugh.

"I don't do it all the time," said Calver. "Only when it's needed. It does take a bit of effort, you know."

Kaleem felt uneasy. He could see that he might be useful even if his ability to read people might be irritating at times, but he didn't have to feel comfortable with it. "Who are you exactly?" he said.

"I think you'd better find out, don't you?" said Calver.

"I guess so," said Kaleem.

"Okay. Let's meet tomorrow. 11.30. Café Colibri, Nav X598."

Café Colibri

It was 11.40. There was no sign of Calver Toms. Kaleem had already been here twenty minutes. As usual he'd tried not to be late and had ended up arriving early. It wasn't the type of place he was used to. It was all glass and polished surfaces. The tables even seem to be edged with some bright white old metal.

The café was in a really good condition considering what had happened everywhere else. The people here were well dressed, most of them in silky executive blue. The only people his age wore their hair very short, usually a sign of having made good progress for their age. It was actually quite difficult to tell the men from the women. They all looked like they were at least executives anyway, maybe some even higher ranks.

It was busy here. There were few places that weren't taken and Kaleem wondered how Calver might find him. If he turned up at all.

A server droid approached him and he ordered a chofa. The droid insisted on taking an iris reading straight away.

Oh, so it's that sort of place, is it? thought Kaleem.

When the chofa eventually arrived, it was very small. He noticed at the tables around him that the portions of everything were very small.

It took a long time for his drink to appear and when it did it was disappointing in other ways too. It was almost cold and was nowhere as nutty in flavour as the really good chofas you could get in the Refreshment Park. Despite it taking so long to arrive he had almost finished it completely when he saw Calver arrive at last.

Kaleem's stomach lurched. He'd actually begun to hope that Calver wouldn't show up.

He appeared in the doorway, nodded to one of the waiter droids and moved straight over to Kaleem.

How on Zandra could he know where I was that quickly? thought Kaleem.

Seconds later Calver was sitting opposite him and looking at him with his disturbing dark eyes. "Sorry I'm so late," he said. "I hope you don't mind me making you come here." He looked over his shoulder than turned back to Kaleem and smiled. "Only I thought it would be better if we met where no one was likely to recognise either of us."

A droid waiter came and hovered by their table.

"Frega?" asked Calver.

Kaleem nodded. Why on Zandra not? This was all so bizarre, what did it matter if the frega addled his brain?

"Oh, and reverse my friend's bill: put it on my account." He offered his eyes to the droid's iris scanner.

"So," said Calver, as the droid moved away. "Will you let me help you?"

"I don't know who you are," said Kaleem, "or what you can do."

Calver looked round at the other tables. "See those two women over there?" he said to Kaleem. "The ones in the pink tunics next to the window."

Kaleem looked to where Calver was pointing.

"The tall one will leave in a moment," he said. "The older one will follow her and the younger one will try to get away."

Seconds later the taller and younger of the two women stood up from her chair and rushed towards the exit of the café. Then the other woman stood up, fussed about a little as she gathered her belongings and followed. She couldn't move as fast but she seemed to be making an effort to catch the first one up.

"They've just had an argument," said Calver. "They are mother and daughter. The daughter wants to make a permanent attachment; the mother does not like her – the attachment she has chosen."

"Ah," said Kaleem. "There are still prejudices?"

"Yes, indeed," said Calver.

"So how do you know all of this stuff?" asked Kaleem.

"Just careful observations," said Calver. "Their body language says a lot. And I listen intently."

"You listen?" said Kaleem. "Isn't that... well... Just plain nosy?"

"It's not really that I listen," said Calver. "I just can't help hearing. I don't tune in, exactly. The sound just falls on my ears."

"You mean you've got some sort of super hearing?" asked Kaleem. This guy was getting to be more of a puzzle by the minute.

"No, I'm just more aware. I keep my ears and my eyes open," said Kaleem. "I never know when I'm going suddenly to need information that I'll have to act on."

"Why, though?" asked Kaleem.

"People expect it now," said Calver. "They ask me if they can't understand what is going on."

"But how did you get to have to do this?" asked Kaleem.

"It started off as a bit of a game when I was younger," said Calver. "I could work out what was going on between people. I became a bit of a peace-maker."

Ah! thought Kaleem. *That!*

"And gradually I got more and more interested and started to study psychology and detective work. And just got better and better at it," said Calver. "Ah, our drinks will be next."

Kaleem watched the droid sweep past their table with a tray full of drinks. "Two minutes, gentlemen," it called. "Please excuse the delay."

Two minutes later it came back and deposited two glasses of frega on their table.

Calver was staring at Tom with one eyebrow raised. "See, it comes in useful sometimes," he said.

Kaleem took a sip of the frega. It was good. It slid down his throat smoothly. He had the impression it was quite strong. Calver Toms, he noticed, wasn't touching his. "Another reason I suggested coming here," said Calver. "They have possibly the best frega on Zandra, though the chofa is certainly less good."

"It's creepy, the way you seem to know what I'm thinking all the time," said Kaleem.

"You'll get used to it," said Calver.

"How do I know I can trust you?" asked Kaleem. "You'll know so many secrets about me, about everyone really."

Calver shrugged. "I always have to be discreet about my clients. I'm used to it. I take my work seriously." He took a small sip of his frega.

"So, who else have you worked for?" asked Kaleem.

"I can't give you details," said Calver, "but let's just say they're just as important as you!"

"So, executives and the like?" asked Kaleem.

Calver laughed. "And I'd bring you here?" He looked around the café and then back at Kaleem, his eyebrows raised.

"Oh!" said Kaleem. What was there apart from executives? Did they have something on Zandra like the elders on Terrestra, and things like Golden Knowledge and Hidden Information?

"And I've worked beyond Zandra," continued Calver. "Wherever I've been needed."

"So, a sort of mercenary," said Kaleem.

"Never," said Calver. "Only for the greater good. Always."

You could be doing my job, thought Kaleem.

Calver stared at Kaleem. "You can trust me, you really can," he whispered.

He sat up suddenly. "Do you want to be recognised?" he asked Kaleem.

"Not particularly," said Kaleem. He still hated that.

"Well, we'd better make a move," said Calver. "Come on."

Kaleem put his glass down and stood up. The room seemed to spin. Yes, that frega had definitely been strong.

"Come on. Now!" hissed Calver. He guided Kaleem out to the walkway outside. His eyes darted here and there.

Kaleem wondered what he was looking for.

A transporter suddenly stopped in front of them.

"Come on. Get in quick," said Calver.

The two of them shuffled into the vehicle.

"See," said Calver. He pointed back towards the café as the transporter drew away. Two smartly dressed men were pointing towards them and nodding. "They'd been speculating for several minutes about where they knew you from. The tall one was just going to realise."

"I suppose it wouldn't have mattered," said Kaleem.

"No, it probably wouldn't have," said Calver. "But do you see? You can trust me. I am usually right."

The transporter moved away. It gained speed quite quickly.

"Where are we going?" asked Kaleem.

"Somewhere quiet. Somewhere where we won't be disturbed," replied Calver. "Into the deep Zandrian countryside.

More like deep holoed-side, thought Kaleem.

"Don't you think it's convincing?" asked Calver.

Drat him. Why was he anticipating his every thought? "Why can't we just talk in the transporter?" asked Kaleem.

Calver looked around the vehicle. "It could be bugged," he said. "And we need more time. It's best if we don't talk now and just admire the scenery."

Kaleem shrugged looked out of the window. Okay, so Calver Toms was right. The Zandrians were very clever. It was convincing. And it was also clear that they'd soon reinstated the holoscenes after the landquake.

The transporter stopped at what looked like woodland.

"Come on," said Calver.

They walked into the woods a little way. The ground was convincingly uneven beneath their feet. Calver kept a little ahead of Kaleem. He seemed to know where he was going.

How come they can't bug holoscenes if they can bug transporters?" thought Kaleem.

Calver turned to face him. "This isn't a holoscene," he said. "This is real. It's on the edge of one of your father's plantations. One that went wild. And, being wild, it resisted the 'quake. There are no bugs – except maybe ones with six legs. We can talk freely. Sit."

Kaleem did as he was told. Calver Toms settled himself down as well. "So," he said, "what's bugging you, pardon the pun? Why is Edmundson getting to you almost as much as your father?"

Drat the man, thought Kaleem.

"I suppose all that business with the droid is a little off-putting," said Calver.

You bet, thought Kaleem. The man was some sort of pervert wasn't he, making a machine into some sort of romantic – or worse – companion. "Well, don't you think it's odd?" he said.

Calver laughed. "It's really no different from other people's insecurities. She – it – is actually only a machine. Highly and perhaps inappropriately programmed, but a machine all the same. He isn't leading the type of life you might think. He's just a bit lonely so he likes to play a game. But he is extremely clever and you should take notice of him."

Kaleem sighed.

Calver stared at him. He narrowed his eyes as if he was looking very closely at something very small. "The droid is clever simply because she has been programmed by Edmundson. But it isn't just their cleverness that bothers you, is it?"

Kaleem remained silent, as if saying what he was thinking would only make it even worse.

"You're scared, aren't you?" said Calver. "Scared of what he's asking you to do. Scared as always of what you're expected to do."

Yeah, that was it.

"How do you always know?" asked Kaleem.

Calver shrugged. "It's just what I do." He stared at Kaleem for a few seconds more. "You really should trust Edmundson," he said. "And you should trust me."

"I don't really know you, though, do I?" said Kaleem.

Calver was staring out in front. "Is that so?" he said. "You might know me more than you think," he said.

He turned to look at Kaleem again. Now his pupils were round and large and he was looking deeply into Kaleem's eyes. Kaleem had the impression that he could read his every thought.

"I certainly know you much better than you would ever imagine," said Calver. "And anyway, haven't you already seen that I read you well, that I read everyone well? If you can't trust me, can't you trust my ability?"

Kaleem guessed he could certainly trust Calver Toms to read everything very accurately. Very accurately indeed. But could he trust him not to give anything away or not to use what he'd found out in a harmful way?

"It's never in my interests to double-cross or to give away secrets," said Calver. "But if you don't believe me, why don't you test me?"

"How?" asked Kaleem. "And how will I be able to tell that just because you've done the right thing once you'll always do the right thing?"

"You'll think of a way," said Calver. "You'll think of a sure way of knowing. But let's go now. You take this transporter and I'll summon another."

He all but pushed Kaleem into the transporter.

The coordinates were already set. The journey back took very little time. Kaleem spent most of it puzzling about how he could test Calver. As the transporter came to rest at the safe-box settlement he still had no idea.

Trust Games

"I think he will be good, and he will help with the mission," said Kaleem. "He's quite clever. He knows what people are up to. The trouble is, I don't know how much I can trust him. He could find out such a lot and give something away."

He'd already spent just over an hour explaining all that he knew about Calver. They'd gone round in circles about how good he could be and how dangerous as well.

"Who is he really?" said Charlek. "Say again, how did you meet him?"

"He just contacted me," replied Kaleem.

"Never heard of him," muttered Alistare. "I can't get over how this looks so – well – ordinary." He was looking round the meeting room Charlek had arranged. He'd never been inside the prison before. He'd been more interested for the whole of the meeting in how the prison worked than in contributing ideas about how to solve Kaleem's dilemma.

They'd had to meet there because Charlek had two shifts with only a couple of hours between them. Kaleem had thought it better to meet in person. But he didn't feel all that comfortable being there. He remembered only too well being a prisoner there himself, not all that long ago. It was decidedly odd now being here as an invited guest.

"Yes, you will have to test him," said Charlek.

"Yes," said Kaleem. "But how? He'd probably see through anything I tried to do."

Kaleem was aware of someone moving past Charlek's door. He could see a shadow of whoever it was through the narrow veriglass panel. He could not be sure whether it was a prisoner or a human or droid guard. He put his finger to his lips.

"Tell me again," said Alistare, "how do you stop people leaving?"

"Force fields, tags," mumbled Charlek, frowning and shaking his head.

Alistare frowned too and then he looked up at Kaleem and Charlek, his eyes round and wide open. “Ah!” he said. “That’s it! Put Kaleem in prison again. Pretend you need to get something out of him. Get this Calver Toms to visit. Charlek, you can try to get him to get something out of Kaleem.”

“No,” said Kaleem. “He’d know what I was up to. So, it wouldn’t be a genuine test.”

Charlek bit his lip. “Unless it was another prisoner,” he said slowly, “who has some information that both the authorities and Kaleem needed.” He turned to Kaleem. “Do you think you could act a little bit?” he said.

“I think so,” said Kaleem. It would be tricky fooling Calver but he would try.

“Is there someone you could use?” asked Alistare.

Charlek shook his head. “No, I couldn’t use a prisoner like that. And they’d have to act as well. If this Calver Toms is as good as Kaleem says he is, he wouldn’t be fooled for a minute. But we could pretend to be tricking Kaleem and see if he works that out. And see what he tells Kaleem. I can tell the people here I’m doing research on the effects of confinement on law-abiding citizens.”

“So, who would you use, then?” asked Alistare.

Charlek grinned. “Fancy a spell inside?” he said.

“Me?” asked Alistare.

Charlek nodded.

“Wow!” said Alistare. He pushed his hair back from his face. “Okay. Bring it on.”

Charlek glanced at the dataserve.

“12.51,” it said.

“Right, gents,” said Charlek. “We have just nine minutes to work out exactly what our friend here is going to say to Mr Toms, and then I’ll take you, my other friend, and show you your room and get you tagged.”

The Info Drop

Kaleem had spent a long time the evening before working out exactly what he should say to Calver Toms. He knew he'd got to be incredibly cunning. He must not let Calver get the slightest idea that this was a trick. And Calver was precisely the person it would be difficult to fool. He had to be absolutely sure he knew what he was doing.

He went over it all in his head again. He would call up Calver. He'd tell him that Alistare was being held at the prison and that he didn't know why. He would ask him to find out what he could.

Once he was sure he'd convinced Calver, he would let Charlek know. Charlek would then seek out Calver and also ask him to find out what Alistare was trying to hide. Alistare would reveal to Calver an aspect of the Terrestran mission that was not general knowledge. Kaleem would then check later with Charlek to see what Calver had told him.

But would Calver see through it right from the beginning and just play along? Kaleem guessed he couldn't really be certain. At least, he supposed, if Calver came out squeaky clean, it would prove he was good at his job. Kaleem suspected that he would never know, even with this elaborate trick they'd thought of, whether Calver was absolutely loyal or just even cleverer than he'd thought.

Which was why he'd got to get this absolutely right.

He sighed. "Calver Toms," he said to the dataserve.

Almost at once Calver's face appeared on the screen. "Kaleem," he said. "How can I be of help?"

"Alistare Rogerin is being held at the prison and I don't know why. Would you be able to find out?" said Kaleem. His heart was beating fast. He hoped he wasn't blushing.

Calver frowned. "Can't your mate Charlek Smithin help?" he asked.

"Not really," said Kaleem. "Even if he knows something, he can't be allowed to say anything."

"A little awkward, I think," said Calver. "As both of them are supposed to be on the Terrestran mission."

"All the more reason why I need to find out as soon as possible," said Kaleem.

"Yes, I understand," said Calver. "I'll see what I can do." He hesitated. He looked straight into Kaleem's eyes.

It was really odd how he could do that, even from a screen.

"This wouldn't be part of the test, would it?" he asked.

Kaleem started his counting backwards routine. Razjosh had taught him how to do this to empty his mind.

"Very clever," said Calver. "You'll be using the red dog next."

How on Zandra did he know that? Razjosh had also taught him to think of the red dog's activities when the numbers didn't work.

"Well, never mind. Either way, I promise I won't let you down."

His face snapped from the screen and the screen went blank.

Charlek and Calver

"So we're not treating you too badly?" said Charlek.

"Nope!" said Alistare. "Everything's cool. I don't know what Kaleem was complaining about. Even the food's not bad."

Charlek laughed. "Well, he was here a bit longer than you're going to be. And he was confined to his room most of the time. The food, though – darned Terrestrans. Still, I got a few extra portions."

"Has he contacted you?" said Alistare.

Charlek shook his head and put a finger on his lips.

"I mean, are you and he still in contact?" said Alistare.

"Oh, he's much too busy for the likes of me these days," said Charlek.

Alistare was smirking.

He'll never fool Calver at this rate, thought Kaleem. *Nor even anyone here who might be watching.*

His personal communicator buzzed three times, stopped, then buzzed twice again. Kaleem. That was the signal they'd arranged.

"If you'll excuse me, I've got work to do," said Charlek. "Unless you've got anything to tell me?"

Alistare raised an eyebrow. Charlek allowed himself to give the slightest nod.

Alistare's eyes widened.

Careful, careful, thought Charlek.

He left Alistare's room and hurried back to his office.

Charlek was surprised to find that he was shaking as the dataserve started searching for Calver Toms. It wasn't like him to be nervous. About anything. But he'd got to get this right. He was even more surprised when the ping a few seconds later told him that Toms was found. But the screen remained disappointingly dark.

"I hope you don't mind me remaining on vocals only," said a disembodied voice. "I currently have no clothes on and I don't believe in avatars. How may I help you?"

Charlek couldn't help smiling to himself. Prude then, this boyo. Now if he'd been sitting there nude, he'd have been only too glad to reveal all. Impress the other men. Enchant the ladies.

"Well?" asked Calver. "Can I be of help?"

"We've got a prisoner who won't talk," said Charlek. "I've heard you're good with people. You know, finding out what's going on, even if they won't speak."

"And how did you find out about me?" asked Calver.

What the... Charlek realised he knew the voice but he just couldn't place it.

"Well?" asked Calver. Charlek could hear the impatience in his voice.

"I can't really remember," said Charlek.

"Oaky, fine," said Calver. "I can come the day after tomorrow."

"Good," said Charlek. "You know we could really make it worth your while. What this prisoner is hiding is of immense value to us."

"I'll see what I can do," said Calver. "Day 132. 2.30."

"Fine," said Charlek. *Got you, baby,* he thought.

Deception

He would be here any minute. Charlek felt decidedly queasy. It wasn't like him to let anything get to him. But this was so incredibly important. He didn't want to let Kaleem down. Just five more minutes and he would be here. Four minutes ticked by. Seeming like four hours.

The dataserve buzzed.

Must be him, thought Charlek.

It wasn't. It was a droid guard. "We need your presence, sir," it said. "There is a security malfunction in G5 section."

"Have you checked it out?" asked Charlek.

"Sir, we cannot establish what caused the alarm. We need a senior officer," replied the droid.

"Must it be me?" asked Charlek.

"Sir, you are the only appropriate officer available," said the droid.

This was all he needed. He'd better go, he supposed. It was probably a false alarm, perhaps a bit of wiring gone wrong. But if he didn't check it and it was genuine he could get into a lot of trouble. Hopefully it wouldn't take too long. It was a bit of a trek to G5, though.

He decided to take the hover-scooter. At least that would speed things up a bit. If Toms arrived he could soon scoot round to meet him.

Ten minutes later, as he turned into F wing, his personal communicator pinged. "Charlek Smithin," he announced. He slowed the scooter right down. It was a bit noisy. The signal would be weak on his communicator down here and it might be difficult to hear. Yes, it really was weak. There were no visuals and Charlek had no idea who he was speaking to.

"Well, I'm here with Rogerin," said that voice again. Who did Toms remind him of? And how had he got into the prison so easily? "I'm sorry I didn't get to see you first. But your reception droid seemed to know all about it and brought me straight here."

That shouldn't have happened, thought Charlek. *Time to reprogramme, I think.* But at least it meant the visit could go ahead even if he couldn't get there.

"Okay," said Charlek. "I'll be back in my office soon. Pop along and see me when you're done." He turned the scooter back up to full speed and was soon in sector G5.

It all seemed calm. Two droid guards were looking at the alarm panel.

"Have you counted the prisoners?" he asked.

"Yes, sir," the more senior droid answered. "All present and correct, sir. All confined to their rooms."

"Have you reset the alarm?" asked Charlek.

"Every time we do," said the lower-ranked droid, "it goes off again."

"There must be something wrong, then," said Charlek. "We may have to override."

"Sir, protocol may be compromised," said the senior droid.

So why on Zandra did you send for me? he thought. "Come on then," he said. "Show me the prisoners."

The tour of the section took about ten minutes. All seemed well, though a few of the inmates were getting impatient.

"Will we be allowed out again soon?" grumbled one. "This is supposed to be an open prison."

Charlek had a go at resetting the alarm himself. Just as the droids had said, it went off again straight away.

"I'll just have to get permission to override," he said. He turned to the nearest dataserve.

"Commander Watkins," he said.

Watkins' face appeared on the screen within seconds.

"So, you've checked all of the men and there's no reason to suspect a problem?" said Watkins after Charlek had explained the problem to him.

"No, sir," replied Charlek, "but I think there will be problems soon if we don't let the men back out into the open areas."

"Very well," said the commander. "You may override. We'll get maintenance to come and have a look. But you'd better stay down there until the alarm is reset. I'll send a couple of extra droids along as well."

This was a disaster. He would not be able to meet up with Toms now. It just all seemed so unnecessary. It was so obviously a circuit fault. He wondered what was going on in Alistare's cell.

"We've found the problem," said the maintenance operative. "It'll take about ten minutes to fix."

"Good," said Charlek. Dare he leave now? Better not, just in case.

Ten minutes later, the maintenance man and his droids started to pack away. "All done," he said.

"Thanks," said Charlek. "Return to central," he said to the two extra droids.

Just as he pressed the power switch on his scooter his personal communicator buzzed.

"Calver Toms here," said that voice. "I've interrogated your prisoner and I'm afraid I have nothing to report."

"Can you wait and debrief me properly?" asked Charlek. "I'll be about ten minutes."

"I'm afraid I can't," said Calver. "I have another appointment now. I must leave straight away." He ended the communication before Charlek had time to say good-bye or thank you.

Still, hopefully, Alistare had done his bit. If he had, it looked now as if they could trust Calver Toms. According also, of course, to what he said to Kaleem. They would see.

He set off towards Alistare's cell.

Daring to Trust

"So, what did he say, then?" said Charlek, sipping his chofa. They were sitting in the Refreshment Park. It was early afternoon and therefore quite warm. Although Kaleem knew it was just a holoscene it was pretty convincing and actually quite pleasant.

Charlek had insisted they should come here even though Kaleem had protested. "Look, I need some fresh air," he said when Kaleem had pointed out that they might be overheard. "And anyway, as the heat kicks in people will keep away."

Kaleem pressed the pad on his minicompu. He'd managed to record the conversation he'd had with Calver Toms.

"Hi, Kaleem. Sorry about the lack of visuals again. I rarely bother with clothes when I'm home alone," said Calver.

Charlek shook his head and frowned then grinned. "Poser," he mumbled.

"I was actually called to the prison to interview Alistare Rogerin. I told him first that I knew something about the Terrestran mission and he told me a little more about how he was involved and what your plans were about the Terrestrans. He also said that no way would the prison guards get anything out of him. I worry a little that he trusted me so easily."

"Why were you called to the prison?" asked Kaleem.

"They wanted me to find out what he knew," said Calver.

"And you didn't tell them anything?" said Kaleem.

"Of course not," said Calver. "Now do you trust me?"

"I'll think about it," said Kaleem. "Give me twenty-four hours."

"Oh, and by the way," said Calver. "Take care with Charlek Smithin. He does not seem trustworthy."

"Thanks for that," said Kaleem. "I'll be in touch."

Charlek was really grinning. "Not trustworthy, eh? I'll show him," he said. "What about my acting skills, then?"

Kaleem stopped the recording. "What do you think?" he asked. "Did we convince him?"

“Whether we did or not,” said Charlek, “at least it seems we can trust him. Either to keep a secret or to understand exactly what is going on. Hopefully both.”

“What did he actually say to you?” Kaleem asked Alistare.

Alistare shook his head. “The stupid thing is,” he said, “I can’t really remember. It was all a bit bizarre. I can remember him talking to me, all right. I guess I must have said those things if he said I did. I do know about all of that stuff after all. But I can’t even remember what he looked like. All I can remember is the droid coming in and saying I had a visitor. And then, yes, I was talking. I think he must have hypnotized me or something. It was all a bit like a dream. And I woke up after he’d gone.”

“I didn’t get to see him either,” said Charlek. “It would be easier to decide if we had. That voice as well. I wish I could remember where I know it from.”

“His voice?” asked Kaleem. What was wrong with that? As far as he could tell, it was just a fairly standard Zandrian voice.

“Just seemed familiar,” mumbled Charlek.

“So what do I do?” said Kaleem.

“Tell him it was a test and that it looks as if he’s passed it?” suggested Alistare.

“He seems a useful sort of guy,” said Charlek. “Can’t hurt to have him on board. We’ll help you keep an eye on him.”

“Right,” said Kaleem. “I’ll get rid of this then.” He deleted the recording on his minicompu.

“I’m going to get going before it gets too hot,” said Charlek getting up from the table.

“Me too,” said Alistare, joining him. “Enjoy my newfound freedom a bit.”

Guess I’m paying for the chofas, then, thought Kaleem. He looked for the droid, but there was no sign.

His personal communicator buzzed.

Calver Toms. Right on cue. How did he know? Annoyingly, he was on full visuals this time.

“Well, have you decided?” asked Calver.

“Yes, I’ve decided to trust you – sort of,” said Kaleem.

"Sort of?" asked Calver.

"Well, did you know we were testing you?" he said. "Were you just playing along?"

"What do you think?" said Calver.

"That I can trust you," said Kaleem, "even if it's only to know a lot about what is going on."

"It's up to you how you make use of me," said Calver.

"How come Charlek recognises your voice?" asked Kaleem.

"I have a standard neutral Zandrian pronunciation," said Calver. "I've cultivated it because it inspires confidence. It's common enough, though."

"Okay," said Kaleem. "You're in. I'd like you to join the Terrestran mission."

"Good," said Calver. "I think you're needed now to settle your account."

The screen snapped to black.

The waiter-droid was hovering at Kaleem's side. "Sir, we close in ten minutes because of the heat. Would you care to settle your bill?" it said.

How does he do it? thought Kaleem.

Meeting of Minds

Kaleem sat in the small meet room with Charlek Smithin, Alistare Rogerin, Ella, Petro and Tulla. Calver had said he would be there but he was running late. They all looked awkward. Kaleem felt awkward. Petro looked tired and pale. He had only been back from his other meet an hour ago and had had to come straight here. They were linked to an almost identical meet room on Terrestra. Frazier Kennedy's face dominated the screen but in the background Kaleem could see Ben-Alki Mazrouth, Saratina, Pierre Lafontaine, Stuart Davidson and Sandi Depra. For once Sandi and Saratina seemed to have nothing to say. And they were clearly staring at the Zandrians trying to make some sense of them.

The only person who seemed to be at all at ease was Frazier Kennedy. In fact, he seemed to be really enjoying the occasion. He had the huge grin across his face that usually meant he was about to make a ludicrous suggestion.

Kaleem, of course was used to this type of awkward meeting but he was struggling today because he was concerned about three of the important women in his life. First of all, where the heck was Rozia? Sure, he'd not managed to communicate with her but he'd asked his grandfather to do that on his behalf. At least with her not there he was avoiding some awkwardness. But where was she, though? Was everything all right with her or not? And he did have Tulla Watkins in the room with him. Her hair was blond compared with Rozia's normal dark Terrestran hair but she acted so much like Rozia. And he couldn't help remembering the black Tulpen again and all that that meant… and it set off a longing in him – for Rozia again.

And of course there was Ella. Being with her, thinking of her, aroused certain similarly strong feelings. But he wasn't in love with her – in fact he was fairly certain he could never ever be in love again.

Frazier's face calmed. He quickly introduced the Terrestran

team and Kaleem did the same with the Zandrian one. A few tentative smiles and greetings were exchanged.

Then the broad grin burst back across Frazier's face. "You need another Terrestran," he said.

"What, do you want to join the group?" said Kaleem.

"No, no, no, much too busy," replied Frazier. "And you need someone who knows about these matters. Someone who is not committed elsewhere."

"Who then?"

"Obvious, really," said Frazier, his grin getting even broader. "Razjosh!"

"I don't know…" said Kaleem. Razjosh was enjoying a quiet domestic life now. Besides, he was doing all of that investigation into the Davina Patterson files. Kaleem didn't want to drag him away from that.

"I only mean that he should help entertain the Zandrian guests," said Frazier. "Not necessarily go to Zandra."

Would it, though? thought Kaleem. Just a few months ago he'd been worrying about no longer having Razjosh's support. Now, though, he'd got used to thinking for himself. The elder who had been saved from switch-off wanted to make the most of his remaining time. Kaleem would have to cope without him sooner or later.

"I think it would be a good idea," said a voice behind Kaleem.

Charlek. The young prison officer pushed back his wavy blond hair and drew his sessel closer to Kaleem's so that the camera would pick him up more easily. "He was really impressive when he spoke that time, just after you'd found your father. And we don't need to bring him here. He can come in hologram."

"I didn't know you could actually do that between planets," said Kaleem.

"What, you still don't understand Zandrian technology at all, do you?" said Charlek. "All the more reason, if you ask me, to get your Terrestran friends to get to know us better."

Then Kaleem remembered what even a couple of Z Zoners had managed when he'd been imprisoned on Zandra.

"You know he'd be good," said Charlek, slapping Kaleem's back.

"I suppose so," said Kaleem. Was he ever going to learn to work on his own?

Enthusiastic clapping came from the screen. Saratina was jumping up and down.

"Ess. Azos. Goo. Good. An alk," she cried.

Kaleem's heart sank as he noticed how uncomfortable Pierre and Stuart looked behind her. Sandi Depra was still unusually quiet. He heard Alistare clear his throat and out of the corner of his eye he could see Tulla and Petro staring at the screen. They were used to meeting other people but it seemed that Saratina bothered even them.

"Well, I'm glad I'm not the only one who is keen on this guy," said Charlek. "He really is great."

"Course he is!" shouted Sandi. Seconds later her face framed with her head of crazy dancing red hair was filling the screen. She seemed to have come alive now. "And this woman here is a star for seeing it before the rest of you. Even before me." She hugged Saratina.

Saratina giggled.

"I was just racking my brain to think who we might have had as well, and hey, you know what? He's about the best choice," said Sandi.

"I thought I thought of it," said Charlek.

"I meant amongst the Terrestrans," said Sandi.

"And what exactly am I?" asked Frazier.

"An elder," replied Sandi. "Amongst ordinary Terrestrans, then. Come on guys; let's get on with this thing."

There was a general mumble of agreement from both sides.

"Okay, we'll get ahead," said Frazier. "I just need to talk to Kaleem on a private matter."

The others all made their way out of their meet rooms. As soon as they were alone, Frazier's face lost its grin.

Oh no, thought Kaleem.

"I'm afraid we've not been able to talk to Rozia," said Frazier. "We've tried to communicate with her several times and we've even visited her home and place of work."

"What's the matter? Is she missing?" said Kaleem. His heart was beating fast and his mouth was dry. Why did he still care so much? He wasn't supposed to care like this any more. What she did was really none of his business.

"No, no, nothing like that," said Frazier. "She's well they say. Fully recovered, in fact. She just doesn't seem to want to talk to anybody. They say she's not taking on any new projects at the moment. There are some sort of personal problems."

So, she was all right, more or less. Thank goodness. But then if she was having personal problems... maybe something was going wrong between her and Julien. Maybe he could... no, that would never be possible again.

Now Kaleem was digging his finger nails into his palms.

"What is she actually doing now?" asked Kaleem.

"She's working on the education programme in the New Zone," replied Frazier. "And doing very well by all accounts."

That figured. Kaleem nodded his head. "Not surprising," he whispered.

"I just thought you should know," said Frazier. "It's a pity. She would have been ideal. Especially with her being able to understand Saratina. And I'm sure you'd have been all right about her, wouldn't you?"

Kaleem managed to whisper, "I would have thought so."

"Oh well, can't be helped," said Frazier. "I'll take my leave now. We'd better get on with this, I guess."

They said their goodbyes and the screen went blank. Kaleem could hardly move or hardly breathe. He was glad that he was alone now. He sat down on one of the sessels and put his head in his hands and closed his eyes.

All he could see was Rozia's face the day he left her. Not understanding and full of pain. Was it his fault whatever was wrong with her now? Or had Julien done something even worse? Was there just the faintest hope that...

No, he mustn't go there. That could never ever be. Never ever again.

Why did he still have to care so much?

He took a deep breath. He really had got a lot to do and he must get on with it. He took another deep breath. The extra oxygen in his body seemed to help. His hands relaxed.

He managed to stand up and walked purposefully out of the room.

He was surprised to find Tulla, Petro and Ella waiting for him. It was agony to look at Tulla, made worse by the look of concern in her eyes. She looked so much like Rozia had on the day he'd left her. Petro's arm was round her waist and that helped a little.

"Everything all right?" asked Petro. "The ladies were a bit concerned."

Tulla nudged him.

"Well, I was too," he added.

"Was it to do with Rozia?" asked Tulla. Her cheeks went bright red.

Kaleem nodded.

"Nothing's happened to her, has it?" asked Tulla.

Why did they have to talk about her? The lump was back in his throat. He managed to shake his head. "She just doesn't seem to want to have anything to do with the project," he said.

"Tough one, mate," said Petro. He slapped Kaleem's back. "Still, I think we're going to be quite a merry little gang. A good mix of talents and personalities."

"Never mind that," said Tulla, nudging Petro. "Kaleem's upset." She looked straight at Ella.

Ella raised her eyebrows and pursed her lips.

"Not, it's all right, I'm fine," said Kaleem breathing deeply again and straightening his back. He couldn't let them think he wasn't ready for this. "And we'd better get on."

Ella came up to him and kissed him on the cheek. "I know exactly what you need," she said. She looped her arm through Kaleem's.

She seemed to bring him back to the ground. They marched smartly along towards the safe-boxes. This felt good. All these tiring emotions were quickly dissolving.

"We'll soon get you sorted," she said. She squeezed his arm a little tighter and stopped walking to pull him into a kiss.

You probably will, he thought.

Then he remembered that Calver Toms had not turned up. "Wait a bit, though," he said. "There's something I must do first."

Calver Toms

The dataserve was already buzzing when he got inside his own safe-box. He wasn't surprised to find that it was Calver.

"Sorry I didn't make the meet," he said. "Something came up."

"We could have done with you there," said Kaleem. "I could have done with knowing what was really going on."

"I can guess," said Calver. "Your grandfather charmed everyone as usual. You're worried about what has happened to Rozia and you find Tulla's presence awkward. You're shit-scared about the whole mission but you're putting on a brave face. You're glad you've got Charlek and Sandi Depra there. Ah yes, Charlek and Sandi Depra..."

"What?" said Kaleem.

"No, you probably haven't seen that coming."

"Charlek and Sandi?" said Kaleem.

"Yes, oh yes," said Calver. "And Ella is seducing you. You had better get to her."

"How do you know all of this?" growled Kaleem. "And why weren't you there?"

"The usual way," said Calver. "I couldn't get there because I had to look into something else for another mission."

Well, I wish you'd tell me something useful, thought Kaleem.

"Take care with the new girl," said Calver. "End it now, before there is trouble."

It's only a game, thought Kaleem. *It's not doing any harm.* "And you've nothing more useful than that?" he asked.

"No," said Calver. "But take my word for it. It's important."

"Okay, fine," said Kaleem. *But let me go now.* He just wanted to be with Ella.

"Fine. We'll talk again soon," said Calver. He disappeared from the screen.

Kaleem set the dataserve to standby. He hurried to Ella's safe-box. Everything else could wait.

Travelling Light

Kaleem still couldn't get used to it. Charlek had insisted that they practise it in turn. Oh, he appreciated all of the benefits of holocommunication: you could be with people when you needed to talk about important matters, and it was quick and relatively easy. But it was disconcerting. He really felt as if he were in the room with Razjosh and Anthea until he went to touch something. Then he seemed to be separated from them by a type of veriglass bubble. And also, very disturbingly, he was very aware of the Supercraft and of Charlek and Alistare who were all waiting for their turn. If he turned his head slightly to the side he could see them.

"So you see," said Razjosh. "I've really been busy. It will be good when you can come in the flesh and see them closely for yourself."

"Yes, it looks like a complete collection of all of her work," said Anthea. "And it's all truly beautiful."

Kaleem remembered the Babel book. That was now also with Razjosh. He could see it just about but this screen through which he seemed to be looking was distorting it. And he wanted to touch it. Even though it would remind him of Rozia and would cause him pain.

"You'll be able to get a much better look at when you're here for real," said Razjosh. "And I don't think I can show you the fascinating audio files because the technology is too weak to make them audible to a holo. We haven't transposed them yet. But you'll be here soon enough."

"Come on Kaleem, let somebody else have a turn," said Alistare.

"I'd better go," said Kaleem. It was hard to believe that Anthea and Razjosh couldn't hear what the others were saying and that those on the Supercraft couldn't hear or see the people on Terrestra.

"Yes, we'll see the real you soon," said Razjosh.

Anthea waved. "Don't forget to lift the screens in the last stage. You all really do need to see Terrestra from space. Not to be missed!"

Kaleem braced himself. He hated the jolt that happened each time he transported into or out of a holo. It made him feel dizzy and slightly nauseous. He gratefully accepted the beaker of water Charlek handed him.

"Right," said Charlek to Alistare. "Where to this time?"

"The Peace Park?" suggested Alistare. "Will you come along as well?"

"No, I'd better not this time," said Charlek. "Petro's the only other one who can operate this device safely. And he's catching up on some sleep."

"We've all got to learn, though, haven't we?" said Kaleem.

"Yes, and you can send him down this time," said Charlek. "But only under my supervision."

Kaleem operated the controls. It really was quite easy. Or so it seemed.

"Steady on," said Alistare. "You're bumping me round a bit."

Kaleem could not work out what he was doing wrong.

Charlek took the control panel back off him.

"That's better," said Alistare, his voice slightly less high-pitched than before. "Oh wow! It's amazing here. The colours – even through this glass bubble thing. It's going to be even better seeing it for real."

"Try moving around a bit," said Charlek. "But don't speak to anybody if you can avoid it. They may realise you're a holo. It might spook them."

It went very quiet as Alistare went into the holo. It was always a tricky moment. But within seconds he was surrounded by the bubble and was moving excitedly.

"It's unbelievable. Even through the holo," he cried. "There's so much green." He breathed in deeply. "You can taste the green," he said.

"You can't actually," said Charlek. "You aren't really there at all."

"Yeah, but even so," replied Alistare. "Can't wait to see the real thing."

"It will seem very real to him," said a voice. Kaleem noticed that Calver Toms had just walked on to the public access deck. "Because although he's in a holo, he's looking at a real scene. He will have seen very little of the real plantations on Zandra."

Kaleem guessed that Calver was right as usual. Everyone else, though, seemed to be ignoring him.

"Don't you think you should stop this now?" Calver asked Kaleem. "Practising holo transporting isn't our only priority."

And right again. He would be infuriating if Kaleem didn't like him so much.

"I suppose that is enough for one day," said Kaleem.

"Okay," said Charlek. "Back you come."

There were the seconds of silence as the holo bubble closed in on itself. It wasn't that he really thought it was dangerous. It was just that nobody was really certain exactly what was happening at that precise moment.

"Hi guys," called a voice. "Are you still playing?"

Ella had wandered out of their room. She'd been catching up on sleep too. She was wearing an emerald green tunic and very tight leggings a shade paler. She had on the same perfume that she'd had on the first time Kaleem had met her. She took his breath away. For the first time since they'd set off, he wanted her.

They hadn't really needed to keep watch. This was a fully sanctioned trip with the blessing of both the Zandrian and the Terrestran authorities. The Supercraft crew had everything under control. They could actually just sit back and enjoy the journey. But Kaleem had insisted on them being vigilant. And he'd made sure the patterns of who was on duty with whom changed constantly – it helped then to get to know one another. Charlek was used to changing shifts as a prison guard, Alistare loved the mathematical purity of it all and Calver really appreciated seeing his predictions about how certain people would be together coming true. Petro and Tulla, though, had insisted on being together all the time. Ella had complained about not spending enough time with Kaleem. He'd actually been relieved to get away from her as often as he could. Oh yes, she could certainly still seduce him, persuade him to make love to her and generally he'd enjoy it – until a few moments afterwards. Then it felt so wrong and Tulla, especially as happy as she was with Petro, was a constant reminder of why.

"Take care," Calver whispered. "She will soon realise what you are thinking."

Today was different though. She looked stunning. All Kaleem wanted to do now was take her back to her cabin or go to his and make love to her for hours and hours. Forget about holotravelling, forget about treaties between Zandra and Terrestra, and acorns and vaccine and the whole Peace Child scenario. He only had one thing on his mind.

"Watch it," whispered Calver. "You'll lose her. She's not dressed like that for you."

Ella smiled briefly at Kaleem and then looked at Charlek. Her eyes grew wide. "You seem to be so good with the holo tool. Will you teach me how to use it?" She laid a hand on Charlek's arm. She turned her head to one side and half smiled up at him. She was standing with one hip turned out.

Great elders, thought Kaleem. *She's too gorgeous to lose.*

Charlek laughed and pushed her arm away. "We're all going to have to get good at using it," he said, "and I wouldn't dress like that if I were you… not for lessons in holo travelling. You never know what might happen to you." He pushed her away gently. "Mind you," he said, "if you weren't already spoken for…"

Ella turned to Kaleem and flashed a full smile at him. "Come on you," she said, grabbing his hand. "I know what you need."

"Hey, don't do anything I wouldn't," Charlek called after them.

Alistare laughed.

"Careful," Calver mouthed.

Kaleem didn't care. There really was only one thing on his mind now.

They went to his room. It was thankfully a good distance from the main deck, a safe distance from the others.

"Come on, quickly," she said, as soon as they were through the door. That increased his excitement even more. And yes, it was as good if not better than ever. And it worked, again. Soon he had forgotten anything threatening or difficult about where he was now.

And when they wandered out of his room and back to the deck a couple of hours later, where thankfully the others were too deep in conversation for them to be amused at the thought of what he and Ella had been doing, he had to admit, Ella was good for him.

He sat on a double sessel and pulled her towards him. He kissed her lightly on the cheek. She responded by squeezing his hand. He hoped the others had noticed but he doubted they had. Everyone was listening intently to what Tulla was saying.

"That's the problem, though," said Tulla. "People in different cultures have different values. You have to respect whatever they believe in."

"Yeah, actually, even if it seems wrong to us because it goes against what we think," added Petro. "We've had to learn that one, haven't we?" he shook his head. "It can be hard. Very hard."

"But there are some things the same, aren't there?" asked Kaleem. "A need for food, shelter and friendship."

"Yes, that," said Tulla. "But when that's all in place, what next?"

"That's where the problems are," said Petro. "And you don't always have the luxury of a Peace Child to help."

Tulla looked up and caught Kaleem's eye and blushed again. "But it's great if you can have one, of course," she said, getting redder by the minute. "And we know you'll be great."

Just the sort of thing Rozia would have done. Tried to make it better. He took his arm from round Ella's waist and pulled away from her slightly.

"You know what?" said Charlek. "I've got an idea. We should have a jug or two of frega tonight – not too much of course – and all get an early night. We really don't need anyone to stay up all night. Then we can all be up early tomorrow to enjoy the whole of the approach to Terrestra without the screens. We really can't miss that!"

Calver was gripping the side of his landing seat. His knuckles were white with the effort.

He's the last person I'd have thought would be scared like that, thought Kaleem.

Everybody else, he noticed, was quiet as well though. It was the usual way, when a Supercraft was about to enter the atmosphere of another planet. It was always a tense moment. Tulla was holding Petro's hand tightly. Alistare and Charlek were staring at nothing in particular and not getting eye contact with anybody. Charlek was taking deep breaths.

I suppose I've done this a couple of times before, thought Kaleem. No, there was nothing particularly scary about this. After all, the first time he'd travelled on Supercraft the crew had been just two members of the Z Zone who's had only a little experience of navigating large beasts like the vehicle they were on now. And he'd got a lot more to worry about. This was going to be the first time for centuries that Terrestra had openly received visitors. His father's expedition party did not count – no Terrestrans other than Razjosh and a few other elders had known about this. This mission was public and he didn't know how the public was going to react.

"Do you think they'll be okay with us?" said Tulla.

Ah! She was even managing to read his thoughts just like Rozia always did. No, it probably wasn't that. She and Petro had gone interplanetary often enough – and not always by Supercraft. The smaller spaceships must have been even scarier. At least you had the impression with a Supercraft that nothing could destroy it – even a planet hitting it at high speed. She wouldn't worry about the landing, though she might well worry about what was going to happen afterwards.

"Well, it's my job to see that it is, isn't it?" mumbled Kaleem.

Great elders, he was only too well aware of that. Again.

A soft whirring started.

Thank goodness, thought Kaleem. *That should distract everybody.*

The screen walls slid out of place so that they were now looking through the robust veriglass walls.

And there she was: Terrestra, blue, with patches of green and brown and white swirls of mist and cloud.

Everyone seemed to relax. Tulla let go of Petro's hand and leaned forward. "Wow!" she said. "Most planets look beautiful from space, but that's about the best I've ever seen."

"Worth the trip just for that," said Charlek.

"I should say so," said Alistare.

"Lucky guy," said Ella, "coming from such a beautiful place. No wonder you're so good looking." She placed her hand on Kaleem's thigh and moved it up and down.

Not now, Ella, thought Kaleem. He brushed her hand away.

"We'll be doing a couple of orbits," a droid voice said. "Then the burn shields will be raised. Estimated time to touch down – fifteen minutes."

"So here we go folks," said Kaleem. "From now on, Terrestran English only."

Calver Toms, he noticed, was still frowning slightly.

Beginnings and Ends

Astrid Wellmanner sat as still as she could, willing herself not to be sick. She'd been to a funeral before, but not one like this. The first and last time was that of her grandmother's, possibly the last person who was going to be allowed to die of old age. The Crematorium looked exactly the same as it had done then. They'd even used the new lasers on her grandmother. There was so much concern about the emissions that were causing the poison cloud to get worse that they were avoiding adding any more carbon to Earth's atmosphere.

"We'll all have to go underground soon," Arnold Pullarney used to keep saying, "if we carry on farting everything into the atmosphere like that." And he'd worked all his life fighting against the pollution that greedier inhabitants of Earth were causing. He'd been such a great man. Astrid was so proud of him. He'd done so much work in medicine that people were living for longer and longer now. Well, it wasn't just him. But he'd had a very big part in it all.

And now this crazy idea.

Patrick slid his arm round her waist. He didn't say anything. There wasn't anything to say. But that felt good. It seemed to take the nausea away a little.

Not for long, though.

She couldn't believe that her grandfather was actually going to be given a lethal injection and that he would die in front of them.

"It will be painless. It will be dignified," he said. "Even for those who have to watch."

A young violinist now stood one side of the small platform where later the minister would speak.

"No religious nonsense," Arnold had said. "Just a celebration of a life that's going to have a dignified end."

She didn't know how she was going to bear it. She wanted it to be over and done with. But there were still people coming in.

The violinist finished and bowed slightly to the audience. People began to clear their throats and shuffle in the embarrassing silence.

"My mother used to say it's an angel passing when it goes quiet like that," Patrick whispered. He kissed Astrid lightly on the cheek.

The music from Fauré's requiem began to play. This was the signal that her grandfather, massively sedated, was about to come in. It was his favourite piece of music. She thought she was going to faint. In fact, she wished she could.

There was a bit of a kerfuffle at the back of the room.

How can they do that? she thought. *This is such an important moment.* She turned to see what was going on. It was Miriam Pullock and her entourage. What on Earth was she doing here? Now, of all times? Astrid had wanted a mother for so long. But she couldn't call this woman mother. Mothers didn't look like that. They didn't act like that.

Astrid felt as if she were spinning faster and faster out of control and everything was becoming a blur. The room came in and out of focus. Patrick was saying something to her but she couldn't understand. Then she was watching a film. It all seemed to be happening behind a glass case. Her grandfather coming in. The medic giving him an injection. One by one they went up to his bed and he gave them a final message. She couldn't take in what he was saying. Then all those people who talked about him. She could just hear and understand snatches of words… "the first to face switch-off… dignity… great discoveries, heritage," but none of it got anywhere near the truth. *He was just my grandfather,* she thought. *They don't know him.*

She was aware that Patrick was holding her tightly. At last a large tear escaped and slid down her cheek. Patrick tightened his grip. *Thank goodness I've got him,* she thought.

Then it was all over and like a zombie she talked to the other well-wishers. She saw Miriam leave. She looked angry. Astrid hadn't the energy to care.

"I get it now," said Astrid. "That's why she was so cross."

"Incredible," said Patrick. "What made her think she'd get any of this?"

"Who knows?" said Astrid. "I've never understood how her mind works."

She took another of the paintings out of the box that the solicitor had given them. They were lovely, with all the rich blue, silver and gold. She would keep them forever. Well, until it was her turn for switch-off. Ugh! She shuddered at the thought. Maybe they would change the law again by then. *What have you done, Gramps?* she thought. Yes, she would keep them until she died and then she would pass them on to her children and her grandchildren.

She looked at Patrick. Would he be the father of her children? She hoped so.

"Do you understand any of this?" he asked. He was looking at one of the books. Its cover showed a baby in a basket that was floating in some rushes.

Yes, she could understand it a little. But she knew she wasn't really deciphering it. She just knew the story so well because her grandfather had told it her so often.

"Not much, really," she answered.

"So he was really the last person who could read Wordtext?" said Patrick.

"Mm," replied Astrid. Strictly speaking, that wasn't true. Gramps had told her that there would be a few people who would be taught how to read Wordtext. But that was secret information and should not be told to anyone.

"Let's put it away," she said. She loved it all but it reminded her of Gramps and she still wanted to cry every time she thought of him. He'd showed her the contents of this box and told her about the stories in it so often when she was a little girl.

Patrick was fiddling with the strange little machine and the little discs that seemed to go with it.

"Do you know how this works?" he asked.

"No idea," said Astrid. Gramps had always told her they were some type of recording that Davina Patterson had made. He'd always said that she was much too young to understand it. Not even now that she was twenty-five. And now she had no idea how to make the little machine work. He'd never shown her.

"I wonder if you just..." Patrick said as he tried to jam one of the discs into the opening.

Astrid didn't want to hear. She was afraid that the discs contained some terrible secret.

"Can you see the book that goes with the pictures of the tower?" she said, changing the subject rapidly. She knew Patrick would not be able to find them. The book had never been reunited with rest of the contents of the box. There was some story of Davina having given it to the child of a friend, and that that friend was going to give it to Davina's granddaughter because the child had died. Yet the book had never arrived. Davina's friend had been killed in a car accident on her way over to bring the book back to Davina Patterson's family. No one had ever found out what had happened to the book.

It was all too much. That was such a sad story and she still could not believe what her beloved grandfather had done. She could not help a loud sob escaping and within seconds the tears were streaming down her cheeks.

Patrick was by her side in an instant. He held her tightly. Thank goodness he held her tightly. It seemed to reconnect her with the ground somehow.

"We'll put these away now, sweetheart," he said. "This is not doing you any good."

"Tell me," said Astrid. "I want to know."

"Well," said Patrick. "I don't know quite how to say this."

He seemed to be hesitating. He looked so serious. Was he about to break up with her? Perhaps he couldn't stand how depressed she'd become. She wasn't being fair to him. But she must keep him. She must do whatever it takes. She couldn't get rid of the lump in her throat. She couldn't tell him how important he was to her. She couldn't tell him that she loved him. He'd never told her that he loved her but he'd always seemed so caring. But perhaps she'd got that wrong.

This was it then. This was going to be the end. She tried to swallow but the physical pain in her throat brought tears to her eyes.

Patrick pulled her round to face him. He held both of her arms quite firmly and looked straight into her eyes. "I think we should… I think we should go and raise our children outside of normal society," he said. "Become self-sufficient. Then we can ignore switch-off. We can let nature do its job."

What was he saying? Was he really saying what he thought he was saying?

"You don't have an answer for me?" he said. He was still holding her arms and in fact he squeezed them a little harder. "Don't you want to be my wife?"

"How can we do that?" she said. "How can we be self-sufficient? How can we live outside of society?"

"They're chopping the planet into zones," said Patrick. "I've seen the plans at work. It's so that they can manage the changes in the most logical order. The least needs doing the longer they're leaving it."

Astrid's heart was beginning to thump now.

"I guess they won't even get round to completing the Z Zone," he whispered. "And it's the most fertile place on the whole of the planet. If we could find some others… some others who feel the same way as we do…"

She tried to pull away from Patrick.

"I can't believe what my Gramps did," she whispered hoarsely.

"Hey, hey, hey," said Patrick now pulling her to him and holding her tightly in his arms. "He was a good guy. A really good guy. But it doesn't mean that you have to agree with absolutely everything he did." He kissed the top of her head.

She could feel him breathing, could feel his chest going up and down. It was comforting somehow.

"You haven't answered my question," he said. "The really important one." He pushed her away and looked straight into her eyes. "Well? Will you be my wife? Will we raise lots of children and bring them up in a good world?"

Astrid couldn't help laughing. "Of course," she said. Why wouldn't she?

"This is it then," said Patrick. "This is where it will all begin."

"Do you think the others will come?" asked Astrid.

"They'll come," said Patrick. He put down the box and sighed.

"I'm sorry," said Astrid. "We couldn't leave it behind."

"Of course not," said Patrick. "It's fine."

What a day it had been. The wedding had gone well. There'd been the normal white dress. The speeches. The presents – all left behind until after the honeymoon. And such a great excuse for what they were doing now. "Taking a honeymoon to an unknown destination."

Astrid looked at her surroundings. It was beautiful here. It was hard to believe that they were on a planet that had been affected by climate change and pollution, that they were threatened by an atmosphere that was gradually becoming more poisonous. The air felt and tasted fresh and clean. There were all sorts of flowers and trees growing here. In the distance, she could hear the waves crashing on to the sands. It was hard to believe that they were living on a sick planet.

"You're sure they won't come looking for us when we don't go back?" said Astrid.

"They'll be too busy by then," said Patrick. "It's all happening more quickly than they'd imagined."

Someone shouted.

Astrid couldn't make out where the sound was coming from.

"Over there, look," said Patrick.

They'd come from a different direction from the way she'd arrived earlier with Patrick. There were about twenty of them.

"There'll be twice as many again tomorrow," said Patrick. "I hope it won't spoil our wedding night, Mrs Mariah." He placed his arms around her waist and kissed the top of her head. "Only it's a bit important. It's the beginning of the Z Zone. Refuge for all of those who object to switch-off."

She didn't mind. She was with Patrick. They were doing the right thing.

Astrid couldn't sleep that night. They had all worked hard making their new home as comfortable as possible. There had been no question of a proper wedding night. That would come later. There was too much to do now. It was exciting and frightening at the same time. She and Patrick, forming a new society. Rebels.

Someone moved behind her. She was pleased to see that it was Patrick.

"It's great here, isn't it?" she said.

"Hmm," he said.

In the moonlight she could see that he was frowning.

"It is, isn't it?" she asked.

He shook his head. "Can't you see? There are no stars."

She looked. It was true. You couldn't see any stars.

"And look at the moon," he said. "Can you see how it looks sort of green?"

He was right. If you looked hard enough. "Why can't we see the stars any more?" she asked. "Why is the moon such a strange colour?"

"It's the poison cloud growing. Soon it'll be too bad for us to breathe. That's what they're working on now," he replied. "Making underground homes and systems for extracting oxygen from the air. It'll be complicated."

"How long have we got?" she asked.

"A couple of years. Or maybe just a few weeks," said Patrick. "Who knows? That's why they'll be too busy to worry about us."

Astrid shuddered.

"Shall we go down to the sea? While we still can?" said Patrick. "It's warm enough to swim. And afterwards…"

"Yes, I'd like that," said Astrid. So maybe they were going to get a wedding night after all. The Z Zone and the poison cloud could wait. She was with Patrick.

False Promise

On Terrestra

Kaleem looked at all of them. It was all right after all, he supposed. The Zandrians seemed quite at ease in the Executive Suite at the Citadel of Elders, though he noticed they had hardly touched their nectar. Alistare had stopped staring at Saratina. Charlek was now managing to look at Stuart and Pierre without getting embarrassed. Sandi Depra was grinning widely. Ben Alki looked quite serious still but no longer quite like when he used to conduct the switch-off ceremonies. Kaleem could have sworn, anyway, that his face had got a bit softer, a little friendlier, and he did now smile occasionally. Tulla, as he might have expected, understood every word that Saratina said and Petro shook his head in amazement as she interpreted for everyone else. But Petro, because he was Petro, was kind enough to smile at everything Saratina said. Calver hadn't said anything. He just sat with his hand clasped together and his two index fingers resting on his lips. And, as usual, he was frowning slightly.

And Rozia was missing. She still would not talk to the group. Well, Kaleem guessed he didn't blame her. Why on Terrestra would she want to come near him?

Yes, the introductions were complete, there had been a mixture of Zandrian and Terrestran handshakes, there was the normal small talk and now Kaleem knew he needed to steer the discussion around to the trading programme between the two planets.

"EE mus oofu, oosin all tree," said Saratina. "A eer ake."

"Yes, it is," said Tulla. She only had the slightest Zandrian accent. "We really need your help now. We really need even more supplies of acorn."

"As ee fitanin?" asked Saratina.

"Not if you could get into a safe-box," said Tulla.

Saratina looked alarmed.

"Oh, most people did," said Tulla with a smile.

Kaleem thought he could guess what Saratina had been saying. He wished Tulla wasn't so much like Rozia with Saratina.

That hurt.

"The trouble is," said Stuart Davidson, "we don't actually need to increase the amount of vaccine we take."

"That is so true," said Sandi, shaking her head and rolling her eyes, "unless you also have got a vaccine that brings back people's common sense. Now that would be something."

"Isn't there something else that we have and you don't?" asked Alistare. "Nothing else you Terrestrans would like."

"I know what would be really useful," said Sandi. "Some of your holotechnology. That's what we need. And Terrestrans should go to Zandra to find out about it. Well, of course, some of us are. Going to Zandra, I mean. And I can't wait to see some of your medical equipment and processes."

"I think holotechnology would be pretty cool, too. Ours must seem pretty primitive to you," said Pierre.

Kaleem had to agree. The holoscenes on Terrestra were not really at all convincing. When you went to Zandra or even travelled on a Zandrian Supercraft the scenes were much more realistic.

"Maybe," said Charlek. "But probably because we need it more. You have far more real landscape – despite having had the poison cloud for all those years."

"I think Terrestra should import frega," said Kaleem, blushing with embarrassment as he saw the empty glasses of the Terrestrans and the still almost full ones of the Zandrians.

The Zandrians laughed.

Mighty elders, thought Kaleem, *they actually think I'm funny.*

The Terrestrans, though, exchanged puzzled looks.

"Oh yeah," said Ben Alki. "I remember now. You could hardly touch the nectar, not even the wheat and rye. So what is this frega then? And you are the only Terrestran to have tried it."

And my mother and Razjosh... and, thought Kaleem. It was almost like a physical pain that shot through him as he thought of the one other Terrestran who had drunk frega on Terrestra. Rozia. The first time they had slept together.

"Ah, frega, yes," said a voice from behind them.

Kaleem jumped. He still did that every time he met Razjosh. Even though the elder was now getting frail, and even though he'd passed on all of the Peace Child responsibility to Kaleem.

Everyone scrambled to their feet. The Zandrians found it quite hard to get out of the advanced Terrestran comfisessels without looking awkward. Saratina, on the other hand, stood up smoothly and elegantly despite her deformities.

"No, no, no," said Razjosh, gesturing that they should go back to their seats. "I am an elder in name only these days. No need for this exaggerated politeness. I am merely another Terrestran. A quite elderly one at that and probably past my usefulness."

Yet he caught Kaleem's eye and Kaleem knew that he most certainly was still useful. "But frega, yes," he continued. "That would be something. Not yet, though, I think. That will have to come later. There will be too many who will not see pleasure as something useful."

"Huh!" said Sandi.

"Indeed," said Razjosh. "But sadly true. Well, welcome, all," he said, looking around the group. "Welcome to the Citadel of Elders. I trust those of you who have come from Zandra had a pleasant journey."

"It's good to meet you again, sir," said Charlek.

"Very good to see you too," said Razjosh in Zandrian, offering a Zandrian handshake.

The other Zandrians smiled at Razjosh and Pierre and Stuart exchanged a glance.

"Look at that," said Ben Alki. "Guys, we ought to learn Zandrian."

"Oh, wise, very wise indeed," said Razjosh in Terrestran. "And you'd have an excellent teacher here," he said, nodding towards Kaleem.

Kaleem blushed and looked down to the ground.

Razjosh grabbed his arm. "That was a compliment," he whispered, "so take it gracefully. And I have some really interesting news. Come and see me soon – in a holo if need be, though better in person."

Kaleem looked up and straight into Razjosh's eyes. The elder nodded slightly.

What now? What on Terrestra had Razjosh found out?

The elder looked at the rest of the group.

"So," he said. "What do we all think?"

"Holotechnology," said Stuart, Sandi and Pierre together.

"Ah, yes, a wise choice," said Razjosh. "Zandrian holotechnology on Terrestra, something to be had indeed. Maybe I myself could get back to Zandra that way."

"You'd be welcome any time, sir," said Alistare. "In person, we mean."

"Oh no, I don't think there'll be any more trips on a Supercraft for me," said Razjosh.

Kaleem went to protest.

Razjosh looked at him sharply. "No, Kaleem is perfectly capable of doing all the diplomatic activities," he said.

"But you'd still be welcome just as an ordinary Terrestran guest," said Charlek.

"Oh, no, no, no," said Razjosh. "We'll leave it to all you young people. Anyway, the main reason I came to meet you here is to invite you all to my home for a meal. Anthea wants to meet you." He turned to Kaleem. "You come half an hour earlier," he whispered. "If you can't get to me sooner." He turned back to the others. "So tomorrow at seven," he said.

He bowed slightly and left the room.

"What a lovely man," said Tulla.

"Enn't ee?" commented Saratina.

"I wouldn't have thought an elder would be so friendly," said Petro.

"That's Razjosh for you," said Kaleem.

"Don't you have to call him Razjosh Elder?" asked Ella.

"I haven't for a long time," said Kaleem. *But you should,* he thought. Why was she irritating him so much?

As Razjosh went out of one door a pair of droids came in through the other. They steered in trolleys obviously containing food.

"Aha!" said Charlek. "Terrestran food. I can't wait to try this."

"Don't hold your breath," said Sandi. "It's nowhere near as good as Zandrian food."

"How can you know?" said Charlek. "Surely, you've never been to Zandra."

"Oh, funny head two over there told me all about it," she said, pointing to Kaleem. "And I believe him."

"It's strange," said Alistare. "You Terrestrans ought to be able to produce better food than we do. You've got more choice."

"That must be what the trouble is," said Sandi. "Makes us lazy."

By now the droids had finished laying out the food.

"Please," said the more senior looking of the two. "Supper is served."

Charlek poked at one of the pastries. "Interesting," said Charlek. "What is it?"

"That's a Cornish pasty," said Sandi. "A Terrestran delicacy."

Charlek took a bite. He chewed it carefully. Then he frowned and pulled down the corners of his mouth.

Sandi laughed. "Oh here," she said. "Try this. Our food isn't all terrible." She took a sliced of red pepper and dipped it into the dish of humus. Then she turned to Charlek. "Open wide," she said, as she popped it into his mouth.

"Hmm, not bad," he said leaning towards her.

Kaleem found it difficult to tell whether he meant the humus or Sandi. Knowing Charlek he probably meant Sandi. Charlek and Sandi. What a thought. But it looked as if Calver had been right again.

"They're getting on well, aren't they?" Ella whispered to Kaleem, as she slipped her hand into his.

Well, yes they were.

"Hmm," he said, squeezing her hand tightly. "And we are, aren't we?" He suddenly felt guilty about how he'd been avoiding her and he also felt a rush of gratitude to her for how kind she'd been to him in her own way. Of course, it wasn't anything like the way things had been between him and Rozia, but it was something. It was a pleasant distraction. It kept him going.

She gave him one of those looks.

"Later," he whispered. "The first time on Terrestra." He tapped her nose.

She giggled. "Real Terrestran sex, then. As long as we don't have to celebrate with that awful nectar."

"Sorry to interrupt," said Calver, grabbing Kaleem's elbow. "But I need a word."

"Now?" asked Kaleem.

"It's important," said Calver.

Kaleem let go of Ella's hand.

"Where are you going?" she said.

"Calver wants to speak to me," said Kaleem.

"Calver?" asked Ella, frowning.

"Couldn't this have waited?" asked Kaleem as they moved away from the others. "We're all tired and hungry…"

"And you can't wait to get back to bed with Ella, yes I know, but if we're going into the New Zone tomorrow there's a few things you need to think about."

"Okay," said Kaleem. "What then?"

"Well for a start, there's Charlek and Sandi. It's a pity that didn't happen until later," said Calver.

"Oh?" said Kaleem.

"Yes, because even though the New Zone has no doubt improved since you knew it as the Z Zone it will be a shock to all of us Zandrians. The whole concept."

"Go on," said Kaleem.

"So, they'll fall apart again. There will be blame – especially as you've got Saratina there. A constant reminder."

He was right, as usual. "And Ben Alki, and what he used to do," Kaleem added.

"Yes," said Calver. "That too."

"Oh dear," sighed Kaleem.

"Alistare, Petro, Pierre and Stuart will balance well," said Calver. "Tulla, however, will be totally shocked." He paused.

"And it could be quite painful for you because... well, you know."

Putrid elders. So all the polite conversation and all the friendliness were not going to mean anything after all.

"And what about you?" asked Kaleem. "What do you make of it all?"

"I can't really judge," replied Calver. "I can only see what others think."

You might make a better Peace Child, thought Kaleem.

"You'd better go back to your food," said Calver, "and your woman."

When he got back to the others just looking at the food made Kaleem feel sick. He couldn't be bothered to use the diastics system. Feeling sick seemed about right. Ella was waiting for him and twinkling at him. The pleasant feelings he'd had before had gone. He'd have to be a performing monkey later on. He forced a smile for her.

The others had finished eating now and were saying their goodnights and he reluctantly allowed himself to be led back to their room by an enthusiastic Ella.

The New Zone

Kaleem found it hard to take it all in. This was not the Z Zone he was used to. For one thing, they were not travelling by kartje. They were using a normal transporter. Just a few months and they had achieved all of this.

"I thought you said it was really deprived," said Pierre. "This doesn't look at all bad to me."

Ah! So, this was a lesson even for Terrestrans. Normal Zone Terrestrans. Or was the point that the Terrestrans were now doing something right for the Z Zoners? Were they trying to show off to the Zandrians?

And bless all the elders, he shouldn't be thinking of it as the Z Zone. It was the New Zone now.

"Eet ood at we done ha o in atrya aee ore," said Saratina. "Ansorta moo etter."

Kaleem couldn't be sure about what she was saying but he did find himself wondering whether she missed driving around in kartjes. She had been such a good kartje driver.

They travelled on and he became even more amazed. The poor little cottages had been replaced already with modern houses just like those in the Normal Zones. Everybody looked cleaner. There were fewer children running around. He presumed they were being schooled via dataserves. There were still more open spaces in the New Zone and fewer people and transporters around than in the Normal Zones. The people who were there still looked older and more worn than Normal Zoners. Yet on the whole it was beginning to look more and more normal, and actually, Kaleem realised, less exciting than it used to be.

"So how long did you say they'd been working on upgrading this area?" asked Tulla.

"Just eighteen months," said Kaleem.

"So what was it like before?" asked Petro.

"Poor," said Kaleem. "You wouldn't believe it."

No, he couldn't believe it himself. And what made it worse

was that he knew Rozia had somehow been involved in making things better here. He didn't know the details, but he expected she had been involved with the Adulkis and with the general education programme.

"So, what was the problem in the first place?" asked Charlek.

Sandi sighed. "The Z Zoners didn't like switch-off."

"Ah yes," said Charlek. He let the arm he had had round Sandi's waist drop.

Just like Calver said, thought Kaleem. He caught Calver's eye. Calver nodded.

"I didn't like switch-off either," said Sandi. "I was part of Operation Hippocrates."

"Yeah, I know," said Charlek. "But what was all that about? You can't…"

"Well, we'd have been overpopulated if we'd have let people go on and on. There's no knowing when they would have died… with our healthcare system."

"Isn't that what you're responsible for?" Charlek said to Sandi. His voice was a little cold.

"I do my best," she replied. "But I don't think being healthy is just about physical health. Terrestrans need to get out more."

"I know. I know that's what you think," he said. He rubbed her arm. "But what about the people that lived here?" he asked. "If they didn't have switch-off, then how come they didn't get overpopulated?"

"Er, life wasn't quite so healthy here," said Kaleem quietly. "They didn't have diastic monitors or much else of the newest Terrestran technology."

"Ah, I see," said Charlek. He exchanged a glance with Alistare.

Kaleem noticed that Petro and Tulla were also speaking very fast and very quietly.

"Ell ee o a ee aulkees?" asked Saratina. She seemed to guess that something was not quite right, that there was some disagreement.

Kaleem wasn't sure.

"She wants to go and see the Adulkis," said Tulla, suddenly alert to what was going on. "Who are they?"

You don't want to know, thought Kaleem.

Saratina began to set the transporter. She'd picked that up quite quickly, Kaleem noticed. He couldn't stop her.

The ride was not that comfortable. Not that they were shaken about all that much like they would have been in a kartje. It was just that no one was speaking. Charlek, Alistare, Ella and Calver just stared straight ahead. Saratina was bright red. She seemed to have realised that she had made a mistake. Sandi looked as if she was about to cry. Sandi, fun-loving, strong-minded Sandi was hurt. Petro and Tulla and Stuart and Pierre just kept giving each other worried looks. Ben Alki just sat with his arms firmly crossed over his chest. Kaleem managed to exchange a glance with him. He shrugged and shook his head. This was looking bad, very bad. But Kaleem guessed that dealing with situations like this was just part of his job.

It seemed to take an age to get to the park but when he checked he realised it had only been about fifteen minutes. The transporter was so much faster than the old kartjes. Yet it had seemed like hours. The atmosphere had been so strained.

The park didn't look any different. Kaleem's stomach turned over as he saw the tower. It just didn't go away. It was always there, reminding him of the Babel prophecy. So was his fear of those strange children in adult bodies. He had got quite used to them before but now he'd not seen them from some time. And of course, he no longer had Rozia with him.

Saratina bounded out of the transporter. She started calling. No one appeared.

"Air ar ay? Air ar ay?"

The others slowly made their way out of the transporter.

Ella sidled up to him. "Is that the place you keep dreaming about?" she whispered, sliding her hand into his.

No, not here, not now, thought Kaleem, pulling his hand away.

Saratina suddenly let out a loud cry and started hurtling down the slope. Then Kaleem too could see them in the distance. Nothing much had changed here then – except, maybe, were they moving a bit more slowly? Then one of the adults with them waved. He recognised Greta, one of their carers. He waved back.

The Adulki who had seen him came racing up the hill, ignoring Saratina. The others had knocked Saratina to the ground and were piling on top of her. Two carers were pulling them off, but they were jumping back on to her as fast as possible. They were all giggling. But the other Adulki kept on running.

Kaleem held his arms out ready to catch the Adulki but he ran right past him and straight up to Tulla. "Rozia," he called. "You've changed your hair."

Kaleem didn't think he could stand it.

"No," he managed to say softly. "This isn't Rozia. This is Tulla. She just looks like Rozia."

He thought he was going to faint.

Ella tried to put her hand back into his, but he kept his fingers tightly closed.

The Adulki looked disappointed.

Tulla beamed at him though. "Oh, I've heard that Rozia used to play with you a lot," she said. "I can play with you, too, if you like."

The other Adulkis were now making their way over to them. Then Kaleem spotted that one of them was carrying the big orange ball that Rozia had made. So, that was still going strong. Well, of course it was: she would have made sure that it was robust enough to last a long time. When they spotted Tulla they began to run. They were all making the same mistake. But when they realised that Tulla wasn't Rozia they didn't care anyway. Because she was so much like her. Soon the ball was being launched down the slope and they were showing her how they chased after it. She and Petro joined in and they and the Adulkis and even the Adulki carers were soon giggling.

Kaleem thought he was going to burst. He'd never seen the Adulkis with the ball in the end but he knew that was exactly how Rozia would have used it. He knew Tulla wasn't Rozia and that anyway she belonged to Petro. That wasn't the problem. Why couldn't he still be with her, watching her doing what she liked most: working with these poor damaged people?

He reminded himself that he had got work to do. Concentrating on that might help him to stop thinking what could have been. He turned to face the others. Charlek, Alistare, and Ella were watching with a look of horror on their faces. Ben Alki, Stuart and Pierre had faint smiles on theirs and Saratina and Sandi were shouting, screaming and laughing, egging them all on.

Finally, the Adulkis flopped to the ground and Kaleem was able to talk to Greta.

"What's being done for them?" he asked. "There doesn't seem to be much change. In fact…"

Greta's face clouded over. "Well, we have done a lot," she said. "Rozia's been fantastic."

Kaleem felt as if he was being stabbed in the chest.

"It's a real pity that…" Greta continued. She looked away from Kaleem.

"A pity that what?" asked Kaleem.

"That she couldn't continue," said Greta.

"Why couldn't she?" asked Kaleem. What was wrong? What had happened to her?

"I… I can't say," said Greta, blushing and looking to the ground.

One of the Adulkis came up to then and started shaking Greta's arm.

"I want to go home," he said. "I'm tired."

"Soon, very soon," Greta replied. She ruffled his hair and pulled him towards her.

The Adulki stuck his thumb in his mouth.

"Yes," she said. "Rozia worked really hard." She looked towards Sandi. "And the health programme she devised with you was really impressive – all that better nutrition, all those vitamins. And there were the education programmes as well. They have all done so well. But you know, I think that tired them out even more. And it was a little too late. They haven't got long now I don't think."

Greta's eyes filled with tears. "Come on my lovelies," she said. "We'll take you all home to bed." She turned without saying another word and she and the other helper and all the Adulkis started making their way back towards the tower.

It occurred to Kaleem that he'd never known exactly where they did live. He'd only ever seen them in the park. Could Rozia be wherever that was, waiting for them?

Then he realised something else. He had not seen Thoma. Kaleem hoped he wasn't ill. He shuddered as he remembered Greta's words.

The others, he realised, were already making their way back to the transporter. Everyone was looking rather serious. Even Saratina was quiet. Charlek seemed to be avoiding Sandi just like he was avoiding Ella.

"So what happened to them?" asked Alistare.

"There was an accident," said Sandi. "The Normal Zoners did it."

"An accident?" asked Charlek.

"They were working close to edge of the Z Zone with some sort of gas," said Pierre. "And some of it escaped."

"So, they were careless?" said Charlek.

"It was an accident," said Stuart. "They were negligent, yes, but it wasn't deliberate."

"Seems funny, though," said Charlek "to work that closely to other people with something dangerous. Or didn't your Normal Zoners count the Z Zoners as people?"

"We know," said Pierre. "It was wrong. But we're trying to put it right now."

"Ormal oers oo oo thin ow," said Saratina.

"Yes, they may be now, but what happened to you?" asked Tulla. "Did the Normal Zoners hurt you?"

Saratina looked to the ground.

"That was deliberate," said Ben Alki. "Saratina and her parents were attacked. For no reason. Yes, I'm afraid the Normal

Zoners used to be very bad."

Calver caught Kaleem's eye. His look said I told you so.

Kaleem knew he should be doing something to put this right. He couldn't concentrate, though, because he couldn't stop thinking about what might have happened to Rozia. All he could manage was to slide his arm around Ella's waist. He had no real desire to touch her but he had to attempt some sort of reconciliation with his Zandrian friends. This time, though, she pulled away from him.

Kaleem couldn't speak. The others didn't seem to want to. So much for being a Peace Child then. The journey back to the Citadel seemed to go on forever.

The Babel Book

Jonty held the strange object carefully. He'd thought it was a picture for his room but there was no hook on the back, just another picture and some strange marks.

"It's very, very old," said his mother. "And yes, you must take care of it, but you must also look inside."

Look inside? What did she mean? It just seemed to be a flat picture.

"It's a book," said his mother. "Look."

She sat next to him on the sofa, put her arm around him and opened the pictures so that it was flat. It was nice sitting with his mum like this. They never did that when they watched movies. There were more lovely pictures inside but also some more of the strange marks and some even curlier, squigglier ones right at the beginning.

"These are words," said his mother pointing to the darker, straighter squiggles, "and they are in Wordtext. Words are what you say. People used to draw them and other people could understand what they meant. These days we just have movies."

Yes, the pictures did remind Jonty of a movie he'd seen. It had been just like these pictures. As his mother opened up picture after picture, Jonty recognised the story of the tower that was built so that people could show the god they believed in how clever they were. But the god had become angry and made the tower fall down and made all the people speak different languages so that they couldn't understand each other. Jonty loved the blue, silver and gold on the clothes of the people in the story. He thought he could almost hear them talking in all those different languages as the tower fell down. The story was a bit frightening though. It made him shiver.

"You shouldn't play with this like you play with your other toys," said his mum. "But you can look at it sometimes. I'll put it somewhere really safe and you can ask me when you want to see it." She cuddled him closer. "It's nice sitting together like this, isn't it? We can always do that when we look at the book, can't we?"

Jonty nodded. "Why have I got the b… book now?" he asked.

"Well, you know Grandpa Goodmanner had his switch-off last week?" said Mum. "He used to own the book and whenever the person who owns the book has their switch-off, it is passed on to the youngest child in the family. That is you this time." She tickled Jonty's tummy. "Aren't you a lucky boy?"

Jonty's eyes filled with tears. He blinked to try and stop them falling. He wanted Mum to think he was a big boy. But he knew he was going to miss Grandpa Goodmanner.

"I know it's very sad about Grandpa," said Mum, "but that's why you have the book. It's to remember him by."

Jonty took a big breath. "Why do we have to have switch-off?" he said.

"This really is a very special book," said Mum, touching one of the pictures very gently. It was obvious she wasn't going to answer his question. "A lady called Davina Patterson made it. Lots of the movies you've seen were based on her books. But nobody knows what happened to the rest of them. This is the only one left on Terrestra. It's worth a lot of credits."

"Why didn't Grandpa sell it then?" asked Jonty. "Then we'd be rich."

His mum laughed. "We have more than enough credits. Don't you want to keep the book?"

"Yes," said Jonty. "But how come Grandpa had it?"

"Well, he was the youngest child once," said Mum, "when his grandma died."

"But how come this is in our family?" asked Jonty.

"Somebody from our family was working on one of the old rubbish mountains. One where there was a lot of scrap metal. Probably from old transporters they used to call cars. They didn't go on their own like our transporters do. The people who worked at the rubbish mountains found the book there. They offered it to Davina Patterson's family, but they said our family should keep it as long as we promised to look after it well. They wanted to forget all about the books. They're still upset because Astrid Mariah disappeared with all of the rest of Davina Patterson's things."

"And did we look after it?" asked Jonty.

"I think so, don't you?" said Mum. "It's lovely, isn't it?"

"I think I want to go and play now," said Jonty. "Will you put the book away for me?"

"I will," said Mum.

Jonty went to his room. He decided he wanted to play on his own. He didn't bother calling up any of his friends. He wanted to think for a bit. Why, he wondered, did they build that tower in the first place? How did they build it? It was a long, long time ago, wasn't it? *They didn't have the machines and droids that we have now, did they?* thought Jonty. *It must have been hard work.*

Jonty had some building blocks. He had a go at building a tower, but as he put more and more bricks on, it was harder to balance them.

"You will not build a tower up to me!" he shouted. "I am your god and I will make you not able to understand each other." He smashed the tower down. "That will teach you!" he shouted.

"Jonty, you're being very noisy," Mum called from the corridor outside.

"I'm playing Babel Tower, Mum," Jonty called.

"I see," said Mum, popping her head round the door. "Didn't you want to call up Tommy and Aidan?"

"No," said Jonty. "I want to work it all out about the tower."

"Well, I know," said Mum, coming into the room. "Why don't we see if we can find the movie and you can watch it nice and quietly before you go to sleep? Get into your jimjams, go under the laser brush and clean your teeth and I'll find it for you."

It didn't take Jonty long to get ready. They'd got the latest laser and toothbrushes at their house, and the house droid had already found his clean pyjamas for him.

Even so, Mum had already found the Babel film on his dataserve when he came out of the bathroom.

"Can I watch it with you?" his mum asked.

"Of course you can, Mummy," said Jonty snuggling up to her as she sat on his bed. "This is nice, but it's not as nice as when we were reading the book."

He began to feel sleepy as he watched the people dressed in their lovely gold, blue and silver clothes making their way up the tower. He woke with a start as the tower started falling and the voice of the angry god boomed out. There was a lot of panic and a lot of noise.

"You're not frightened, are you?" asked his mum.

"A bit," said Jonty.

"Okay," said his mum. "Serve off," she commanded the dataserve. Then she turned back to Jonty. "I'll tell you a different ending to the story. There was one man, a very brave young man, like my Jonty will be one day, who said to the angry god: 'No, we didn't build the tower so that we could show how good we are. We built the tower so that we could get closer to you, sir.' Then the angry god scratched his head a little. 'Mm,' he said. 'Now that is a good idea. I would like it very much if some of you came up the tower every day to see me. And I'll even help you to rebuild the tower and let you all speak the same language again.' So, you know what happened?"

"No, what?" said Jonty.

"The tower was built again. And it was beautiful. The children played around it and in it and they climbed up it. And they told the god how good he was. The god saw how good they were, and they all lived together and understood each other, and they are probably still all living there very happily."

"I like that story, Mummy," said Jonty.

"Good," said his mum. "Now it's time for sleepyhead Jonty to get to bed." She tucked him into his bed and kissed him on his forehead. "Sweet dreams, little one."

Although he'd been sleepy earlier, Jonty wasn't able to get to sleep at first. He couldn't help thinking about the tower and the young man his mum had talked about. The man who would rebuild the tower. He sounded really brave. Jonty hoped he would be like that when he grew up.

He did drift off to sleep eventually. Then he began to dream. It was just as his mum had said. There was a young man rebuilding the tower. He had soft blond hair just like Jonty's. But he wasn't actually building the tower. He was telling other people to build it. The people looked like children and grown-ups at the same time. And he was telling them a story or something, Jonty thought, but he couldn't quite understand the words. Not at first anyway. Then he could. The man was making marks on something that looked like a book.

"What are you doing?" asked Jonty.

"I'm writing," said the man.

"Writing?" asked Jonty.

"Using Wordtext. Just like they used to." The man smiled at Jonty.

Jonty knew he was in the story about the tower because all the people were wearing the blue, silver and gold, just like in the book. Well, some of them were. The funny children and the man with the blond hair were wearing clothes a bit more like the ones Jonty and his friends wore. Jonty liked the young man.

"Do you want to help me to rebuild the tower?" the man asked Jonty.

Jonty nodded.

"The masterbuilder will write the instructions for you," said the man. "You'll have to learn to read Wordtext."

"How can I do that?" asked Jonty.

The man smiled again. "You'll know how to when the time comes," he said. Then he turned round and carried on talking to the funny-looking children.

The sun suddenly came out from behind the clouds and Jonty had to shut his eyes. When he opened them again he was in his own bedroom and his mum was changing the light setting on his window. The morning sun always woke him up.

There was something of the dream still with him but the details were fading fast. There was something he had to do. What was it?

He noticed his building blocks in the corner. His mum looked in that direction at the same time. "Oh, Jonty, you didn't tidy away properly last night," she said. She started fussing with his bricks.

Then he remembered the tower and the funny children. What was it he had to do? It was something to do with the book, wasn't it? He closed his eyes and tried to remember the story.

"Aren't you going to help me, Jonty?" his mum asked.

No, he couldn't. He had to think. He closed his eyes even tighter and put his hands over them.

"Hey Jonty, are you going back to sleep?" his mum asked. She shook him gently and laughed. "Sleepyhead. Still, they say people who sleep a lot don't get wrinkles."

Wrinkles. That was it. All those wrinkles on the book.

"Mummy, what are those funny marks again? On the book?"

"Words," replied his mum.

"I want to be able to know what they say," said Jonty.

"Oh Jonty, nobody bothers with Wordtext these days," his mum said.

That was it. Wordtext.

"I want to learn how to understand Wordtext," said Jonty. He looked straight into his mother's eyes. *Don't you laugh at me,* he thought.

"Oh, Jonty, why?" she said softly. She wasn't going to laugh at him, he could tell.

"So that I can read how to rebuild the tower," he said.

She didn't say another word. Her eyes were all wet and it looked as if she was going to cry. No, she certainly wasn't going to laugh at him.

Suddenly she was hugging him really hard and he could only just breathe. He knew, though, that somehow she would help him to learn Wordtext. She just had to.

Decisions

"We've listened to every single audio file," said Razjosh. "Every one. It wasn't easy. This little contraption has its own power supply. Of course it ran out." He held up the little machine that had been found in Narisja's box and a small tube which had an even smaller tube on top. "We had quite a job hooking it up to our power systems. There was every chance we might have burnt it out. But we managed, and I have to say, it made very interesting listening – in places. Lots of boring bits too, of course."

"Was there any more… about…?" asked Kaleem.

"No, there was only that one mention of you. Only that one time. And really, it could have been just an amazing coincidence. You know, just like how we've talked before about how prophecy can be used as a satisfying explanation for an unusual event. Would you like to hear it?"

"I don't think we'll have time before the others arrive," said Kaleem. No, he definitely did not want to hear a description of his mother going into the Z Zone carrying the Babel book. It just might seem too real.

"I don't think there was actually anything wrong with Davina Patterson either," said Razjosh. "All of this happened at a time when she was stressed by her work and it was rather fashionable to hypnotise people to try and find out what was going on in their minds. It is all very interesting, though, and you should certainly listen to the recordings sometime."

"I will," said Kaleem.

"Will you take all of the collection back to Zandra?" asked Anthea.

"No," Kaleem answered quickly. "It should stay here. Perhaps there should be some sort of exhibition."

"A good idea," replied Anthea. "Though wouldn't your mother like her Babel book back?"

"Oh, I think she'd rather everything stayed together," said Kaleem. "I expect she'll come back to Terrestra sometime and can see it all then." Would she though? Terrestra hadn't been particularly kind to her and she and her parents were not completely reconciled. He got on with his grandparents Louish and Frazier very well but their relationship with their daughter was as strained as his was with his father. It must be a generation thing, he decided.

The communicator buzzed.

"Ah, here they are," said Anthea. "Now let's see what's what."

The house droid showed the visitors in. They all seemed like strangers. Kaleem noticed that the Zandrians were wearing Terrestran tunics. They'd obviously made an effort. He himself was wearing the strange hybrid outfit he'd devised for such occasions. Sandi, Saratina, Ben Alki and Charlek looked more serious than they'd ever looked before. Pierre, Stuart and Alistare seemed anxious. Ella was very pale. Calver as usual looked perfectly calm and was totally unreadable.

Kaleem suddenly felt guilty about the way he'd been with Ella. Yes, all she'd wanted was a very casual relationship but maybe he'd taken that a bit too literally. He didn't have to be unkind to her, did he? He slid an arm around her waist and smiled at her. She returned a faint smile.

"Well, come on in and make yourselves comfortable," said Anthea.

This time the Zandrians actually succeeded in sitting down quite elegantly in the comfisessels. The droid busied itself pouring glasses of nectar.

"It's wheat and rye," Anthea explained. "Perhaps not too sickly sweet for our Zandrian friends."

The Zandrians seemed to cope with the nectar better this time and even the Terrestrans seemed reasonably content with the unpopular flavour. Kaleem sensed that everybody was beginning to relax, if only a little.

The droid eventually announced that the meal was ready. Whilst they ate, Razjosh told the Zandrians about the production methods for the different types of food they were consuming.

Anthea asked lots of questions about how food was produced on Zandra. For Terrestran food, what they were eating was pretty good and the Terrestrans ate with relish. If there was anything wrong with it the Zandrians were too polite to let that show. The atmosphere eased a little more. But Kaleem was only too well aware that they were not dealing with the real problems.

"Well," said Razjosh at last as the droid began to clear away the dessert dishes. "Have you all agreed on any strategies to increase trade between Terrestra and Zandra?"

After a long silence Ben Alki finally spoke. "I still think the best Zandra could do would be to show us how their holotechnology works."

"Yeah, that would be really cool," said Pierre.

"O tees it atualee?" said Saratina.

"Oh, it's just a sort of pretending," Tulla answered quickly. "Our planet is nowhere near as beautiful as yours. We have to build it up with holoprogrammes."

Saratina still looked puzzled. "Estra? Ootiful? Een aer oosio low?" she said.

"We're trying to avoid getting a poison cloud," said Tulla. "That's why we still need your acorns. Especially now after the landquake."

"We'd still need some vaccine. A smaller but still regular supply," said Sandi. "We'd need to keep our diastic systems topped up."

Charlek was sitting with his arms crossed. "The trouble is," he said, "I'm not sure I want to trade with any planet that can cause that." He pointed to Saratina. "And what about those funny children?"

"Yes, a result of Normal Zoner carelessness," said Razjosh. "But tell me, Charlek, you're a prison guard, aren't you? Are you're saying that everybody on Zandra is perfect? Why do you have prisons if that is the case?"

What is he doing? thought Kaleem. *That's not the way he taught me to handle these things.*

"Our prisoners are usually political," replied Charlek, his

arms still folded across his chest. “Just like Kaleem.”

“And our Z Zoners became Z Zoners for political reasons,” Razjosh said. “At least we gave them a space where they could be free and think what they liked.”

No, this is not the way, thought Kaleem. *I’ve got to do something.* But he didn’t know what.

“Funny sort of freedom,” Alistare mumbled.

Razjosh caught Kaleem’s eyes. There was a half-smile on the retired elder’s face.

Calver began to chuckle. “Can’t you see what he’s doing?” he whispered to Kaleem. “He’s goading you. Doing it all wrong on purpose. Go on, Kaleem, tell them all: how every single Terrestran and Zandrian sitting round this table is doing the best they can, and always has done and always will do.”

Yes, thought Kaleem. *The eternal message. We mean you no harm. Let my ways be your ways and my people be your people. We shall not compromise, but will find the way that goes beyond either of our ways.*

“The Z Zone started off because some people didn’t want switch-off,” said Kaleem. “And it became neglected because the Normal Zoners wanted to leave the people there in peace. Later, they became lazy and didn’t bother trying to communicate. And then they became a little afraid of the Z Zoners.”

“We only had switch-off because our medical control became so good,” added Sandi, looking at Charlek, a question in her eyes. “And we’ve only taken on isolation so that it could stay that way.”

“Only it didn’t,” said Alistare. “Because the Starlight Racer disease happened.”

“And some of us realised that switch-off wasn’t needed any more, and also that it was wrong,” said Ben Alki.

“Not everybody, though,” added Sandi. “Not everybody thought that way.” Kaleem had never seen her look so angry.

“Air are oo eepal a a eepal in zed zoe a noall zo a o andra,” said Saratina.

“Yes, you’re right,” said Tulla. “It’s the same everywhere

we've been, isn't it, Petro? A mixture of good and bad."

"Most of the bad ones, even if they do terrible things, do it because they are afraid," said Petro.

"That was my father's problem," said Stuart. "That, and he was very bitter."

"Bitter?" asked Kaleem.

"Ah, so your mother never told you," said Stuart. He blushed a deep red and looked away from the others. He took a deep breath and looked up at Kaleem again. "Didn't you know? He used to be in love with your mother. He tried… he tried to seduce her just before she disappeared."

What!

"Kaleem," said Razjosh gently. "Tell them."

Kaleem swallowed. *Put the personal aside,* his training reminded him. "There is a way to understand this," he said. "Everyone does do their best. And more often than not, people only do bad things when they're afraid or hurt. So, what do we think? Holotechnology in exchange for a doubling in the number of acorns shipped?"

There was general agreement.

"Which just leaves the little problem of how to persuade everybody else," said Kaleem.

"Oh, you'll manage," said Pierre with a grin.

The conversation now became animated as they discussed plans for bringing Zandrian holotechnology to Terrestra.

"Do you think it will make our food as good as Zandrian?" asked Stuart.

"Better, I would have thought," said Alistare. "You've got better ingredients to start with."

"It's just a relief that your father will be able to restart the reforestation," said Tulla, looking up at Kaleem and smiling warmly.

Kaleem's heart skipped a beat. No, that was not to be. He mustn't even go there. Both Rozia and Tulla were spoken for. And it was no good, anyway, him having that sort of emotional relationship anymore. Much better to stick with what Ella had to offer.

He slid his hand on to her leg. No one could see what he was doing as their legs were hidden by the table. She returned his touch by sliding her hand right up the inside of his thigh. A wave of desire hit him. Would this dinner party please come to an end soon? He turned to smile at Ella. She returned the smile but her eyes were dull. She gave his thigh a quick squeeze and then removed his hand from her own. *Oh, don't go all cold on me now,* he thought.

"Well, I don't know about anybody else," he said. "But I'm shattered. And we've another big trip and a lot to do over the next few days. I think we should get some sleep."

The others mumbled in agreement and they took their leave of Razjosh and Anthea.

"Come again soon," said Razjosh, to all of them.

"You take care of yourself," said Anthea to Kaleem in particular. She shook her head slightly and drew him into a tight hug.

It was just a short ride in the transporter to the unit where they were staying. Kaleem suddenly felt weary. It had been a long day and a lot had happened. He was actually looking forward to the comfort of citadel standard luxury sheets, to the smoothness of Ella's skin and the excitement he knew she could whip up for him. And then physical exhaustion, sleep and oblivion.

No one said much on the journey back. It was clear that they all had a lot to think about. Kaleem noticed though that Charlek and Sandi were holding a whispered conversation and that he was playing with her hair. Sandi smiled suddenly and touched Charlek's cheek. They walked into the building holding hands. They walked straight past the room assigned to Charlek and made for her room. Kaleem caught Sandi's eye and smiled. She flushed bright red.

I should think so too, thought Kaleem. She worked so hard and did so much for other people. It really was about time she had some fun. She never made much time for herself.

"Hey, come on you," said Ella softly. "Never mind them. We've got business to attend to as well." She grabbed his hand.

Suddenly he was aware of her perfume and a very strong desire for her. "I'm coming," he whispered.

Irritations

Kaleem could have done without this meet. They'd just got back from Terrestra the night before and he'd barely had enough sleep. They'd been late and Ella… well, Ella had just been Ella. Emmerline was fussing around Edmundson and generally being no use whatsoever. And he was worried about the Terrestrans. It was one thing taking Zandrians to Terrestra – they were used to travelling. But bringing Terrestrans to Zandra – that was not so easy.

"The thing is," said Edmundson. "We could really do with your help in another matter."

Emmerline walked over to Kaleem, swaying her hips and batting her eye-lids.

"Only the Terrestran Peace Child can help us with this problem," she purred. "Can't he?" she asked, turning to Edmundson. She placed her arm around Edmundson's waist and laid her head on his shoulder.

Edmundson beamed.

Oh please, thought Kaleem. *This is so sick.* He suddenly thought about him and Ella. That was different, though, wasn't it? She was human after all.

"It's the Zenoton," said Edmundson. "We just can't get them to understand that we must use universal credits for our trade."

"Ah!" said Emmerline, suddenly pulling away from Edmundson. "They are here!"

"Will you speak with them?" asked Edmondson.

Kaleem guessed he hadn't any choice. He shrugged his shoulders.

"Show them in," Edmundson commanded Emmerline.

The doors swished open and the Zenoton delegate walked in. At first sight he didn't look all that different from a Terrestran or a Zandrian. He had the same sort of complexion and he was quite tall but no taller than some Terrestrans and some Zandrians. His clothes were a little odd; his tunic seemed tighter than a Zandrian and looser than a Terrestran one but actually not all that unusual at all. Most striking were the snake-like curls that covered his head. Hair it wasn't.

Kaleem did know a little about the Zenoton: he knew they were from an independent planet and not one of the former Terrestran colonies. He guessed, though, there might be other, more subtle differences apart from what was on top of their heads. They were after all from a different race.

"Greetings, Zandrians, greetings Terrestran Peace Child," said the Zenoton in broken Zandrian.

At least he's making an effort, thought Kaleem. "How can I help you?" he asked. It was odd. He was speaking what for him was a foreign language as well yet it felt perfectly natural.

The tall Zenoton jumped slightly. "I am Rogin Xavier. I am the chief negotiator from Zenoto. We find ourselves unable to trade with you and yet we have come this far."

"Yes, your planet is a long way from here," said Kaleem. A crazy journey actually. Probably quite uncomfortable. What was so important that they wanted here? "I'm sure we can find a way of trading with you. What do you require of us? What can we offer you?"

"Are you offering to trade for Zandra or Terrestra?" asked Rogin.

"It could be both," replied Kaleem. What was he saying? "Do you need acorns as well? Or other vegetation?"

"No, we have plenty of our own. Our planet thrives. We also want Zandrian technology," said Rogin. "I believe Terrestrans want it to."

"I don't think that will be a problem," said Kaleem. There would surely be enough for everyone, wouldn't there? "But what can you offer in return?"

"We have no physical commodity," said Rogin. "And your credit transfer system is incompatible with how we work on Zenoto."

"That's a problem, I guess," said Kaleem. "But can you maybe offer a service instead?"

Rogin sighed and looked straight at Kaleem. "Your leaders have already rejected our offer. That is why we asked to speak to you. We need the services of a multicultural guru."

A what? thought Kaleem.

"Yes," said Rogin. "I think you say – Peace Child?"

Okay. Multicultural guru. Even worse than Peace Child.

"Someone who sees beyond their own culture," said Rogin. "We offer to teach you the ways of Zenoton credit."

"Go on," said Kaleem slowly.

"We have a sun," said Rogin. "Very similar to your Terrestran sun and the two Zandrian suns. It too is the source of all of our being. The planet and the creatures on it survive because of it. It costs no credits. And we have the rule that every sentient being is entitled to the five freedoms.

"The five freedoms?" asked Kaleem.

"Freedom from hunger and thirst, freedom from discomfort, freedom from pain, injury or disease, freedom to express normal behaviour and freedom from fear and distress," said Rogin.

Well that sounded reasonable, and oddly familiar to Kaleem. He thought about himself for a moment, though. He'd not done too badly on the discomfort, hunger, thirst and physical pain front recently, but fear, distress and normal behaviour? Especially the last. Just how possible was that for intelligent beings? "That sounds quite familiar to me," he said. "And a bit like common sense. So, are you saying we don't at least try to give every living creature those five freedoms?"

Rogin shut his eyes. He mumbled to himself for a few seconds. Kaleem could not make out what he was saying. Then the Zenoton took a deep breath. "It only seems to be your second priority," he said. "It is our first. Both Zandra and Terrestra seem to regard credit balancing as the main driving force behind everything you do."

Did they? Did they really do that? Kaleem knew he would have to think about that carefully for a bit.

"Your suns still shine," Rogin reminded him. "Everything is possible. You've worked with the Hippocratic oath for medics.

This is a type of Hippocratic oath for everybody."

"So what if something goes wrong over which you have no control?" asked Kaleem. "What if something upsets you? What if something is uncomfortable?" *Like that journey from Zenoto,* he thought.

"You take control. You talk yourself out of it. But you also look out for other people," replied Rogin. "Stories, droids, proper planning – they all help."

"So how does work fit into all of this?" asked Kaleem. He could see Edmundson shaking his head. Emmerline winced, too, at the mention of droids. So they were taking notice as well.

"It's part of intelligent life's nature to want to contribute and each individual has to find a way of doing that that does not compromise one of the other four freedoms either for himself or others. It's the equivalent of a tiger feeling grass beneath its paws," said Rogin.

It seemed incredibly reasonable to Kaleem.

"How can we trade, then?" asked Edmundson.

Is he missing the point? thought Kaleem.

"We can go through your trading systems and make them work on these ideas," said Rogin. "And you can show us how some of your holotechnology works. We'll select what delights us."

"So simple," whispered Kaleem.

Emmerline looked at him blankly. Edmundson was frowning. Kaleem wished everything he had to do could be so simple.

The communication buzzer sounded.

"I understand what you're saying," said Kaleem. "I'll do my very best to make my colleagues and friends understand your request. But I'm afraid you'll have to excuse us now. We have another visitor." *It's not going to be that easy,* he thought. He shouldn't be making promises he couldn't keep. But he had to say something, hadn't he?

The Zenoton bowed and walked towards the door just as it opened and the new visitor walked in. Kaleem's heart sank as he recognised Nazaret. Unmistakably his father, but with his face blanker and his back more stooped than normal.

Edmundson caught Kaleem's eye and signalled that he would leave him alone with his father. He and Emmerline followed the Zenoton out.

"It's even worse that we thought," said Nazaret, without waiting for Kaleem to speak first. "We've more or less got to start all over again."

Kaleem found himself feeling sorry for his father. This man was distressed and in pain. He remembered Rogin's words. His own problems with Nazaret were not important now. What could he do, though? The droids were already helping. His father was good at planning and he'd done quite a bit already himself as well. So, all that was left from Rogin's list was to tell him a story.

"I'm sure the Terrestrans will help," he said to Nazaret. "There'll be plenty of acorns. You can build it all up again very quickly." He knew for certain that Nazaret was good in that area. But the Terrestrans… he couldn't be so sure.

"But what if it was over-planting that caused the landquake in the first place? What if it happens again?" Nazaret's voice was getting higher and higher.

"Surely they'll have looked into that already?" said Kaleem.

Nazaret nodded. "They've found no evidence that it had anything to do with the plantations directly," he said.

"Well then," said Kaleem.

"But what if that was the cause and we just can't see how?"

"Then it's still not your fault," said Kaleem. He suddenly felt as if he was father and Nazaret was the son. "Listen, you're tired. Why don't we all relax together this evening – me, you and Mum? Have a nice meal together? My Terrestran friends can look after themselves for a while."

Nazaret nodded. Kaleem was surprised at how pleasant that actually seemed. A quiet evening with just him, Nazaret and Marijam. Was this just because he'd seen that Nazaret was so down and wouldn't be his usual too cheerful self? He hoped not.

Nazaret suddenly straightened up. A trace of a smile passed across his face. "That sounds good," he said. He looked a little more like his normal self though the dark rings around his eyes still showed that he was tired.

Kaleem was surprised that he didn't feel uneasy about spending time with his mother and father. "So, I'll see you later," he said.

Nazaret had hardly left when the doors swished open again. Stuart and Pierre rushed in, followed by Sandi. Kaleem couldn't decide whether she looked concerned or amused. Stuart, though, looked terrible. His face was grey and his forehead was covered in sweat.

"It just better not be Starlight fever," said Pierre. "It just had better not be."

Kaleem had never seen Pierre look agitated like that. He was usually so calm and accepting of everything.

"It won't be," said Sandi. "Just let me treat him. Or take him to one of the Zandrian medics."

"How can you know that?" snapped Pierre. "Great elders, they don't even have diastics here."

"It really is unlikely to be Starlight," said Sandi. "Everybody here is vaccinated. You have both been. It's probably some relatively harmless virus that's affecting him more keenly because he's not used to illness."

"Well, he looks pretty bad to me," said Pierre.

Stuart groaned and then fell to the floor.

"Putrid elders, do something!" shouted Pierre. He had now gone white as well.

Sandi was already down on her knees listening to Stuart's chest and feeling his pulse.

Kaleem went to command the dataserve to fetch help but before he had opened his mouth it had already whirred into life. "Medic units here in seven seconds," it said.

"It's okay," said Sandi. "His pulse is quite strong and his airways seem clear. I'm sure he'll be fine. Probably just a grippa. A bad one."

The doors swished open again. It wasn't the medics. Saratina and Ben Alki walked in. Calver seemed to hover behind them.

"What's happened?" asked Ben Alki.

Kaleem shook his head and shrugged his shoulders.

"ee ort uming," said Saratina. "Ut ooo play ee eel. Oo medy."

Two Zandrian medics hurried in, pushing the others out of the way.

"Okay, we've got it," said one of them.

Sandi stepped aside. She watched without flinching as the medics examined Stuart.

"Okay," said the other after a few minutes. He pressed his wand to Stuart's chest. He looked up at Sandi and grinned. "Just a grippa. He'll be fine. You Terrestrans just can't take it, can you?"

"I knew it!" said Sandi. She grinned at the others.

"We'll soon get him right. He'll have to come to the medical centre though – probably needs some fluids and some anti-virals. He'll probably have to stay a couple of days," said the first medic.

"Can we come along as well?" asked Sandi.

"What, all of you?" asked one of the medics. "There won't be room!"

"We can take another transporter," said Ben Alki.

"Okay, I guess," said the other medic. "Only don't get in the way."

The medics had now managed to get Stuart on to a hovering mattress. The wand seemed to have done something already. There was more colour in his cheeks. He now seemed to be sleeping peacefully.

They all started moving out of the room.

Kaleem went to follow. Calver laid a hand on his arm.

"They'll really find this hard," he said. "Oh, yeah, it's all right in theory. Illness as an acceptable consequence of mixing with others and a prerequisite of switch-off not being needed – but the reality is somewhat harder to bear. Illness is not nice if you've not met it before. Well, it's not nice anyway." Calver bowed slightly and he too left the room.

He was right, of course. Kaleem remembered when he'd been ill – the first time on Terrestra and then later on Zandra. Although the first time he'd been really very ill and it was such a shock he really couldn't say that the second time was all that much better. Still, he'd been well treated on Zandra and he knew Stuart would be too.

And the rest of them would all be so agitated. Oh, he just didn't want to go there. He slumped down into one of the chairs. He suddenly felt very weary.

"Summon transporter?" asked the dataserve.

"Yes please," said Kaleem with a sigh.

"So how long did they say they'd keep him there?" asked Marijam.

"They weren't sure," replied Kaleem. "But they said at least two days."

"Oh, it brings back some bad memories," said Marijam. "Of when you were so ill."

Kaleem shuddered at the thought of it. He remembered how scary it had been. And it had been scary as well when Marijam had also been sick.

"It's nowhere near as bad as that," said Kaleem. *Though you'd have thought it was, by the fuss they made,* he thought. He'd only got back from the medical centre half an hour ago. The other Terrestrans had been so wound up he'd not been able to get them to leave the medics to do their work or to let Stuart get some rest.

"It must be pretty scary, the first time you encounter illness," said Nazaret, "when you come from a planet where you're not even allowed to get thirsty."

"Saratina ought to understand about illness, though," said Kaleem. "Even she was agitated."

"Isn't that just because she cares so much about other people?" said Nazaret. "She was just worried about him. She's such a lovely person to have on board. She's going to be a real asset to the exchange programme."

Ah! So you're being the Peace Child now, are you? thought Kaleem. But he realised that his father was right. He ought to try to be more understanding.

"And it's definitely just a grippa?" said Marijam. She still looked quite worried.

"Oh, yes. Nothing more. But with our useless immune systems…" said Kaleem.

"It always happens when you go interplanetary," said Gabrizan. "It's not just Terrestrans."

The kitchen unit pinged. The safe-box was suddenly filled with the smell of onions, garlic and some indefinable meat. Kaleem realised only then how hungry he was. Marijam got up and busied herself with serving the meal.

"I'm sorry it's so late," said Kaleem. Nazaret, he knew, would want to be up early again the next day.

"Not a problem," said Nazaret. "It's all beginning to come together again. If Terrestra will help us with even more acorns… we should be all right."

"And we'll be able to move back to the apartment in a week," said Marijam.

"So, we thought we'd better have some of this," said Nazaret, opening a bottle of special frega.

Nazaret poured the frega into the glasses that Marijam had put on the table.

"It's so nice having you spend the evening with us," said Marijam to Kaleem as the sat down at the table. "It really is," she added, stroking his arm.

She was right, Kaleem realised. They were just sitting together like a normal family and for once he didn't feel uncomfortable. This was so easy compared with all of the Peace Child stuff. The food was good. The frega relaxed him. Nazaret didn't irritate him for once. And Nazaret was beginning to lose the rather worried look he'd had for the last few days. It really was a pleasant evening.

"That's one thing I really like about Zandra," said Kaleem, as he finished his second portion of the fruit crumble. "The food's so good. Just how do you do it, considering the planet's so infertile?"

"Ah, I'll let you into the secret some time," said Nazaret. "It is actually getting a bit late. It would take hours to go over all of that."

"Yes, I shouldn't stay too long," said Kaleem. "I'll need to talk to people about what I discussed with the Zenoton."

"Oh?" said Nazaret. He had stopped eating. "What did they want?"

"They want us to adapt their no-credits system," said Kaleem.

"What?" spluttered Nazaret. "It would never work. Look how finely balanced we've had to keep the trade between Zandra and Terrestra."

"But just suppose you didn't have to keep it balanced like that," said Kaleem. "Suppose you could just have what you needed exactly when you needed it. Like you could have all the acorns now and needn't worry about whether Terrestra needed vaccine. Just think how much easier it would be."

"I suppose… in extreme circumstances…" said Nazaret. "Everybody usually does help out when things go wrong… I'm sure Terrestra will help? Surely?"

"Yes, of course," said Kaleem. He hoped so. He didn't feel too confident, though.

"But all the time?" said Nazaret. "People would be too greedy. Or lazy. Wouldn't they?" said Nazaret.

He might be right. Look how he'd just reacted himself. Doubting that Terrestra would help even though the Zandrians were in desperate need. The Zenoton had all made it seem so easy. People just didn't behave the way they'd suggested. Not on Zandra and Terrestra, anyway.

There was an awkward silence.

"It's a dream, isn't it?" said Nazaret. "I can't see it actually happening, can you?"

He's probably right, thought Kaleem. But he'd promised the Zenoton he would talk about it and he ought to do that. What was it going to be like putting the Zenoton's case to others if it was this difficult talking to his own parents? He couldn't think what else to say to them.

“Are you seeing Ella later?” asked Marijam.

Kaleem shook his head. They’d agreed not to meet tonight. Ella was tired. She had stayed at the medic centre with him. She had not attempted to hide how irritated she was with the Terrestrans’ panic. He’d thought a night apart would do them good. Now he wished he had got the excuse that she was waiting for him.

“I’m feeling a bit tired,” he said. “Do you mind if I get back now?”

“Of course not,” said Marijam. “Take care.”

“We know you’re doing your best,” said Nazaret. “Sleep well.”

“You too,” Kaleem just about managed to say as he left his parent’s safe-box.

Monetarism

"It'll never happen," said Charlek. "Not here, nor on Terrestra. Definitely not on Terrestra."

"Say again," said Alistare. "How is it supposed to work?"

"Nobody pays for anything," said Kaleem. "Everybody just uses or takes what they need."

"Paradise!" said Alistare. "Only paradise didn't work because humans didn't know when they were well off."

"Ho, ho!" said Charlek. "It's beginning to sound like one of the old religious stories."

Alistare leaned back in his chair. His eyes swung to the top of his head and to his left. He closed his eyelids as the sun blinded him.

"Look, he's calculating again," said Charlek. He took a sip of his chofa. "Maybe he's working out how many Zandrian credits you would need to get real vegetation into this place."

"At least the sun's real," said Kaleem. "And the Zenoton make the point that that's all we actually need. Everything else follows from that."

"Seventy-three billion, two million, five hundred, one thousand one hundred and twenty-five," said Alistare. "We could never afford it."

"But that's the whole point," said Kaleem. "We take it because we need it. We give what we can."

Charlek took another sip of his chofa. "Well, I hope they'd let us keep this," he said. "Could you imagine it, life without Zandrian chofa?"

Kaleem knew what he meant. Chofa was much better than coffee. And the chofa here at the Refreshment Park was particularly good. The park was amazing, anyway, and it was really hard to believe that it wasn't real. The only two things that were real about it were that it was outdoors and that the sun was actually shining. And it was extremely pleasant, sitting here in the late spring morning sun. The park had hardly been touched by the landquake.

"Yeah, but how do you make people give what they can? What about all the things that no one wants to do?" said Alistare.

Kaleem shrugged. "They have droids, just like we do," he said.

"But who makes them and who programmes them?" asked Alistare.

"People who like making droids and who like programming?" said Kaleem. "Just like you like twisting numbers around."

"Not sure I'd do it though, if I didn't have to," said Alistare. "I might just sit in the Refreshment Park all day and drink chofa."

"Unless you had something even better to do," said Charlek, grinning. He looked over Kaleem's shoulder.

Kaleem turned to see what he was looking at. Ella was coming towards them. She was wearing an emerald green tunic and her hair and make-up were immaculate as usual. She looked less tired than she had done. Her normal sparkle was back.

"Come on," said Charlek to Alistare. "Let's get out of here. We'll leave you to settle the bill, shall we?" he added, tapping Kaleem's shoulder. "Wouldn't want to be in the way, would we?"

Ella shaded her eyes from the sun and looked up at Charlek. She smiled sweetly.

Charlek turned to Kaleem. "Just remember, the Zenoton are different from us. They're not actually human."

He and Alistare made their way towards the exit of the café.

"Ooh, that sounded a bit serious," said Ella, leaning forward and kissing Kaleem lightly on the lips.

By all the elders, the perfume of her! Kaleem pulled her towards him and kissed her back hard and long. Talk about taking what you wanted! How did that all fit in with the Zenoton way?

"Steady on," said Ella, pushing him away gently. "I think you ought to pay this bill first, and anyway, I'd quite like a chofa as well."

The waiter droid was already making its way over to them.

"But then we can go back to yours or mine," said Ella softly, sliding her hand along his thigh under the table.

Kaleem wished she wouldn't do that. She took her hand away

abruptly. *Please don't stop,* he thought.

The droid was whirring gently, looking expectant.

"A large chofa," said Ella. "Do you want another?" she asked Kaleem.

He shook his head. Why did she have to order a large one?

"And bring the bill straight away," she said to the droid. She turned to Kaleem. "While we're waiting, you can tell me what you were talking to Charlek and Alistare about that made you all look so serious."

By the time the chofa arrived and he had paid the droid, he had explained about the creditless Zenoton economy. By the time she had drunk half of it, she was intrigued.

"It would be good if it we could make it work," she said. "But I can't see it happening."

He wished she would hurry up. There was nothing now that was going to stop him having what he wanted.

She finished her chofa at last, wiped her mouth and took his hand. "Come on," she whispered.

It had been good to be lost in the moment with her, to be taken out of himself so completely. But now, as was more and more often the case, he felt guilty that he should have been doing something else. That he should be trying to talk to others about the Zenoton's wishes. That the way he was behaving towards Ella somehow wasn't right. And stupidly, unbelievably, it wasn't right mainly because of Rozia.

He got out of the bed and started to dress.

"Do you have to go already?" she asked.

"Yes," said Kaleem. He sighed. "I have to see Edmundson." That wasn't the half of it, he knew. And that made him feel even worse.

"Just can't be done," said Edmundson. "Everything's too involved. If we started unpicking that all now, whole systems would collapse." He looked over towards Emmerline. "Bring up those calculations about what would happen if we gave Terrestra vaccine instead of trading it against acorns."

Kaleem was relieved that for once Edmundson was treating Emmerline as nothing more than a droid. He didn't think he could stomach passionate droid / human interaction on top of his mixed up Ella-Rozia feelings.

Green light came from Emmerline's chest and then a screen opened up on the wall. "Complete deforestation from lack of acorns within five years," said her electronic voice. "No credits left to purchase food materials from Bezen Two within six years. Death of planet within seven years. Evacuation recommended three years from now."

Well, there's an explanation about the food, then, thought Kaleem. The images projected from the droid's chest kept repeating, showing nearer close-ups each time. It became more and more distressing.

"Seen enough?" asked Edmundson.

Kaleem nodded.

Emmerline became silent. Even the normal droid whirring stopped.

"But it wouldn't come to that if we took on board the give-and-take of the Zenoton, would it?" said Kaleem.

Edmundson laughed. "Well, Zandrians might be willing to play that game," he said. "Even Terrestrans might – under your persuasion – but I think you'd have your work cut out there. And the Bezen? And the others we trade with? I don't think so. Not in our lifetime."

"But in emergency situations?" said Kaleem.

"Yes, of course," replied Edmundson. "Most people are human, even the non-humans. But they won't do it all the time."

Kaleem tried to swallow but he couldn't. His throat seemed to be swollen. Here he was, failing again.

"Anyway, if you'll excuse us, Emmerline and I have some other business to attend to," said Edmundson.

Emmerline suddenly switched from droid mode. Her eyes grew wide and she smiled at Edmundson. She sauntered over towards him, her hips swaying. She slid her arm round Edmundson's waist and laid her head on his shoulder.

Nothing's changed here then, thought Kaleem. "I'll get going then," he said, wondering how he was going to stop himself from throwing up.

Come on, come on! thought Kaleem. It was taking forever to complete the connection to Terrestra. Just when he needed it most. Maybe he should have gone in a holo. But he actually wanted to have a private conversation with Razjosh.

At last, though, the elder's familiar face appeared on the screen. The dataserve's tinny voice told him the connection had actually only taken forty seconds.

"Well, I can see you're bothered about something," said Razjosh before Kaleem had time to utter a single word. "Do tell."

I wish he wouldn't do that, thought Kaleem. *He knows me too well.* "The Zenoton want me to convince everybody to take on their credit system. Actually, their lack of credit."

"I see," said Razjosh. "And what do you think?"

"I can see the point of it," said Kaleem. "But everybody else is so against it. I've no idea where to go with these suggestions."

"Yes, indeed," said Razjosh. "The Peace Child's fate. Always to be caught in the middle, always to see both points of view at once. But it isn't your job to convince. You are only meant to understand and clarify. Do you truly understand both points of view?"

"I think so," said Kaleem.

"Well, there you are, then," said Razjosh. "Nothing to worry about. It may not be comfortable, but you can do the right thing."

You make it sound so easy, thought Kaleem. "What do you think, though?" he said. Surely Razjosh could now have his own opinions. He didn't have to act as a Peace Child any more.

"I don't really know enough about it all to be able to judge," said Razjosh. "But I gather that it's all to do with abandoning balancing credits. That everything is done according to need, desire and aptitude? Am I right?"

"That's about it," said Kaleem.

“It does sound good,” said Razjosh. “But some human weaknesses may get in the way. I suspect you would have to complete all of your work before it was really possible. And actually, is a Peace Child’s work ever really finished? It may well work for the Zenoton. They are very similar to us but not completely the same. They are not human. They may be more robust.”

So, you’re no different from the others, thought Kaleem. “I see,” he said.

The dataserve indicated that he had another call coming through. The flashing red light told him that it was urgent. A still picture of Calver Toms appeared.

“I’ll have to go,” said Kaleem. “I have to take another call.”

“Go ahead,” said Razjosh. “I won’t wish you luck. I know you’ll do the right thing.”

Razjosh’s face disappeared from the screen and Calver’s appeared.

“I’m sorry to disturb you so late,” said Calver. “But this is rather important.”

Havoc

The communicator buzzed on the door in Kaleem's safe-box. It had only taken Calver ten minutes to get there but to Kaleem it seemed more like two hours. What could be so urgent at one in the morning? He was wide awake now but minutes before he had felt pleasantly drowsy from the good food and the frega.

"Okay," said Kaleem. "What is it?"

Calver grinned then shook his head. "Oh my, such a lot," he said. "You will be really earning your credits soon." His eyes seemed almost to be on fire.

Kaleem's stomach plummeted.

"Yes," said Calver. "You need to get a grip."

Great elders, I'm trying, thought Kaleem. "Why in particular?" he mumbled through gritted teeth.

"Yes, you'll really be earning your credits and you might not be able to get them," said Calver.

"What?" asked Kaleem.

"Your friends, the Zenoton," replied Calver.

"What are they doing?" asked Kaleem.

"They're not. But this is what they want to do. If they really did overhaul our credit systems," replied Calver. "And if they were any good at persuading other people. This is what they would have achieved. Just in the few hours since you met them."

"What do you mean?" asked Kaleem.

"If they persuaded the executives that all inhabitants on Zandra should have the basic credits to allow individuals the five freedoms – without having to work," replied Calver.

"How would they do that?" asked Kaleem.

"Er, by being persuasive, I guess," replied Calver, "and by being as charming as ever."

"Well what have you found out?" asked Kaleem.

"Using my usual powers of observation," said Calver, "and especially from a conversation I overheard in a frega bar. Then a droid almost blew a fuse because he could not get the system to take our credits."

"Why?" asked Kaleem.

"Because I'd made a local projection of what would happen if we adopted the Zenoton system. And there's more," replied Calver.

"Go on," said Kaleem. Yes, he was really wide awake now.

"Despite their saying there would be no credits any more, they would have to claim credits from Zandra's account to cover their effort of coming to us," said Calver. "If they did that, Zandra could be bankrupt within forty-eight hours."

"What can we do?" asked Kaleem. "I've said I'd look into it."

"Ask them to go slowly. Look." Calver called up some charts on the dataserve. "It will all actually work – but it just has to go slower. See the blue bar? That is where Zandra could be in three years if they do everything in an orderly way and if Terrestra will supply the acorns."

"And if not?" asked Kaleem.

"The orange bar shows what would happen to Zandra in two days time," said Calver.

"Do you think I can ask them to be reasonable?" asked Kaleem.

"Yes," said Calver. "But you must talk to them at breakfast tomorrow. They're leaving just after that."

"What time do they have breakfast?" asked Kaleem.

"Five thirty," replied Calver.

No. The clock already showed that it was almost two.

"And there are other problems," said Calver.

More? Kaleem didn't think his heart could sink any lower. "Go on tell me," he said.

"I predict that our Terrestran friends will want to return home at once," said Calver.

"At once?" asked Kaleem. "You mean leave Stuart here?"

"No," said Calver. "They'll take him with them."

"That's madness."

"Yes, Terrestran madness."

I'll let that pass, thought Kaleem. "What about if some of the others become ill?"

"Well, they've got a medic with them, haven't they? And I'd imagine she'll want to get back home soon," replied Calver.

"Oh?" said Kaleem.

Calver ignored his question. "One will stay," he continued. "Saratina."

"Why? Why will she stay?" asked Kaleem.

"You don't realise?"

"No."

Calver shook his head and sighed. "Because she wants to support you, of course. You are her prize."

Kaleem went hot and cold in quick succession. He could never understand why people wanted to support him. He always seemed to make such a hash of things. "Is there anything I can do to stop the others going?" he asked.

"I'm afraid not," said Calver. "And they will probably need your help before they are home again."

"What?" asked Kaleem.

"And there's another thing," said Calver, ignoring Kaleem again.

"So, what is it?" asked Kaleem as coldly as he could. It really couldn't get any worse, could it?

"Ella will leave you – very soon," said Calver.

Ah, so it could get even worse, though Kaleem was surprised that he suddenly felt that way. He'd always thought Ella was just a bit of fun. He'd always thought he could manage without her if need be. "Why?" he asked.

Calver laughed. "You really have no idea?" He shook his head and sighed. "You just can't treat women like that and get away with it."

"What?" asked Kaleem. "What have I done wrong?"

"You don't have a clue, do you?" said Calver. "You can't go blowing hot and cold like that. She doesn't know where she stands."

"But she said she didn't want any complications," said

Kaleem. "She just wanted a… she just wanted a bit of fun."

"Yes fun, Kaleem," said Calver. "Not misery. Oh, she's very clear that you're both only in it for one thing. But you're just so ill-mannered sometimes."

"I am?" said Kaleem.

"Yes," said Calver.

"How long then before…?" asked Kaleem.

"Not long," said Calver.

"And there's no chance that… she might…?" asked Kaleem.

"None whatsoever, unless I'm losing my touch," said Calver.

Kaleem doubted that he was.

"Look, it's getting late," said Calver. "I'd better go. You've got a big day tomorrow." He cuffed Kaleem's shoulder. "I'll help all I can. Just send for me if you need me."

Kaleem had a lump in his throat. He swallowed hard but it would not go away. He nodded.

Calver left and he was alone.

He thought about Ella. The one thing that would bring him some comfort now would to be lying in bed with her, tasting her sweet kisses, feeling the smoothness of her skin… He was very well aware that in three and a half hours he was going to be doing some quite tough negotiating with the Zenoton. He felt too agitated to sleep, but spending time with Ella… in their own special way, now that would relax him and give him some energy at the same time.

He looked over towards the safe-box. There was no light on, no sign of life. He sighed. He ought to try to get some rest. He went to clean his teeth and take a quick shower.

His personal communicator buzzed.

It was Ella! His heart started beating quickly.

"Hi!" he said.

She looked pale, he noticed.

"I guess you couldn't sleep either. I saw your light on." she said.

"Do you want to come over, after all?" said Kaleem. "Or shall I come over to you?"

"I'll come to you," she said.

Seconds later she was there.

"Oh, come here," said Kaleem taking her in his arms. He kissed her firmly and she returned his kiss. He wanted her so much. "Oh, you're so gorgeous," he mumbled.

They started undressing each other and she guided him towards her then suddenly she pulled away. "Stop," she said. "Stop. I can't do this anymore." Tears began running down her cheeks. "It's too hard."

Kaleem stepped back and covered himself up. "I thought you wanted it like this," he said. "Just casual."

"Casual's fine," said Ella. "But you're still in love with Rozia. I wouldn't mind that so much, but it makes you cruel at times. And I wouldn't mind if I hadn't fallen in love with you a bit."

Ah. Kaleem couldn't think what to say. "I'm sorry," was all he managed.

She started to dress again as well.

"I have to forget. I'm going to move back home tomorrow," she said. She leant over and kissed him on the cheek.

"Someone's waiting for me," she said. "He's going to help me move. He can cope better with casual that you can."

He watched her leave and walk slowly back to the safe-box. Before she got there, the door opened and someone was standing in the entrance. The man stepped into the light and waved. Kaleem recognised the tall confident Zandrian. Charlek! Ah, so that explained why Sandi would want to go back to Terrestra.

He went back in, commanded the lights to low and lay on his bed. He wished he could go to sleep straight away. He wouldn't have to think then. All he could think about if he stayed awake was how being the Peace Child sucked.

Confusions

The Zenoton Way

The three Zenoton had almost finished breakfast when Kaleem arrived at their quarters the next morning. That was a relief. He didn't feel like eating at all. He hadn't slept. The whole Ella situation worried him. He felt such a failure that his friends had panicked and rushed home and he was worried about Stuart. It was only a grippa but he shouldn't be travelling – not even with Sandi on board.

"Ah, good morning," said Rogin. "May I introduce my companions, Trindan Astley and Godran Muset." He stood up and offered Kaleem the Zandrian handshake.

The other two Zenoton did exactly the same. It really was hard to see any difference between them and Zandrians or Terrestrans – apart from the slightly odd accent, the not quite standard clothes and the snake-like curls on their heads. Yet they weren't from one of the colonised planets. Life seemed to have sprung up on Zenoto just like it had on Terrestra. Similar conditions, Kaleem guessed.

He accepted the handshake and bowed slightly.

Trindan Astley, and Godran Muset, he noticed, were slightly less sure of themselves than Rogin.

"Well, what is your opinion now?" asked Rogin. "Have you had time to think how different your economy might be if you adapted our ways?"

"There would be a problem," said Kaleem, "if it happened too quickly."

Rogin's face fell. Then he grinned. "You're just out of sorts," he said. "Come, on sit down. Partake of this glorious Zandrian food. That is something else we'll have to learn from you. But as we're making such fast progress…"

Kaleem did sit down. He pushed the offered food away, though.

"How can you refuse?" asked Rogin. "Oh, I guess you're used to it. Well, have some coffee at least."

Kaleem accepted the coffee. It was good. He'd rather have had chofa – it was slightly less bitter – but the coffee was doing the trick. His head was beginning to clear and he was beginning to think he could communicate with these people. "What exactly do you want to achieve with knowing about our technology?" asked Kaleem.

"We want to create a world," said Trindan, "where everyone's dreams come true as soon as they just think it. Like 'Your wish is my command'."

"And a world where we can have food like this and smart surroundings like yours," added Godran.

"What, a world that is about to get a poison cloud, like Terrestra had?" asked Kaleem. "A world that's just lost almost all of the vegetation that it had recreated? You think all this technology is worth that?"

"Oh, well…" started Rogin.

"Listen," said Kaleem. "We can teach you about that technology. And we would like to learn about your credit exchange systems. But we have to go carefully."

Trindan's face suddenly lit up.

"We have acorns, too," he said. "And other plants you could use. It's a longer journey, but we could freeze the seeds…"

That could be the solution then. Perhaps it didn't matter after all that the Terrestrans had gone home. "Okay," said Kaleem slowly. "Tell me what you propose."

Kaleem could suddenly hear urgent footsteps and then people arguing outside. The door swished open and the sound of arguing grew louder.

"Systems will melt-down and economy will close," said an electronic voice. A tall young woman in a low-cut tunic whirled into the room. Emmerline.

"Have you loaded all of those figures?" shouted a gruff male voice. Edmundson.

Emmerline paused and turned to face the Zenoton.

What's she going to do now? thought Kaleem. *She's not going to try and seduce them, is she?*

"Ah, gentleman," she said in a very human voice. She fluttered her almost human eyelashes. "I trust you are enjoying your breakfast." She moved swaying her hips and her eyes blinked.

The Zenoton's mouths were dropping open.

"You can stop that right now," snarled Edmundson. "They just want to pull us into a right mess."

Had they found Calver's predictions, Kaleem wondered.

"We mean no harm," said Rogin, standing up. He exchanged a worried glance with the other two.

"Yes, we are only trying to help," said Trindan.

Edmundson scowled.

"Now, now," said Emmerline, making her eyelids flutter again. "Remember they are our guests."

Edmundson raised his eyebrows, and then shook his head. "Now is not the time, woman. Being polite won't get you anywhere, let alone flirting."

Being polite would be good, actually, thought Kaleem. *I was beginning to get somewhere.*

"You see, you silly man," said Emmerline. She walked over to Edmundson and ruffled his hair. "Now there you are. Calm down then." She placed a kiss on Edmundson's forehead.

Great elders. She's just a machine, thought Kaleem. *And she's behaving like that.*

"Hmm," said Edmundson, closing his eyes. He slipped his arm round Emmerline's waist. "But I think we'd better leave that until later."

Putrid elders, thought Kaleem. *What will he do next?*

As he opened his eyes, Edmundson looked at Kaleem and went bright red. "Well, it's no worse than you," he whispered. "I heard about you and the Raymond girl. At least as she's only a machine and no one will get hurt." He nodded towards Emmerline. *Better than the real thing,* he whispered.

So, thought Kaleem, *all the rumours about him and Emmerline are true.*

The Zenoton were looking even more uncomfortable now.

"Well gentlemen, what are we to do?" said Edmundson, offering

Rogin, Trindan and Godran a Zandrian handshake.

The Zenoton shuffled on to their feet.

"Please remain seated," said Edmundson, sitting himself down as well.

"They had just begun to think of a better plan," said Kaleem. "Why not let them tell us?"

The three Zenoton looked at each other.

"Well, we could offer just as many new plants as Terrestra has been doing," said Rogin. "And in return we ask that you teach us all about your technology."

A jolt went through Kaleem. That was exactly what his friends had said they wanted to do. But their suspicion about the New Zone and Stuart's illness had now driven them away.

"Tell us what you want to achieve by that," said Edmundson.

"They want to have a world where everyone's dreams come true as soon as they just think it. Like 'Your wish is my command'," Kaleem replied for them.

Edmundson threw back his head and laughed. Emmerline made a sound that was almost like a human tut. *You don't do that,* thought Kaleem.

"I don't think even the advanced holotechnology on Zandra can really do that," Kaleem explained calmly. "But it can do a lot, I'll give you that."

"It is amazing," said Rogin, "how your machines seem to know exactly what you're thinking."

"It can be annoying, actually," said Kaleem.

"We have nothing else we need on our planet," said Trindan. "We had the idea, though, that, you might need something from us."

"We didn't think it would be as simple as vegetation," said Godran.

"What do you mean?" asked Edmundson.

"It's always worth listening," said Kaleem. "They may have something."

Rogin stood up and started pacing up and down the small space. "What do your credits stand for?" he asked.

"Labour and raw materials," said Kaleem slowly.

"Yes, that is the case on many planets," replied Rogin. "But there is not much labour now. Not here. Especially with your fantastic technology. There is only intellectual work. And the raw materials belong to everyone. They come from the sun."

Trindan and Godran were nodding enthusiastically.

They were right, Kaleem could see that.

"There is no need even for bartering now," said Trindan.

"We can create paradise," said Godran.

But on a dying planet? thought Kaleem.

"We can set your systems straight again," Rogin said quietly.

Impossible, wasn't it? He looked over to Edmundson.

Edmundson shrugged.

"Wonderful," said Emmerline, standing up and clapping her hands. "I can show you some forecasts," she added in her electronic voice. Her chest started whirring.

"Yes, okay," said Edmundson. "We'll take them in the inner dataserve room."

His eyes were glistening.

Kaleem felt slightly sick.

There was another kerfuffle outside. Kaleem recognised Saratina's voice straight away.

The door swished open and she burst in.

"Oo ot oo hel. OO ot to hel," she cried. She rushed up to Kaleem and started shaking his arm.

She started punching Kaleem and stamping her foot.

"I'm sorry," said Kaleem. "I can't understand what you're saying."

Calver Toms came into the room.

"She says you've got to help," he said.

"I've got to help?" asked Kaleem. "You can understand her?"

Saratina nodded.

"Not really," said Calver. "I mean, I can't understand the words she says but I can work out what she's talking about. Just the same as with anybody else."

"Why does she need me to help?" asked Kaleem.

“Oo ar. Ou ar airy ee. Ani ot ayl oo hel. Ee axee,” Saratina said.

Emmerline came back into the room. “Problem on the Terrestra bound Supercraft,” she said in her electronic voice. “Suspected case of Starlight Racer disease.”

“What? So it wasn’t a grippa,” shouted Kaleem, jumping to his feet. He was surprised that she was working in this mode. He’d thought that she and Edmundson… well, he wasn’t really sure what he’d thought.

“It’s not confirmed that it isn’t,” said Calver quietly. “The medics aren’t sure either way.”

“They shouldn’t have gone,” whispered Kaleem. “They should have waited.”

Saratina was crying now. Suddenly she stopped.

“Vaccine!” she cried out loudly.

Kaleem understood her clearly. How had that happened? And she was right. Of course there would be vaccine on the Supercraft. They could use that. Of course they could. Surely it would help, even if he’d got the fever already, wouldn’t it?

“There is no vaccine on that Supercraft,” said Emmerline and Calver at the same time.

“The Terrestrans claim they no longer need it,” said Edmundson.

Saratina fell to the floor, curled up and started rocking. Kaleem felt his heart sink. What now?

Death Threat

"It's conclusive," said the medic. "Just a grippa. Nothing more. Nothing less. He does seem to be having an odd reaction though. That is hard to explain."

The medic set the screen of the dataserve to blank. Kaleem guessed he wanted their full attention. Not that all the diagrams and pictures had made much sense to him anyway.

"What can we do though?" he asked. "How can we help?"

The medic sighed. "I think it's just a matter of convincing them. If your friend believes he has the Starlight Racer disease he'll probably experience the symptoms of it. His grippa is a spectacularly bad one. I suspect you Terrestrans have extremely weak immune systems. Normally, I'd say that the disease will just take its course. This time, though, I'm afraid it looks as if there are complications. If he'd stayed here we could have made him comfortable and treated the symptoms."

You think I don't know that? thought Kaleem. "These symptoms that he has," he said, "will they have the same consequences as if they really were from the Starlight disease?"

"They could well do," said the medic. "And besides, the complications he may have from the grippa could also kill him." He sighed again. "Especially on board a Supercraft without any specialised medical assistance. And with his poor immune system."

"What do you mean, no medical assistance?" said Kaleem. Surely all Supercraft these days carried a full medical team and besides there was Sandi as well.

The medic exchanged a glance with Edmundson who was sitting at the back of the room with Emmerline.

"The Terrestrans ordered the departure of the Supercraft before the medical team had boarded," said Emmerline's electronic voice.

"And no offence," said the medic, "but I doubt that a Terrestran medic will be able to do much. Their knowledge is not extensive.

Neither is their experience. They're a little theoretical. They just don't get enough practice."

But we are trying to change. Especially Sandi, thought Kaleem. "Would you talk to her, though?" he said.

"Yes, I suppose I can," said the medic, sighing again. "Though I'm not sure what good it will do. They really should not have gone."

I know that, thought Kaleem.

He called up Sandi via the medical centre's dataserve. Within seconds her face was on the screen. She was hardly recognisable. Only her red hair showed that it was her and this time it was just naturally untidy and not woven into some statement-making deliberate mess. She looked pale and much older than usual.

"Hi Kaleem," she said, her voice crackling with tiredness. She managed a thin smile.

"How is he?" asked Kaleem.

"Bad. Really bad," said Sandi. "He's unconscious most of the time. But when he is awake he's in a lot of pain. I'm getting worried about Pierre as well now."

"Is he showing symptoms of the grippa?" asked the Zandrian medic.

Sandi shook her head. "No, he's just worried and upset. He thinks his partner is going to die. He's not eating or sleeping."

"It's unlikely, just from the symptoms of the grippa," said the medic. "But the complications… and if those around him and he himself think that it's really Starlight… And of course there is also the possibility that the rest of the group could become infected."

"Are you absolutely certain that it isn't Starlight?" said Sandi. "From what I've read and heard about grippa, it doesn't normally behave like this."

"People who get the grippa don't normally have such weak immune systems," said the medic. "Look, here is the data."

The dataserve loaded up Stuart's files again and minimised Sandi into a small window in the top right hand corner of the screen.

"I see," said Sandi, as the presentation finished and she again filled the screen. "So why is he presenting so badly? Ben Alki says he looks so much worse than people do just after they've been switched off. I tend to agree."

"Oh, come on now," said the medic. "How often on Terrestra do you see the corpses of people who have died naturally? And even so, corpses can look remarkably peaceful even after the most terrible illnesses. The fact that you can see that he's suffering is actually a sign of life."

"I've seen quite a few corpses actually," said Sandi, regaining some of her normal sparkle. "Because I've worked in the Z Zone."

Now that I didn't know, thought Kaleem. Gosh, she was a force to contend with. *Not a wimp like me then,* he thought. The thought of switch-off alone had made him vomit. Ben Alki had actually seen post switch-off corpses. Plenty of them. And Rozia had been with Narisja when she died. Rozia! Why did he have to think of her now of all times? He shuddered though he wasn't sure why – was it the thought of death or his disgust at his own ineptitude – or both? "So what can we do?" he said.

"I think your best bet is going to be convincing him and all of those around him that he merely has a grippa," said the medic. "Then good medical and nursing care. That should be possible even on a Supercraft without a medical team." He turned to Kaleem. "I think you could be very useful here. You have had both Starlight fever and normal Zandrian grippa. You know the difference. You need to convince your friends."

That was it, though. They'd both felt exactly the same to Kaleem. Except that the grippa had passed more quickly, thanks to the Zandrian medication and it had been slightly less scary because he already knew what illness felt like.

It must be awful for Pierre. And so painful for Stuart when he was conscious. Was he also having terrible dreams while he was asleep?

"I'm convinced at least," said Sandi. "But I don't know whether I can convince the others."

"I should talk to Pierre," said Kaleem.

Emmerline's chest suddenly started whirring.

"What the…?" said Edmundson.

"Suggest project Super Holo," said the droid's electronic voice.

"No, we couldn't," said Edmundson. "It's not been properly trialled. It might be dangerous."

"Well, Kaleem's not afraid of a little danger, is he?" said Emmerline, going into human mode. "That's what he's all about."

"Project Super Holo?" said the medic. "What's that, then?"

"New holo technology which allows the transportation and use of objects at the destination setting," Edmundson explained. "Not the sort of thing we can let novices loose on."

"Seventy-five per cent of trials conducted," said Emmerline's electronic voice. "Ninety-eight per cent success rate."

"See, that's not enough," said Edmundson. "It's got to be made a hundred per cent safe and it's still got a lot of tests to go."

That would be so good. If he could get on to the Supercraft and get some Zandrian medication on there, Sandi would know what to do with that. And he'd be able to talk to them all face to face. "What was the two percent failure?" he asked.

"Food had no taste," said Emmerline. "And paint did not cover properly. Colours came out several shades lighter."

"Have any wand injections been made via this Super Holo project?" asked the medic.

"Several pigs have been vaccinated against swine red pox," replied the droid.

"And did the vaccine take?"

"One hundred per cent."

"And what are the trials that still need to be done?" asked Kaleem.

"Only droids have superholoed," said Emmerline. "We do not yet know how the human physiology will react to the more intense transportation. We are having difficulty finding human volunteers and we no longer test on animals."

“Okay. I’ll do it. I’ll be your volunteer,” said Kaleem. “There’ll be no problem superholoing to a Supercraft will there?” What was he doing? He hated holo travel. But this was what he was about, wasn’t it? Emmerline was right there. And if it went wrong and something happened to him… well, that might save him a heap more other trouble.

“Trial 275: superholo to Supercraft, 100% successful,” said Emmerline.

“Definitely, then,” said Kaleem.

“It would certainly help,” said the medic, “getting the medication into him and having you talk directly with your friends.”

“You’re sure about this?” said Edmundson.

Kaleem nodded.

“Way to go, funny head two,” shouted Sandi, grinning. She suddenly looked more like the Sandi he’s always known.

“You darling boy,” said Emmerline in her human voice. She swaggered over to Kaleem and kissed him on the lips.

“Oy!” shouted Edmundson as Kaleem tried to pull away from the over-sexed droid.

For the Sake of Terrestra Again

"I think you've got the hang of it," said Drewd Atkins, the medic who had been showing Kaleem how to use a medi-wand. "Just as long as the superholoing is good at that distance."

"Well, we need to get on. It should be fine. It will have to be," said Edmundson. "He looks as if he might know what he's doing. Just."

I should think so too, thought Kaleem. It had been a tedious two days, going over and over using a wand, getting used to the superholo and then using a wand transported by the cradle. It was actually all relatively easy. If anything the superholo was a little more comfortable than normal holo travel. You didn't feel as much as if you were looking through a glass bubble when you got to the other end.

So far, he'd given fifteen children a booster anti-grippa wand-shot and used a diagnostic wand on five elderly females and found that they had bone-mass deficiency. They'd all been at another medi-centre fifty kilometres away.

"Easily treatable," said Drewd. "Good that you've caught it."

"Yeah, but it's going to be a bit different with a group of Terrestrans who are scared and don't understand the technology," said Kaleem.

"Well, you're Terrestran, so that should help," said Edmundson.

"And I'll be right beside you all the time," said Drewd.

"As shall I," said Calver.

"Ooo an oo ee," said Saratina, beaming at him.

He guessed she was wishing him luck or some such.

"And we'll have normal communication with them as well," said Edmundson. "We'll all be able to see exactly what is going on."

This is going to be bizarre, thought Kaleem. *They'll be looking at me on the Supercraft yet I'll actually be right next to them here.*

"Well," said Edmundson. "Are we all agreed? Want to give it a go?"

"Well, Kaleem?" asked Calver. "Are you ready now?"

As ready as I'll ever be, thought Kaleem. "I guess," he replied. "Let's go for it."

Kaleem felt decidedly nervous as he watched Drewd charge a new wand with the anti-viral drugs and some other substances.

"That should do the trick," he said. "Anti-grippa-drugs, some supplements and rehydration remedies to help build up his immune system. Pity we can't send some fresh food. That would help as well."

"Out of the question," said Edmundson. "The trials on food transfer are not complete."

"Surely if the drugs work…" said Kaleem.

"No," said Edmundson. "We won't risk it. Not even with you, Kennedy."

"Well the food they have on the Supercraft ought to be nutritious enough, I guess," said Drewd. "It's just that, psychologically…"

"It won't be a problem," said Calver. He turned to Kaleem. "No need to worry, my friend. You are well prepared."

"We have contact," said Emmerline.

A view of the Terrestra bound Supercraft appeared on the main dataserve screen. A still worried-looking Sandi Depra came forward.

"Is there any improvement?" asked Drewd.

"No, but he's stable," she replied. "Kaleem, I'm sure he'll be fine. We'll all be fine. You don't have to do this if it's dangerous."

"It's not dangerous," said Edmundson.

"And I've had plenty of practice," said Kaleem.

"Here we go then," said Drewd. "The wand's ready."

Kaleem took it from Drewd and slotted it into the carrier in the holochamber. He lined his feet up with the footplates and took a deep breath.

"Ready?" asked Edmundson.

"Yes," said Kaleem bracing himself.

There was a roaring in his ears, the usual slight feeling of nausea followed by the disturbing light-headedness. Then everything normalised and he was standing in the Supercraft. He could see clearly as if he were actually there.

"You do look real," said Sandi. "We can't see the holoframe at all now. I feel as if I can touch you."

"Try it," said Kaleem.

She stretched her hand out. He could almost feel her touch him. Not quite, though. And he knew it was really only the wand that had actually travelled to the Supercraft.

"Don't take the wand out of the cradle until the last minute," warned Edmundson.

"She's on your side," whispered Calver. "The others will need persuading."

"Best get on," said Kaleem. "Take me to him."

They were already in the same cabin as Stuart. Sandi pointed to the bed where he was lying and went over to it. Kaleem followed. It was actually so much easier to move in the superholo than it had been in the ordinary one. It was just very confusing being able to see the Supercraft and the medi-centre at the same time, out of the corner of his eye. He could see and hear everything clearly in both places. He could only feel – and smell – the medi-centre on Zandra – if there was a smell at all. It was more of a lack of smell. A sense that everything was completely clean. And missing from the Supercraft was the smell of illness.

"How is he actually?" asked Kaleem.

"His fever is still far too high," said Sandi. "The usual treatments for bringing fever down have not worked. There may be an infection that has taken hold."

"She's probably right," said Drewd. "But the wand treatment should deal with that as well."

Sandi sighed. "Not that I've had all that much experience in bringing down fevers," she said. "I know the theory but that's about it."

Kaleem was standing right next to Stuart now. He could see that his skin was grey and his chest rattled with each breath. Pierre was sitting next to him. He looked almost as grey and there were dark circles around his eyes.

Kaleem wanted to ask Drewd about Stuart, but he didn't want to risk the other Terrestrans hearing anything he said.

"The wand will fix it," said Drewd. "But it'll really help if you can convince the others that this really is only a grippa. It will make their immune system stronger if they become infected, which we really can't rule out."

Ben Alki came into the room at that moment. He nodded at Kaleem. "Do you think you can help him?" he asked.

"We're going to try," said Kaleem. "It is only a grippa."

"How can you be so sure of that?" asked Pierre, suddenly jumping to his feet. "He shouldn't be this bad, should he? How can you be sure it's not the Starlight Racer fever back? I can't lose him. I can't lose him."

"Tell them about the wand," whispered Calver. "And the tests."

"It's all there, in the tests," said Kaleem. "Stuart only has a grippa."

"But it doesn't say a lot for our immune systems, does it?" said Ben Alki, looking as gloomy as when he used to be a switch-off attendant.

"I don't know," said Sandi slowly. "They must be good for something. I mean, none of the rest of us have come down with it." She turned to Kaleem. "And is Saratina all right as well?"

Kaleem nodded.

"Why is he so ill, though?" asked Ben Alki.

Kaleem had to stop himself from making some remark about how taking him from a well-equipped medi-centre and putting him on a Supercraft without a medical team had probably not helped.

"You should get that wand on him as soon as possible," said Drewd.

"Remember the drill," said Edmundson. "Don't take it out of the cradle until the last possible minute."

"Let me use the wand on him now," said Kaleem to Sandi.

She exchanged a brief look with Pierre and Ben Alki. Pierre

sighed and nodded.

"Okay, steady now," said Edmundson.

Kaleem remembered how to remove the wand carefully from the cradle. It did feel real and solid in his hands. It was hard to believe that it was on the Supercraft, picking up an imprint of movements he was making on Zandra.

"Good," murmured Edmundson.

"You've remembered how to feel the wand finding the right spots?" asked Drewd. "The superholoing shouldn't make any difference to that… though we've never tried it over this distance before."

It had better work, thought Kaleem.

He was now at Stuart's bedside. Sandi pulled back the sheets. The greyness, Kaleem noticed, had spread all over Stuart's body. He was covered in bruises.

"What are those?" he asked Sandi.

"It's caused by the weakness in his immune system," she said. "It's because he's become short of the blood cells that usually clump together to stop bleeding. The bruises have formed quickly when he's become restless and thrashed around or when we've had to move him."

Kaleem swallowed hard. Stuart looked even worse than he'd imagined.

"The sooner you get to work on him with the wand, the better," Drewd said. "He needs that boost real fast."

Kaleem lowered the wand over Stuart's chest. It still felt solid in his hand. He was amazed at how his own arm looked just as real. So bizarre! The wand was really on the Supercraft and he wasn't; his feet were still firmly standing on the floor of the Zandrian medi-centre.

"Good. Feel for the latching point," said Drewd.

Even more amazing, the wand felt no different from the one he'd used just fifty kilometres away on Zandra. He could feel the slight vibration as it searched for the exact point on the lung meridian. Then he felt the tug as the wand began to discharge into the first point on Stuart's chest.

"If there's any charge left, go to the right arm, then the left," Drewd reminded him.

Kaleem could feel the charge getting weaker. Even so, as he worked over both of Stuart's arms, he was aware that there was still quite a bit left. Drewd must have packed a heck of a lot of medication into this wand.

"Best go for the gonads," said Drewd. He chuckled. "If he's conscious at all it'll give him a bit of a thrill." Then he became more serious again. "But it is actually one of the best ways in – after the heart, lungs and arms."

Kaleem pushed the sheets even further down, exposing all of Stuart's manhood.

"Be careful what you're doing down there," said Sandi.

Kaleem looked quickly at Pierre who continued to stare at Stuart with a slight frown on his face. He just about blinked, pursed his lips and nodded.

Kaleem didn't have to move the wand. It seemed to find its own way and was hovering over Stuart's penis and testicles. A sudden surge of energy escaped from the wand, then it juddered so violently that Kaleem almost dropped it.

"Ah, yes," said Drewd, laughing. "I forgot to tell you how quickly the energy releases when you work on those parts."

I wish you had, thought Kaleem.

Now, though, the wand was completely spent.

"It's okay," said Drewd. "You can leave it as a souvenir for your medical friend. Yep, it's expensive equipment, but not, they tell me, as expensive as getting it back here. Or she can bring it with her when she comes visiting again."

"Does that mean you've finished?" said Edmundson. "So, can we get him back, talking of expenses?"

I think the Zenoton might disagree, thought Kaleem.

"Would you look at that?" said Sandi. She uncovered Stuart's stomach. Already the bruises were fading and his skin was beginning to go pinker.

Pierre stood up. "Thank you," he mumbled.

"Right," said Edmundson. "Standby. We're bringing you back."

"Can't I stay and see what happens?" asked Kaleem.

Apparently not. The nausea and the disorientation kicked in again immediately. He was soon whirling and floating. The Supercraft and its occupants disappeared. Seconds later there was nothing but the medi-centre.

"Still nothing?" asked Kaleem.

The droid shook her head. As soon as the superholo had been deflated there had been a massive power surge that had cut off the communication with the Supercraft. He'd gone straight to bed and slept for about six hours; it had partly been exhaustion after a few sleepless nights and partly the effect of the superholo – it seemed to make your body think it really had gone that far. Emmerline had been working on restoring communication ever since.

Kaleem had assumed it was just a blip. But now to find Emmerline still struggling to get through to them was really worrying. Had something gone wrong? Had it been caused by the superholoing? Or had he done something wrong with the wand and maybe something really bad had happened to Stuart?

Edmundson wandered up to the console where Emmerline was busy. "And?" he asked. "What news?"

"All internal Zandrian communications restored," said Emmerline's electronic voice. "Interplanetary connections will take some time more."

That was something, at least. They were probably all right then. It was just that the communications weren't working.

"Any idea what caused it?"

"Extreme sunspot activity," said Emmerline.

Good. So it wasn't because they used the superholo.

"That is probably what also caused the landquake," Emmerline continued.

"Really?" said Kaleem. Nazaret would be pleased to hear that. So, it hadn't been because of all the extra planting. It would probably mean they could get Zandra back on track pretty quickly.

"Communication from Supercraft," said Emmerline.

Sandi's face appeared on the screen and she was grinning.

"He's conscious already," she said. "Still weak, but the wand shot is obviously working."

"Good," said Kaleem. It was a relief it had all worked so well. "What do the others think?"

"It's all fantastic, man," shouted Ben Alki. His face loomed up on to the screen. "We should start trading again. Pronto!"

Sandi pushed him out of the way. "Ben Alki, you should not be drinking frega whilst travelling. It's not good."

"Well, you've got to celebrate somehow," shouted Ben Alki, off-screen.

"Seriously," said Sandi, "I think we should re-open trade. Maybe even more acorns in exchange for holo technology *and* medical technology. What do you think?"

Oh dear. After what he'd agreed with the Zenoton.

"Well, can we?" asked Sandi.

"Urgent communication from Elder Razjosh on Terrestra," said the dataserve suddenly.

"I'm sorry," said Kaleem. "I'll have to take this." He didn't know whether to be relieved that the conversation about the acorn trade had been interrupted or worried about what Razjosh had to say.

Seconds later, the elder's face appeared in the screen. He looked shaken.

"Kaleem," he said. "I have the most disturbing news about Rozia."

The room began to sway. *Please don't let her be hurt,* thought Kaleem.

"I think you should come and see her as soon as possible," said Razjosh.

What? What was it?

Kaleem could not speak.

"She needs you," said Razjosh.

The Tower Falls

It was the best day it could possibly be for this. The sun had lost some of its heat yet it still shone brightly. There was a refreshing breeze.

"Why do we need cloaks?" asked Benjamin. "It is so warm. They'll be too much trouble to carry."

"You'll be glad of your cloak, believe me," said Enmerkar, "when you get to the top of the tower. Especially in this breeze."

Naomi smiled. She looked radiant, now in her seventh month of pregnancy. Enmerkar was worried, though. He didn't really want her to go on this long journey. There had been the two miscarriages and the two still-births since Benjamin had come along. He would be thirteen soon. He would soon be a man himself.

Naomi brushed some fluff off Enmerkar's robe.

"Husband, stop worrying," she said. "If I get tired I'll rest at one of the side stalls and wait for you to come down. This baby is stronger than the rest. She will be fine."

"Oh, she's a girl, is she?" said Enmerkar.

"Definitely. I know."

"That's a pity," said Benjamin. "She won't be able to join the family firm."

"But you will," said Enmerkar. He looked at Naomi.

"Go on," she said. "Tell him."

"I'd like you to start working with me. On your thirteenth birthday. As a partner, not as an apprentice," said Enmerkar.

"Really?" said Benjamin. His eyes grew round.

Naomi laughed and stroked her son's cheek.

Benjamin brushed her hand away. "Mother, I'm almost a man now. Stop it."

Enmerkar looked at his son and felt pleased. Yes, he was still a little thin and his muscles had not yet hardened. But he was clearly strong and healthy. He was reliable and a polite boy as well. They had done well, Naomi and he, raising this child.

Naomi smiled at him.

The bugle sounded.

"This is it, then," said Enmerkar. He and the other three thousand people started their long climb up the tower.

They were all wearing the king's colours. Nimrod had commanded that they should. The blue suited Naomi. The silver and the gold had cost a fair amount. But that money had been easy to find. Nimrod may have been demanding in what he wanted for the tower, but at least he paid his workers generously, and Enmerkar in particular.

Some people overtook them. Naomi had to walk slowly. Who were all these people, Enmerkar asked himself, who had been invited to the opening of the tower? How had Nimrod chosen who should come and who should be left behind?

People became quieter as they made their way further up the tower. It was quite hard work. Even for Enmerkar. He was quite used to scooting up and down and he'd even climbed up the outside on ropes. This slow pace, though, was very tiring.

Naomi stopped suddenly and shook her head.

"It's no good," she said. "I can't go any further."

There was a refreshment wagon surrounded by jugs at the side of the walkway.

"You can stop here with me if you like," said the old woman who was selling the wine and water. "A woman in your condition shouldn't be climbing the tower. And I'd be glad of the company."

"It might be an idea," said Naomi. She held her hip and sighed. She winced.

"It's not…" said Enmerkar. She couldn't be going into labour. It was two months early. He knew she should never have come.

"No, it's all right," she said. "It's just a stitch and a little indigestion. She's lying a little awkwardly." She sighed again. "I so wanted to see the view from the top."

"There'll be plenty of opportunities for that," said Enmerkar. "After the baby is born."

"Maybe, maybe not," said the old woman. "But one thing is

sure: this young woman needs some rest now."

Naomi laughed. "Too true," she said. "I'll be fine," she said, turning to Enmerkar.

He didn't want to leave her.

"Go," said the old woman. "Your king expects it." She raised her eyebrows and shook her head.

"Come on, Father," said Benjamin. "You ought to be the first to get to the top."

Naomi nodded. She settled herself down next to the refreshment wagon.

Reluctantly, Enmerkar carried on with Benjamin.

Actually, though, it was easier without Naomi. He'd been right. Benjamin was fit and strong. Soon they were overtaking others. And so many people recognised him and greeted them as they made their way up the tower that his mood lightened. He began to feel quite pleased with his work. And he was certainly very proud of his fine son.

As they went up further and further, more and more people were resting at the side of the walkways which were now becoming narrower and narrower. They were taking deeper and deeper breaths. Enmerkar smiled to himself. Yes, he remembered the first few times he had come up this high. He had become light-headed and he had found it hurt to breathe.

God manages with little air, he thought to himself. *He probably doesn't need to fill his lungs as we do.*

He, too, was used to this thinner air now.

Suddenly, Benjamin stopped. He gasped. His face had become green.

He fell to the ground and began to judder. Foam began to form at the corner of his mouth.

"Help! Help me," cried Enmerkar.

A man moved slowly towards them from a little further down the tower.

"He has the falling sickness," said the man. "Caused by the thinness of the air up here."

The falling sickness? Benjamin? No! A man with the falling

sickness could not be a master builder. It was too risky. If he were to have a fit when climbing the outside of a tall building… It was unthinkable. Was this a punishment from Yahweh? For daring to try and build a tower so high?

"It will pass," said the man. "Don't hold him. Let the seizure take its course."

Enmerkar watched in horror as his son continued to jerk and the foam carried on coming from out of his mouth. His eyes rolled until you could only see the whites. It seemed to Enmerkar that it would never stop.

"It will stop," said the man. "I know it is alarming. But it will stop. Then you must let him rest and as soon as he has his strength take him back down from the tower. This thin air is dangerous for those who have the falling sickness."

It didn't stop, though. Benjamin's shaking became even more violent. It seemed then suddenly to Enmerkar that the whole tower was shaking with him.

A shout came from further up the tower.

There was a huge rumble. What was it? An earthquake?

Suddenly bricks were flying and people were screaming. The tower was falling. Enmerkar was pushed aside as people began to try to get down. He lost sight of his son.

"Benjamin, Benjamin," he called.

He saw the man who had been helping him carrying him. The man gestured with his head that Enmerkar should follow him, but within seconds he had lost sight of them both. People were really beginning to panic now.

And what about Naomi? She was further down. That might mean she would escape more quickly or it could mean that she would be crushed with falling debris. Whichever happened, it would not be good for the baby.

Why was the tower falling? Had he not built it well enough? Was Yahweh angry with them?

I built it to try to reach You, he offered as a silent prayer. *I did not do it be boastful.* But he knew his prayer was false somehow. He had gone along with Nimrod's wish to show Yahweh how great man was. This was the punishment. That was for sure.

Despite everything, he had time to look to the ground. Was it shaking? It was difficult to tell. Was that the ground wrinkling or was it just heat haze? Was it just the hand of God directly pushing over the tower? Or was it really an earthquake?

It didn't matter either way. It was Yahweh's doing and he and all the others were being punished.

Enmerkar watched in horror as some people began to jump from the tower. What were they thinking? Were they wishing for a quicker death? Surely there was a small chance that some of them could get down to the bottom before it fell completely? Who would die and who would be saved?

I built the tower with the talents You gave me, he prayed again. *I built it as much to please You. Please, Yahweh, spare me, my son, my wife and my unborn child.*

A man pushed him roughly out of the way. Enmerkar fell. The man tripped over him, fell to the ground as well, and yelled an expletive Enmerkar had never heard before. As both men got to their feet, the man gabbled something else that Enmerkar could not understand.

The panic was getting greater. People all around him were yelling. Enmerkar could not understand one word. Anyone he answered looked at him blankly.

Perhaps I took a blow to the head when I fell, he thought. *Or it is the heat, or the thinness of the air?* Yet he could see a new fear growing on the faces of the people who were running. They were failing to understand each other.

Yahweh is angry indeed, thought Enmerkar.

The wall holding the section of the tower where he was standing suddenly gave way. He and several others moved backwards so that they could lean against the central core of the tower. Enmerkar could still think clearly enough to know that this core would hold and if they could somehow climb down it they might be saved.

Yet as he desperately hung on he knew this was not to be. He'd heard it said that just before you die the whole of your life flashes in front of you. Then he must be about to die for he started remembering. Remembering how his father had taught him to build his first wall, how Nimrod had persuaded him to build the tower, how he had come to love Naomi, Benjamin's first faltering steps, the day Naomi announced she was with child again and the day he personally cemented in the last brick of the tower.

Still he clung to the core, searching for the next foothold.

Then briefly there were some strange images: the woman painting again, the children with the adult faces and then the man in the odd tunic and leg clothes, writing on great white scrolls as the bricks continued to tumble, around him in reality and in this strange vision.

Enmerkar's foot slipped and his fingers lost their grip.

He was falling, falling forever. The ground was taking a long time to meet him. He knew that as soon as it did there would be at best oblivion, at worst an angry Yahweh to reckon with. Whichever it was, may it come sooner. But he was still falling.

Then he stopped falling and it all went black.

No More Happy Families

"I really wish you wouldn't go," said Marijam. "They probably won't be too pleased when you know about the arrangements you've made with the Zenoton, anyway."

"I just have to go," said Kaleem. "Rozia needs me."

"Rozia is nothing to do with you any more," said Marijam.

"Razjosh says she needs me."

"Oh, and what about Ella?"

"There never was that much about me and Ella." said Kaleem.

"Really? You think it's all right to treat a woman like that?"

"I'm not doing anything wrong," said Kaleem. "Ella and I were clear about things from the beginning."

"Not what I heard!" said Marijam.

"She broke the rules," said Kaleem. He wished she hadn't. It had been going along just fine, hadn't it?

"And why do you want to go getting involved with Rozia again?" said Marijam. "I thought she'd found someone else as well?"

Ouch! Great elders, why did that still hurt so much?

"Yes, but she needs me now," said Kaleem. "Razjosh said so."

"Well, didn't he give you any more details?" said Marijam. "I could shake that old fool."

"Razjosh is not an old fool!" Kaleem shouted, though he was slightly irritated too with the elder who as ever had refused to say much on an open communication channel.

"I don't think there's any need to speak like that to your mother," said Nazaret.

"Isn't there?" muttered Kaleem. "Are you sure it's not because you're just trying to stop me leaving the planet, mother? You've just got to stop this. There are things I need to do sometimes, places I need to be. You just have to let go."

Marijam shook her head. Her already chalk-coloured face went a shade whiter. She sighed. Kaleem could see that she was trying to hold back the tears.

"Mum, I'm so..." he started to say. She waved him away dismissively and rushed out of the lounge area of their newly repaired apartment.

He shouldn't have spoken to her like that. Nazaret was right. And she was right too. He needed to take more care with the way he treated women. It hadn't really been going well with Ella at all, if he was honest.

Yes, he would have to be careful with Rozia. But he trusted Razjosh and if Razjosh said she needed him, she needed him.

And now it was just him and Nazaret.

"She's right," said Nazaret. "Rumour has it that Terrestra has stopped all Supercraft docking on their planet."

"Well, that's just rumour, isn't it?" said Kaleem. He hoped. They had said they wanted to learn more about medicine and holotechnology. But that was before they'd found out that Zandra was getting its supply of acorns from the Zenoton. And that was just people like Sandi and Ben Alki. And even Stuart and Pierre. Other Terrestrans could well be still like Stuart used to be. It was always such a struggle to persuade Terrestrans to do something different.

"You would be foolish to try," said Nazaret. "Even if they are still receiving Supercraft, they're hardly going to welcome you with open arms. Not now that you've sold out to the Zenoton."

"Well, aren't you at least pleased that I found you a supply of acorns?" shouted Kaleem. "Even though it might have cost me some of my only friends?"

"I think a little patience might have been in order," said Nazaret. "There's no knowing if they will survive such a long journey and the freezing process. And it will take far longer to get them here than it would have from Terrestra. Then there's the thawing process."

"Oh, well, excuse me for trying," shouted Kaleem. How dare he? How dare he complain? Hadn't he just also saved his planet from a diplomatic incident? Hadn't he restored peace between Zandra and the Zenoton? Even though it was nothing to do with him. He was the Peace Child for Terrestra, not for Zandra.

Nazaret sighed. "You are right," he said. "And it is helpful, what you've arranged with the Zenoton. Especially with matters with the other Terrestrans being so unclear. I think I'm just concerned about how worried your mother will be when you go off again. She found it hard last time and things were still good then between the diplomatic parties. I would still have rather had the acorns from Terrestra. But acorns from Zenoto are better than no acorns."

"I have to go," said Kaleem. "I'll always have to go somewhere." Surely Nazaret would understand that? He felt a little calmer.

"As part of your Peace Child role, yes," said Nazaret. "But to do with a young woman you no longer have a connection with? That seems to me less wise."

"Well at least I'm not abandoning her like you did my mother," said Kaleem as calmly as he could. How dare his father say anything about him and Rozia after he had left Marijam and him to fend for themselves?

"You know I had no control over being fetched back," said Nazaret, his voice now quite cold. "But if I'd had a message saying she needed me I'd have been back at once."

"Really?" said Kaleem. "You don't seem to have made much effort."

"I always felt that I wasn't as important to her as she was to me," said Nazaret. "She seemed like she wanted a fantastic career, perhaps following in Frazier's footsteps. But we didn't break up. If she'd called me, I'd have come back. I wouldn't have played with her feelings."

"Oh, so you think I'm going to play around with Rozia's feelings, do you?" shouted Kaleem. This was so unfair. "Do you really think I wanted to break up with her? That was the last thing in the world I wanted. I just thought it was for the best."

"And how on Terrestra do you think my mother would have been able to contact you? You didn't even tell her who you were or where you came from."

"There was nothing I could do…" said Nazaret.

"And I can do something, so don't try to stop me," shouted Kaleem.

"At least I never stopped loving your mother," said Nazaret.

"And I still love Rozia," said Kaleem. There. He'd said it now.

The two men stared at each other. Kaleem was throbbing all over.

"Don't do anything foolish… or unkind," said Nazaret quietly.

"Oh, I won't," said Kaleem. He was having great difficulty not punching Nazaret. "I won't let her need me for sixteen years."

Nazaret's shoulders sagged and he looked defeated. But Kaleem could not feel sorry for him. He just could not. He turned his back on his father and left the room, left the apartment in fact.

Help by Strange Women

It had been easy enough to track her down. Now that he was used to Zandrian technology it had been easy to find Edmundson's private apartment where Emmerline kept him company when not on duty. It had been easy enough as well to call Edmundson away with a story about a problem left over from the Zenoton's interference in the Zandrian monetary system. It had even been quite easy to switch Emmerline from mistress mode into worker droid. She'd even confirmed that Nazaret had been right: all alien Supercraft had been again forbidden to visit Terrestra. Even if they hadn't, this solution seemed better to Kaleem. Now came the difficult part: persuading Emmerline that a human could be transported in a superholo cradle.

She was having nothing of it.

"Trials on human teleportation are not yet complete," she said in her electronic voice.

Oh for the sake of the all the elders, the first time he'd visited Zandra he'd been teleported from a broken Supercraft down to the planet. That had been a very primitive sort of teleportation at that, invented by Z Zoners. Kaleem wondered for a few seconds why there'd been no more progress made with that on Terrestra, and then turned his mind back to the current problem.

Maybe he could use blackmail?

"How would it be if I told everyone about you and Commander Edmundson?" he said.

Emmerline laughed in her human voice. "We would deny it, of course," she said. "And you would look foolish." She sidled over to Kaleem and positioned herself so that her cleavage was very visible. "And there are certain things I can do that will make you not want to do that at all," she added in husky voice, as she placed a hand on his buttock. So much for getting her into droid mode.

It was difficult to believe that she was not human. But he just wasn't in the mood for those sorts of games. It had been a stupid thing to try anyway. Most people had probably already guessed about Edmundson and the droid. They must have thought of a cover story.

She went back into worker droid mode.

"I will not operate the superholo device without the permission of Commander Edmundson," she repeated.

"Alee! Alee!" called a familiar voice suddenly from outside.

What on Zandra was Saratina doing here?

Emmerline turned and jumped.

"What is the deformed Terrestran doing her?" she asked. "How did she find out where Commander Edmundson lives?"

"Alee! A me i!" cried Saratina. "I owe ot oo ooen. O. S aineruss."

"Let her in," said Kaleem, trying to use the usual voice for instructing a droid.

Emmerline hesitated for a few seconds but then did operate the door control and seconds later Saratina was there.

"How did you get here?" asked Emmerline in her human voice but quite coldly.

"Oyo Alee. Oray ollo Alee. A oo oloo Ale ul e ti," replied Saratina.

"She does tend to follow me around," Kaleem explained. He turned to Saratina. "Go back, Saratina. And don't tell anyone."

"I o o. Lee ee umm e u," said Saratina.

Then he had an idea.

"Okay," he said to Emmerline. "Will you at least let me holo to Terrestra?"

The droid hesitated again.

"There's no objection to simple superholoing is there?" asked Kaleem. "Aren't all of the tests complete on that? It's just the cradle device that's tricky, isn't it?"

The droid nodded at last. "That is possible," she said. "Permission has now been granted for the superholo to be used for general transport." She began to work at the console.

Kaleem pushed Saratina towards the holoplatform. "You're to pretend to be me," he whispered. "I'll go in the cradle and you can stand on the platform."

"Ee'll o," said Saratina. She looked at Emmerline and frowned then looked back at Kaleem.

He guessed she was worried abut the droid knowing what they were doing. He shook his head and put his finger to his lips to indicate to Saratina that she should be quiet. If he could just get away with this. He did know that even the most sophisticated Zandrian droids had some problems with peripheral vision in certain light conditions and when they were struggling with that and occupied with other tasks, there was every chance that their other sensors would be less effective as well. All he had to do was create those light conditions.

That was all.

Here goes, he thought. *Let's hope.*

Conveniently there was a large mirror in the lounge area of Edmundson's apartment. Kaleem opened his personal communicator and used the touchpad to make the make the light come on. He shone the light at an angle to the mirror so that it was deflected straight towards the droid's eyes. Just as Kaleem had hoped, the side shields on the droid's eyes raised and she now seemed to concentrate on keeping those in place and on preparing the superholo device.

Kaleem pushed Saratina on to the holo platform and then slipped himself into the cradle. It was a tight fit, but he was in. He didn't speak to Saratina, though it would probably have been fine to do so: everything else that was supposed to happen when you dazzled a droid was happening, so why shouldn't she also lose some of her extra senses as they said she would?

"Stand by for holo to Terrestra, Razjosh Elder's quarters," said Emmerline.

The cradle began to wobble and judder.

Oh putrid elders, thought Kaleem. *Why on all the planets am I doing this?*

Accident

The superholo was obviously working. The wobble and jerk became more intense. Kaleem could not yet see Razjosh's apartment. Edmundson's apartment and Emmerline were still visible. The door slid open. Was that Edmundson coming back?

No, Calver Toms walked into the apartment. Had he been following him as well? He ought to have guessed.

"Kaleem, this is madness," he called. "Apart from it being dangerous, there is actually nothing for you to do on Terrestra now."

"I've got to help Rozia," Kaleem replied.

"She won't want your help," said Calver. "Even if she needs help, you won't be much use to her."

How on all the planets would you know anything about me and Rozia? thought Kaleem as the wobbling and jerking subsided and he began to feel as if he were floating. Yes, Calver was good at working out how people would react to events but he'd never met Rozia and he really knew very little about her.

"Come back before it's too late," called Calver moving over to the console where Emmerline was still adjusting the controls.

"Don't let him interfere," called Kaleem.

Saratina looked to where Calver was standing and then looked back towards Kaleem. A deep frown cut through her forehead. Calver seemed not to be able to move. What had she done? Mesmerised him? Whatever it was, it didn't matter. He needed to concentrate on what was going on here.

"As soon as you see Razjosh's apartment, release me from the cradle," Kaleem called to Saratina.

She nodded in reply.

It went dark. It was just like when he was teleported from the Supercraft to Zandra when he first went there. He felt as if her were being pushed through a very black tunnel. The shaking was much more violent now than it had been earlier. He felt as if his body was being pulled apart. There was that strange humming sound again, and all the rainbows, just like before. At last there was the bright light at the end of the tunnel. Yes, just exactly like before and no less scary even though he knew what to expect.

Then, everything stopped happening and he was standing in Razjosh's apartment. There was no holo glass bubble in front of him. And there was Saratina beside him in hologram form. He could no longer see Edmundson's apartment, even when he looked though Saratina's holo bubble. It had worked then. And Razjosh was now standing just in front of him.

"Well that was a bit of a dramatic entrance," said the elder. "Are you sure you couldn't have found a more dangerous way of travelling?"

"I'd heard that they'd stopped all Zandrian Supercraft landing," said Kaleem.

"I'm sure the powers that be would have made an exception for you," said Razjosh. "And even if that proved difficult, your grandfather and I would have come up with something."

"Well, it was quicker this way," said Kaleem.

"And extremely risky," said Razjosh.

"I've taken bigger risks," said Kaleem.

Razjosh suddenly threw back his head and laughed. "I suppose next you are going to tell me that I taught you to do that," he said.

"Well, actually, yes," said Kaleem.

"Then you have me there," said Razjosh. "And welcome you are. You too, Saratina."

Saratina clapped her hands.

"So, now I'm here, what did you want to tell me about Rozia?" asked Kaleem.

Razjosh sighed. "The news is not good. I'm afraid. Julien has been killed."

"What happened?" asked Kaleem. A part of him felt quite pleased for a few seconds. But he felt bad about that almost immediately.

"It was an accident," said Razjosh. "A complete and utter accident. No one's fault."

Saratina whimpered.

Kaleem swallowed hard.

"A cave collapsed when he was in a meeting there. In the Z Zone. Well, it was a partly manmade cave," Razjosh explained. "It was the manmade part that gave way."

Saratina whimpered again.

"Why on Terrestra was he there?" asked Kaleem. "Surely that was a stupid place to go?"

"Except that it was precisely those sorts of places that were under discussion," said Razjosh. "They were trying to decide whether the old Z Zone cave network was worth preserving."

"Did they try to rescue them?" said Kaleem. "How many were there?"

"Six," replied Razjosh. "There would have been seven. Rozia should have been there. But one of the Adulkis also died that day. The first. She felt she had to stay behind and help."

"Who died?" asked Kaleem.

"Thoma," said Razjosh.

"Ohma? Eeetl Ohma?" Saratina squeaked.

Kaleem heard her begin to sob.

"Rozia has taken it badly, as you would expect," said Razjosh. "She really does need you."

Something was melting inside him. All he wanted to do was take Rozia in his arms and hold her until she had stopped sobbing, even if she was crying over another man. And maybe he would cry with her over the loss of his favourite Adulki. He wondered about Kevik.

"How's Kevik taking it?" he asked Razjosh.

"Naturally, he is upset," said the elder.

Kaleem was glad Razjosh said "naturally". It was good to hear Kevik being referred to as a normal human being. A few months ago who would have thought that?

"But even though he is going about his business as usual, he is handling his grief well this time. He is not afraid to talk to people about Thoma and to show his sadness," Razjosh continued. "Rozia, on the other hand, is in pieces. Of course, she has lost a partner which is naturally worse than losing a brother."

Ouch. Razjosh really knew how to hurt.

"She also considers herself partly to blame or rather she feels guilty about still being alive. She ought to have been with him when it happened."

"So how can I help?" asked Kaleem. By all the elders he wanted to help but he couldn't really see how he could. Marijam's and Calver's warnings came back to him.

"She is in a severe depression," said Razjosh. "She is still working with the Adulkis, but otherwise is speaking to no one and is keeping herself hidden away. She has, however, said she will speak to you. Only if you came to Terrestra in person."

"Why, though?" asked Kaleem.

"Who knows?" said Razjosh, shaking his head.

"Arap ee eel ov oo," said Saratina, clapping her hands.

"Oh, make no mistake, Saratina, she was as devoted to Julien as she had been to Kaleem," said Razjosh, "if not more so."

"So how do I find her?" asked Kaleem. He was now beginning to question the wisdom of coming here. How would he cope with her grieving for another man? How would he be able to provide anything for her but all the love he had for her? And he had already decided that that was an impossible way for them.

"There are one or two trusted friends who can show you the way," replied Razjosh. "And I am one of them."

Saratina suddenly screamed.

Kaleem turned to look at her. Her hologram seemed to be fading in and out of view.

"Are they pulling you back?" called Kaleem.

Saratina shook her head violently. "Ee hers, ee hers," she called, clutching her head.

The holograph seemed to shine brightly. For a few seconds Saratina looked as if she was really there in Razjosh's apartment. Then something snapped and she disappeared completely.

"By all the elders, what's happening?" said Razjosh.

"They've pulled her back, haven't they?" said Kaleem.

"No, look," said Razjosh. "The bubble is still there."

Kaleem looked at where Razjosh was pointing. Yes, it seemed

that the holograph was still there. It was just that Saratina had disappeared from it.

"That's never happened before, has it?" asked Kaleem.

"You tell me," said Razjosh. "You're more experienced with the latest Zandrian technology than I am."

Razjosh's dataserve bleeped. "Urgent communication from Zandra," its electronic voice said.

"Send," commanded Razjosh.

"Has that woman thrown herself into the cradle as well?" asked Edmundson, not bothering with any formal greeting.

"No," replied Razjosh. "She just seems to have disappeared."

"Kennedy, what have you done?" growled Edmundson at Kaleem. "This stuff is dangerous. You knew very well that all the trials were not complete."

Putrid elders, what had he done? This was getting really scary.

"We'll get all of our top scientists on to it straight away," said Edmundson.

"Likewise," said Razjosh.

Edmundson's face snapped off the screen.

"Problems, problems," mumbled Razjosh, turning to Kaleem. He grinned. "What would life be without them, eh?"

Becoming the Peace Child

All the Science Men and Women

"It really is extraordinary," said Danielle Thomas. "That she has disappeared from both the holo platform and the holograph itself. You are absolutely sure she went nowhere near the teleporter cradle?"

"No, she really didn't," said Kaleem. He wished they would believe him. He was glad Danielle was in charge of the investigation though. He knew her quite well from the time she had travelled to Zandra with him the first time he went. Just like Sandi Depra, the Head of Science, she was much younger than a normal head of service. Unlike Sandi, however, she was quite serious and definitely had normal Terrestran looks.

"I can verify that," said Razjosh. "She was most definitely in the hologram and not in the cradle at all."

"I just hope she's not hurt," said Kaleem. "She seemed pretty agitated just before she disappeared."

"Well, we've got all of my best workers looking into it. We'll find her," said Danielle.

Kaleem wanted to believe her but he was finding it difficult. "Does that include the Z Zoner teleport experts?" he asked. He trusted them more somehow.

"No such place as the Z Zone. It's called the New Zone now," Frazier Kennedy reminded him sharply. "Ah, good. Here comes the tea."

A waiter droid pulling a glider tray of tea-cups, a teapot and a plate of cakes moved silently into the room. There was something surreal about this. Here they were in his grandfather's plush apartment in the citadel drinking tea and poor Saratina was missing.

"It might be that somehow the functions of the holo platform and the cradle became confused," said Danielle.

"But why didn't it just deposit her in Razjosh's apartment?" asked Kaleem.

"It could be that the holo transmission was intercepted

somehow," said Danielle.

"I expect we'll get some news from Zandra soon," said Frazier.

As soon as he had finished speaking the dataserve screen sprang into life. "Urgent communication from Zandra," said the electronic voice. It was almost like on Zandra where the dataserves seemed to know what you were thinking.

"Send," said Frazier Kennedy.

Edmundson's face appeared on the screen.

"Greetings, Elder Frazier," he said. "I have some important news."

Well at least he's remembered his manners this time, thought Kaleem.

"Do you have visuals?" asked Frazier.

"Yes, I can see Elder Razjosh and Kaleem Kennedy-Bagarin and I presume the young lady is an official? I can speak freely?"

"Danielle Thomas, Head of Science," said Danielle.

"Ah good. Good that you are all together. We have made an extraordinary discovery," Edmundson continued. "What we thought was an empty holo platform was in fact a holograph itself. A very clever and convincing one. It seems the female Terrestran has been abducted."

"And someone has improved the technology even beyond Zandrian standards," said Danielle.

"Indeed," answered Edmundson.

"Any idea who might be able to do that?" asked Frazier.

"Difficult to guess," said Edmundson. "Ours is the most advanced in the known universe."

"Depending on how well you know the universe," mumbled Razjosh.

"Why would anyone want to abduct Saratina?" said Kaleem.

"Every life has it value," said Razjosh sharply. He sighed. "Though I guess they thought they were taking you," he added turning to Kaleem.

What now? thought Kaleem. Wouldn't that droid know something? He went to ask Edmundson but before he could string his words together the screen went blank.

“So, interplanetary communications are still unreliable,” said Frazier. “Would that be because of the problems on Zandra?”

Kaleem remembered what Emmerline had said about the sun spot activity. “It’s all to do with one of Zandra’s suns,” he explained.

“Ah yes,” said Frazier. “Sol II, is, I’ve heard, becoming unreliable.”

The lights flickered.

“What on Terrestra…?” said Danielle.

“That’s never happened before,” said Frazier.

The lights flickered again and then went out altogether.

“Information, please,” called Frazier.

The dataserve whirred briefly than went quiet.

The corner of the room began to glow. The lights came back up.

“Malfunction not understood,” said the dataserve speaker. “Collecting data.”

There seemed to be someone standing in the corner of the room.

Edmundson reappeared on the dataserve screen.

“What on Zandra am I looking at?” he asked. “Is that a holograph you have there?”

“Air am ay? Ot apapnin?” said the figure in what was now obviously a holograph.

Kaleem had never felt so pleased to see Saratina’s crooked smile. At least she was alive. She didn’t seem hurt. But would they ever be able to make sense of what she was saying?

“Do you know where you are?” asked Razjosh.

Saratina shook her head violently. “Ike oopercra ut ieer,” she replied.

“You must speak slowly and clearly,” said Razjosh.

Saratina shook her head. “Arn eek earer,” she said slowly.

“Are you hurt at all?” asked Frazier.

She shook her head again. “Oee a biinin. Ea hur.” She held her head and frowned a little. Then she turned to the side as if someone was speaking to her. She nodded. “Ozeeah,” she said.

"Ozeeha a unairsta."

"I know who would be able to understand her," said Kaleem.

"My thoughts entirely," said Razjosh. He turned to Kaleem. "And I'm afraid she still won't have any contact with you until Saratina is found."

Kaleem felt as if he had been stabbed in the chest again.

"I'll go back to my quarters and talk to her from there," said Razjosh. "Saratina, I'll come back as soon as I can. I'll see if Rozia will come to interpret. Or maybe they can follow me. Maybe we can even meet in Rozia's apartment." He turned to Kaleem, shrugged his shoulders and shook his head.

Kaleem watched the elder leave the apartment.

The holograph snapped out.

Kaleem had never felt so useless in his life.

Saratina's Story

"Decline," said Rozia. That was the third attempt Razjosh Elder had made in the last twenty minutes to communicate with her. And there were the three attempts yesterday. When he'd first told her about Kaleem's unorthodox arrival and Saratina's disappearance she'd told him in no uncertain terms that she would only speak to the elder, and possibly later to Kaleem, the Peace Child, after she had been assured of Saratina's safe return. And he should inform her of that via a droid messenger, not to her directly but to the Adulki centre. One of the administrators would let her know.

It had probably been a mistake, anyway, saying she would speak to Kaleem at all. Despite Julien, despite all that had happened since, it still made her shudder when she thought of how he'd left her at the medical centre. Now, though, she supposed it was more because she felt sorry for the person she was then than because of any feeling of losing Kaleem himself. She felt more of a sense of loss about the opportunity that was then denied her of helping with the Peace Child's work. The day he'd first approached about that had been the day the cave had collapsed. Then there'd been the problems on Zandra. And poor Thoma dying. Now, though, she needed to do something to drag herself out of this inertia. Possibly, though, it had been a mistake, trying to do something with Kaleem again. Saratina's disappearance had been the ideal excuse yet again to put off meeting him.

These were the thoughts that ran through her mind as she got ready. She showered slowly. It seemed the one time she could allow herself to cry – about the way Kaleem had treated her, about the death of little Thoma and about losing Julien. Funny, kind, courageous Julien. And about what would become of Petri The rest of the time she had to keep on a brave face. For the sakes of the other Adulkis, for those who worked with them and for Petri. And the rest of the time she wasn't working or dealing with Petri she would sleep as much as possible – to try to forget and with the hope that she wouldn't dream, for if she did it was always about Kaleem, Thoma, Julien or Petri.

She took a deep breath and gave her face a final scrub. She must hurry now. Anna would be here any minute. She switched the shower to laser drier function. Seconds later she was dry. She picked the first clothes she found out of her closet. She pulled them on hastily, gave her hair a quick brush and smoothed some camouflage moisturiser all over her face. She took a quick look in the mirror. It hadn't really worked. There were still dark circles under her eyes.

So much for beauty sleep, she thought. *It clearly hasn't done me much good.*

Her eyes looked dull. She seemed to have aged. She didn't really care. Not for herself at least. But she knew she needed to make an effort.

Get a grip, woman, she thought. *You'll frighten the Adulkis. You'll frighten Petri. You'll frighten everybody.*

The tears threatened to fill her eyes again but she pushed them back.

The apartment's communicator buzzed.

Don't tell me she's forgotten the code again, thought Rozia. *I'll kill her one of these days.*

"Visual," she commanded the dataserve.

It wasn't Anna. It was Razjosh. She would have to face him at last.

"Show him in," she reluctantly commanded the dataserve.

The house droid trundled to the front door.

"I had to come," said Razjosh as Rozia indicated that he should sit down.

Rozia felt herself blushing and had to look away.

"I'm sorry to force you like this, my dear," said Razjosh, "but we really do need your help."

Rozia still could not look at him.

"No one will force you to speak to Kaleem," said Razjosh. "But Saratina does need you."

Rozia couldn't hold back the tears any longer. Why did the elder have to say his name? And why was she acting like this? She was over him, wasn't she? The Peace Child? Oh, she must just be feeling sorry for herself. She put her hand in front of her eyes. She didn't want Razjosh to see how upset she was.

"Saratina has been kidnapped," Razjosh explained. "They have sent her holograph but we cannot understand what she is saying."

Rozia took her hand away from eyes and looked at him. Kidnapped was a little better than lost in cyber-space wasn't it? Perhaps?

"How can I help?" she asked huskily.

"Oh, my child, I didn't mean to upset you," said Razjosh.

He was looking at her so kindly. That really didn't help. She felt the tears welling up again.

Razjosh pulled her into his arms and hugged her closely. "I know it all hurts now," he said. "But can you set the pain aside a little and help your old friend Saratina?"

Rozia managed to nod, though how she might be able to help she wasn't quite sure.

The door to the apartment glided open suddenly. Rozia pulled herself away from Razjosh. It was Anna of course.

"I'm so sorry I'm late," she said, scraping back a strand of loose hair that had come from her pony tail. As usual her clothes looked as if they had been dragged on. "Oh, I'm sorry. I didn't realise you had company," she added as she noticed Razjosh.

Don't ask any questions, thought Rozia. She signalled to Anna that she should see to Petri. *And don't give anything else away.* Still, she thought she could trust her. Even though the girl's time-keeping was all over the place, Rozia was fairly certain she would give nothing away and wouldn't ask too many questions about Razjosh. And, of course, she was great with Petri.

Anna seemed to get the message and scuttled off.

"Anna's doing some research for me," Rozia explained to Razjosh quickly.

He nodded. He seemed to believe her.

"So, how do we know that they will send Saratina again and where exactly will they send her? Would they know to send her here?" she said to Razjosh.

"We have to hope," said Razjosh. "Whoever they are, they seem to be very clever and I've no doubt they will find you. I'm sure they're tracking us."

The lights in the apartment suddenly dipped.

"I was right then," Razjosh muttered. "They are tracking us."

"What on Terrestra is happening?" asked Rozia. Lights just never did that these days. Not even here in the New Zone.

Anna appeared briefly at the door to the back hallway. Rozia shook her head and signalled that she should go back. Anna obeyed at once. Rozia looked at Razjosh.

I don't think he noticed, thought Rozia.

The holograph settled. And there was Saratina again.

"Rozia!" she called. "Rozia." Then she started to cry.

"It's all right, Saratina," said Rozia. "It's going to be fine."

"They can't understand me," said Saratina.

"What's she saying?" asked Razjosh.

Rozia shook her head. "Just that no-one can understand her."

"Who is it?" asked Razjosh. "Who is keeping you there?"

"I don't know who they are," replied Saratina. "But I think we're on a Supercraft or something like one."

Rozia relayed the message to Razjosh.

"Have they said what they want?" asked Razjosh.

"Something about a proper agreement with Zandra," said Rozia. "Getting rid of the credit system in exchange for knowledge about technology?"

"The Zenoton!" cried Razjosh after Rozia had interpreted. "The Zenoton have her. Huh! And they want to improve their technology? Seems to me they're already quite competent."

"The Zenoton?" asked Rozia.

"Yes," replied Razjosh. "They were going to supply Zandra with acorns after the… er… problems between Terrestra and Zandra because of Stuart Davidson's illness."

Saratina suddenly became quite agitated. She looked away

from Rozia and Razjosh.

"They must be speaking to her," said Razjosh.

"Why don't they just communicate directly with us?" asked Rozia.

"Kidnappers rarely seem logical or considerate," said Razjosh. "I guess now they have Saratina when they thought they were getting Kaleem they're using her as an emotional weapon."

Why did the mention of his name again make her feel as she was being stabbed? And could that be a slight feeling of relief that it was Saratina and not Kaleem stuck on a Zenoton Super-craft? Surely not? And at the same time she was so cross with him for allowing Saratina to be captured because he did something so stupidly… brave?

Saratina turned back to them.

"They said they will give you some time to think about it all," said Saratina. "Then they will send me back to you."

The holograph snapped shut.

"So, what next?" asked Razjosh.

"They'll send her to me again," replied Rozia. "When we've had time to think about it."

Petri suddenly squawked. Anna came running to the door, her eyebrows raised and her lips pulled into a tight grimace.

Razjosh looked at Anna, then at Rozia.

"I'll be on my way," he said. "I'd like to discuss this with Kaleem and the others in person. And I can see you are very busy."

Rozia's stomach lurched at the mention of Kaleem.

Razjosh nodded and smiled. He put a finger to his lips.

"Take care, my dear," he said. "Take care."

Waiting on the Zenoton

"Well, it's good having you here anyway," said Louish. "And I hope when all of this is over you will come and make a proper visit. One where you can just relax."

His grandmother looked as glamorous as ever in her deep blue silk tunic. She seemed to get younger every time Kaleem saw her. Or was he getting older? And he felt relaxed anyway. He always did around his grandparents. Even Frazier had that air of calm about him and always gave you a sense that everything was going to be fine.

They were at Louish's apartment at the Community of Attachments today. She had arranged a small tea party for themselves and Razjosh and Danielle Thomas. Danielle was still looking at ways of tracking where the Zenoton were – they had managed to hide themselves completely. Razjosh had been working with Kaleem on his diplomacy skills. Other than that, though, it was a matter of waiting until Saratina put in an appearance again. At least she'd seemed well and relatively happy, Razjosh had said, when he'd seen her holograph last week.

Louish beamed.

"Oh, it is so good having the two most important men in my life to tea," she said. "And I'm looking forward to seeing Razjosh again and meeting that very clever young head of science."

Already the small table was covered in plates of cakes and biscuits, which Kaleem knew she had made herself even though the house droid was busily arranging plates, serviettes and teacups. He smiled to himself. Yes, it was good having Louish as a grandmother.

"This all looks excellent, my dear," said Frazier, rubbing his hands together and grinning. "I do hope they will be here soon. I can't wait to sample your delicious cakes again. Those in the Citadel are frankly… boring."

Louish giggled.

It was impossible to be worried with those two around. He was in the middle of this huge crisis and here they were being all jolly and optimistic. This was their just their rather eccentric way of showing they cared.

The communicator buzzed.

"Ah! There they are," said Louish, jumping off her comfisessel. She followed the house droid to the main door. "Let them in, let them in," she called.

Seconds later the house droid had shown them in.

"I am so pleased to meet you at last," said Louish, shaking Danielle's hand. "I really admire what you do. And you are so young as well."

Danielle blushed. "I try my best," she said.

Louish got busy making sure that everyone had tea and cakes. She left very little for the house droid to do. Soon everyone was eating and drinking and had their mouths to full that they could not speak.

"This is all so delicious," said Danielle, as she finished a slice of Louish's chocolate cake.

"Thank you my dear," said Louish. "I do my best too."

Kaleem noticed that Razjosh was rather quiet. He seemed not to be taking much notice of what was going on.

What's on his mind, I wonder? thought Kaleem.

"Well," said Frazier at last. "So, have we found any more out about where the hologram is coming from?"

"It's proved impossible," said Danielle. "We have not been able to trace it at all."

"Now, don't be so modest my dear," said Razjosh, suddenly brightening up. "Tell them what you think you might be able to do."

"This sounds interesting," said Frazier, rubbing his hands together.

"Well," said Danielle, "we can capture the hologram so that we keep a permanent copy of it. We can then have more time to examine it. We might be able to crack the codes of its properties and see where it's come from."

"And what happens to poor Saratina whilst that is happening?"

asked Louish.

"She'll just be wherever she is," explained Razjosh. "We'll just have a still picture of her."

"So what exactly will happen?" asked Frazier.

"Well, we think the Zenoton will send her to Rozia again," said Razjosh.

"And Rozia knows exactly how to attach the freezing device that will hook the last frame of the hologram permanently to Terrestra," added Danielle. "Then we can bring it into our labs and look at it properly. And we should be able to extract a recording of the whole scene from that one still."

Even now hearing her name was painful. Kaleem shivered. Fantastic as his grandmother's chocolate cake was, he'd suddenly lost interest. He put his plate down.

Louish caught his eye. She frowned at him. He smiled back. She looked away again, thank all the elders, and became absorbed in the conversation.

"Sounds pretty good," said Frazier. "Now, take some more cake. After all that work, you need to build up your strength."

"Eat up," Louish mouthed to Kaleem.

He wasn't hungry, though he supposed he'd better to try to eat. He went to pick up his plate. He still had his serviette in his hand. It caught on the cake and wouldn't let go. It suddenly reminded him of how the cradle was attached to the hologram when he arrived on Terrestra.

"Would you be able to attach a cradle to a still from a hologram?" he asked. "And would you be able to send it back when you'd found out where to send it?"

"It might be possible," said Danielle slowly. "Although it would be easier to send a new hologram once we can unpick the information buried in what they send here."

"Either way, I think I ought to go and speak to them in person," said Kaleem.

"It's a bit risky," said Danielle.

Razjosh didn't say anything but nodded his head briefly and pursed his lips.

"What are you saying?" asked Louish.

Frazier put his fingers in front of his mouth and blew through them.

"You can't mean that you'd want to be teleported again?" said Louish, frowning, her eyes wide open. "You can't. It's too dangerous."

"I've done it twice before," said Kaleem.

"Yes, and you got away with it," said Louish. "But it doesn't mean it's safe."

"It's necessary, though, isn't it?" said Kaleem, looking at Razjosh for support.

The elder sat with his fingers on his lips. His eyes narrowed and he just about nodded. As Louish looked over to him, his face became blank again.

"It would almost kill your mother. And me," Louish continued.

"My mother doesn't need to find out, does she?" asked Kaleem. "In fact, if I do it, it's probably best if as few people as possible know."

"Oh, I don't know," said Louish, throwing her arms up into the air. "I don't like it. I don't like it at all. What do you think?" She turned to Frazier.

"I think he's right to want to go," said Frazier grinning. "He's right that somebody should speak to the Zenoton in person."

"Indeed, indeed," said Razjosh, now nodding his head vigorously.

"But it's a quarrel between Zenoto and Zandra, really," said Louish. "Zandra should be risking someone, not us."

"Don't forget," said Frazier, "Kaleem is half Zandrian and the Zenoton are actually holding a Terrestran."

Louish sighed and nodded her head. She turned to Kaleem.

"Just take care," she said. "Take care. All of the time."

"But I wouldn't want you to go unless it is absolutely safe. The cradle I mean," said Frazier. "I know you're perfectly capable of negotiating well with the Zenoton." He turned to Danielle. "Is any more research being done on the cradle?"

"Well, it is a Zandrian product and we are putting all of our efforts into finding where the Zenoton are sending the holos from," she said. "But we have had a look at it and we know a bit more about how it works."

"But not enough to use it safely?" said Frazier.

Danielle shook her head.

"In which case, you keep well away from it," said Frazier. "You only use the technology when it's safe to do so."

Kaleem could tell that Frazier meant what he was saying. His answer was definitive and there was something about his tone of voice and the look on his face that said it would no longer be up for discussion.

Louish busied herself offering more tea and cakes. She beamed at everyone. The company relaxed as she relaxed. Kaleem guessed she thought that he would not dare disobey Frazier. But he had to do something. No one else seemed to be worried, not even Razjosh. Soon everyone was chatting again and the piles of cakes were gradually disappearing. Even he was seduced a little by the almond and apricot pastry. But he kept his mind alert.

"Well, this has been great," said Danielle, beaming at Louish. "I really must be getting back, though, now."

"It's been a pleasure having you," said Louish. "Come again."

"I'd like that," said Danielle.

"I'll leave now as well," said Kaleem. He had to talk to her. There must be something they could do.

There were the usual goodbyes and Frazier said he would arrange for a transporter to pick them up.

"Do you think it can be done?" asked Kaleem as they arrived at street level and waited for the transporter.

Danielle sighed. "Are you asking me whether I think it can be done or whether I'd be willing to help you?"

"Both, I suppose," said Kaleem.

"I thought so," said Danielle.

The transporter rumbled up to them.

"Okay," she said. "We can talk as we travel."

"Well, can it?" asked Kaleem as they stepped into the transporter. "Can we?"

"It's risky," she said. "Quite dangerous."

"It's my job to live dangerously," said Kaleem. "It doesn't bother me." *I wish,* he thought.

"I could get into a lot of trouble if I allowed you to do something so unsafe," she replied.

"I'll get into even more if I don't do something soon," said Kaleem. "Act first, apologise later. You can do that as well, surely."

"Only so many times," replied Danielle.

"Won't you get into trouble if you hold up a peace mission?" said Kaleem. "I'm always getting into trouble for messing about with science I don't understand. Of course, I'd get into less trouble if you helped me…"

Danielle looked hard at him. She shook her head. "Why do I have the feeling that you can do anything?" she whispered. "I guess I'd better help you. You're not safe on your own."

The transporter slowed and stopped in front of her apartment block. She stepped out.

"Give me a few of days," she said, "and then come and see me again in the lab."

The transporter sped on to where Kaleem was staying.

What have I done? he thought to himself. He would have to go through with this now.

Pierre and Stuart

"Give me a few days," she'd said. It was now almost a week. He should be doing something but there was nothing he could be doing. Much. The one thing he could and should do he just didn't want to do. Kaleem ran his fingers through his hair and paced up and down the small apartment he had been given in the Citadel. Comfortable and luxurious, naturally. And equipped with all the latest Terrestran technology which, even though considerably inferior to what he would find on Zandra, was actually pretty good. But nothing appealed. Not the advanced entertainment platforms, nor the holoed participative sports programmes, not even the enhanced information channels, where he was allowed access to a little more Golden Knowledge and Hidden Information than other Terrestrans – no, none of it appealed. He didn't want to go out either. He'd be recognised and questioned, quite probably.

It was so obvious what he should do. He just didn't want to. He flopped on to one of the advanced comfisessels. It moulded itself to him and hovered at the height that allowed his feet to rest on the floor so that his legs were stretched at a comfortable angle.

"Info," he commanded the dataserve.

The sessel hovered forward so that he was at the right angle for viewing the dataserve. The pictures and movie clips loaded. The same routine reports. No dramas. There was a news blackout on Saratina's disappearance and even the suspension of trade between Terrestra and Zandra was not mentioned.

"Same old. The olds, not the news," Kaleem muttered to himself. "Golden and Hidden, Kaleem Malkendy Peace Child," he commanded the dataserve.

The dataserve offered a discussion of the Babel Prophecy, a progress report on the demands of the Zenoton and a discussion of Terrestra's inadequate medical system. The first one he didn't want to go anywhere near, the second would contain nothing new – he would be updated as soon as there was any more news of

Saratina – and the third was too sharp a reminder of what he should really be doing.

Perhaps he should contact his parents. He wasn't looking forward to that either but it was slightly less uncomfortable than the other option. They'd had a few days now to get over the way he'd travelled to Terrestra. It might be all right.

"Nazaret Bagarin or Marijam Kennedy-Bagarin, Zandra," he commanded the dataserve.

The dataserve whirred and grumbled for a few seconds. The screen went grey. "Connection between Terrestra and Zandra unavailable," said its electronic voice.

So much for technology, thought Kaleem. He couldn't help being relieved though. He wasn't really sure he could face his parents yet. "End," he commanded the dataserve.

"Switch-off commencing," said the electronic voice.

Why do they still call it that? thought Kaleem.

He remembered the last switch-off he'd attended, which was hopefully the last there would ever be. It hadn't been a switch-off in the end after he, Ben Alki and his friends from the Z Zone had foiled it. And then he remembered what he had had to do afterwards. It had been right, hadn't it? Ending his relationship with Rozia. He couldn't put other people in danger.

But wasn't that what he'd just done to Saratina?

Oh, he'd got to do better than this. He'd got to be better around people. He really couldn't put off any longer that visit he had to make.

Kaleem left the apartment.

He'd decided to wait outside for the transporter and didn't even call it up until he was out of the building. It would put the inevitable meeting off a little longer. Not that you ever had to wait too long for a transporter in the citadel. His heart sank as the single pod trundled into view. He would be there in twenty minutes.

"Apartment Pierre Lafontaine and Stuart Davidson," he commanded the machine. He shuddered as he said their names. He wished he didn't have to do this.

The journey was unremarkable. The transporter passed without a hitch through the crystalline passages of the Citadel. As it swerved out of the entrance he noticed a dip in his energy. It was amazing how quickly you got used to the feeling of well-being the Citadel gave you and how hard it was when it was suddenly taken away.

He didn't have long to think about that, though. In just a few moments the transporter was rushing him across open country. This was a new vehicle and it could move really fast. He was going to have to have this meeting pretty soon.

He swallowed the lump in his throat. The sun was shining outside. That made it worse somehow. Why did he always have to do things like this?

All too soon the transporter was stopping by the apartment building where Pierre and Stuart lived. Their apartment was in the same block that Pierre used to live in with his parents. How many times had Kaleem been here before? And apart from just a little niggling guilty feeling that he only went to see Pierre when it suited him, he'd always been pretty happy to turn up here. He'd always been made so welcome. This time, though, he didn't know how he would be received.

The transporter was whirring quietly to itself. "Do you require me to wait for you, sir?" said its electronic voice suddenly.

"No," replied Kaleem. "I'll reprogramme when I need to return."

"As you wish," said the transporter's dataserve. The door slid open. He could put it off no longer.

Kaleem made his way up to the apartment block entrance. He announced himself at the door. The dataserve seemed to take an age to respond. When it did, there was no greeting from either Pierre or Stuart. "Please make you way to the sixth floor," said an electronic voice. Kaleem sighed and placed his palm on the command pad of the lift.

The lift glided up the six floors far too quickly for Kaleem's liking. He could have sworn when he'd been there before that particular journey had been much slower. The door to Pierre and

Stuart's apartment was already open when he arrived.

"Hello?" he called through the open doorway.

There was no reply.

He supposed he'd better go in. As he arrived in the hallway he could hear whispered voices that seemed to be coming from the living-room. What should he do? Should he go in? He couldn't just stand there, could he? This was ridiculous. Then Pierre suddenly stepped out of the lounge. He was frowning slightly and he had his arms folded across his chest.

Kaleem swallowed as he remembered how welcoming his friend had always been in the past.

"Your journey may be wasted," said Pierre quietly. "I've had some trouble persuading Stuart to see you."

Kaleem followed Pierre into the couple's lounge. Their apartment couldn't be more different from the one that Pierre used to share with his parents, even though it was basically the same shape. Kaleem could see that the two of them had really made this into a home that reflected their personalities: rich woollen rugs for Pierre who loved the old world and the most advanced dataserve for Stuart who loved everything modern. Scrupulously tidy and clean. That was Stuart, yet with the hints of comfort that Pierre always brought: thick, soft cushions everywhere.

Pierre nodded that Kaleem should sit. A comfisessel hovered over to him and moulded itself around him.

"He's here," Pierre called through a doorway that opened off the lounge.

Kaleem heard a shuffling and a few seconds later Stuart appeared into the doorway. Well, Kaleem assumed it was Stuart because he knew that Stuart shared an apartment with Pierre. But he was totally unrecognisable. He'd always been slim but now he was thin and skeleton-like. His hair had become lifeless and bald patches were showing through. What hair he still had was mostly grey. His face almost matched. There were dark circles under his eyes. He was limping and was using a stick to help himself along. He seemed to be having some trouble breathing.

He struggled over to the comfisofa which twisted itself to accommodate him. He flopped down on to it, laid his head back on one of the cushions and closed his eyes for a few seconds.

Kaleem's mouth was dry. What had happened here?

Stuart opened his eyes. "So," he said, "you've come to see us, at last."

Pierre started to fuss around him, straightening the cushions and tucking a blanket around his legs. Stuart waved him away. Pierre stepped back but remained standing, his arms folded across his chest again.

"I thought…" Kaleem started. Hadn't that shot cured him of the grippa?

"Oh yes," said Pierre, "he's clear of the grippa virus but this is something left over. It damaged his body permanently."

"Well, haven't you…?"

"What, consulted our useless medical facilities?" snorted Pierre. "Of course we have. In fact, Sandi Depra herself has been here pretty much every day since we got back. Nobody here understands what's happening to him."

"Perhaps… on Zandra…" said Kaleem.

"He'd never survive another journey," snapped Pierre.

"Perhaps someone from Zandra could…" suggested Kaleem.

"You have got to be joking," said Pierre. "They'd never allow a Zandrian here. Not now."

They might, though, if it was kept as Hidden Information, thought Kaleem. He shuddered at the thought of trying to persuade all the elders and the heads of service to do that.

Stuart suddenly began to cough and then to choke. Pierre rushed to his side.

"Steady on, love," he said. "Deep breath. Deep breath." He quickly pulled over the diastic monitor. A tube with a mouth piece was attached to this one. Kaleem had never seen anything like it before. Pierre slid the mouthpiece on to Stuart's face. Immediately his breathing became a little easier. Some colour even came into his cheeks. He closed his eyes again and then seemed to fall asleep.

Pierre turned back to Kaleem. Kaleem could see tears in his eyes.

"I think I'm going to lose him," said Pierre. He covered his eyes. The whole of his body convulsed with a silent sob. "Can't you do something?"

"I'll try. I am trying," said Kaleem. "You know that don't you? Hey, come here." He pulled Pierre into a hug. Kaleem held him tight until the tension seemed to fall away from him.

Then Pierre pulled away. Kaleem could see that his eyes were red. "I know. I know you do your best," he said. "I just can't bear to lose him. Have you any idea what it's like loving somebody so much?"

Oh yes, thought Kaleem. He knew what it was like loving someone so much that you had to let them go for their own good. And he remembered how he had almost lost Razjosh. But at least Rozia and Razjosh were both still alive. Kaleem shook his head. "I can see how much you love him," he said.

The door communicator buzzed. "Sandi Depra," announced the dataserve.

"Hi, Sandi, come on up," said Pierre.

Just a few seconds later the young Head of Health arrived.

"So, how's he going?" she said as she came in.

Despite everything, Kaleem could not help but smile at the way she had tied her hair in two bunches that stuck out like horns on the top of her head. Her face was speckled with large freckles that she had painted to match her hair.

"A bit better… perhaps," said Pierre.

"Ah, Funny Head Two," said Sandi suddenly spotting Kaleem. She stared at him. "I'm glad you're here," she said more seriously. "And how are things on Zandra?" she whispered.

"Getting there," said Kaleem. He knew she really meant were Charlek and Ella together and was there any hope for her. There were just so many problems and so much upset because he was failing to do his job properly.

Sandi nodded slowly and pursed her lips. "Well, I'd better see to the patient, then," she said. "That's what I'm here for."

"I wish you wouldn't talk about me as if I wasn't here," said Stuart hoisting himself up into a straighter sitting position.

Was he imagining it or did Stuart look a bit better than when he'd hobbled in from the other room? Oh, even if he was, it was probably just because he'd had a short rest and whatever the diastic monitor had made him breathe had brought him a little relief for a while. He still looked more like an old man than somebody Kaleem's age.

"Well, fella, let's look at you," said Sandi making her way over to the comfisofa. She took out a medi-wand and started to wave it over Stuart's body. "Hmm," she said after about five minutes. "There's a little improvement… but?"

"But not enough?" said Pierre.

Sandi shook her head.

Pierre covered his eyes again.

"Hey, you," shouted Stuart. "Stop that. I ain't going nowhere. Come here."

Pierre rushed over to Stuart who pulled his lover into his arms. "You know I love you, don't you, mate?" he whispered, gulping for air. "You know I'll show you how much again one day."

"Don't you ever leave me," Pierre sobbed.

"Best leave them in peace," whispered Sandi. Kaleem nodded.

They made their way out of the apartment. He couldn't speak as they went down in the lift. Even Sandi was rather quiet.

"Look, we know you're doing your best and that you'll do everything you can to help us all," she said walked out of the building. "Pierre and Stuart know that as well."

Well, yes, it was true. He was doing his best. He was just not sure that his best was good enough. He nodded. He couldn't bring himself to speak.

"Take care," she said as she stepped into the transporter that was already waiting for her.

Kaleem waved to her as she left. He watched until her transporter had disappeared. He turned and started to run. He was not sure where he was going. He just hoped that running might help him to think want to do next.

Narisja's Book

The baby kicked again. Its foot seemed to stick under her rib cage.

"I'll be glad when you're out of there, chum," whispered Narisja. She was so big now she could hardly move and the wretched child kept on bumping around on her bladder, making her want to pee all of the time.

Yes, she'd be glad all right. Not that she was looking forward to the birth itself. This was the one time in her life that she wished she'd been brewed in a tube in a nice clean Normal Zone laboratory not pushed through a birth canal by her own mother who had been kind enough just before she died to tell her how painful childbirth was. If she'd lived in a Normal Zone she and Jojo could still have been parents. They too could grow their child in a test tube. But this method was gross. How on Terrestra anyway was something with such a large head supposed to get through such a narrow space? Bless all the elders, it had hurt enough the first time with Jojo. And he's just an ordinary sort of guy, not especially big in a certain place.

Except at the moment, may the elders grant him peace, he was off mining. He wouldn't be there for the birth. What was he thinking, elders curse him?

Narisja's belly hardened and she had to hold her breath as a pain passed through the whole of her trunk. No, this wasn't it the beginning of her labour, though. Her mother had warned her.

"You get some practice pains," the old woman had said as she lay dying in the poor but roomy cave where Narisja now lived, when Narisja had just told her about her first pregnancy. "You'll think those bad enough but they're not the real thing and they don't hurt as much as the real thing."

As the pain subsided again Narisja made a mental note of two facts. If these were practice pains then there were only a couple of days left before the baby arrived. And if practice pains were this bad, real labour pains would be unbearable. *Maybe they'll kill me,* she thought. *And whether they do or not, I'd better get this place straight before the baby's here.*

Somehow, despite her size and despite the constant discomfort of the baby bouncing on her bladder she managed to move quite energetically. She beat the dust out of all the rugs, then swept it up and threw it into a passage in the cave they never used.

Pity I can't take the wretched stuff outside, she thought. *Mind you, if I went outside we'd both be dead in minutes.* There was no sign of the poison cloud that covered Terrestra ever going away.

The baby kicked. Narisja smiled to herself. "Don't fret, my darling," she said. "I'd never do that to you. I'll give you your chance of life, even if it kills *me* in the attempt."

She suddenly felt a great wave of affection for her unborn child. *You will grow strong and be a great leader. You will make your mama proud,* she thought.

She changed the bed, scrubbed the floors, washed towels and laid out all the clothes she had made and had been given ready for the new baby. Soon the cave apartment was gleaming.

The baby kicked once more, and again its foot seemed to stick in her rib cage, giving her heartburn. She sat down on the edge of her bed. The trunk of books and drawings was still in the middle of the room. She'd moved it when she'd wanted to get the dust out from under the bed.

I wonder what you are all about? she thought. *Maybe my son will find out.* She put her hand on her belly. She was convinced she was going to have a boy.

She touched the old box. It always fascinated her. The box itself, as well as the contents. Its wood was smooth and shiny. She loved touching it. It felt silky under her fingers. It was always hard to open though, with its strange old physical catch. She didn't always manage to get it open and she had thought about not shutting it properly but at least with it shut she knew its contents were safe. Only she, Jojo and Ben Mariah knew how to open it.

She slid the catch back and felt the spring give. It was complying today. The lid clicked open. And there they all were again, the books with the Wordtext pages, the funny black marks on the white background. Such a strange way for people to get their stories. But perhaps nobody needed to understand the Wordtext. The pictures told their own stories.

Her favourite was on top.

She turned the pages of the book slowly. It was the story of the man who built the big house boat and let the animals on. Then came the floods. And eventually the dove returning with the olive branch. Narisja found herself making up the words to go with the pictures. This story seemed so familiar. Maybe because she had looked at this book so often.

She looked at the one about the tiger as well. That was a great one, too, but the story was harder to follow here. Daveen… what was her name again? Patterns? Whoever. She was a brilliant artist.

Narisja sorted through the pictures and the books. So many stories here. Eventually she found the ones about the tower. She touched the picture of the master builder in his sparkling ceremonial costume edged in blue, gold and sliver. The pictures were full of such fine detail that the people seemed real. They looked as if they could come to life and step out of the book at any moment.

"All of the contents of the box are to do with the Babel prophecy," her mother had said. "Keep them safe."

Narisja wished that Ben Mariah was there. He always had such clear ideas about the prophecy. Sure, he was a story-teller but there was always something that seemed so true about his stories. Narisja never felt as if he was really making them up.

Even with his best efforts, though, the Babel prophecy remained a mystery.

I wish you could tell us your secrets, she thought as she carried on rummaging through the box.

Soon all of its contents were strewn across the floor of the cave apartment she had so thoroughly cleaned and tidied earlier.

Well, not quite all of them. Because there it was again. The little contraption and the disk that seemed as if it should fit into it. Right at the bottom of the trunk.

She carefully lifted them out. They were such strange objects. She slid the flat disk out of the case like she had so many times before. There were some black marks scrawled on them. It reminded her of Wordtext but it wasn't quite so even. She slid the disk into the other box, the one Jojo had said must be some sort of machine, perhaps a primitive dataserve for reading what was stored on the flat disk. It seemed certain that that was where it belonged. It clicked as it found its place. Yes, she was sure it was meant to go into the machine like that. But today, as ever, she just couldn't make it work. She had no idea how to get any power to the machine.

I'd better tidy this up, she thought and started gathering together the papers and books. As she went to put the machine back in the box, it slipped out of her hands and fell to the floor. She gasped. She hoped she hadn't harmed it. One day, one day, surely, someone would be able to make it work. But a piece of it had broken off the back of it and something from inside it had fallen out.

"No!" she whispered to herself. As she picked it up she realised that what had fallen away was some sort of hinged door and lying on the floor next to it was a cylinder with a button on top. And inside the machine there seemed to be a corresponding button. Her hands trembling, Narisja slotted the cylinder into the back of the machine. It began to hum.

So simple, she thought. *Why didn't we try that before?*

But the cylinder lost its contact with the machine. *It needs something to hold it in place,* she thought. Then she picked up the little door. Yes, that would do it. She pressed the cylinder back on to its connection and then slotted the door onto the back. It slid in so easily. She was sure it was supposed to come off like that, probably so that you could renew the power supply.

The machine started to hum again. This time nothing dropped off or out of the back. Narisja tentatively pushed one of the buttons. The hum turned into a rumble and a woman's voice stated speaking.

"There's a woman walking into the place where the poorer people live," she said. "She is carrying the book, with its beautiful cover, all silver, blue and gold. She carries the story of the Babel tower, the tower that was built to reach God. And God was angry and caused them to not understand each other.

"She carries the book. She is about to become a mother. Not just yet. In some months time. But you can clearly see that her belly's getting bigger. She holds it, as if the baby has just moved. She seems pleased to feel it alive. I don't think she has had this experience before. I think it is the first time the baby has kicked.

"She is carrying a book. She is dressed strangely. I think this is some time in the future. And I think there is something not right about her being pregnant. This is happening at a time when babies no longer grow in the womb. She is having a natural pregnancy. It's a sort of miracle birth again. This is why she has come here.

"They greet her, these poor people. They seem to treat her better that her own people do. It's like the Good Samaritan.

"It's fading a little. I can't hear what they are saying. We seem to move on. We're going into the future. She lives in the caves. They look after her. There is something very precious about the child she is going to have. He is to be a Peace Child. Days and weeks pass in seconds as I watch.

"Then it becomes clearer again. She goes into labour. The old woman who looks after her tells her not to push, then tells her to push. The baby is born. The mother names him. I can't quite hear what she says. But it begins with K. Kevin? No. Kel – Kal… I don't know. I can't hear.

"Peace Child. I've come across that idea before. They give peace children when they've been at war. The children are born in one tribe and grow up with another. They understand both peoples. They are the go-between. But this is the Peace Child, capital P, capital C.

"I can see further. But it's vaguer. He has to do something

quite spectacular. He is a peace child. But he has to be *the* Peace Child.

"He's ill. That illness makes him be a peace child. He helps the others… the others who are ill. He helps to find the cure.

"I can feel the loneliness. His loneliness. He is isolated.

"But that's it. He understands them. The others. And he understands his own people. He is the bridge.

"And it's to do with Babel. He brings down the tower. He brings down the Tower of Babel. Then they all understand each other. He makes them all understand.

"Yes, then the tower falls down. He has to tell the stories. They can understand because he tells them stories… But they have to understand the words of the stories. They have to be willing to learn the words.

"He has a big mission. But it could save the world. Yes, he is going to save the world and it is all to do with overcoming the tower. They will all be taught to understand each other."

There was a loud click and the voice file ended. So Jojo had been right. It was a sort of dataserve and the disk held a voice file. The machine whirred quietly to itself. Narisja quickly opened the little door and disconnected the power supply. There was no knowing how long that would last. They must preserve it. In the Normal Zones they'd probably easily have found some way of turning the disk into a modern dataserve file. But not here.

Then Narisja went hot all over. Her hands suddenly felt clammy. The room started to spin round. What on Terrestra had she just listened to? She didn't have time to worry. A pain seared through her back and took her breath away. She couldn't move.

The pain suddenly subsided and the baby kicked. Probably just another practice contraction. She carried on putting the books and drawings back into the box. She kept back the picture of the master builder admiring the complete Tower of Babel. What a story! And the prophecy… She held the drawing to her rounded belly.

"Is it to do with you, my sweet," she whispered to her baby. "Are you the Peace Child? If you're a boy shall I name you

Ka…Ke? Which? What?"

"Narisja!" someone called.

"Yes, come in," she cried recognising the voice of Wendy Ampel, her midwife. Why had she come? It wasn't time yet. But she was glad, actually. These practice pains, the whole Babel Prophecy thing, especially now what she'd heard on that strange voice file, all of this was really making her uneasy.

Wendy bustled in, dragging with her bags that seemed to be overflowing with towels and what looked like medical supplies. She had Saratina in tow, the poor disfigured girl who seemed to cling to her. Narisja knew that Wendy was teaching her the art of midwifery. She was still only a child and if you could look beyond the scars and the deformed eyes she was actually quite pretty. It seemed such a serious job for one so young.

"I see," said the older woman as she looked around. "I haven't come a moment too soon."

"What do you mean?" asked Narisja. She hadn't sent for the midwife.

"Oo a ain?" asked Saratina.

"What?" asked Narisja.

"She's asking if you have any pains yet," said Wendy.

"Only practice ones," said Narisja. As she spoke, though, another pain pulled across her back. It was even more intense than the last.

Wendy held her hand and started counting.

"Really?" she said. "Practice pain indeed. And all the housework? That's usually a sure sign."

Saratina was soon busy putting a mattress and clean sheets on the slab of rock that served as a table in the cave apartment.

"Come on, then, up here," said Wendy as Saratina finished putting together the makeshift delivery bed. "Let's be looking at you."

As Narisja tried to move her huge body, she suddenly felt as if she was wetting herself. *I knew that would happen,* she thought, putting a hand to her belly. *I knew you'd get my bladder in the end.* Only she knew really that it wasn't her bladder that had let her down. This was all just part of it. Her waters had broken.

“Very good of you both to get that out of the way,” said Wendy, “before we’d got you installed in this rather grand bed Saratina has made for you. Practice pains indeed. Honey, this is the real thing.”

Saratina clapped her hands and jumped up and down excitedly. Wendy nodded to the pool on the floor. Saratina went off, Narisja presumed, in search of a mop and bucket. She went to call to her, to tell her it was in the alcove off to the right, but she couldn’t get her lips to move. She felt as if she was dreaming.

“Right, lets loosen all of this clothing,” said Wendy after Narisja had struggled on to the bed. “And pop those panties off. You won’t need those for a while.”

Narisja did as Wendy told her. She shivered. It wasn’t from the cold, though. It was the thought of what the midwife was about to do with those sleek metal instruments she would fetch from her bag. And the thought of what was going to come out of that narrow opening in her own body. Very soon, by what Wendy seemed to be saying.

“Bend your knees up for me,” said Wendy.

I’m glad Jojo’s not here, thought Narisja. *This is so undignified.* She tried to think of something pleasant as Wendy slid the hard metal spatula up inside her body.

“By all the elders!” cried the older woman. “You’re eight centimetres dilated. I can see the head.”

Another pain came. This time it was stronger than ever. Narisja wanted to push.

“No pushing yet,” said Wendy. “Breathe through the pain. Pant if it helps.”

Saratina stopped her mopping. She took Narisja’s hand. Narisja squeezed the girl’s hand tightly as she panted. As the pain subsided she let go. Saratina rubbed her arm.

“Aay um oo,” she said.

“Yes,” said Wendy. “The baby will be here soon. Very soon.”

Narisja was floating. She was up on the ceiling of the cave. It hadn’t been long, really. But the pain had been so intense she’d felt as if her body was going to rip apart. It was calm up here, looking down at herself.

"You'll have a lot of pain, afterwards, as well, I'm afraid," she heard Wendy say. "When a birth happens this quickly, it takes more time to recover afterwards than when it's slower. But it suggests a good, strong healthy baby."

Narisja didn't care. It was calm up here. And she was hatching a plot. Well, it hadn't been the Babel book she'd had in her hands when Wendy and Saratina had walked into her cave home, and they weren't really strangers to her. But prophecies were never that accurate, were they, really? And she had been holding a picture from the Babel book. As long as this baby was a boy… he'd be the Peace Child from the prophecy. For sure.

"If you push with this one, as hard as you can," said Wendy, "your baby will be here."

The pain was so intense that she felt it a little even up there on the ceiling. It pulled her straight back into her body.

"Push, push, push," said Wendy.

Narisja pushed. She knew now how to focus her energy in the lower part of her body. She pushed and pushed and pushed. She had never worked so hard before in her whole life and she was known for her hard work.

Saratina wiped the sweat from her forehead and this gave Narisja the last drop of energy she needed to carry on pushing until she felt her baby slip from her.

Wendy caught the baby. She wrapped it loosely in a towel. "Can you see what you've got?" she said softly as she passed to Narisja the new-born who was already crying gently.

Narisja looked at the little creature. Unmistakably a boy. In her mind she replayed the words she'd heard on the strange voice file. Yes, he was here. The Peace Child had definitely arrived.

"His name is Kevik," she whispered.

Capturing Holograms

Rozia settled herself into the comfisofa. She'd been tempted to go straight to bed now that Petri had at last settled down to sleep. Normally Anna didn't leave until Petri was already sleeping, but tonight she had to attend a family birthday party. It was an opportunity anyway for Rozia to spend some time with the child. Julien would have wanted her to do that. He'd loved Petri.

But being with Petri was exhausting. The Adulkis tired her out too. And she still wasn't sleeping properly. Bed was really tempting. But what if the Zenoton chose this evening to holo Saratina to them again? Of course, they could still turn up in the middle of the night but she guessed even they wouldn't be that inconsiderate or at least would realise that you will get more out of people if you talk to them when they're fully awake not just waking up out of a deep sleep. She supposed she ought to try and stay up for normal Mid-Terrestran hours. Just in case.

She settled on the sofa. She would perhaps try looking at some of the entertainment channels. Perhaps watch a soothing romantic comedy movie. Or maybe not. It would set her off on the Julien / Kaleem / Julien / Kaleem train of thought again and that was torture. So, perhaps a children's film? One with a happy ending?

"Children's channel," she commanded.

She was tempted by a vintage classic the dataserve suggested. One about a girl only a little younger than herself who managed to talk to dolphins. Yes, that would do nicely.

"Yes please, 'The Messenger'," she said to the dataserve.

The movie began to play out in front of her. It was soothing – until she realised that she hadn't eaten and that she really ought to. Not that she was hungry. She needed something tasty but not filling. She paused the movie.

"Bring me humus and chips," she commanded the house droid. Should she have a glass of nectar with that? Better not, actually. If something did happen, she wanted to be alert. And there was something not quite right about drinking on your own, she thought. "And a cranberry juice," she added.

The movie was superb: life-affirming, comforting, definitely 'feel good'. Even without the nectar she began to feel relaxed, more relaxed that she had felt for a long time. Perhaps she would sleep well tonight. She began to hope that there would be no appearance of Saratina this evening. She wanted to stay in this cosy cocoon.

The movie was coming to an end. It was clear that Charlie, the main character, had correctly understood Baranco, the leader of the dolphins, and there was about to be a good ending. This was great. The story was making Rozia feel more cheerful. But then the lights dipped just as they had the first time Saratina had been holoed into her apartment. So, it was happening again tonight.

Suddenly she was wide awake. Her heart was thumping, her mouth was dry and she was having trouble swallowing.

She quickly found the device that Danielle Thomas had given to her.

"It's really simple to use," Danielle had said. "Keep it hidden in your hand and point the beam so that it touches the hologram's edge at a convenient point. They won't be able to see the beam or be aware of what we're doing in any other way."

Rozia's hands trembled as she switched on the small gadget and folded it into her palm. Then, Saratina was in front of her and the beam seemed to somehow attach itself to the edge of the hologram.

Rozia's heart calmed a little though her mouth remained dry. And Saratina grinned. She looked well.

"So they're looking after you all right?" said Rozia.

"Yes, they're being kind, really," said Saratina.

Hmm, thought Rozia. *I can't think that keeping you away from the people you know is particularly kind.* But she did look well. Much better, Rozia thought, than she herself must look at the moment. Still she was wide awake now and really nervous. The beam from the box in her hand seemed to be holding on to the holograph. Could she get through this conversation without them finding out what she was doing? "Will they talk to me?" she asked.

"No," said Saratina. "But they've said I'm to tell you they do want to talk to Kaleem. And they really are trying to bring a better way of making everything fair to everyone. He should listen."

Ah! So they've dragged you on to their side, then, thought Rozia. There was a name for this she knew; when kidnappers got their victims on their side, but she was too tired to remember it. "How do you manage to communicate with them?" she asked.

Saratina shrugged. "They just seem to understand me now," she said.

So, I'm not the only one, then, thought Rozia.

"Not the way you understand me," said Saratina, her face dropping slightly. "They just understand when I make lots of gestures."

"Well that's good, then," said Rozia. "And how, when and where do they want to see Kaleem?"

"They will send me to you here again in two days," said Saratina. "He is to be here with you."

The hologram snapped out and the lights flickered. Rozia's heart began racing again and the dryness came back to her throat. Kaleem was to come here. Well, in that case she would go away. But what about Petri?

Perhaps, though, if she got the device to Razjosh and Danielle, they could get to the Zenoton before they sent Saratina again. The little box that she was still holding in her hand was getting very hot. She gently put it down on the table in front of her. Best get onto them straight away, then.

"Razjosh Elder and Danielle Thomas," she said to the dataserve.

Within seconds both the retired elder and the Head of Science appeared on the screen.

"So, they've sent Saratina again?" asked Razjosh. "Is she being looked after?"

Rozia told him how well she thought Saratina looked but also that she was a little afraid that she was getting a bit too fond of her captors.

"I don't think we need to worry too much," said the old man. "It's probably just her normal good nature. She always likes to think the best of everyone, as you well know. Surprising after what she has gone through. But I'm glad they're not doing her any harm."

"And you think the device worked?" asked Danielle.

"Well, it did latch on to the hologram just like you said it would," said Rozia. "And it did get very hot. So I think it did something."

"Excellent," said Danielle. "Listen, I'd like to pick it up myself. I don't want to risk just having the content transmitted. I'll be around in twenty minutes if that's all right."

"Yes, yes, that's fine," said Rozia. Petri was asleep. Once Danielle had come round, she could get to bed herself. That would be wonderful. As long as Danielle didn't want to stay and chat… No, she probably wouldn't. She'd be much too keen to get back to her lab and find out all about the Zenoton's hologram.

"Well done, my dear," said Razjosh. "You can relax now."

Oh, so I look that bad, do I? thought Rozia.

The screen blanked. It occurred to Rozia that she had not mentioned the message Saratina had given about the Zenoton wanting to speak to Kaleem. She'd better call Razjosh back… but she'd do that in a while… perhaps after Danielle had been. Or even perhaps tomorrow morning. They'd said two days, hadn't they? She'd got plenty of time. It wasn't really that urgent.

Petri suddenly started screaming. It sounded as if it the nightmares had come back again. The child was as bad as Kaleem with these terrifying dreams. Rozia hoped by all the elders that all would be quiet again by the time the Head of Science arrived.

"I'm coming, I'm coming," Rozia whispered. "Don't fret, don't fret."

So, no rest for her yet.

Calver's Predictions

It was cabin fever. He was trapped here. Kaleem didn't dare leave his room. So, the Zenoton had sent another holo yesterday. Danielle was working on the data she'd managed to get from the small tool she'd made for Rozia. And of course secretly also trying to find out if they could attach a cradle to this recorded holo and get him to wherever they were holding Saratina.

The Zenoton were really playing hard to get. All that Rozia had been able to tell him –and that only through Razjosh – was that Saratina seemed to be well and had found a way of communicating efficiently with the Zenoton.

There could be a message any moment from any one of them and he needed to be in this private apartment to receive it. The communication system to this room had been made particularly private.

He flicked through the sports programmes. He really needed some exercise. "Rowing programme seven," he commanded the dataserve. Soon he was quite convincingly rowing a canoe against the current on a warm but breezy day. He soon worked up a sweat and could almost believe that he really was on the river – it was just a pity about that faint whir in the background that told him that he was only dealing with a holoscene. That, of course, only served to remind him that there was some big business to do with holoscenes waiting for him and any moment now he was going to have to leap into a different sort of action.

He pulled harder still on his canoe paddle and felt some satisfaction as the vessel cut efficiently through the water. This was better than just sitting about waiting, anyway.

Then the dataserve's communicator buzzed.

"Send," he commanded.

The river scene faded immediately and he was back in his room, staring at the dataserve screen. All there was at first were a few lines.

Interplanetary, he thought. They were still getting delays like that.

Seconds later Calver Tom's face came into view.

Great, thought Kaleem. *That's all I need.*

"Hi Kaleem," said Calver. "I think you're in for a big day tomorrow."

How does he do it? thought Kaleem. "I could be," he said.

"I thought I'd update you about what's been happening here," said Calver.

Kaleem hoped he wasn't about to get more bad news. "How's the replanting going?" he asked.

"Not bad, considering," said Calver. "We do need more acorns, though, as soon as possible. But yeah, everything is now cleared up after the landquake. It's actually something a bit more personal I wanted to mention first. It's about Ella."

"Oh," said Kaleem. He'd forgotten all about Ella.

"She's moved on," said Calver.

A shade of sadness swept through Kaleem but it was followed by something, if he was really honest with himself, that felt more like relief. If she'd moved on, he didn't have to feel bad about her any more. He would definitely have to steer clear of relationships in the future. Even ones that seemed very casual. And he guessed he know who it would be. "Charlek?" he asked.

"No, actually," said Calver. "Charlek is a reformed character. He reckons he's stopped playing the field. He has only one interest at the moment and present circumstances prevent that developing further."

"He's still interested in Sandi, then?" asked Kaleem. That at least was something. Sandi would be pleased about.

"Seems so," said Calver. "So get on to it, Kaleem. We need Zandra and Terrestra working together again." Calver's eyes were twinkling and a grin spread across his face.

"So, what about Ella?" asked Kaleem.

"She is with Alistare now," said Calver. "And they both send their good wishes."

Alistare and Ella? What a thought! But it was about time Alistare had some female company.

"So you can stop worrying about all of your friends and get

on with what you need to do," said Calver.

Well, yes, that was true. "She's happy now, is she, Ella?" asked Kaleem.

"It seems so," said Calver.

Kaleem felt a weight literally lift from his chest. Maybe he wasn't destroying everybody's lives after all. Only his own. All he'd got to do now was get Saratina back safely and negotiate successfully with the Zenoton. That was all. Just those two little things.

"Right, now on to the other woman," said Calver.

Her name's Rozia, thought Kaleem. He looked away from Calver.

"She's keeping something from you," said the Zandrian.

"Surely not," replied Kaleem. She wouldn't, would she? But then, he hadn't really actually spoken to her, had he?

"Well, she hasn't really told you what the Zenoton wanted, has she?" said Calver.

Kaleem shrugged. "I guessed they were really showing us that Saratina was okay."

"Oh come on, please," said Calver. "Don't forget they probably really wanted you. And they probably still do. She's keeping something from you."

Kaleem knew that Calver was right. If he was honest, the lack of information from the Zenoton had been niggling away at him since Razjosh had told him that Saratina had been sent again.

Except it's not really me she's keeping things from, because she's not actually talking to me at all. All my fault again, he thought. "So what do you suggest I do?"

"I don't think there is anything you can do very quickly. Maybe Razjosh can get more out of her," said Calver.

Maybe, thought Kaleem.

"But anyway," Calver continued, "as they're working on the saved holo, you may be able to communicate with them directly."

"That's the plan," said Kaleem. Thank goodness they'd stopped talking about Rozia.

"So, how's Danielle Thomas getting on with that?" asked Calver.

Why are you asking me? thought Kaleem. *Surely you already know.*

"I'm only asking because she hasn't sent any information to Zandra for over twenty-four hours," said Calver.

"Why would she send you information?" asked Kaleem. Really, what happened on Terrestra was no concern of any Zandrians at the moment.

"Because we requested it," said Calver. "Zandra has an interest. It needs a secure supply of acorns. And the Zenoton claim to have an interest in our technology."

"Claim to have an interest?" said Kaleem.

"Well, do you think they need it?" asked Calver. "Look at what they've already been able to do. I think they have a much deeper, more complex motive."

"The credit exchange system?" said Kaleem.

"Most likely," said Calver. "Now I know you agree with it and have already suggested that it needs to go more slowly."

You know everything, don't you? thought Kaleem.

"But they probably don't want to wait that long," said Calver. "And they'll put pressure on you."

And I shouldn't really face them on my own, thought Kaleem.

"I'm a little concerned about you, too," said Calver. "I think you're not telling me something."

"Oh?" said Kaleem. By all the elders, he was doing it again. Mind-reading or whatever it was he did. It was hard to keep anything from Calver.

"It's really clear to me that you are plotting something. You are just not communicating openly."

Kaleem had to look away from Calver's gaze. The man was just so annoying.

"Well, I have a few ideas," said Calver. "But I'll keep those to myself. I can be secretive, too."

Had he really guessed about what he and Danielle were planning to do with the saved holo? "I've got nothing to hide," said Kaleem, suddenly remembering his training and looking straight at Calver. He emptied his mind and just stared at the young

Zandrian, spending a long time examining each of his facial features. No other thoughts were allowed into his head.

"Mm, very clever," said Calver. "Your training is serving you well. But we both know you're up to something. Just be warned. Be sensible and keep yourself out of danger. And remember the Zenoton are very clever people."

The screen blanked.

Oh dear, thought Kaleem. *What am I doing?*

The Cradle

"Well, here it is," said Danielle. "Though we can't pinpoint exactly where it came from, we've at least found the tag that contains the information about where to send a reply."

"Has anyone done that yet?" asked Kaleem.

"No," said Danielle. "No, we don't want to risk them knowing that we've captured the holo. Nothing will be sent until we know exactly what we want to communicate."

"And nobody's worked that out yet," said Kaleem.

"It isn't just that," said Danielle. "We really want to find out where they are first."

"And has anybody replayed the holo?" asked Kaleem.

"No," said Danielle. "We don't know how strong it is. It could be very fragile. It might break up if we keep looking at it."

"And what about the cradle?" asked Kaleem. "Will it work with a record of a holo? Are you still going to help me to try it?"

Danielle sighed. She turned to face Kaleem. He noticed that she had dark circles around her eyes. Her skin was very pale. He knew he was asking a lot of her.

"It might. It might not," she said. "But we'll have to replay the holo to find out. And this may be our only chance to do that."

"So, do we do it? Replay the holo?" asked Kaleem.

"I guess. We'd have to do it sooner or later, I'm thinking." Danielle moved over to a console that looked pretty similar to other holo consoles Kaleem had seen before. She placed her palm on what looked like the main control.

The lights dipped. Kaleem's mouth went dry.

"That's not supposed to happen," Danielle whispered.

Then, there was the glow that normally accompanied a hologram. Seconds later Saratina was there, lifelike and grinning. Except that Kaleem could tell she wasn't seeing them.

"Es, Eelee in a ee," said Saratina.

"We'll only hear her side of the conversation," said Danielle. "And I guess that'll be pretty difficult for us to understand."

It was clear that Saratina was listening to Rozia. And Kaleem thought he could hear something in the background. "Whatever you did to make it record the hologram, could it have recorded other sounds?" he asked.

Danielle frowned. "Maybe," she said.

"Can you turn up the volume?" Kaleem asked.

"I'll try," said Danielle, "but it will mean that Saratina's voice will be louder."

"I think we can live with that," said Kaleem.

Danielle manipulated the controls on the console.

"Will they talk to me?" Kaleem heard Rozia's voice ask.

"O," shouted Saratina. "Ut ay eed eyem o elloe ay wa o tor ka-eee. A eeyee a eein oo bee a eeay ay o achin erryin eer oo eeryon. Ee hood is-hen."

Kaleem thought he could pick out his name. Something for him to do then. But what?

"How do you manage to communicate with them?" he heard Rozia ask.

Saratina shrugged. "Ay us eem o unersan ee ow," Saratina replied. "Ot e a oo unersan ee," said Saratina. Her face suddenly looked sad. "Ay us unersan en I ae os o estus."

"Well that's good, then," said Rozia. "And how, when and where do they want to see Kaleem?"

Kaleem went hot and cold. So, Saratina had said something about the Zenoton wanting to see him.

"Ay ill en ee o oo ee a-en i oo ays," said Saratina. "Ee i oo ee ere it oo."

He just couldn't make out what she was saying. He had been beginning to understand her quite well, but maybe it was all a bit distorted in the hologram. And why hadn't Rozia said anything?

Saratina seemed to freeze in time.

"If you're going to do it, we'd better attach the cradle now," said Danielle. "I'm really not sure about this, though. I really don't think you should try it."

Before he could move, though, the lights dipped again, and there was Saratina again, this time in a live holo.

"I suppose they must have said they would contact Rozia again in a couple of days," said Danielle, "and I think the recording of the holo has somehow attracted their transmission here."

"Alee!" cried Saratina. Her face lit up with a warm smile. "Ere Ozia?" she added, frowning and looking frantically for Rozia.

"At least it will be better fitting the cradle to a live holo, even though nobody has ever tried fitting a cradle to an incoming holo in the hope that it will go back to where it came from," said Danielle. "Are you still up for it?"

"Of course," said Kaleem, although he really did wonder what he was doing. Why had Rozia not told them about the Zenoton sending Saratina again? They needed her here so that they could understand what Saratina was saying. Perhaps he should ask Saratina to tell the Zenoton to speak directly to him. But Saratina was looking really worried now and he didn't think she would be able to concentrate enough to communicate effectively with them. No, the cradle was the best bet.

Danielle was already fetching it. "This had better work," she whispered under her breath. "I'm going to be in so much trouble for doing this. I might still be in trouble even if it does work."

"It'll work," said Kaleem. He'd got to do this. "I'm coming over to you," he said to Saratina. "Don't let them see me."

"O! O!" cried Saratina, putting her hand in front of her mouth and shaking her head.

"Act naturally," said Kaleem. "Laugh. Pretend I've just told you a joke. Tell them I'll speak to them."

Saratina gave one of her wide-mouthed grins. It looked convincing though Kaleem still had difficulty understanding how she could be so cheerful.

Danielle managed to fit the cradle on to the hologram now. Kaleem climbed into it. He nodded to Saratina. "Tell them as best you can that I'll talk to them in ten minutes if they holo me directly. Don't tell them I'll be there sooner."

"Good luck," Danielle seemed to be saying. He could see her

mouth moving but could not hear any sound coming from it.

The other sounds from the lab also faded quickly. Kaleem only realised that the machinery and the dataserves had hummed quietly because now it was silent. Then it went black.

It was quite similar to the last time he'd travelled by cradle, at least at first. The darkness seemed to get even blacker and he had the sensation of being pushed through a very dark tunnel. Then came the feeling that he was being pulled apart as his body jerked and wobbled. The silence was replaced by the humming he'd heard the last time only this time it was louder and less consistent. It came and went in waves. He waited for the bright light that usually came at the end of the tunnel but it didn't seem to want to come this time. Did this mean the Zenoton were even further away from where he was now than the distance between Terrestra and Zandra?

On and on the wobbling and jerking went and the blackness just seemed to get blacker.

Putrid elders, he thought, *when on Terrestra or even on Zenoto will this stop?* He thought he was going to pass out or that his body was going to be shaken to pieces. His brain felt as if it was going to explode and he was sure he was going to vomit. Where would it end up, though, if he did?

Suddenly, though, there was a bright flash and the cradle spilled him out on to some sort of vibrating floor.

Saratina was right by him. "Al-ee," she said, "a oo or eye?" she said.

Kaleem grabbed the hand she held out and pulled himself up. He just about had time to register that he was on a Supercraft when a door swished open and there stood Rogin.

He looked scarier than ever. His icy blue eyes looked straight at Kaleem. The long slimy curls that hung from his head seemed to have a life of their own today and looked like fat hissing snakes.

"So," said Rogin. "Terrestra has been less than truthful about its technological prowess. I hardly think, Kaleem Peace Child Kennedy, that you can reproach us for what we have kept hidden."

"Oh, this isn't normal Terrestran technology," said Kaleem. "This is Peace Child risk-taking."

The Zenoton laughed. "And you think we haven't taken any risks?" he said. "It has cost us. It has cost us much. 7,000 of our scientists have worked on this. We have used up two years' worth of fuel to power this Supercraft and will have to find a way of replacing it or we shall starve and freeze. What we have to say is that important."

"Where are we exactly?" asked Kaleem.

"One day's travel from Zenoto," said Rogin.

Kaleem swallowed. What had they done? They hadn't had enough time to be only one day from Zenoto by now. Maybe an acorn trade between them and Zandra could work. But where would that leave Terrestra? Isolated again, he supposed. They didn't need the starlight vaccine any more.

Then he remembered Stuart. They might need other Zandrian help, though. What could Terrestra offer in return if Zenoto supplied the acorns?

"We are no longer interested in trading," said Rogin. "What we have to give, we give freely. That is our first message. Our second: if you do not accept our gift, we shall all die and you and the Zandrians and the other One-Worlds will follow soon after."

"A oo beelee," Saratina cried suddenly.

Kaleem turned to face her. Her eyes were shining and she was smiling.

She's on their side now, thought Kaleem. Had they blackmailed her?

"Will you let her go?" Kaleem asked Rogin. "Can you send her back to Terrestra?"

"O! O!" cried Saratina. She stamped her foot. She grabbed Kaleem's arm. "Ay I oo. El oo."

Rogin laughed again. "We could," he said. "But I don't think she wants to go."

Saratina was frowning at him now.

Rogin went to leave the deck. He hesitated as he approached the door and tuned to face Kaleem.

“I’m glad you came to us,” he said. “We’ll try to make you comfortable whilst you’re with us. But you must remember you are our prisoner. The disfigured girl is now our guest. Someone will be with you shortly.”

Peace Child Failure

Kaleem took a good look at the deck. In some ways, it looked like the deck of any other Supercraft. Screen shields protected the veriglass windows. The furniture was sturdy so that it could withstand any rough riding. Everything was about the same size as it would be on a Terrestran or a Zandrian supercraft. The Zenoton were probably on average a little taller than the Terrestrans and Zandrians, but the upper limit was the same. This furniture looked as if it would be comfortable for all three races.

Yet there was something about this Supercraft that seemed different. It wasn't just the different colours. The Zenoton seemed to favour cool greens and warm creams and browns. Kaleem had no idea why that might be. But there was something else that was different. He couldn't quite work out what. He touched one of the sessels. Its fabric had a slightly rough feel to it. Yet the cushion at the back was soft and smooth. He touched as well what looked like a good plastikholz table. It was grainier than he expected. That was it. Everything here was made from the old materials.

So it looks as if their lack-of-credit system works, thought Kaleem.

He then noticed the smell. It was not unpleasant. It reminded him of the pinewood scent he was used to on the skiing holoscenes.

The gentle hum that all Supercraft made was definitely there, yet it was quieter than usual.

Maybe it's a superior Supercraft, he thought. *Maybe they don't need Zandrian technology at all.* He just didn't get this.

It seemed like hours until the doors swished open again and another Zenoton appeared. He was a little shorter than Rogin and had darker eyes. He walked with a limp. He circled Kaleem, looking at him so closely that it was almost as he was sniffing him. When he had finished, he stood in front of him so that their faces were just a few centimetres apart. Kaleem had the impression that he was a short-sighted.

"So," said the Zenoton, frowning slightly, "how did you get here?"

Kaleem explained as best he could about how they had intercepted the holo and got him to travel with it by cradle.

"Oh," said the Zenoton, "so Terrestran technology is as good as Zandrian, after all."

"Not really," said Kaleem. "Theirs is so much more advanced. It's just that when we really need something, we usually can invent it."

"I see," said the Zenoton. He turned away from Kaleem and walked to the edge of the room.

Why are we having to go over all of this? thought Kaleem. *Surely there are more important matters to be dealt with?*

The Zenoton came back to him. "Why did you come, though?" he asked.

"Because I was worried about Saratina," said Kaleem.

"We have been taking good care of her," said the Zenoton.

"But you're keeping her prisoner," said Kaleem. "And you're keeping me prisoner now, as well."

This man was beginning seriously to irritate him.

Steady, steady, Kaleem could almost hear Razjosh speaking to him. *What happened to all of your training?*

But this is unreasonable, thought Kaleem. *What right have they got to keep us here, just because we don't agree with their way of doing things? Especially as most other people agree with the Zandrian / Terrestran way.* "It might be just about all right for you to keep me here," he said to the Zenoton. "But it's not all right to keep Saratina. And I thought Rogin said something about making me comfortable? This isn't exactly comfortable."

"I'm sorry," stuttered the Zenoton. "I was just curious. Can I get you some refreshment?"

Kaleem noticed that the Zenoton was beginning to tremble. What was the matter with him? He was ugly and apparently weak. Why did he dither so much? He was seriously annoying Kaleem now. "Refreshment!" he shouted. "Do you really think that that would make a lot of difference? Do you really think that

that's what matters here?"

"No, I suppose not… but I'm sure you would like to rest, maybe have something to eat… you can't really go anywhere from here."

"No, I can't," said Kaleem. Something was taking over. He felt as if he was going to burst. Why did he keep on ending up in these situations? Why did everybody always expect so much? "And that is so wrong!" he shouted. He felt as if he wanted to punch the Zenoton. He punched the wall instead. He felt something crack and a pain shot through his finger up into his arm. Putrid elders. He'd really done some damage.

"I think I've broken my finger," he called out.

"Oh, let me look," said the Zenoton. He limped over to Kaleem and took the finger into his hand.

The pain shot through Kaleem again. He yelped and pulled the finger back. As he did so, he caught the side of the Zenoton's face. The Zenoton gasped and put his hand to his cheek.

"I'm sorry," mumbled Kaleem. "I didn't mean to…" What had he done? This wasn't the way a Peace Child was supposed to behave. What had he been thinking?

The door to the deck swished open again. Rogin reappeared. He was frowning deeply and he seemed to be taller than ever. His eyes flashed around the deck.

"What's been going on?" he boomed.

"Just a… a slight misunderstanding," the other Zenoton said. He took his hand away from his face. There was an ugly red mark with black edges. It looked as if the Zenoton were quicker to bruise than Terrestrans.

"Did our Terrestran friend do this to you?" demanded Rogin.

"It was an accident," said the older Zenoton. "He's hurt his hand. I was just looking at it. I'm afraid I hurt him even more."

"How did he hurt his hand?" asked Rogin.

"I hit it against the wall," said Kaleem. "I was angry. Angry that you are keeping us prisoner. Me and Saratina. Especially Saratina."

Rogin's eyes clouded over and narrowed. "It wasn't our

intention to keep you for very long. We only wanted to show you what might be possible. It looks as if you'll have to be shown the hard way." He looked at the other Zenoton. "Take him to the deprivation room."

"The deprivation room?" asked the elderly Zenoton. Kaleem could have sworn he went a shade paler.

Rogin turned to Kaleem again. "We've hardly ever used our deprivation rooms."

Kaleem could not guess as to what he would be deprived of but he was sure he was going to be uncomfortable. His hand was really beginning to throb now. "Could you help me with this?" he said, holding his hand up to Rogin.

"I'm afraid not," said Rogin. "That is one of the deprivations. You are not to be free of pain and suffering." He nodded to the Zenoton. "Take him away."

Freedom One Returned

Kaleem guessed they were now at one of the extremities of the Supercraft. They'd walked for about twenty minutes and it was quite quiet here compared with how busy it had been on the way. Lots of the Zenoton stared at them as they walked by and started whispering to each other. Kaleem could not make out what they were saying but presumed that someone being frog-marched by two guards was quite unusual.

The two Zenoton guards opened a hatch in the floor of the corridor. A staircase led down. The guards nodded to Kaleem. He placed his foot on to the first step. One of the guards gave him a gentle push and he had to run down the remaining steps. The hatch dropped shut behind him and pushed him to the floor as it did so. It became completely dark.

His eyes adjusted and he could see a little. Not that there was much to see. He was in a low-ceilinged, absolutely bare room. No, room was too grand a name for it. The space was tiny. He could just about sit down. He would never be able to lie down. He couldn't hear anything though he could feel a faint vibration from the Supercraft. How long were they going to leave him here? Just what were they going to deprive him of? Comfort, company and light, that was for sure.

It soon became obvious what else. There was some sort of air control in the room, but it was erratic. It would be too hot, then too cold and even once or twice it felt like Terrestran rain as water showered down on him from the ceiling. Sometimes the air stream became quite violent so that it felt like a Terrestran wind. He tried to sleep but the pain from his hand and the localised weather system kept waking him. He was soon very thirsty and his clothing began to stick to him and made him even more uncomfortable.

They came to see him, now and then, a different Zenoton each time. They asked him how he was getting on.

"Can you give me anything for this pain?" he asked, or "Can I have a drink?"

"Not yet," they would reply. "But we won't let you actually die."

You reckon, he thought.

Occasionally they took him out through the hatch up on to the deck and let him walk round a little. The light was so bright up there that it hurt his eyes and although he was glad to stretch his legs, he was also glad to get back into the dark. It worried him that he had become so sensitive to light.

"How long have I been down here?" he would ask them every time they came for him.

"Not long enough," they said.

"I'm so thirsty," he said.

"You can't drink yet," they would reply, "but we won't let you die."

He tried to keep count of the time by how often he needed the toilet, but he guessed he was holding back: it was a matter of either wetting and soiling himself or using a bucket in full view of the guards and anyone else who happened to be passing. The former wasn't really an option: there would be no way of getting cleaned up.

Just how many times does a Peace Child have to be kept prisoner in a life time? he thought.

It got worse each time. It was actually physically no worse this time than it had been in the Z Zone. It was possibly a little better. But it felt worse because this time he knew he deserved it. He'd got to live with that as well, if you could call this living.

He began to feel really ill and then he did manage to sleep for longer stretches. But when he woke up his body was so cramped that he was in agony. His finger still throbbed and he could tell that it was swollen. It was numb, too, and he was afraid that he was going to lose it.

He woke from a disturbed sleep as he heard the hatch being opened. Light flooded the room and made a pain shoot through his head. He screwed his eyes up.

"Well," said a familiar voice. Rogin. "I am here to see whether you can have the first freedom restored."

What? thought Kaleem.

"I've brought you a drink," said Rogin. "Whether you get another one soon, and even perhaps something to eat, depends on how our conversation goes now." He handed a bottle of water to Kaleem. "Only a few sips now," he said, "but you can keep the rest for later, whatever happens. As we said, we don't want you to die. You can still go several days without food but you are at your limit for lack of fluids."

Kaleem gulped down two mouthfuls of water. By all the elders, that tasted good.

"Careful," said Rogin. "Not too much at first."

"Okay," said Kaleem, wiping his mouth. Already he felt much more alert.

"So, tell me," said Rogin. "Where does your food come from on Terrestra?"

"From the glasshouses. The farms. The cultured-fields," answered Kaleem.

"Yes, I believe that is correct," said Rogin. "What about Zandra?"

"That I'm not so sure about," said Kaleem. "Some is imported. Some is forced in super-glasshouses."

"Yes, they're clever with it, aren't they?" said Rogin. "On Zenoto we use very similar methods to you Terrestrans. We grow in raw soil, and in glass houses. We rear animals for food. We actually share many natural plants with you, though. And just like on Terrestra, it all actually comes from our sun. Either directly through photosynthesis or indirectly through energy from our light and wind farms. And do you know something about the sun?"

"It shines?" said Kaleem. *Stupid thing to say,* he thought.

"It most certainly does," said Rogin. "Without our interference. And no Zenoton owns it, nor has any right to deprive another Zenoton from any of its benefits."

"But what about the work? With the plants and the animals?" said Kaleem.

"Done freely by those that love that type of work," Rogin

said. He paused and then smiled. "Though much of the tedious work is done by the droids. Before you ask, yes there are Zenoton who love building and programming droids."

"Yes, but we humans…" said Kaleem.

"Have you ever tried it?"

"No, but…" said Kaleem.

"That's all we ask," said Rogin. "That you at least try it."

His blue eyes seemed to cut into Kaleem's head and he almost felt a physical pain. He couldn't think what to say. He could see the sense of it – he had from the beginning – but he couldn't speak for anyone else on either Terrestra or Zandra.

"What do you most need now?" asked Rogin.

"More water, I guess," said Kaleem.

Rogin nodded. "And probably some food."

"But do I have to do something to deserve that?" said Kaleem.

Rogin sighed. "No," he said. "That is the whole point. You have the right to it. We only deprived you of it to make you appreciate it. What you contribute is up to you. When you're ready." He touched Kaleem lightly on the shoulder. "Think about what I've said."

He made his way up the steps and Kaleem was once more alone.

It seemed an age before anyone came to him again. He sipped the water. At last the hatch opened.

It was the elderly Zenoton who had been with him before. He struggled down the steps carrying a tray which held a large bowl of something steaming, a large bread roll and another bottle of water.

"We weren't properly introduced," he said, as he set the tray down on the floor. "My name is Albasto."

"I'm sorry… about before," said Kaleem.

Albasto waved his hand and shook his head. "You were in pain," he said. "You couldn't help it. How is the finger? May I look at it again?"

"Are you sure? I might hit you again," said Kaleem. "Actually, I can't even feel it now."

"If you can't feel anything, you're unlikely to feel me touching it," said Albasto. "I'll risk it."

The Zenoton took Kaleem's finger and prodded it. Kaleem had no sensation.

"Well," said Albasto. "Despite everything, I think it's healing. Hold on there. Next the freedom from discomfort will be returned to you and after that comes the freedom from pain and injury."

"Good," said Kaleem.

"Oh, right," said Albasto. "Better not forget your food. Eat up while it's still warm. And knock on the hatch when you've finished. Or if you need the lavatory. And if you need more to drink."

"Thank you," said Kaleem.

Albasto scuttled back up the stairs and dropped the hatch down again.

Kaleem allowed his eyes to adjust to the dark and then pulled the tray towards him. He couldn't balance it on his lap because of the way he had to sit. He had to crouch down rather like a dog to feed. He didn't care, though. It was delicious. It was a type of chicken soup, smooth, creamy and flavoured with herbs but not too rich and the bread was soft and fluffy. It was just right.

When he'd finished he felt so sleepy that he couldn't even be bothered to let them know. He pushed the tray as far away as he could, rested his head on his knees and fell asleep.

Freedom Two Returned

The meals started coming regularly now. They gradually built up the proportions and made the food more interesting. Soon his meals were normal-sized. Very rarely did the same Zenoton bring his food. And none of them wanted to be drawn into conversation. His "What have we got today, then?" was more often than not answered with a grunt if anything at all. He guessed the Zenoton had decided to keep him isolated in more ways than one.

The food was good, though. He had to give them that. Balanced and tasty. Always some fruit. Good coffee and even on occasion good chofa. Every third day there would even be something that was a little like Zandrian frega. He began to look forward to his meals. The patterns of them helped him to keep count of the days, more or less. He was fairly certain that it had now been three weeks since he'd spoken to Rogin.

He was beginning to feel the lack of exercise. He could hardly stretch in the small space. Every time he woke up, some part or other of his body would be really stiff and it would take ages to get rid of the cramps and other aches and pains. The food, delicious as it was, would sit heavily in his stomach for ages. Yet he would always eat it: satisfying his taste buds helped him deal with the boredom.

The changing temperatures in the small space made it all worse. One moment he'd be unbearably hot. The next it would become icy cold and he would start shivering. Some sort of sprinkler system would often kick in and he'd be drenched. It was only because that this was followed by the air control being switched on for a few moments, and set at a high temperature, he was certain, that he didn't get pneumonia. He guessed the Zenoton had carefully calculated it all: they never left him cold or wet long enough to make him ill. It was all just to make him uncomfortable. Well, they were succeeding.

A warm breeze was drifting through the space today, though. It was actually quite pleasant for once. Kaleem could almost persuade himself that he was sitting somewhere outside, near water, in the real country side. Well, at least he could if he closed his eyes.

He'd just finished his lunch. The midday meal was always a little bit lighter than the evening one. This time there had been some grilled fish and a potato salad. The fish had seemed fresh. Had they got fish tanks on the Supercraft, then? Where were they actually? The Supercraft had been so close to Zenoto? Why hadn't they landed there?

The dessert had been a light chocolate mousse, subtly flavoured with something Kaleem had not recognised. He guessed it was some sort of fruit and whatever it was, it tasted good. But it had all been a little too much even so. Lack of exercise for days and just too much food had left him feeling bloated and now he'd got indigestion as well. Thank goodness, at least, the air control was actually being pleasant for a change instead of tormenting him.

He tried to wriggle around to get more comfortable. It was impossible, though, especially with the tray still there. He wished they'd hurry up and clear it away, but they were really taking their time today.

At last, the hatch opened.

"Come on up, Kennedy," said a voice. Rogin. "We're taking you somewhere else. Bring that tray along."

The light dazzled Kaleem as he made his way up the steps. As his eyes adjusted, he could see Rogin standing there with two droids. One of the droids took his tray and disappeared through a doorway with it.

"Can you walk?" asked Rogin.

Kaleem nodded his head. It was difficult, though. His legs didn't seem to be doing what he wanted them to do. He couldn't feel his feet properly and he kept slipping.

"It's not far," said Rogin. "We're putting you into one of the crew rooms. It has a real bed, a bit more space, and it is properly controlled air. You'll find a fresh supply of clothes in the wardrobe. You'll have your own shower – laser or water, as you wish."

They walked another fifty metres. Rogin turned into another corridor.

"It's just along here," he said.

They walked past five doors. A sixth was already open. Rogin nodded that Kaleem should go in. "We are restoring the freedom from discomfort," he said. "All your physical needs will be catered for here. You will even be allowed some holo exercise programmes. But you will still have to put up with pain and injury, lack of normal contact with others and you still may have to face fear and distress. You remain our prisoner." He waved his arm around the room. "Well, what do you think?" he asked.

Kaleem nodded. It looked luxurious compared with the hole he'd been shut up in. There was what looked like a comfortable bed, soft carpeting on the floor and certainly enough space for a holo-exerciser, even though he could not see the dataserve that would drive it.

"The dataserve is not in the room," said Rogin. "It will be operated by the droid from outside and you will only be allowed to use it for programming the exerciser. When you want to use it, you can call the droid by using this button here." He pointed to a button just above the bed.

"Good," said Kaleem.

"I'm sure you will appreciate this," said Rogin, "after your time in the hatch-hole. Now let me look at that finger."

Kaleem held up the broken finger. The swelling was going down now. It hurt less, and it had gone back to its normal colour. But it was still numb and he couldn't use it properly. And occasionally, when he did try to use it, it would let him down.

"Yes, well," said Rogin. "You'll have to live with that a while longer. The freedom from pain and injury will be returned to you next. We will be able to cure the finger, but not until then." He looked around the room again. "You will be comfortable here," he said. "Make sure you appreciate it."

Rogin turned and walked out of the room. The door swished to and then Kaleem heard another swish which he assumed was a force field being activated. As if he would try to get away. Well, not just yet anyway. That bed looked way too inviting.

It was great being able to move properly. Even just crossing the couple of metres from one side of the room to the other was a luxury. Not to mention stretching out on the firm but supportive bed.

Kaleem lay there for about an hour, staring up at the ceiling of the cabin. The shields were still on, but he could see that when they came off he would have a view of the galaxies. Something to look forward to. It was great, too, being able to stretch as much as he wanted to.

He moved at last. He took a look in the wardrobe. Seven sets of underwear, tunics and leggings – some Zandrian, some Terrestran style, and a different colour for every day of the week by the looks of it. How would they manage his laundry? No doubt that would become apparent.

He stripped off and left his clothes in a neat pile on the floor. He made his way into the bathroom. Should he have a laser or a wet shower? Why not both? Laser to get him clean, and then a water one, just for the sheer luxury of it.

Twenty minutes later, he felt much cleaner and was enjoying the sensation of warm water cascading down his back. He ought to move, but this was just too enjoyable.

He forced himself at last to get out of the shower and dried himself first on one of the thick yellow towels and then under the laser–drier. Naked, he went back into the room. The pile of clothes he had left on the floor had already disappeared. He assumed the droid had taken them.

He opened the wardrobe and decided he would wear red today. He stretched out his arm to take down the red tunic and leggings. As his injured finger brushed the cloth, a pain shot through it and up into his shoulder. He pulled his hand back quickly and then tried to manage with one hand.

It was so awkward, getting dressed with one hand, that by the time he'd finished, he was exhausted again and feeling a little hot and sticky despite the air control.

He flopped down on the bed and fell fast asleep.

Freedom Three Returned

There was hardly a moment now that Kaleem could forget his finger. Now that he could move around so much more, he kept catching it on things. Then it would hurt again and it kept on swelling back up for a short while. He was comfortable enough in every other way. But this finger was a pain. In more ways than one. He could only use about one third of the holo-exerciser programmes and even those he had to keep down to a speed that was actually far too undemanding for him.

If it's not one thing it's another, he thought.

Sometimes the finger would just ache for hours on end. It helped if he kept his hand really warm, but as soon as it cooled down it started throbbing again.

Just how long are they going to let this go on for? he thought.

And he was bored. It was all very well being comfortable again – relatively, at least, though with the finger being so useless and hurting so much, he didn't feel all that easy – but he needed a bit more than just this.

He'd only seen droids for the last ten days. At least he thought it was ten. There were four outfits in the wardrobe now. On the day he'd put on the seventh a droid had come with seven new outfits.

So let's call first outfit day Sunday, he'd thought.

How long would it be now before they fixed his finger? He looked at it again. It was bent at a slightly odd angle. It wasn't swollen at the moment and it wasn't bruised but he couldn't move it.

I bet it's set wrong, he thought. *I hope they know what they're doing.* Oddly, though, he trusted them. He was sure they had the right medical technology to be able to fix it, even at this late stage. He was sure as well that that was their intention.

"Would your people be able to fix this finger if the wanted to?" he tried asking one of the droids who delivered his food.

The machine remained silent.

He'd not had much appetite for breakfast that day. It had included fresh orange juice, chofa, fresh fruit and toast.

The shields were still on his skylight. He guessed though that they must still be near Zenoto if they were able to get such fresh food, so they couldn't be travelling fast enough to need the shields to be activated. They'd probably decided to deprive him as well of a view of the universe.

He slid the tray to near the door. That would save the droid coming right into the room. He flung himself down on the bed. Perhaps he could try and sleep a bit more? He might at least have an interesting dream? Or should he go on the exerciser again? Oh, no, for goodness sake. That was such a bore. He'd done to death all the simple programmes his damaged hand would allow.

He turned over so that his face was to the wall. That way he wouldn't even have to look at the droid when it came in. He closed his eyes and started counting backwards. He would concentrate on the numbers and put all other thoughts out of the way.

He got to twenty. *I'm going to have to use the red dog,* he thought.

He heard the door swish open. He tried to ignore the sound. He would not listen to the droid taking away his tray. He would concentrate on the last few numbers and then would sleep, hopefully.

It must have worked. Kaleem woke with a jolt. He had dreamt something but he couldn't remember what. That was a pity. He could have carried on the story in a day dream.

There was something different about his room, he thought. He couldn't put his finger on exactly what, though. Had someone other than the droid been in? He looked around. The tray had gone. Well, that was hardly surprising. Nothing else seemed to have moved. He couldn't help feeling, though, that someone had been in there.

This wasn't the first time that this had happened. He would often wake up suddenly and feel absolutely scared. Yes, of course he was being held captive. Yes, of course he had a lot of responsibility being the Peace Child. Most of the time, even though he always felt slightly uneasy, he just got on with it and it was fine. So far, also, the Zenoton had done everything they promised they were going to do and they had not been unduly unkind, at least for any length of time. He hoped, and was actually pretty sure, that they were looking after Saratina all right.

No, this just seemed to be one of those irrational moments again. He guessed it just felt worse each time because he didn't have anyone at all he could talk to. And that was also what made it happen more often. He suddenly thought of Ella and then of Rozia. How was Stuart getting on now? And his parents? Would he ever get used to being around his father? Why hadn't he tried a bit harder when he'd had the chance?

He took a few deep breaths and tried to calm himself a little. His breathing became slower and he did feel a bit more peaceful. He just wished he knew what was going to happen next. The anxiety about that never quite went away.

The door swished open. Kaleem's heart started to beat fast. He had no real idea what the time was but he sensed it was too early for the lunchtime droid visit.

Rogin and two other Zenoton came in. The strangers were carrying some odd looking instruments.

"We've come to look at that finger," said Rogin.

The two Zenoton Kaleem supposed must be doctors came over to him. One of them placed what looked like a small paddle over the finger. It hummed gently and Kaleem felt a slight tingling in his finger.

The two Zenoton started talking excitedly. Kaleem could not follow what they were saying. Then they turned to Rogin. The one who had held the paddle spoke more slowly but Kaleem still could not understand what he was saying. Rogin kept nodding his head.

I bet it's dead, thought Kaleem. *I bet they're going to have to amputate it.*

Rogin leant forward and touched Kaleem lightly on the shoulder.

"I'm sorry," he said slowly. "We miscalculated a little. The finger has started to set wrongly. We shall have to rebreak it and even do some plastic surgery on it."

Ouch! thought Kaleem. "You can do that on board a Supercraft?" he said.

"Oh yes, easily," said Rogin. "Besides, we're currently orbiting Zenoto. We could take you down there if we had to and we can certainly get supplies up here."

Ah. So he had been right. That explained the fresh fruit and fish.

"We don't need to, though, and I shall now leave you in the capable hands of doctors Ramski and Colant. I wish you a swift recovery."

"We'll take you to our medical deck," said Doctor Ramski, now speaking more clearly, though he was still more difficult to understand than Rogin.

"But we'll give you an anaesthetic now," said Doctor Colant. "You'll be asleep by the time you're there."

"And that means you won't be able to do any spying," said Doctor Ramski. "You'll be asleep before you can see anything important." He chuckled at his own joke.

Doctor Colant waved the paddle over Kaleem's head.

He was vaguely aware of a hover stretcher arriving, and he remembered seeing the swirling patterns of the corridor ceilings gradually going black.

Next there was nothing.

Then he woke up. He was back in his room, in his own bed and wearing a fresh Zenoton medical gown. His finger, he could tell, was held in place by some sort of splint and a light dressing. But it felt normal. No aching. No numbness. Doctor Ramski was sitting next to him.

"You should feel no more pain," he said. "In two days time you will be able to use it as normal, though the splint will hamper you a little. In five days, the splint comes off and your finger will be as good as new if not better. You can get up and get dressed now. A droid nurse is there for you. Just press your buzzer if you require any help."

Ramski bowed, got up from his seat and left the room.

Five days later, just after Doctor Colant and the droid nurse left, Kaleem waved his hand in the air. He waggled the finger that had been broken. It seemed fine now. He could move it. It had sensation. He had no pain.

"Now then," he said loudly to no one in particular, but hoping that the dataserve that programmed the holo-exerciser, or the droid outside would hear. "Find me some decent exercise."

Pictures started to flash across the dataserve screen.

That'll do, he thought as he saw an image of canoes on the open sea. "Rowing Level Five," he said.

Freedom Four Returned

He was now on Level Seven rowing. He had played Champion's League football and stopped five goals from a premier league holo-striker. He had run two marathons. All on the holo-exerciser. And all in under 48 hours. He felt better for it. The bloated feeling was gone. His body was functioning perfectly. He felt pleasantly sleepy. His bed looked inviting.

Best shower, first, though.

He peeled his clothes off and went into the bathroom. He quickly cleaned his teeth and then within seconds, even though he didn't know how he was managing to make his legs move, he was under the shower, feeling the silky moisturised water cascading over his skin.

He felt good. Over the last ten days he'd really upped his exercise regime. He would soon be back at his normal fitness level. Maybe even a little fitter.

He laser-dried himself, wrapped himself in one of the large yellow towels and made his way over to the minibar. Yes, they'd installed a small fridge with drinks in his room. He took out a small bottle of frega, poured it into a beaker and put that on his bedside table.

He dropped the towel on the floor and slipped into the bed. The duvet felt cool and soft. He took a sip of the frega. It tickled his tongue and already he could feel the active ingredients pumping through his veins. Oh that was good. He closed his eyes. Yes, it was all good.

He opened his eyes with a start. There was something missing. He would have liked to watch some movie clips on the dataserve, or even read some Wordtext. Maybe speak to somebody. By all the elders, yes, speak to someone.

He buzzed for the droid.

"Sir," said the machine, when it arrived. "How can I be of assistance?"

"I want to talk to someone," said Kaleem. "Can you fetch

someone to talk to me? Or can you talk to me."

"Doubly not possible," said the droid and whirred out of the room.

Kaleem, sighed, drank the rest of the frega and commanded the lights to dim. He counted backwards from 100 and then thought about the red dog. Finally he fell asleep.

He woke suddenly. He was damp with sweat but felt cold. *This is not right,* he thought. *This can never be right.* He screamed.

The droid came running. Then there were other footsteps.

Snatches of the dream now came back to him. It had been about the tower again. Only this time everyone had moved silently. It had seemed that no one wanted to speak to anyone else, especially not to him. He had felt a type of despair. At least when there had been panic, people were still capable of wanting to change their circumstances. It was the complete acceptance of what was happening that had been so terrifying.

But it had been just a dream.

He slowly came back to reality. He was a prisoner in a small cabin on a Supercraft that was circling Zenoto. Wasn't that even worse?

A droid and Rogin were in the room with him.

"Go to standby," Rogin ordered the droid.

The droid whirred, bowed its head and its lights went out.

"Was it the isolation that caused the bad dream?" asked Rogin.

Kaleem nodded. "Yes, I think so," he said. "Being on my own so much made it worse this time."

"Ah, one of those," said Rogin.

"Hmm," mumbled Kaleem. "I wish it would stop, actually."

"Now, that is the one that is the most difficult of the freedoms to return," said Rogin. "The freedom from distress and fear is very much the matter for humans, and for the Zenoton as well, of individual perception. But we might be able to help you see things differently."

Rogin paused and looked around the walls of the cabin. "A bit small here, isn't it?" he said. "We'll move you to a better cabin tomorrow. We'll restore full dataserve usage to you straight away and you have the freedom of the Supercraft. The shields are off and the view is glorious. Why don't you come and have a look?"

Two hours later Kaleem was back in his cabin. The shield on his skylight had also been removed. He couldn't see as well from there the galaxy in which Zenoto found itself. It was a fascinating part of the universe. The constellations were even more intricate and complex than the ones in Terrestra's and Zandra's galaxies. He'd caught a glimpse of Zenoto and even though it had been shrouded in mist it reminded him of Terrestra, for there were glimpses between the clouds of colours swirling together.

Now he was flicking through pictures of Zandra on the dataserve screen. Nazaret was making progress in clearing up after the landquake. He hadn't felt quite like communicating with them yet. It was good to know that he would be allowed to do that though, and he would do it soon. He needed a little time yet to formulate what he was going to say.

His door buzzed. "Alee, oo ao rie? An ee om i? I wa see oo."

Saratina! It was late but her company would be good for a while. "Come in," he called."

Reclaiming Freedom Five

Kaleem sat on the viewing deck of the Zenoton Supercraft. It certainly was a very well equipped vessel. It was even more luxurious than the ones he'd travelled on before, even better in fact that the Zandrian ones with all their fascinating technology. At Rogin's suggestion, he'd walked around the whole of the public areas: five kilometres of passages and not a dirty mark or inferior material anywhere. Now he sat enjoying a chofa and some of the extraordinarily light Zenoton bread. His seat moulded itself to him even more efficiently than any Terrestran comfisessel he'd used before.

He could not fault the Zenoton. They were treating him well. But everything was nagging away at him: Stuart's illness, this Peace Child role that was always such a pain, this huge change the Zenoton were asking for, the plantations on Zandra and Saratina. Above all, Saratina. It was so unfair that she was trapped here.

"E ice eein ow?" said a voice.

Saratina. Right on cue. She limped over to him. Kaleem could not help but notice that she looked very well and very happy too. "I don't know how you can be so cheerful," he said to her. "I'm really sorry I got you into this."

"Ay os elpe oo," said Saratina. "Ay os aee o he loo." She smiled and stroked Kaleem's cheek.

"Have they been treating you well? Really?" asked Kaleem.

Saratina nodded her head vigorously. "Ay arr ine oo mee," she said. "Ude eely goo," she said. "Ay eah mee oo coo. Ay o woo. Aer."

He wished he could understand her but it was impossible for him most of the time. If only they could find a way of helping to make her speak properly. Now, that would be something.

She nudged him and laughed.

He couldn't help but laugh back.

She really did seem well-looked after and very content.

"Eets ay ine. Or ine," she said and scuttled away. As she went from the deck, Rogin arrived.

Kaleem watched her say something to Rogin. The Zenoton laughed. She grinned and carried on her way. So, Rogin could understand her too. Why couldn't he?

"She's an amazing person," said Rogin as he sat down beside Kaleem. "You are so lucky to have her."

"I know," said Kaleem. "And it really annoys me that she has had to be kept here all because of me."

"So, it's causing you some distress," said Rogin.

Kaleem nodded. Some? It was causing him a lot of stress.

"She doesn't look very stressed," said Rogin. "So why are you worrying about her?"

"Well, with her not being able to make herself understood... and being far away from home."

"What is her home like?" asked Rogin. "Is it more comfortable than here?"

He had to be kidding. Even though the Z Zone was now rapidly becoming the New Zone it was nowhere near as luxurious as here. Nowhere on Terrestra or even Zandra was. "No," he replied. "But I expect she's missing her friends."

"She seems to get on very well with everyone here," said Rogin. "Why don't you ask her?"

"I have," said Kaleem. "Yes, she seems fine."

"Then perhaps you need to stop worrying," said Rogin. "And you need to let her know that too. Look, we can't let her go just yet. But you can at least do that. Set your mind at rest. And hers. Then we can peel the next layer off."

He stood up ready to leave and then hesitated. "You know," he said, "you might even find it a little easier to understand her if you relax around her a little." He turned and left.

He found her in one of the kitchens. She was chopping up vegetables.

"Make the pieces smaller," said the Zenoton chef. "And take care when you work with the green snaps. The juice can sting.

Wash your hands afterwards."

Saratina nodded. She noticed Kaleem and beamed.

"Ain oop," she said. "Eno on oop. Do oo wan oo el?"

"You can if you want to," said the Zenoton. He was the smallest Zenoton Kaleem had seen. He moved quickly. His dark brown eyes looked carefully at Kaleem. "Wash your hands first, though."

The Zenoton threw an overall and cap at him as he finished drying his own hands. "You can help Saratina with those. If you're half as good as she is you'll be fine and we won't starve. I'm Clix, by the way, and I suppose you must be Kaleem."

Kaleem put on the overall and cap.

Clix nodded. "You'll do. Now, get chopping."

Saratina grinned at him. "Ureeps, eepers. Eno-o uff. Lots o do." She pointed to a large tray of vegetables.

Kaleem took one of the turnips and began to peel it. He watched how Saratina held her knife. She made it look so easy. He found it difficult. Great chunks of the flesh came away as he tried to cut the skin off.

"Dear, oh, dear," said Clix. "It's a good job we don't have to worry about credits here."

"I'm surprised you don't get droids to do this sort of work," said Kaleem.

"Oh, we do," said Clix. "But never when we're trying out a new recipe. And personally, I love handling the food. I mean, just smell this."

He picked up a handful of a green herb Kaleem didn't recognise. He held it up to Kaleem's nose. It was certainly startling. It seemed so fresh and green.

Clix handed some to Saratina. She took a deep breath. She closed her eyes and smiled. "Hmm," she said. "Ovely."

"Zenoton water spinach," said Clix. "It only grows by certain of our lakes. It will make such a difference to the taste of our soup."

Kaleem closed his eyes and took another sniff at the herb. He could almost taste it and he could see it, he thought, growing at the side of the lake.

"Well, come on," said Clix. "No time to waste. We have to have this recipe completed and tried in time for the next main course sitting."

"Om on," said Saratina.

They chopped and peeled. Kaleem slowly got the hang of it and there was less flesh stuck to the peel than went into the compost bins. Then came the smell of something good cooking.

"Don't you get homesick?" he said to Saratina.

"Ot eally," she said. She looked at him and shook her head. "I'm a ome erever I am. Epecially en I'm ith oo."

He thought he was beginning to understand her. Her speech was beginning to sound almost normal.

She laughed. "Zeno-o ood. Oup ood as ell."

Rogin had been right. He didn't need to worry about her. She was fine and possibly all the better because he was not worrying about her so much.

"So, are you two going to come and help me cook, now?" asked Clix.

Saratina gave a little jump and clapped her hands. "Es lease," she said.

Kaleem picked up the tray of chopped vegetables and followed her over to where Clix was stirring two pots of boiling liquid.

"Put half into each pot," Clix said. "Mix them up a bit so that each pot gets a variety of the vegetables." He stood back to let Kaleem get to the pans.

"That's it," he said as Kaleem slid the vegetables into the pot. "Nice and gently so that you don't splash yourself."

Kaleem still wondered why they didn't get droids to do that if it was so dangerous. But he could tell that Clix was enjoying the cooking and Saratina was watching, her eyes and mouth wide open.

"Are you two going to stir?" asked Clix, handing them each a large ladle.

"It smells lovely," said Saratina.

Kaleem was amazed. He could actually understand her

suddenly. Perfectly now.

"That's because the water-spinach has already gone into the water," said Clix. "It will get even better as the vegetables soften."

He was right. At each turn of the ladle the smells became even more enticing. Saratina, he noticed, was struggling a little. She wasn't as tall as him and couldn't stir as effectively. Every so often liquid would splash over the side of her pot.

"Be careful," he said.

"It's okay," she said.

He stopped stirring himself to watch her for a while. She was determined to finish making the soup but he could tell it was hard work.

"On strike, are we?" said Clix laughing.

"Just making sure Saratina's all right," said Kaleem.

"She's done fine," said Clix. "You both have. Time to taste, I think."

The liquid in the pans gradually stopped boiling. Clix gave them a spoon each. "Ladle some out and then use the spoon," he said. "Take care, though. It will still be hot."

It was. Kaleem burnt his mouth on the first spoonful. He remembered to blow the second to cool it down first. This time he could really taste it. It was absolutely delicious.

"Not bad," said Clix. "Not bad at all. A little more pepper perhaps."

He added some to the pot, stirred the liquid a little, and then offered Saratina and Kaleem another spoonful each to taste. It was even more delicious now.

"I made this," said Saratina, grinning.

"You most certainly did," said Clix. "Now, we'll leave it to cool a little. Then we'll add cream and liquidise it. It will stand for a while before we reheat it and serve it."

"What next?" said Saratina.

"Oh you are keen," said Clix. "Maybe you could help with the dessert."

"Yes please," said Saratina.

"What about you?" asked Clix.

Kaleem couldn't think what to say. He really wanted to go away and think about this whole bizarre situation a bit. It was so odd, how he could suddenly understand Saratina. And how he also now understood that he did not need to worry about her.

"It's all right," said Clix, laughing. "I do understand that not everyone is as mad as me and Saratina. Doing work that droids are perfectly capable of doing."

"Yes, you're right," said Kaleem. "But I did enjoy it. I just wouldn't want to do it all the time."

"I want to take some of these recipes back to Terrestra," said Saratina.

"Whenever we get back there," said Kaleem.

"It's all right, Kaleem," said Saratina. She walked over to him and hugged him. "I need to stay a bit longer with the Zenoton so that I can learn more about their food."

"I guess it is okay, then," whispered Kaleem.

"Go off and do what you have to do, Peace Child man," said Saratina. "Get out of my kitchen."

They all laughed as Saratina waved him out of the way with her apron.

As the door to the kitchen swished shut behind him, Kaleem realised that everything Rogin had said had been true.

Life on a Zenoton Supercraft

Kaleem had got into a routine now. He would get up relatively early. Then he would go to the hologym on the fourth deck. He particularly liked that one because you had a good view of Zenoto from there and you even got a sense of the speed you were travelling at. It was always better using a real hologym than just using the holoprogrammes on the dataserves. Then he would have a good brunch. He'd spend some time talking to whichever Zenoton had time for him. He would stay in his room for some part of every day, looking at news broadcasts, keeping an eye on Nazaret's work and checking for any progress in Stuart Davidson's condition. The Zenoton were willing for him to communicate with Terrestra and Zandra as much as he wanted to. However, as he had little to report, he'd only spoken to his parents once or twice, Razjosh a few times more, Charlek about three times and Ella never. He'd tried to call her up once but she'd refused his call. He'd not contacted Calver Toms at all. He didn't think he could stand Calver's clever remarks.

"We're only keeping you here until we feel you really understand how our creditless society works," said Rogin. "Once we're sure you understand, we'll let you go."

So, he carried on talking to as many people as he could and spent a lot of his time studying their language a bit more and finding out more about their culture.

He only had a light lunch every day. He'd exercise again before dinner and he'd try to dine with a different Zenoton every time.

Often Saratina would join him and tell him all about the food he was eating, how it was made and how good it was for him.

"Do you think we'll be able to grow water-spinach on Terrestra?" she asked.

"I've no idea," said Kaleem. "I guess that's the sort of question my father might be able to answer.

"Well, ask him," said Saratina. "Next time you speak. And make that soon."

He'd sometimes spend the evenings joining in the Zenoton entertainments. He now understood their language and their culture well enough to find some of their movies and live shows entertaining.

If it hadn't have been for the feeling he had that he ought to be doing something else, life was very pleasant on the Zenoton Supercraft. Everything was very comfortable. The food was superb and the company of the Zenoton was very rewarding.

"You'll understand better," said Rogin, one evening as they dined together "when you find out what you really want to do. When you find out how you want to spend your time. For in the end, even in your society, it comes down to how you end up spending your time."

Kaleem decided not to go and watch a movie or go to a live show this time. He wanted to try and work out the answer to the puzzle Rogin had set him. What did he really want?

He remembered being with Rozia. He'd been so happy then, until she got hurt. What about Ella? She was great company and a real turn on, but she was a bit like a glass of fine wine. Great whilst you're drinking it, but you wouldn't want to drink it all the time and really you only enjoyed it if everything else was all right as well, or just occasionally, if everything had gone wrong and you wanted to forget for a while. Being with Ella was not like being with Rozia.

Rozia had been more like a permanent shelter. If he was honest he would like that back but his head told him it was wrong. It was too risky for her. She'd already been badly hurt because of being with him. No point in even thinking about that, then.

Besides, even with Rozia there, he still had to occupy himself somehow.

"Do you eat to live or live to eat?" Rogin had asked him one day at dinner. "Do you live to work or do you work to live? Can you really call what you do work if it is your vocation, what you feel called to do and you are passionate about?"

No, this was no good. This was doing his head in. He could not make up his mind what he, Kaleem Kennedy, Malkendy,

Bagarin, – Detran Malthus as the Zandrians first knew him – putrid elders, it was hard enough getting his name right – really wanted to spend his time doing.

He decided to spend the rest of the evening looking at more Zenoton files. Perhaps go back in their history to the time when they became creditless. Find out what had triggered it, how it had happened.

He searched for hours and gradually became tired and stiff from sitting in the same position. He couldn't seem to pinpoint a time when they brought in this regime, but he'd come across some fascinating stuff and now felt that despite not being able to answer that one crucial question, he understood the Zenoton even better now. He was even quite pleased with himself because it was clear that he was getting more and more mastery of the Zenoton language.

That was it! What he really liked doing was finding out about other cultures and languages. It was more than just that, though. It was something really deep. It was gaining that real understanding about how other people worked. A true Peace Child thing, then. It was the negotiating that he had to do that he did not like.

He suddenly felt the need to speak to Calver Toms after all.

"Request communication with Calver Toms," he commanded the dataserve. Within seconds, Calver's face appeared on the screen.

Kaleem tried to explain what he had noticed. It was hard putting it into words. Calver, of course, understood straight away.

"It's not surprising that you like finding out about other cultures and learning other languages," said Calver. "That is why Razjosh picked you out."

"Are you sure it's not because I'm part of a prophecy?" said Kaleem.

"Do you believe that?" asked Calver. "Does Razjosh?"

Kaleem didn't know what to say.

"Never mind," said Calver. "That probably isn't important. It seems to me that there is one good thing: that you enjoy doing what you have been called upon to do."

"Only in part," said Kaleem. "It's fascinating finding out about all of these different people. And I really enjoy learning other languages. That comes fairly easily. But it's the negotiating between people. I can see both ways of looking at things and I can also see why the people would find it difficult to accept the other point of view."

"Are you beginning to understand the Zenoton?" asked Calver.

"Yes, I am," said Kaleem. "I can see that their system works for them and I wish it could work for the Terrestrans and the Zandrians, but I don't really see how it can."

"So what are the most important aspects of the way the Zenoton see things?" asked Calver.

"That everybody should have what they want and that everybody should contribute what they can," replied Kaleem.

"And why don't you think that can't work for everyone else?" asked Calver.

"Greed, laziness," replied Kaleem.

"So that must be what you most fear in yourself," said Calver.

Kaleem could not reply. Was he likely to be greedy? Or lazy?

"What stops the Zenoton being greedy and lazy?" asked Calver.

"I'm not sure," said Kaleem.

"You'll just have to watch them more closely."

Why was he being like this? Why was he not telling him what was going to happen next like he normally did? "How will this all turn out?" he asked Calver.

"However you want it to," said Calver. "You can control it all. The Zenoton will show you how."

Then he was gone. He never did finish a conversation with a "good bye" or "take care". Just like Edmundson, he always went when he'd decided there was no more to say.

Kaleem sighed. Calver had not really been a lot of use. He was even more puzzled now. What should he do next?

Calver was infuriating. Kaleem did not know what was worse – when he knew everything that was going on or how he was now – not giving away a thing and making it all to do with him.

And yet, he felt oddly calm. Calver had at least acknowledged that he was on to something. That he had been right in recognising what he was good at and what he enjoyed. And he felt glad that this idealised way of life seemed to work for the Zenoton. All he had to do was watch how they did it. Well, he'd been doing that for a while. It wasn't onerous. It was pleasant, in fact. The Zenoton were really easy going and they had made him very comfortable.

He suddenly felt confident that he would find a way. And very soon, he was sure, the Zenoton would realise that he did understand how their systems worked.

He was beginning to feel quite sleepy. He suddenly felt free of all worries. He would go to bed and sleep, and tomorrow he would have even more ideas.

The dream was different again this time. The tower didn't fall, although the ground rumbled and shook, and Kaleem could tell that the people could not understand each other. But he could understand them, every single one.

"We must leave the tower," he found himself saying. "We must hope it doesn't fall, but we must leave in case it does."

"But the stories?" said one of the Adulkis.

"I can tell you the stories," said Kaleem, taking the little man-boy's hand. "I don't need to write them."

When he woke up, he was not covered in sweat like he usually was after one of the dreams about the tower. In fact, he felt more as if he was waking up from a pleasant dream.

"Time?" he asked the dataserve.

"Six forty," replied the electronic voice.

That was something else that was different. He'd not woken in the middle of the night. This was more or less his normal waking time. In fact the alarm would go off in five minutes.

It's all so simple, he thought. *I get it now.*

Maybe he wouldn't go to the gym this time. There was someone he wanted to see.

Rights and Duties

"It was different in the dream this time," said Kaleem. "I knew exactly what to do." I just had to get them out of the tower, quickly, calmly and safely. And I could understand what they were all saying though they couldn't understand each other."

"So, is that it then? The key to it all?" asked Albasto.

"Well, I always knew it was about understanding other people even though they couldn't understand each other," said Kaleem. "But I never knew what to do about it. This time, though, I knew we were all in danger and whatever else, I had to get them out. Being able to understand what everyone was saying and being able to make myself understood just made it easier. I gathered information and acted on it."

Albasto smiled and nodded. He topped up Kaleem's coffee cup. "What about the other bit?" he said. "The bit about the stories."

Kaleem frowned. That was trickier. "They wanted stories written down and some were already done. That little Adulki was scared we were going to lose them."

"But you wouldn't because you had them in your head?" said Albasto.

Kaleem nodded. "And there was a sense that they could come later. There was something more urgent to be done first."

Albasto nodded and smiled again. "There is something I would like to show you," he said. "It's only stored on my dataserve for security. You need to come to my quarters. But please, finish your breakfast first."

Kaleem looked at plates of fruit and rolls still on the table. He'd had two coffees, already, some fruit and a couple of rolls. He was feeling inexplicably excited. He couldn't eat any more. "I'm fine," he said. "Thank you. Breakfast was delicious."

"Very well, then," said Albasto. "Follow me."

Kaleem was conscious as they walked to Albasto's quarters that other Zenoton bowed slightly to Albasto. He smiled at many of them and greeted them by name.

They really respect him, thought Kaleem. *I just don't understand why I didn't at first.*

Twenty minutes later, Albasto showed Kaleem into large airy lounge, one wall of which was veriglass and looked out towards Zenoto.

"Please, take a seat," said Albasto.

Kaleem sat on one of the wide leather comfisessels. His feet rested in the thick pile of pale blue carpet.

"You read Wordtext, don't you?" said Albasto.

Kaleem nodded.

"Good," said Albasto. "I'd like you to see this," he said. "It was actually created on Terrestra in 1948 and has never been revoked."

Kaleem started to read out loud the Wordtext document that scrolled down on the screen in front of him.

"What is this exactly?" he asked. "Where did it come from?"

"They are the laws by which your society is supposed to live," said Albasto. "They were put together a few years after one of the worst wars on your planet. Their formation was overseen by the attachment of one of your presidents."

It all made a lot of sense. He shuddered a little when he read Article 1 and thought of the Z Zone and the Adulkis.

> *All human beings are born free and equal in dignity and rights. They are endowed with reason and conscience and should act towards one another in a spirit of brotherhood.*

Article 2 was tricky as well.

> *Everyone is entitled to all the rights and freedoms set forth in this Declaration, without distinction of any kind, such as race, colour, sex, language, religion, political or other opinion, national or social origin, property, birth or other status. Furthermore, no distinction shall be made on the basis of the political, jurisdictional or international status of the country or territory to which a person belongs, whether it be independent, trust, non-self-governing or under any other limitation of sovereignty.*

Article 25 really made him squirm.

> *(1) Everyone has the right to a standard of living adequate for the health and well-being of himself and of his family, including food, clothing, housing and medical care and necessary social services, and the right to security in the event of unemployment, sickness, disability, widowhood, old age or other lack of livelihood in circumstances beyond his control.*
>
> *(2) Motherhood and childhood are entitled to special care and assistance. All children, whether born in or out of wedlock, shall enjoy the same social protection.*

"So what do you think?" asked Albasto.

"It makes a lot of sense," said Kaleem, "though I guess we didn't do so well on 1, 2 and 25. I guess 'born in or out of wedlock' is to do with whether their parents are formally attached or not?"

"Yes, that's right," said Albasto. "And we've been going against number 3 a little lately."

True, thought Kaleem. They had taken his freedom away from him for a short while and in a sense they were still doing that, though it was nothing compared to the way Terrestrans had treated the Z Zoners.

"But we mean you no harm," Albasto continued. "What I'd really like you to look at are numbers 22 and 23."

The dataserve picked up on what Albasto was saying and the two articles appeared on the screen. Kaleem read them silently this time.

> *Article 22.*
>
> *Everyone, as a member of society, has the right to social security and is entitled to realization, through national effort and international co-operation and in accordance with the organization and resources of each State, of the economic, social and cultural rights indispensable for his dignity and the free development of his personality.*

Article 23.

(1) Everyone has the right to work, to free choice of employment, to just and favourable conditions of work and to protection against unemployment.

(2) Everyone, without any discrimination, has the right to equal pay for equal work.

(3) Everyone who works has the right to just and favourable remuneration ensuring for himself and his family an existence worthy of human dignity, and supplemented, if necessary, by other means of social protection.

(4) Everyone has the right to form and to join trade unions for the protection of his interest.

"We don't need points two to three," said Albasto. "In fact, we don't need any of this at all, because that is the way the Zenoton operate anyway. Without having to define it."

Kaleem thought about the two articles and what Albasto had said. "So, it's a right to do what you feel you want to do, in the way of work, and a right to enjoy what life has to offer?" he said.

"You are so close to understanding now," said Albasto. "Eleanor Roosevelt was more than a millennium and a half ahead of you. You would almost think she had been sent subliminal messages by the Zenoton."

Kaleem nodded.

"You're almost ready to be let loose on this," said Albasto.

"So how come the Zenoton are so good at this sort of thing?" asked Kaleem.

"Zenoton nature is more trusting," said Albasto. "We believe that as long as our sun still shines there is enough for everyone. Only a lack of political will could stop that abundance. And why would we want it to stop? It doesn't make any sense."

Kaleem understood what he meant. Yet he still couldn't quite see it working with the people he knew, with the Terrestrans and Zandrians.

"Why don't you just try trusting us and see what happens?" said Albasto.

"Oh yes," said Kaleem. "After you've kept me and Saratina as prisoners?"

"Trust us that we mean you no harm," said Albasto, "and that we do it for your own good?"

"Okay," said Kaleem. "I'll give you that."

"Really trust," said Albasto. "Not try to catch us out. You know, actually, it's even more comfortable for you to trust."

This all suddenly reminded Kaleem about his experiences with Calver. What harm could it do, actually? And deep down he felt that he could trust the Zenoton.

"Will you give it a go?" asked Albasto.

Kaleem nodded.

He could certainly trust Albasto anyway. He actually liked the Zenoton and from what he had seen he was some sort of authority amongst the others. He wondered briefly how any sort of hierarchy worked on Zenoto. Was there anything like the elders on Terrestra or the executives on Zandra? He had a feeling that even that worked differently here.

"Well?" said Albasto. His deep brown eyes seemed to smile warmly.

Yes, Kaleem knew he could absolutely trust this person. "Yes," he said, "but I don't know whether I'm not too human to work on Zenoton standards."

"You will be fine," said Albasto. Now he was smiling with his whole face.

Kaleem felt a lightness in his chest as if a weight had literally lifted from him.

The Zenoton Way

Kaleem stared through the huge veriglass walls of Supercraft. The shields were still raised and he could see Zenoto. It was almost as beautiful as Terrestra, but not quite. It lacked the swirly marble effect: Zenoto was a much drier planet and its redness, though startlingly rich, was not as breathtaking as the subtle mixture of Terrestra's blue, green, brown and white.

The Supercraft was still orbiting the planet. Even though it seemed as if they'd finished negotiations. He'd agreed to try it, hadn't he? But now he was still waiting. They still didn't seem to want him and Saratina actually on the planet.

I still wonder what they've got to hide, thought Kaleem. He stared again at the red planet. *It looks all right down there.*

In fact, it looked a little like the old pictures they had of Terrestra's neighbour, The Warrior, before they'd cultivated an atmosphere there. But the Zenoton claimed that Zenoto did have an atmosphere even though you couldn't see it. It was bizarre. There was surely something they weren't telling him.

One of the smaller Zenoton walked over to him.

"Would you like some coffee, sir?" he asked, behaving just like a Terrestran droid.

"Yes, please, that would be nice," Kaleem replied.

It was really quite pleasant here, circling another planet and looking out at the stars. There was nothing more he could do until Rogin gave him some indication of what he should do next. He couldn't wait now to get back to solving the problems between Zandra and Terrestra and he wished he could get Saratina safely back home.

"Oh. Lovely," Saratina cried suddenly.

She was looking in a mirror. Alixia, one of the young female Zenoton, had been doing something to her hair. She now had some Zenoton curls and her otherwise raggedy blond-grey hair was swept to one side. Alixia had applied a gel that made the hair shine. It did look rather good. Why hadn't anyone ever thought of doing something like that for Saratina before? It made all the difference. And seemed so simple.

Yes, it was very comfortable here. But Kaleem could not enjoy it. There was too much that needed to be put right and it was, as usual, down to him to do it.

The door swished open and a Zenoton walked in with the coffee. He was followed closely by Rogin. Kaleem felt his body tense. Rogin was always pleasant enough though he rarely smiled. The sheer size of him made him very scary. Those eyes, too, always seemed to look right into you and Kaleem was sure this particular Zenoton always knew exactly what he was thinking. He was the one who seemed to represent authority here, even more than Albasto. Now Kaleem needed to be careful.

Rogin did almost half smile. "I take it you are still being looked after well?"

"Yes," said Kaleem.

"Good," replied Rogin. "Then there will be no complaints from Terrestra when we return you there."

He turned to face Alixia. He nodded towards the exit of the deck.

Alicia took the hint. "Let's go and take a walk through one of the holoscenes," she said to Saratina.

"Will you be all right, Kaleem?" asked Saratina.

"It'll be fine," said Kaleem. "Rogin and I have to talk business."

"It's a shame about the woman," said Rogin as soon as Alicia and Saratina were through the doors. "But there will be many more like her soon if we don't all do something about it."

"What do you mean?" asked Kaleem.

Rogin sighed. "If you don't do something about it soon," he said, "the whole interplanetary credit system will collapse. We're not just talking nice ideas about exchanging commodities any more. We Zenoton have realised we need to take more direct action."

Kaleem could hear his heartbeat thudding in his ears. He knew that Rogin was telling him something really serious.

"We were just being diplomatic before," he explained. "Giving you all the chance to try this out and feel that you were taking on our methods in exchange for something you have."

"So you didn't need Zandrian technology?" said Kaleem.

"No," said Rogin. "In fact, our technology is even more advanced than Zandrian – and largely because of our attitude to credit."

"You do make it all sound so simple," said Kaleem.

"It is simple," said Rogin. "Everyone works according to their strengths and joy. What no-one wants to do we give to the droids. We keep a high vision of how we want our world to work. We always go for abundance, never for reduction."

"Yes," said Kaleem. "I've already told you I can see it's a good idea. But we can't change overnight, and what about the darker side of people? What about those who are lazy, unskilled, those who are… different?" He could suddenly see Rozia playing with the Adulkis. How would the Zenoton deal with people like them? And hadn't other Terrestrans found the Z Zoners difficult enough to comprehend?

Rogin made a fist and tapped rapidly on the side of his comfisessel. He pursed his lips and frowned. "We've treated your friend well enough, haven't we? Our education system prepares us adequately for a world full of otherness. Yours could do the same."

That's a bit of a challenge, thought Kaleem. "We can't do that overnight, either," he said.

"No, but the Terrestrans and Zandrians have a good role model," said Rogin. He stared hard at Kaleem for a few seconds. His face softened slightly. "That's why we wanted to speak to precisely you," he continued.

Kaleem blushed.

"But it really isn't a matter of what you should do – it is what you must do," said Rogin. "Let me show you." He operated a control in the side of his chair.

A dataserve screen slid into place and covered the largest of the veriglass panels. A movie clip started playing. It was a scene from Zandra, looking a little how it did after the landquake, and as if you were looking down from a high hill. This time, though, there were no droids clearing up the rubble. The clip zoomed down to the ground. Some emaciated Zandrians in tattered clothing lay groaning on the bare earth.

"What's happened?" asked Kaleem.

"Overspending of inter-planetary credits. No-one willing to trade. No reforestation. No more self-sufficient farming. Nothing to offer in return."

The scene faded and was replaced by another, clearly at a Terrestran medi-centre and one that was startlingly full of people. Most of them looked at least as ill as Stuart had last time Kaleem had seen him. A few tired-looking medics were rushing round from person to person without really doing anything.

"What's happened to the diastics?" asked Kaleem.

"They can't be maintained," said Rogin, "without the help of the Zandrians and they are too weak to be of any help. Terrestra does not have enough inter-planetary credits to call in help from further afield."

"But isn't this just because of the problems between Terrestra and Zandra?" said Kaleem.

"Well, they don't help, but look at this," said Rogin.

Several more clips now followed each other on the screen. More pictures of starving and ill people, devastated landscapes, deserted cities and finally Zenoto, with its people looking reasonably well but definitely poor.

"All of our futures," said Rogin.

"But isn't this just one version of the future?" asked Kaleem.

"Our futurologists are usually very accurate," said Rogin. "They are free from commercial restraint."

"I just don't see that it can work," said Kaleem. "Won't people get greedy? Or lazy?"

"What do you most want, Kaleem?" asked Rogin. "What would give you the greatest joy?"

That was easy. He saw himself leading a normal life with Rozia. She would still work with the Adulkis and they would have children of their own. “What I want isn’t possible,” he whispered.

“What aren’t you contributing that makes you think you don’t deserve whatever it is that you want?” said Rogin.

Something like a physical shock went through his body. Kaleem suddenly knew exactly what he needed to do.

Rogin’s eyes penetrated right into him again. “Just take the first step,” said Rogin. The Zenoton stood up and went out of the room.

Rogin

Kaleem struck at the punch-bag. What on Terrestra, Zandra or Zenoto was he supposed to do about this? Rogin had promised he would release neither Kaleem nor Saratina until Kaleem showed that he understood. Hadn't he done that? Rogin seemed to be going back on what he'd promised. He'd made it seem so simple earlier that morning. Then he'd seemed to go back on his word and implied that detailed plans had been drawn-up, universe-wide, about the reform of the inter-planetary credit-transfer system. Now it was up to Kaleem again to do something about it.

Oh, he'd faced plenty of situations like this before. But this was by far the biggest and the one about which he had the least clues as to what he could do. He wasn't even sure, this time, if he agreed with what the Zenoton were asking for. Well, maybe he had actually agreed but had no idea how what they wanted could be put into practice.

He swung again at the punch-ball. It returned to him and he pelted it with punches. He was beginning to work up a sweat. He pushed himself. He was working faster and harder than he ever had before. He felt his heart rate increase. He punched and punched, and then punched some more. He became breathless, his sides began to ache. He had to give up finally and he flopped down on to the bench at the side of the gym.

"Reset programme?" asked the electronic voice of the dataserve.

Kaleem shook his head and waved dismissively towards the machine.

His hair was damp from the exertion and was sticking to his forehead. He pushed it away from his skin. His breathing gradually became more regular and his heart rate slowed. He took a deep breath. There would be a solution, he guessed; he just didn't know what it was yet. Yes, there would be a solution. There always was an answer. The work with the punch-bag had helped. Physical exercise always did. Some fresh air would now be good, too, but he guessed there wouldn't be too much chance of that.

He wiped the sweat from his face. He would take a shower, get dressed and then talk to someone. Who though? Who would be best for this? Razjosh? Calver Toms? Saratina? He shuddered as he realised the one person he really wanted to talk to now was Rozia. That, of course, was impossible.

The door slid open. Rogin entered. "I'm sorry to disturb you," said the Zenoton.

Kaleem blushed. "I'm sorry I'm a bit of a mess," he said. Why couldn't he have come a few minutes later?

"It doesn't bother me at all," said Rogin. "I'd wait for you to shower but I have to go down to the planet for an urgent meeting about developments. There is little time…"

"Are there any developments?" asked Kaleem.

"You tell me," said Rogin. "Are you willing to discuss this with your people? With both Zandra and Terrestra agreeing to what we propose, the rest of the universe is bound to follow."

"Terrestra's really that important?" asked Kaleem.

"The universe envies Terrestra's diastic system," said Rogin. "And anyway, before it became so isolated, Terrestra was a leading planet. After all, many races first came from there."

"The diastic system's not that good, really," said Kaleem. "It only copes with Terrestran diseases."

"It can be improved," said Rogin.

"Oh, and then wouldn't we get back to the problem about switch-off?" asked Kaleem. That he would not allow. There was to be no more switch-off.

"Doubtful," said Rogin. "New diseases will come. Old age will probably eventually happen anyway. It will mean all deaths will be peaceful ones. Bodies will just give up, eventually."

"And we'll be back to problems of over-population again," said Kaleem.

"It's hardly likely," said Rogin. "There are still many unpopulated planets."

"Yes, but the cost of making them habitable and sending people there," said Kaleem.

"There would be no cost if everyone adapts the Zenoton system," said Rogin.

"But how can you make that work?" asked Kaleem. "I still can't see what you would do about the lazy and the disillusioned?"

Rogin's eyes glazed over. "We have to build a society where no one is disillusioned and where everyone wants to contribute."

It still sounded ideal but improbable.

"But how?" asked Kaleem.

Rogin sat down on the bench next to Kaleem. He looked straight into Kaleem's eyes.

"Consult, offer, allow, make allowances, see the best everywhere," he said.

Kaleem laughed. "How can I see the best in people who keep me and a very vulnerable friend hostage?"

"You'll thank us for it one day," said Rogin. "Call it tough love."

Maybe, thought Kaleem. This wasn't actually helping much. "How do you suggest we start?" he asked.

"Get it working on Terrestra and get it working on Zandra," said Rogin. "We have it in place too. Three planets can then show the world. Start small. Start with yourself."

"How?" said Kaleem.

"Tell me what is the most important for you at the moment that we can influence," said Rogin.

That was easy. "I want Saratina to be returned safely," he replied.

"It will be done within the hour," said Rogin. "Would you like to speak to her first, though?"

Kaleem nodded.

"What else?" asked Rogin.

That was hard. He wanted the problems between him and Rozia and Ella to be solved. He wanted Stuart to get better. So much of that, though depended on them. They had to be involved, too. The Zenoton had no control over that.

"Any physical need right now?" asked Rogin.

"Well, I could do with a shower and I'm pretty hungry," said Kaleem.

Rogin laughed. "I'll leave you in peace in a moment, and you are invited to the executive suite for lunch."

"Yes, okay, I get that," said Kaleem. "But shouldn't I give you something in return?"

"No!" cried Rogin. "That's the point. Everyone takes what they need and gives what they can. If there's a mismatch, then we look for a way around it. We have had this on Zenoton now for two centuries. And we have no prisons and no one has been ordered off the planet."

It sounded fantastic.

"Try it now," said Rogin gently. "Try it whilst you're with us,"

Rogin left.

Kaleem took his shower. He opted for water rather than laser. He was able to think as the wet warmth caressed his skin.

He felt lighter as he stepped out of the shower. Sure, a laser shower would have left him cleaner but he doubted he would have felt so good afterwards.

So Saratina was going to go home. It had been that easy in the end. What was he going to have to do now to get himself released?

As he dried himself, he thought about Rogin. He was determined and obstinate, that was for sure. But he was also warm and little bit humorous. He would get his way, but his way would be well thought out and he would be absolutely sure he was right.

Kaleem liked him.

Then he realised: Rogin was just like his grandfather, Frazier Kennedy.

Kaleem's personal communicator buzzed. It was Rogin.

"If you go back to your room, Saratina will come to see you. We'll keep your table for lunch," said Rogin.

The screen went blank.

Kaleem waited in his room. He felt oddly restless. He didn't have to wait long for Saratina, though. She buzzed at the door a few moments later.

"I'm going home soon," she said. "I hope they'll let you go soon as well."

"I'm glad they're going to let you go," said Kaleem. He could see tears in her eyes.

She hugged him tightly. "I'll miss you, Kaleem," she said. "I'll miss you."

The door buzzed again.

"Come in," called Kaleem.

Two Zenoton droids and a Zenoton were standing there.

"We've come for Mz Saratina," said the Zenoton.

"I'm worried, I'm worried," said Saratina, her eyes suddenly darting backwards and forwards.

"Can I watch the transportation?" asked Kaleem.

"Of course," said the Zenoton.

A few moments later, they were in the holotransporter room. Saratina looked scared.

"You'll be fine," said Kaleem. He hoped he was right. The Zenoton seemed very capable, but you never knew, really.

The droids led Saratina gently on to the holopad. A cage came down from the ceiling and surrounded her. The room began to hum.

The Zenoton manipulated some controls. "Good morning," he said. "We are sending Mz Saratina back to Terrestra. Will you receive?"

Kaleem could not hear the reply, though some noises came from the dataserve.

There was a high-pitched squeal and the humming he'd heard earlier became louder.

Then she was gone.

The Zenoton turned to Kaleem and smiled. "Your friend is back safely on Terrestra," he said.

Kaleem felt a weight lift from his chest. Seconds later, he realised that he was now totally isolated, again. And still a prisoner.

"Sir, your lunch is waiting," said the Zenoton.

Calver's Take

Kaleem knew he had to speak to Calver. Yet he didn't want to. He didn't want to know what was happening on Terrestra or Zandra. Well, he wanted to know that Saratina was fine after her ordeal, he wanted to know that Stuart Davidson we getting better and he wanted Calver to say that yes, the Zenoton idea was great and it would be easy to implement. He somehow thought none of this would happen.

He wanted Rozia to at least speak to him again.

That wouldn't happen either.

He really needed to talk to Calver. He didn't want to talk to Calver.

He sighed. "Calver Toms, Zandra," he commanded.

Seconds later, Calver was on screen. His dark eyes stared at Kaleem. "So, the Zenoton insist," said Calver.

By all the elders, this was annoying. Calver could still read him like a book.

"They'll keep me here until at least Zandra and Terrestra try to use their trade methods," replied Kaleem.

Calver nodded.

"So what are the chances?" asked Kaleem.

"It's a big step," said Calver. "But they'll do it if you persuade them," he continued. "Start with Terrestra."

"Why?" asked Kaleem.

"You've got more at stake there," replied Calver.

"But what about my parents, and Ella? And the oak plantations?" asked Kaleem.

"Rozia, Davidson, Saratina, Razjosh, your grandparents?" answered Calver. "You'll work harder on Terrestra."

"Will I?" asked Kaleem.

Calver nodded. "Especially when you discover her secret," he said.

"Her secret? Whose secret?" asked Kaleem.

"Rozia is keeping something from you."

There was an awkward silence.

"So, how? How can I start?" asked Kaleem.

"Just as the Zenoton told you," said Calver.

"It can't be that easy."

"They seem to think so, don't they?"

Kaleem had to think for a moment. He tried to remember exactly what Rogin had said. That everybody just did what seemed right? Didn't think about cost? Was that it?

"They see it all so simply, don't they?" said Calver.

How does he know? thought Kaleem. *I haven't even told him what they said yet. How can he read me so well?*

"Why don't you try it?" said Calver. "Tell them you'll take it to Terrestra. Tell the Terrestrans you'll show them what the Zenoton want. Then just do it."

"Will the Zenoton accept that?" said Kaleem. "It seems a bit of a cop out."

Calver shrugged. "Why not try them and see?"

"But won't it take a long time?"

"Does that matter? Will they care? As long as you've started," said Calver. "Remember the water wheel on Polynket."

The screen went blank.

The water wheel on Polynket? Yes, the water wheel on Polynket. Where instead of raking around in the muck they'd just thrown more and more clean water at it and suddenly it started moving again. How did Calver know about that? Perhaps Razjosh…?

Kaleem's heart began to thump.

Babel Questions

Kaleem's heart was still pounding ten minutes later. Calver had been even worse than usual this time. He seemed to know things that he couldn't possibly know unless he could mind read.

But if Kaleem had really understood what Calver had said, and it really did tie in with what Rogin meant, like it seemed to… well, it was really easy, wasn't it?

It was getting late now. Too late to speak to Rogin and he didn't want to speak anyone on Terrestra or Zandra until he'd made absolutely certain with the Zenoton, that he and Calver had really understood it right.

Besides, always better to sleep on it.

He looked around at the Supercraft cabin. It certainly was really comfortable. Droid-made, presumably? He touched the edge of one of the beige tables. Convincing plastikholz – or something remarkably similar. Really well finished off, smooth, thick, no expense spared, apparently. Except that the Zenoton would argue it had cost nothing but an act of will.

He looked through the veriglass porthole. Zenoto looked even more like Terrestra tonight. Why wouldn't the Zenoton let him visit the planet properly?

Well, he could bargain as well. He'd ask them that tomorrow.

He suddenly felt weary. Yes, sleeping on it might be the answer. He got himself into bed as quickly as possible and fell asleep straight away.

He knew he was dreaming as soon as he saw the lawn covered in daisies. They were there, of course. He waited for one of them to turn and braced himself to confront again the slightly ugly, wrinkled face with the questioning eyes.

It was a girl who turned this time. He was a little less shocked than usual.

"Kaleem," she said. "The tower's gone."

She was right. There was nothing at all left of the tower,

except the red bricks scattered over the ground.

The girl took his hand and pulled him towards where the door into the tower had been. Some of the other Adulkis began to follow slowly. Occasionally one of them would look into his eyes. The question was still there.

Kaleem could only look away.

The girl who looked like Rozia was gathering together the fragments of the book. She turned to face Kaleem and smiled. Her almond eyes looked deep into his and as usual he felt as if she knew everything that he was thinking. It was Rozia and yet it wasn't Rozia. No, she wasn't Rozia. But he knew her just as well, just like he knew Calver Toms. There was something there that was deeper than in all the other friendships, including what he used to have with Rozia.

"You will need the book," she said. "You will still need the pages that turn and refresh themselves."

"Why?" asked Kaleem.

"I don't know the answer to that," she said, "but they do." She pointed to the Adulkis.

The little girl who was still holding his hand smiled shyly at him.

"But I do know this," the girl with the almond eyes continued. "Now that the tower has fallen, the people will scatter and they will understand each other less and less. Only if the tower is rebuilt will that be stopped. Only if the tower is rebuilt can they all live in harmony again."

Kaleem looked back down at the bricks.

"The tower is not built by bricks alone," she said. "And this time it must not be built to challenge God but as a symbol of the peace only the Peace Child can bring."

"How?" said Kaleem turning to face her.

"You will find a way," she said. "And you must ask them what they want." She nodded towards the Adulkis.

The little girl tugged at his hand again. Kaleem turned and smiled at her. "I just don't know…" he said turning back.

The Rozia girl had gone.

Two more Adulkis came up to him. “You have to help us,” one of them said.

“What do you want me to do?” asked Kaleem.

“Tell us the stories,” said the other. “Tell us the stories from all the places and in all the words. So that we can know all the people.”

“And we have to rebuild the tower,” said the girl who was holding his hand. She let go of his hand and bent down and picked up a brick. “Only our hands are too small.” She held the brick out to Kaleem.

He took it and examined it. “I don’t think I’d be very good at building a tower,” he said. *It would probably be better droid-built,* he thought.

“We need a master-builder,” said one of the other Adulkis. “And you will find, him, Kaleem, in one of the stories.”

“Tell us a story, Kaleem,” the Adulkis began to chant. This time, again, it didn’t sound like a nightmare.

He woke with a start. The communicator on his door was buzzing. “Seven twenty,” the electronic voice of the room dataserve informed him as he looked towards the machine. “Zenoton Rogin to see you.”

The dream came back to him. *Find the master builder in one of the stories,* he thought to himself. *Rebuild the tower. Read them all the stories from all the places and in all the words so that they can know all the people. Okay.*

And what does Rogin want?

“Oral contact only,” Kaleem commanded his dataserve. Rogin had seen him in his sweaty gym wear two days ago. Now he was dishevelled from a drama-filled sleep. He had to preserve some dignity.

“Kaleem, come and get breakfast,” said Rogin. “Then afterwards go to the landing deck. We’re going down to Zenoto.”

Zenoto

"So, what do you think?" asked Rogin.

Kaleem was sitting on something that was just a little more sophisticated than a comfisessel. It was even more comfortable. They were at the home of Rogin Zenoton, enjoying a small second breakfast.

The landing on Zenoto had been smooth and the planet had been almost as spectacular as Terrestra as they'd approached it. But where Terrestra looked mainly blue and white with touches of green and brown, Zenoto was mainly a deep red with splashes of emerald green, lemony yellow and pale blue.

A droid came into the room bringing a fresh jug of coffee.

"Thank you," said Rogin and smiled.

Kaleem had never seen that before. On Terrestra and Zandra and on the planets he'd visited in his hololessons, yes, sure, you always acknowledged the droids. Occasionally you might even thank them if they belonged to some high-ranking official, but to actually smile at them? Apart from Edmondson's Emmerline of course. Definitely bizarre.

The droid served the coffee and made its way out of the room.

"So what do you think of my little home?" said Rogin.

"It's er, it's great," said Kaleem. He knew he was making an understatement. This was the most luxurious home he had ever been in. It didn't have the energy-giving crystalline walls of the Citadel of Elders on Terrestra but in every other way it was just as fabulous.

He gazed out of the veriglass window. On one side were snow-capped mountains and below them was rich green meadowland. In the distance a green sea's waves caught the light of Zenoto's sun.

Kaleem took a sip of the coffee the droid had just poured. It was possibly the best he had ever tasted. It was hot, though, and burnt his tongue a little. He quickly put down his cup. His seat adjusted itself with even more precision than the comfisessels at the Citadel on Terrestra and his hand brushed against its soft surface. His shoeless feet sank into the thick-piled carpet.

“It’s good, isn’t it?” said Rogin. “I wonder whether you will ever get anything like this on Terrestra? I somehow think not, even when you become an elder. And you know what, Kaleem? It’s all droid-built. I’ve not had to work hard for this. Work yes, but my work is more like what you would call a hobby. I have made no sacrifices to be able to live here.”

“It’s good,” said Kaleem. “Very comfortable.”

Rogin grinned. “Come on, Kennedy,” he said. “It’s more than comfortable and you know it.” He laughed again. “I think we’d better send you shopping à la Zenoto.”

Forty minutes later Kaleem was climbing into a transporter destined for the centre of Zenoto’s commercial area.

“You mean you don’t just call up stuff on the dataserve?” said Kaleem.

“Well, we can do that,” said Rogin. “Of course we can. But we also like to go and inspect our goods. Touch. See them. Feel them. Smell them. Just go sometimes and browse.”

“How do I…?” Kaleem had begun to ask before he remembered.

“We have no credit system,” said Rogin. “But remember: take no more than you actually need.”

“I don’t actually need anything,” said Kaleem. “I just *want* to get home.”

Rogin smiled. “And so you shall, if you choose wisely.”

The transporter made its ways smoothly to the commercial centre. As he gazed out of the window, Kaleem realised that it wasn’t that different on Zenoto from either Terrestra or Zandra. The buildings were just as tall, there were railed roadways for public transporters and small airborne transporters, like the one he was travelling in, that flew at four distinct levels. It just all seemed a little calmer.

The transporter slowed and entered a large opening in one of the buildings. It came to rest next to a platform that looked just like the ones from which public transporters departed on Terrestra. "Good morning, sir," said a droid, as the door slid open. "Can I be of any assistance?"

"Thank you," said Kaleem, remembering what he had seen at Rogin's home that morning. "I really don't know exactly what I'm looking for yet."

"Then, sir, might I suggest that you go to Wester Mall. That is second level. Your personal communicator will guide you as you come out of the elevator. I have already programmed it and also programmed in my call sign. Just say 'droid assistance' if you require any more help and I will be at your service."

The droid accompanied Kaleem to the lift. Seconds later he was walking along the Wester Mall.

From what he could tell, people were really enjoying themselves. Shopping seemed to be a leisure activity on Zenoto. They weren't just getting things that they needed as Terrestrans and Zandrians did. And Terrestrans and Zandrians would never have gone and chosen things like this. They would just order them through the dataserve. People here were pulling small hoverbags behind them and were looking extremely pleased with themselves.

The shops were certainly colourful and invited you in. As far as he could tell, they were mainly looked after by droids. It seemed you selected what you wanted and took it to a droid who stood behind a counter. The droids seemed to quiz people about why they wanted the goods but they didn't seem to be refusing people. The machines than packed the goods into the hoverbags.

Occasionally, he spotted Zenoton working in one of the shops. Usually they would be speaking to a few of the droids or chatting to one of the customers. Kaleem suspected they were just checking everything was going well and helping to make things even better.

But there was nothing that attracted his attention. There were many things he liked the look of – some of the Zenoton clothing looked very elegant but wouldn't look right on Terrestra or Zandra. There were some bits and pieces that would look good in a home, but as he wasn't sure where his home was going to be in the future, it wouldn't be right to take anything from those stores.

There was food as well – both shops where you could find items to take home and cook and places where you could have a snack or a meal. Kaleem's feet were aching by now. He decided to stop at one of the small cafés in the centre of the wide Wester Mall. The dataserve screens showed pictures of the food and drinks and described them. There was no mention, of course, of any prices.

As soon as he sat down, a droid was at his side. "Might I suggest, sir," said the machine, "orange juice, lemon pancakes and double-brewed coffee with a slug of firewater?"

"Perfect!" said Kaleem. So, they had mind-reading machines here just like on Zandra. All that about wanting Zandrian technology had been a trick, definitely.

"Just the Zenoton way, sir," said the droid.

The food was delicious when it came. Kaleem had not realised how hungry he had become. Soon he was full, though. The droid hovered and asked him if he needed anything else.

"No, that's all, thank you," said Kaleem. That was the third time now he'd thanked a droid.

"Have a nice day, sir," said the machine as it began to clear the table. No mention of any credit transfer.

As he walked out of the café he noticed the other tables. There were a few empty ones and one or two people were coming to fill them. There were a few people waiting for food and some were already eating. There were no plates piled high. People weren't being greedy. All of the food looked fresh and colourful.

It did seem to work, then.

But now he had to find something to take back. He felt that Rogin was testing him. If he went back without the perfect item he would not be allowed back to Terrestra.

He decided to go to the far end of Wester Mall and work backwards. He took the moving pavement and fifteen minutes later he stepped off at the end of the mall. Some of the shops seemed to repeat ones he'd seen earlier, but as he walked back towards the other entrance, he did notice one or two new places.

One drew his attention. It was a small jewellery shop. In the window there were lots of brooches, ear-rings and necklaces, all made from tiny holograms of flowers. Perhaps he might find something there to take back for Marijam, Ella or Saratina. They'd all had to suffer because of him. He might be able to make it up to them this way.

The shop was almost empty. A droid was rearranging some of the displays. A Zenoton was sitting at the counter. His greying Zenoton curls and a slight stoop in his back suggested that he was quite old. His face, however, was completely wrinkle-free and his eyes were bright. He gave Kaleem a cheery smile. "Are you looking for anything in particular?" he asked.

"Maybe something for some of the women in my life," said Kaleem.

"Yes, that's normally why the men come in here," said the Zenoton. "I suggest a brooch for an older lady and maybe ear-rings, a necklace or a bracelet for a younger woman, unless she's really special then why not all three? Look at these." He pointed to the case that the droid had just rearranged.

They were all beautiful, Kaleem had to admit that. But there was nothing that screamed Marijam, Saratina, Ella or even Louish.

"Nothing?" said the Zenoton. "I wonder…" He turned to the droid. "Fetch the special."

A few moments later, the droid returned with a small box. The Zenoton took it and went back to the counter and unpacked it.

Kaleem gasped when he saw what came out of the box. It was a large brooch, the sort that might hold a scarf in place at the neck. On it was the most delicate hologram of a bunch of black Tulpen and red roses. It was exactly like the bouquet he had given Rozia the first time they'd made love. In fact it could have been a hologram of that very bouquet. The background colour was a pale blue, one of Rozia's favourite colours and one that suited her well.

"How on Zenoto did you manage to make this?" asked Kaleem.

"Oh, we have some very clever artists," replied the Zenoton. "The question for me has always been why. Why did Zarifi make this brooch? I have the answer now, I think. No need to explain why you want this one. I don't know the full story, nor do I need to know it, but it's obvious from that look on your face that this brooch absolutely belongs to you."

The Zenoton put the brooch back in its box and then put the box into a hoverbag that he attached to Kaleem's wrist.

"I think you've probably finished your shopping now," said the Zenoton. "Perhaps you will take some tea with me before you return to where you're staying? I have a feeling that you have some questions and I would like to tell you more about the brooch and find out a little about how you intend to use it. As I said, I don't need to know, but I am curious."

Yes, he did have some questions. Lots of them. He accepted the Zenoton's offer.

"I am Pendalon, Zarifi's brother, by the way," said the Zenoton as he led Kaleem out of the shopping centre. "We'll go to the Tea Parlour. It's much quieter than the Mall cafés. You can hear yourself think there."

It was just a few minutes' walk to the tea shop. It overlooked the city, but beyond the tall buildings and the transporter roads, you could see a green lake and the snow-capped mountains. Kaleem wondered whether this was the same one he could see from Rogin's home.

"That is indeed the same one as you saw this morning," said Pendalon. "Though that is a coincidence. All of our lakes are green like that. The colour comes from a weed that grows in the lakes. It is a real asset to our planet. But tell me now; who will you give the brooch to?"

"Rozia," said Kaleem. "My ex-girlfriend. If she'll have it. And if she won't take it, I'll know it's definitely over forever."

"Well, yes," said Pendalon. "The flowers of love and lust. I knew there was a romantic connection. The roses of course are from Terrestra, as are you, and that is intriguing as I know Terrestrans don't travel easily. And to choose something that has so much work put into it."

Kaleem gulped. "So that would be something that, if you actually did use credits, would cost a lot?" he said.

"Yes," said Pendalon. "Zarifi actually grew the black Tulpen and the red roses here on Zenoto in order to be able to make the holograph. Not easy. Our ecosystem does not support such flowers normally. I have no idea how he got the seeds. But he was such a perfectionist. He always found a way to do these things."

"Was?" asked Kaleem.

"Yes, he died, four years ago," said Pendalon. "Overworked. Some of us do work too hard. But it wasn't out of anxiety about not making a big enough contribution in Zarifi's case as it is with some folk. It was because it was always so important to him to get things absolutely right."

"I'm sorry," said Kaleem.

Pendalon shrugged and shook his head.

The tea arrived. Pendalon poured.

"So it really works, then, this no credit system?" asked Kaleem. "I mean for the ordinary things as well?"

"See for yourself," said Pendalon, waving his arms round at the room. "Most things are droid built. We've learnt not to be greedy and we just check that the droids do things to a very high standard. And surely, you've seen it all in action in the shops today?"

Kaleem nodded.

"And then just occasionally something really special happens," said Pendalon. "Like you and this brooch. So tell me all about her."

Kaleem touched the package next to his wrist. Suddenly it was very easy to talk about Rozia. The fact that he'd found this brooch seemed to give him permission.

"Well," he started, "Rozia was in my school group and I always liked her. But we didn't get together until after I got back from Zandra."

Pendalon's eyes grew round. He poured more tea and then sat back into his comfisessel.

"Do tell all," he said.

Rogin handed the brooch back to Kaleem. "It is truly very beautiful," he said. "Yes, Zarifi was one of our finest artists. His death was tragic."

Kaleem carefully wrapped the piece of jewellery back up and placed it in the box. It still felt as if it was very precious. Even though it had not cost him any credits, it had cost Zarifi a lot of hard work and had probably contributed to his dying so young.

"So everything isn't perfect even here, then?" said Kaleem.

"Zarifi's death was tragic for us, not for him," said Rogin. "He worked too hard, used up his two million heartbeats too quickly. He was happy all of his life. He loved his work and he was excited by it. He just needed more balance."

"Balance," repeated Kaleem.

"Is that what you can bring, Peace Child?" said Rogin. "Balance between the Terrestrans and the Zandrians? Balance into a whole universe?"

Kaleem gulped. "That wouldn't be easy, for one person," he said.

"It doesn't have to be just one person and it doesn't have to be hard, either," said Rogin. "You have seen the Zenoton way. All we ask is that you now go and practise it. Go back to Terrestra. See what's needed that you can provide. Take what you need, but only what you need. And do it all in joy. And what you can provide is more than good enough."

Rogin stood up and looked out of the window. It was beginning to get dark and the whiteness of the snow was catching the last light from the sun. It was like on Terrestra, yet it was different as well. "Do you like our planet?" he said.

"Yes, I do," said Kaleem.

Rogin turned to face him. "Then you must spend two more days here before we send you back," he said. "And when your work on Terrestra is done, you must come and visit for a longer time." He nodded towards the box with the brooch. "Perhaps you might bring a companion with you."

Back to Terrestra

"We won't tell you the secret of how we manage to do this," said Rogin, "until you Terrestrans are ready to use the holotransporter or really have a need for it. You don't even want to leave your planet yet. And we certainly wouldn't let you use it just to get people to Terrestra more quickly – except you and Saratina, of course."

Kaleem wished he would get on with it. He wasn't looking forward to this. But if they could only get started, he would be back on Terrestra within the hour.

"So I'm guessing that next time we see you, you will come by Supercraft. A three Terrestran month journey. A real opportunity to spend quality time with a special companion."

"So, you don't think I'll be successful with changing Terrestran habits?" said Kaleem.

"Not that quickly," said Rogin. "But you will change them. You're changed yourself. You just need to hold on to that. Remember, just do what needs to be done, and be yourself."

"Okay," said Kaleem. "What I need to do right now, I think, is get back to Terrestra."

Rogin grinned. "Good. If you would take your place on the holopad…"

Kaleem's legs were trembling as he stepped on to the pad. *Why do I keep doing these things?* he asked himself. This would be the fourth time he had used a form of teletransportation. It ought to be less risky this time – the Zenoton seemed to have pinned down the science of it and he would be doing it with their blessing. But it was still scary. What if he got stuck? And it had not been particularly pleasant the other times… though that weighed against three months on a Supercraft…?

He'd got to do it, so best just get on with it.

"Okay," said Rogin. "We're activating now."

The pad began to vibrate a little. A loud hum surrounded him. Then he was no longer looking at Rogin. Colours swirled around him. He felt as if he was turning head over heels over and over. His ears were ringing and he felt nauseous. The noise in his ears and the hum outside got louder and louder.

He thought he wouldn't be able to bear it a moment longer. He screamed. That seemed to help a little, but the dizziness and the noise just got worse and worse. The screaming now seemed to add to it so he stopped.

Then there was as sudden jolt. Now it was completely quiet. He felt solid floor beneath his feet. His mouth was dry and he was incredibly thirsty. His vision cleared and he could see he was in a holoroom on Terrestra. It seemed to be whizzing round as well but gradually it slowed down and eventually stopped.

"Welcome back," said Danielle. "Thank goodness you're okay."

I've never felt so thirsty, thought Kaleem.

"He should go on diastics," said the droid that was assisting. She walked over to Kaleem with a hand set.

His legs gave way and he sat down on the floor. The droid put the pad to his hand. An alarm sounded immediately.

"Great elders," said Danielle. "You're setting off alarms again."

"It's massive dehydration," said the droid. "A side-effect of Zenoton teletransportation. He just needs water."

Seconds later, another droid appeared carrying a beaker. Kaleem took it and gulped down the water.

"More?" asked Danielle.

Kaleem nodded. He drank the second beaker full just as quickly. The droid brought him a third. Half way through that, the thirst began to subside.

Danielle sighed. "We should be debriefing you about the Zenoton now," she said. "But I'm afraid I've got some rather bad news about Razjosh."

Kaleem's heart started to beat violently.

"What about Razjosh?" he asked.

Danielle sighed and shook her head. "Razjosh Elder suffered a massive stroke two days ago," she said.

“I should go and see him,” said Kaleem.

“He may not know you,” said Danielle. “He’s barely conscious and he cannot communicate at all.”

“How come diastics didn’t stop it?” asked Kaleem. “Why didn’t you let me know?”

“They are not programmed for old age,” said Danielle. “This is the beginning of the end of Terrestran perfection. And we didn’t want to let you know because you wouldn’t have been able to do anything from Zenoto.” She sighed. “You can’t do anything anyway.”

“I’d still like to see him,” said Kaleem.

The dataserve screen lit up. Edmundson’s face appeared. Emmerline was visible by his side.

“Well, Mz Thomas, have you begun the debrief yet?” he asked. He didn’t look at Kaleem.

“I, er, think there’s something he’d rather do first,” said Danielle.

“Oh?” asked Edmundson.

Emmerline nudged him. “He wants to go and see Elder Razjosh,” she said.

Edmundson frowned. “Very well then,” he said, sighing again. “One hour only. Then I want to know everything you’ve discussed with the Zenoton.”

Thoughts tumbled around Kaleem’s head. Was Razjosh about to die? Was it going to be a painful death? One that would make him want to cry and scream that they should bring back switch-off? And did this mean that diastics, after all that, weren’t that much use? Would Terrestrans now be more willing to leave the planet and let others come here? He guessed it wouldn’t happen overnight. And surely nobody would expect him to make that whole change go more quickly than it wanted to go?

“Go on then,” said Edmundson. “Get him over there.”

Kaleem remembered what Rogin had said.

“What the Zenoton want will actually be very easy to provide,” he’d said. “There will be change. But it will happen gradually.”

Edmundson raised an eyebrow. “Okay. Call me up when you’re back from seeing Razjosh.” The dataserve screen went blank.

Kaleem dreaded what he now had to do but knew that he must.

Razjosh

The room in the Citadel was darkened, and beyond the clinical smell Kaleem now associated with medical centres, there was something else he also recognised: the smell of illness. It wasn't really a smell as such, more a sort of atmosphere. One of hopelessness and weariness. He remembered it from when he was ill himself and from when he had watched his mother and then Rozia in their comas. He felt it too, when he'd visited Pierre and Stuart. Narisja. And now it was Razjosh. That was quite a lot of illness considering he lived on a planet that was supposed to know no illness.

Anthea was sitting at the elder's bedside. She was holding his hand. A medic droid was pottering in the background. Anthea smiled at Kaleem and gestured that he should sit down.

"How is he?" asked Kaleem.

Razjosh looked grey and his lips were tinged with blue. Anthea also looked very pale. There were dark circles round her eyes. Kaleem guessed that she had not slept since Razjosh became ill.

Anthea shook her head. "Not good," she said.

"Is he in a coma?" asked Kaleem.

"No," said Anthea. "He wakes quite often and the really sad thing is that he wants to tell me things and he can't."

Anthea put her hand over her eyes. Her shoulders began to shake. Kaleem knew that she was crying.

He put his hand on her shoulder. She patted his hand and turned and smiled at him again. "I'm sorry," she said. She looked back at the sleeping elder and stroked his face. "I'll miss him so much."

"I'll miss him, too," said Kaleem.

"Of course you will," said Anthea. She turned back to face Kaleem. "It's such a pity he didn't have time to tell you all that he had found out about the Babel story. This happened just as he'd finished going through the last of those strange voice files."

“Did he talk to you about it?” asked Kaleem.

“All the time,” said Anthea. “Don’t worry about it, though, it is all recorded. Some on movie clips and sound files but a lot of it in Wordtext. He seemed confident that you would understand.”

Kaleem nodded. “Oh yes,” he said. “I can read Wordtext. It’s one of the most useful things I’ve ever learnt to do.”

Anthea turned to face him. “There was one thing he said that really surprised me,” she said. “He said he thought there might be something in it after all. The Babel prophecy. But that it wasn’t the way anyone supposed. The main point was that the tower needs to be rebuilt, not to be brought down.”

That again. Kaleem tried to get his head round it. The story said that people built the tower to show off to God and that God was angry so he made the tower fall and made people speak different languages so that they couldn’t understand each other.

Right, well first of all, there was no such thing as God. And even if there was, wouldn’t he / she / it get angry again if the tower was rebuilt?

The language thing? Perhaps people started off in the same place and then moved away from each other so their language changed? And their customs and habits and ways of seeing things. That was a bit more believable. It was Kaleem’s job to bring them back together…

“Yes, there’s a lot to think about, isn’t there?” said Anthea. The tears were forming in her eyes again. “And he would have so liked to talk to you about it.”

Razjosh moved and groaned. His eyes opened. He saw Kaleem and managed to smile. He opened his mouth and tried to speak. No words came, though. All he managed was a strangled croak. He managed to lift his arm a little and pointed to the dataserve screen.

What did he want?

He managed to grab Kaleem’s hand and pushed it out flat. The elder then traced a W onto Kaleem’s palm. He then traced an O.

Wordtext! thought Kaleem. “Load Wordtext alphabet,” he

commanded the dataserve.

Razjosh managed to nod his head.

Kaleem pointed to the E. Razjosh nodded. He pointed to other letters and Razjosh would either nod or shake his head. Letters started appearing on the top half of the screen.

Both Kaleem and the dataserve managed to guess some of the words Razjosh was trying to say. Gradually a message started appearing.

E BD

RE BUILD

"Rebuild tower!" cried Kaleem.

Razjosh nodded.

PATTE

"Patterson," said Kaleem.

Razjosh nodded.

AN

The dataserve offered AND.

Razjosh nodded.

OTHE

The dataserve offered OTHERS.

The dataserve managed to work out SAME IDEAS. THEREFORE DREAMS

"RE BUILD TOWER. PATTERSON AND OTHERS SAME IDEAS. THEREFORE DREAMS," Kaleem read from the dataserve screen. It sort of made sense, he guessed.

Razjosh nodded and sighed. He seemed to whistle as he breathed out. Then he kept gasping for breath.

"No," whispered Anthea. "No!" She covered her eyes and her shoulders shuddered.

A strange rattling sound now came from the elder's chest.

Kaleem felt as if there were a tennis ball in his throat.

The medic droid hovered near the bed.

Anthea took Razjosh's hand. The colour drained from his face and the very slight pinkness in his cheeks turned to blue.

"The elder's life systems are failing," said the droid. "No reversal possible."

Kaleem leaned forward and put his arm around Anthea. He placed his other hand over those of Anthea and Razjosh.

The rattle in Razjosh's chest became even more alarming. It seemed to go on and on. Then it stopped suddenly. The elder gave a little cough and some yellow bile escaped from his mouth. The rattle started again only louder still and then turned into a constant creak. Then it stopped. There was a silent pause and then a final sigh, and Kaleem saw the life leave the old man. Razjosh now looked like a piece of paper.

"The elder has passed," said the droid. "In ten minutes I shall return to lay him out. Please say your goodbyes."

The machine trundled out of the room.

Kaleem looked at Razjosh's body. That was no longer his friend and mentor. That was just an empty piece of flesh.

He knew he should try to comfort Anthea but he had nothing to offer. The most important person in the world to him after Marijam and Rozia had gone.

"I'm afraid the elder has passed," Kaleem heard the droid say.

"Oh," a voice gasped. "So I'm too late?"

Kaleem's heart started to race. He would know that voice anywhere.

"I'm afraid so," said the droid. "Mizz Anthea and Mister Kaleem are saying their goodbyes. Do you wish to join them?"

"I don't know," said the visitor.

The droid had already opened the door.

"Would you mind if Mizz Rozia joined you?" asked the droid.

Kaleem stood up. His hand went instinctively to his pocket and the small box containing the black Tulpen and rose brooch.

"Of course not," whispered Anthea, her voice hoarse with suppressed tears. "Please come in."

Rozia gasped as her eyes met Kaleem's.

He swallowed.

"I'm so sorry," said Rozia, turning to Anthea. "I'm so very, very sorry."

She put her arm round Anthea and then leant forward and squeezed Kaleem's hand.

It was too much. Kaleem had to turn away. He could not stop the tears that began to pour down his cheeks.

A Wake for an Elder

The Ceremonial Temple was very different from the last time he'd seen it. That had been at Razjosh's attempted switch-off. Now that switch-off was no more, the Temple was being used in an entirely different way. They were calling it a wake.

"They used to have wakes," Ben Alki explained, "in the days when they were not so good at diagnosing death. They would watch the body for several days, just in case the deceased really wasn't. Dead, that is. They'd make a lot of noise. We've turned wakes into parties. Post-switch-off celebrations."

Frazier Kennedy had thought of the idea. "They used to call it lying in state," he said. "It will give people who didn't manage to see Razjosh after he became ill the chance to say goodbye."

Kaleem had been astounded at the number of people who had trooped into the Temple to walk slowly past Razjosh's open casket. On the first day, he reckoned the whole population of London Harbour had been there. Today, two days on, it looked like mainly Z Zoners – or should he say New Zoners?

All sorts of people came. Some wept, some put flowers in the casket and some even leant over and kissed the elder. Kaleem had not yet managed to bring himself to go and look at his former teacher. All he could remember was how the last time he'd seen him, Razjosh had seemed to turn into a piece of paper and how the vile yellow bile had come out of his mouth.

The crowds were thinning a little now. He would go just before they closed the Palace for the evening.

The door opened and Louish bustled in.

"Come on, grandson mine," she said. "You can't put this off any longer."

The last few of the New Zoners were making their way down from the platform where Razjosh's coffin lay on a table.

Louish hooked her arm through his and led him up the steps. She walked quickly. He could not help but keep up with her. He couldn't breathe. He thought he was going to pass out. He did not want to look at what was in that casket. It would not be Razjosh.

He closed his eyes as they got nearer. Louish stopped walking. She freed herself from his arm.

"Oh, he looks so peaceful," she said.

Kaleem opened his eyes. She was right. Razjosh did look peaceful. He could just have been sleeping. The greyness had gone and his cheeks even had a little tinge of pink in them.

Louish leant forward and kissed the elder's forehead. "Sleep well, old man," she whispered. She stepped back.

"Go on," she said. "Touch him. It will help."

Kaleem leant forward and touched Razjosh's face. It didn't feel cold and hard as he'd expected. It was cool, yes, and although not exactly soft, it wasn't rigid either. Just like paper, in fact.

Everything that he'd done with the elder suddenly flashed in front of him, the lessons they'd had, the harsh words and the kind ones that he'd spoken and all the wisdom Razjosh had given him. He wanted to say something, but he couldn't find any words. Then he could almost hear Razjosh's voice.

"Enough, young man. Go on. Get on with it, then."

Louish rubbed his back.

"Are you all right?" she asked.

Kaleem managed to nod. He touched Razjosh's hand.

The door to the Temple opened. Kaleem turned to look. Three people crept in: Rozia, Pierre and Stuart.

His heart leapt.

"I thought you'd need your friends around you this evening," said Louish.

She turned and hurried out of the Temple.

Pierre, Rozia and Stuart made their way slowly up towards Razjosh's coffin. Kaleem noticed that Stuart was walking a little better. Rozia kept her eyes on the ground, but when they arrived level with Kaleem she looked up and smiled at him.

His heart leapt again. She blushed and looked away.

Stuart and Pierre nodded to Kaleem and went up closer to Razjosh.

"He was a good elder," Kaleem heard Pierre say.

"Yeah, I didn't always think so, though," said Stuart. "I used to think he was really suspect. That stupid father of mine."

"He was a really nice man," said Rozia. She looked up at Kaleem. "You're really going to miss him, aren't you?" she said.

Kaleem nodded.

"Goodbye, old man," said Pierre.

Stuart continued to stare at the coffin. Pierre made his way over to Kaleem.

"Look, I know we didn't part on the best of terms," he said. "But I'm really glad you got back all right. And I'm really sorry about Razjosh. I shouldn't have shouted at you like that. I was just worried about him, that's all."

"I understand," said Kaleem. "How is he, actually?"

Pierre grinned. "He's a little better. Listen, why don't we all go to a nectar bar? We can have a natter about old times. And Razjosh. What do you say?" He turned to Rozia. "And you of course as well, Rozia," he said.

"I'm sorry, I can't," said Rozia. "There is somewhere I have to be."

"You'll come, though, won't you Kaleem?" said Pierre.

Kaleem nodded.

"Kaleem," said Rozia, "can you come and see me tomorrow? There is someone I want you to meet." She blushed bright red and looked at the floor. Then she looked up at him again. "Please," she said. "It's important." Her eyes danced, just like they used to. But she wasn't smiling this time.

Something sank in Kaleem.

She turned and made her way out.

"Poor old thing," said Stuart as he limped over to Kaleem and Pierre.

Kaleem had the oddest feeling that Stuart meant him and not Razjosh.

"I'll see you tomorrow, then," said Rozia. "First thing?"

Kaleem nodded.

"The New Laguna?" asked Pierre.

Kaleem nodded again.

They set off slowly to towards the exit of the Temple.

I'm doing it again, thought Kaleem. *Hanging around with Pierre when everything else is black.*

He put his hand in his pocket again and touched the brooch. He guessed he wouldn't need that, then. He supposed he was going to have to meet the new man in her life tomorrow. She'd moved on. There'd been Julien and now there was someone else. That's what he'd wanted her to do. But it still hurt.

Next Steps

The New Laguna was full when they got there. It was impossible to get to the bar and the droids could not get through to serve them. People were shouting their orders over the heads of others and then passing over the drinks and iris readers. People stared at Stuart, though: it was so unusual to see anybody walking with a stick, even though several New Zoners were now visiting the Normal Zones more often and many of them walked with a stick.

Some people got up from a table near the door and nodded to Stuart. The three of them were able to sit down.

"The silver lining," said Stuart with a grin.

"That's a terrible thing to say," said Pierre. But he was grinning too. "It's funny, isn't it?" said Pierre. "How everybody comes to this particular bar when something big happens?"

"Don't they go to the other ones as well?" asked Kaleem, and then immediately regretted it. That was a sure way of showing them just how pathetic he was, socially.

"Well, yes, they do get pretty full," said Pierre. "But this always seems to be the most popular place when the most important stuff happens."

Kaleem nodded. It was true, he guessed. His parents had met here the day the poison cloud disappeared. And he had come here when Elder Joshran Kemnat had been switched-off. Now the information screens were full of pictures of Razjosh. His was the first natural old-age death after switch-off had been abandoned. And he had been a great elder.

Kaleem swallowed. He wasn't sure he was going to be able to drink or talk.

"What will you have?" asked Pierre." My shout. Huh!" He looked towards the bar. "Literally by the looks of it."

"Wheat and rye," Kaleem managed to say.

"Yuk!" said Stuart. "I don't know how you can!" He turned to Pierre. "Make mine an apricot and vanilla."

Pierre frowned. "But your meds," he said.

Stuart shrugged. "Well get me a water to drink alongside. It won't hurt for once, will it? Anyway, they've probably watered it down to make it go further tonight," he said. He hoisted himself up out of his chair. "I'm going to go and take a leak or I'll wet myself if I start drinking. Can't control the old bladder so well these days."

Pierre ordered the drinks. They'd arrived before Stuart got back.

"It's affected his waterworks, then?" asked Kaleem.

Pierre shrugged. "A bit, maybe. He's milking it you know. You know what he's like."

"And what about…?" *Putrid elders,* thought Kaleem. *What a thing to ask him! Perhaps they've made the nectar stronger, not weaker.*

Pierre grinned again. "He's just started to manage again," said Pierre. "I can tell you, I was missing that. But he seems to be getting better."

Not quickly enough, though, thought Kaleem. *If only he'd let me get them some help from Zandra.*

"He still has to take a lot of medication, though?" he said.

"Not too much, actually," said Pierre. "But yes, some, and he shouldn't mix it with alcohol."

"Can doing that hurt him then?" asked Kaleem. "Or does it stop the drugs working?"

Pierre shook his head. "No, it just makes him get drunker quicker. Which, of course, he quite enjoys."

It sounded as if the old Stuart was coming back.

Pierre nodded towards the door. Stuart was walking quite quickly towards them. As soon as he saw them, though, he began to limp.

"See what I mean?" said Pierre.

"Right, you two, you can stop talking about me," said Stuart. He sat down at the table and took up his glass of apricot and vanilla. He swallowed a mouthful. "So, do tell. What's the goss?"

Pierre leant over towards Stuart and stroked his head. Stuart pulled Pierre over to him and kissed his forehead. "I was just telling Kaleem here how you're coming back to me," said Pierre.

"Oh, yes, coming," said Stuart. "You know, you're wicked, Pierre LaFontaine, talking dirty like that in front of Kaleem. He is the Peace Child, you know."

Kaleem laughed. "Don't mind me," he said.

Take it easy, he could hear Rogin saying. *Just what they need, not what you think they ought to have.* He couldn't help himself, though. "You know they could cure you completely on Zandra, don't you?" he said to Stuart.

Pierre and Stuart both sat back stiffly. The comfisessels drifted away a little from the table. They looked at each other.

Pierre cleared his throat and took a sip of his nectar. "We know you're right," he said. "But…"

"Travelling in those Supercraft scares the shit out of me," said Stuart.

It was that simple? There must be a way round it.

"Well, maybe the Zandrians could come here," said Kaleem. "Or we could put you out for the whole journey. Or we could get the Zenoton technology to work here. You know, the way they got me back."

Both Pierre and Stuart were staring at him. Was he going on too much? He took a gulp of his nectar. It was sickly sweet and very strong. His head began to spin. He started to splutter.

Pierre thumped him on the back. "Steady on," said Pierre. "We know you're right. But, you know, he was so bad just before you disappeared. I really thought I was going to lose him." Pierre's voice was hoarse.

Stuart leant towards Pierre and pulled him towards him. He kissed him on the lips. "I told you I wasn't going anywhere," he whispered as he pulled away.

Kaleem felt awkward. Not because they were complex-gendered, but because he could see they were so much in love. He envied them. This wasn't likely to happen for him again. But he knew what it was like and he missed that.

"Hey," said Pierre, rubbing Kaleem's arm. "You know, we calmed down just after you left that day. And we were really worried about you while you were away. Both of us were."

Stuart nodded. "I'll be brave," he said.

"You do want to get better, then?" said Kaleem.

"Yes, I want to stop feeling tired, I want to show this fine young specimen here what I really think of him and I want to get rid of that damned stick."

"Oh, so you really do need it?" said Kaleem.

"What have you been telling him?" said Stuart. He punched Pierre's arm.

"The truth," said Pierre.

"Well, he's right about one thing," said Stuart. "I do put it on a bit. I do try to look better than I actually feel. Yes, I am better than I was, but I could do with feeling less lousy than this." He turned to Pierre. "Sorry, mate, I'm really tired now."

"I think we're going to have to go," said Pierre.

"Oh, but we'll finish the drinks first," said Stuart. "Will the Zandrians help?" he asked Kaleem. "Will they start accepting our acorns again?"

Kaleem thought of the devastated woodlands on Zandra. "They could certainly do with them," he said. "I'm sure we can arrange some sort of exchange. We needn't even have any credits involved."

Stuart suddenly went white and then slumped forward unconscious on to the table.

"I'll have to take him home," said Pierre. "Don't worry. He still does this quite often."

A few moments later, Kaleem was helping Pierre get Stuart into a transporter. "The sooner you can set something up the better," said Pierre.

"I'll get on to it first thing tomorrow," said Kaleem.

The transporter set off. As he watched it disappear into the distance, Kaleem felt lost. He thought about the half-finished glass of nectar. He still didn't like the stuff, but he didn't mind the effect it had.

He pushed his way back into the bar. It seemed even more crowded now, if that was possible. Amazingly, though, his drink was still there and the three sessels were still empty. He sat down and took a sip of the wheat and rye. At least sitting in a bar with other young people made him feel a bit more normal. Maybe he would manage to get talking to somebody else. He looked around. No, it didn't seem likely. Everybody was totally engrossed in their conversations.

He settled to looking at one of the information channels. There was nothing particularly interesting at the moment. Just some news about the latest holoholidays.

He may as well just go back to his the apartment. He was staying in his grandparents' old place. Maybe he would be able to sleep now. And Louish had been right. It had helped seeing Razjosh, appearing to be fast asleep. It had been so horrible watching him die.

He took a final sip of his nectar and got up to leave.

A news bulletin came on to the screen.

"Thousands of visitors have streamed to the wake of Razjosh Elder," said the droid presenter. "His departure ceremony and life celebration will take place in two days' time. Only a fraction of the people who would like to be present may attend but every public place will accommodate people who wish to watch the ceremonies in the company of others. Large screens will be provided.

"The passing of Razjosh Elder means that we must have a new senior Peace Child and of course that means that Kaleem Kennedy will be inaugurated as a slightly young elder."

Oh yes, that, thought Kaleem. He suddenly felt very conscious again of his bright blond hair. He went to leave. He hoped he could get out before they started showing pictures of him.

"His inauguration ceremony will take place in six weeks time," said the presenter.

Nice of them to tell me, thought Kaleem.

The first photo came up on the screen. Out of the corner of his eye he saw someone look his way and then nudge the person standing next to them.

Kaleem walked out of the bar as quickly as he could. As soon as he was up on the surface, he resolved, he would send for his grandfather's transporter.

Rozia

Rozia stared out of the apartment window. But she wasn't really seeing anything that was going on in the town below. She was glad she'd seen Kaleem. She didn't hate him anymore. Not that she ever had really. She could never hate him. He'd looked so fragile tonight. Now he was going to take on this huge responsibility and she longed to help him through it. He wouldn't let, her, though.

It was almost as if Julien had never existed. No, that wasn't true. She missed him still. He had been so funny and always so cheerful. Despite all of the problems with Petri. It was terrible what had happened to him.

She wondered how Kaleem was getting on with Stuart and Pierre. She smiled to herself. It would be good for him to have a bit of pleasant company. It wasn't ever easy for him with all of his Peace Child duties, especially now that he was going to become the Peace Child Elder. Gosh, what she wouldn't give for an evening out! But it just wasn't possible. Not with Petri.

At least she'd been asleep when Rozia got back. If she'd have known that she could have stayed out longer. She just didn't have the energy though. Not anymore.

Still, it was peaceful looking out at the lights of the city at night. All those people still busy and up and about and doing things. And here she we quiet and cosy in her apartment. And Petri was asleep.

She decided to have a glass of nectar while she could. There was some apple in the fridge, she thought. That would do nicely.

As she walked through the lounge she caught her reflection in the mirror. Even in this dim light she could see that she looked dreadful.

That won't do at all, she thought. Her hair looked dull and matted. There were dark circles around her eyes again. Could she get away with an early night? Would Petri let her sleep? The nectar would help. *Frega would be even better,* she thought.

She poured herself a glass and then started to run a bath. She chose a really good conditioner for her hair. She remembered she had some of that perfume that Kaleem liked so much.

The hot water felt good. Her hair was silkier and had more body after she'd washed and conditioned it. She felt altogether much livelier. She took another few sips of the nectar. Yes, it was all good. And tomorrow she would see Kaleem again. She would have to get rid of those dark circles around her eyes, though.

The water began to cool. She pulled herself up out of the bath and switched on the laser drier. It was better than a towel. It actually moisturised the skin at the same time. That too was soothing.

She looked at herself in the mirror again. The dark circles looked if anything even blacker.

Suddenly she was wide awake. What was she thinking? Her mouth went dry and her heart began to thud. She could not get into another relationship with Kaleem. She had Petri to think about now. She wouldn't be able to support him the way he needed her to. She would need his help more than he needed hers. It wouldn't be fair to him.

Oh, and for the sake of all the elders, why was she even thinking that way? What about Julien? Thinking about Kaleem like this meant that she was being disloyal to Julien. He was such a good man. He didn't deserve that.

Putrid elders, she was still in love with Kaleem, still loved him and she'd forgiven him. She understood. She really did. He had his Peace Child work just as she had Petri. And the Adulkis. It was actually so similar.

What about Julien, though? What had that been all about?

Hmm. It had been a different sort of loving, actually. Just as valid. He'd been good for her and she'd been good for him and they were both good for Petri. But what she felt for Kaleem was something totally different. There could never be anything like that again. Maybe she should put him off coming.

Petri screamed. She was clearly in pain again. Worse than ever, by the sounds of it.

Rozia rushed towards the child's bedroom. "I'm coming, I'm coming," she whispered. "I'll try to make it better."

No, she couldn't give her attention to anybody else, except when she was working with the Adulkis and that was work, after all. So she should let Kaleem come. He needed to see Petri and understand about her.

Petri screeched. "It hurts, Rozia," she cried. "It really hurts."

"I'm coming, I'm coming, Pet," called Rozia dimming the lights before she opened Petri's door.

Yes, Kaleem must definitely meet Petri so that he could understand all of this.

Connections

The flat seemed emptier than ever when he got back. He sighed as he remembered watching the activity at London Harbour with his arm around Rozia in the mornings. The big dining table looked absurd for one. It had been much more inviting when Louish had piled it up for breakfasts for herself, him, Rozia and Frazier.

Soon, he supposed, they'd be trying to persuade him to move to the Community of Elders. Well, why not? It wasn't as if he would be a prisoner there. And this place was too big for him. He'd spend some time on Zandra anyway.

Yes, time to move on.

He shuddered at the thought of what he was going to have to do the next day. But once he'd seen her again, with the new man in her life, he could let her go once and for all. Her second new man after him. She was doing so much better than he was. There had just been that pathetic attempt at goodness know what with Ella. Yes, he'd get absorbed in his new responsibilities. With what he'd learnt from the Rogin and the Zenoton he would probably be fine. There was always Calver as well.

Calver! He should call him up. He'd probably have some idea how tomorrow might go. "Calver Toms," he commanded the dataserve.

The machine sprang into life. However, instead of Calver's call-sign ID being announced straight away, the dataserve seemed to spend a lot of time searching. *Must be a dodgy connection to Zandra,* thought Kaleem. But the machine carried on chuntering to itself. It went on and on. Normally, if there was a problem with getting a connection, a dataserve would report it after five minutes.

"What's going on?" asked Kaleem. "Is there a problem with reaching Zandra?"

"Connections to Zandra are stable," answered the machine. "Tracking identity of one Calver Toms is proving impossible."

"What do you mean?" asked Kaleem.

"Calver Toms does not exist," said the dataserve.

"That can't be right," said Kaleem. "There must be records of when I spoke to him before."

"No Calver Toms files," repeated the machine.

"What, has someone deleted them all?" asked Kaleem.

"No record of any files. Search of databases for Calver Toms identity in place." The machine whirred and clicked for another ten minutes. "No matches found," it said.

"That's incredible," said Kaleem. "Get me Don Edmundson."

The machine whirred again and Edmundson's face appeared on the screen.

"Evening, Kennedy," said Edmundson. "You look a bit agitated."

A bit, thought Kaleem. *You'd be a bit agitated if someone had disappeared on you.*

"I can't get hold of Calver Toms," said Kaleem. "The dataserve here's telling me he doesn't exist."

"Interplanetary blip, I should think," said Edmundson. "Emmerline," he called. "Call up Toms' files and call him up as well."

Edmundson was clearly watching what the droid was doing. He frowned slightly.

"Seems there is a problem," he said. He turned back to Kaleem. "So what are your plans, then?"

Kaleem sighed. "I'll probably come to Zandra for a short while, after the ceremony," he said. "We need to get some more medical help for Stuart Davidson. I need to look at the acorn situation and see what I can negotiate." *And I'll have to get away from her,* he thought.

He heard Emmerline's electronic voice say something but he couldn't make out what.

"Really?" said Edmundson. "Great elders and executives." He turned to Kaleem. "It seems you're right, Kennedy. Your friend Calver Toms does not exist, nor ever has. What on Zandra have you been playing at?"

"I didn't do anything," said Kaleem. Where was Calver? He seemed to have been, – well, deleted. Or even not have been there at all in the first place.

The dataserve peeped to tell him that he had an incoming call.

"I'll be watching you," Edmundson said.

The screen went blank then opened up to show Nazaret.

The usual frisson went through Kaleem as he stared at an older version of himself. Nazaret looked tired.

"Hi Kaleem," said Nazaret. "Will you be coming home soon?"

My home's here, thought Kaleem. *Has to be. No, wait a minute.* If he was the Peace Child, he had two homes.

Always just do the next thing, he heard Rogin's voice in his head. The next thing had got to be getting the acorns flowing again to Zandra. Getting the Terrestrans and Zandrians to talk to each other again. Easy, then.

Just the next thing, he heard Rogin's voice again.

"Well?" said Nazaret.

"I'll come back with you for a couple of weeks after the ceremony," said Kaleem.

"Good," said Nazaret. "Your mother will be pleased."

"Is she all right?" asked Kaleem. Why hadn't she come to the communication console?

"Absolutely fine," said Nazaret. "But she wanted me to ask you without her there. You see, we'd like another child. How do you feel about a brother or a sister?"

Nazaret looked even more worried now.

Another freak like me? thought Kaleem. *I wonder if he or she will have blond hair.*

"Strictly the new way," said Nazaret.

"Cool," said Kaleem. He meant it. It would be really great.

The tension went out of Nazaret's face.

"How are the plantations doing?" asked Kaleem.

"Good," said Nazaret, now grinning. "But we could still do with more acorns."

"So, I'll just have to get you some," said Kaleem. He stared at

Nazaret. He was okay, actually. And hc was his father.

"Good," said Nazaret. "And good about the baby. See you soon."

The screen went blank.

So, he would just have to work out how to get the rest of them talking again.

Petri

He'd left the transporter at the corner of the road and walked the last 500 metres to Rozia's apartment. Now he was worried that he might be a bit sweaty. But his blue satin tunic and leggings still looked smooth and smart, he noticed, as he checked his reflection in the glass of the apartment block door.

All he had to do now was press the buzzer and she would let him in. He was exactly on time.

He didn't think he could speak though. His stomach churned. It was like when they'd first got together. He'd felt like that every time they met. Today, though, there was the added worry about how he'd react when he met this new man of hers. Would he be able to keep his feelings in check? Would he be able to be polite?

He pressed the buzzer. The dataserve sprang into life at once. She hadn't put it on visual.

"Kaleem?" he heard that familiar voice say. His heart sprang. Was there a trace of excitement in it? Certainly, there was a little breathlessness.

"Hi, yes, I'm here," he managed to say.

"Come on up," she said. "Fourth floor."

The door slid open and he walked in. His heart was bouncing off his rib cage now.

The lift seemed to take forever to arrive and even longer to crawl to the fourth floor, and yet at the same time it seemed to be arriving too quickly. Then he was there. The lift stopped. He stepped out. The door to her apartment was open already and then there she was, even prettier than usual in a deep pink silky tunic.

He wanted to rush forward and scoop her into his arms and smother her with kisses, but couldn't give himself permission to do that. What would he think, the other guy, who was no doubt waiting behind the door?

She blushed. That made her look even more beautiful. "Come in then," she said. Her voice was hoarse. So, she was nervous too.

He followed her into the apartment. It was neat, and tidy, and

Rozia-like, but seemed to lack the fun that she normally brought to everything she did. A small table, he noticed, was set with coffee cups and small plates for two.

Where was the other guy, then? Was he coming later?

"It's good to see you again," said Rozia. "You look very well, especially considering. Everything. The Zenoton. Razjosh."

"You look good, too," he said.

She did, but he thought there was something not quite right. Sure, she had put as much effort into looking good as he had. But beyond the carefully and minimally applied make-up, the pretty tunic and her normal graceful movements, Kaleem sensed a tiredness. It was there in her eyes and in a slight stoop in her shoulders.

"Will you have some coffee?" she said. "And I've bought some stottie rolls." She blushed really deeply again.

Kaleem remembered the first time they had had stottie rolls with their breakfast. That had been just as they were getting to know each other. He wished he could go back to that time.

"So where's…?" asked Kaleem. He had to know who this man was.

"Petri?" said Rozia. "Oh, she's still asleep. She'll be awake soon enough and then we'll have no time to talk. I just wanted to enjoy a few minutes peace and quiet with you first."

Kaleem thought he was going to choke on the piece of stottie in his mouth. She? Surely Rozia wasn't complex-gendered?

Someone screamed loudly. It sounded as if it was coming from the corridor just outside.

Rozia's shoulders sagged. "So much for peace and quiet," she said.

The door from the back corridor slid open. A small figure wandered in. A very little girl with long frizzy ginger hair and very pale skin covered in freckles hobbled into the room. Her legs seemed to be supported by metal tubes.

"This is Petri," said Rozia. She moved towards the child and picked her up.

Petri squirmed and struggled.

"Calm down, there's a good girl," said Rozia. She kissed the child's head. "This is Kaleem. He's come to meet you."

Petri leant forward and touched Kaleem's face.

"She's in constant pain," said Rozia. "Diastics don't help. The medics can't do anything for her. I'd like to get her to Zandra. But how do I explain all of this? She wasn't supposed to be born."

Kaleem watched as Rozia soothed the child. She was good with her, just like she'd always been good with the Adulkis. He could see that the little girl was in pain. And the way she looked. She was even more freakish than him. How had this child ever been allowed to come about?

He guessed she was about two years old.

Two years old? That could mean… "Who is she?" he asked. Could it have happened again? No tube baby would be allowed to grow into this.

Rozia shook her head. "Not what you think," she said. "She's not even mine."

So what had happened than? Was this another project that Rozia had taken on, a bit like she had with the Adulkis? Was she hiding this… this freak?

Petri screeched.

"Shush, shush," said Rozia, stroking the little girl's hair. "I'm here. Let me have some of the pain." She rocked her backwards and forwards and gradually the child's eyes closed. Rozia turned to Kaleem. "We let her sleep as much as possible," she said. She sighed. "Any form of light is torture to her. Even inside light. Daylight could kill her. She plays at night. In the dark. I stay up with her most of the time. She still has pains from when any light touches her. Do you mind if I darken the room?"

"Of course not," said Kaleem. He wondered who the "we" referred to.

"She's older than she looks," said Rozia. "She's actually seven years old."

Kaleem didn't know whether to be relieved or disappointed. "So, who is she?" he asked.

"She is Petri, Julien's child," answered Rozia.

"How?" asked Kaleem.

"He'd applied to be a single parent," said Rozia. "They didn't find the problem until she was quite advanced. He couldn't bear to have her destroyed."

"So, how did he manage that? Surely she would have been rejected?" said Kaleem.

"He found a medic through Hidden Information," said Rozia. "She oversaw the remainder of the gestation. And helped a bit afterwards."

"But isn't it cruel?" said Kaleem. "If she's in so much pain?"

"You have some pain, don't you, because you're different?" said Rozia sharply. "And what about Saratina, and the Adulkis? Aren't you glad they exist?"

"But it can't be as bad for them – for us – as it is for her, can it?" said Kaleem. It was strange sitting in the dark talking to Rozia. He wanted to see the expression on her face.

"But she is intelligent and kind-hearted and even happy when it's not hurting," said Rozia. "Her life is worth the pain. And if we could get her to Zandra, she could get help there. We know she could."

"We?" asked Kaleem, dreading the answer.

"Me and just a few other people who know about her, and who help me to look after her," said Rozia.

Kaleem felt a huge weight lift from his chest.

"But it's no good. We daren't let people know about her. They might… they might suggest switch-off," said Rozia. She began to sob quietly.

Kaleem touched her face. He could feel the wetness of the tears on her cheeks. She took his hand in hers and kissed his fingers.

"You must get her to Zandra. Of course you must," said Kaleem. "We'll take her with us when I go back."

"We?" said Rozia. She squeezed his hand and then let go of it.

"Yes," replied Kaleem. "You must come along too."

“We can’t,” said Rozia. “What will they do to her when they find out?”

I wouldn’t let them do anything, thought Kaleem. *Haven’t we learnt yet?* “Maybe we could get someone from Zandra here first to look at her,” he said.

Petri started to scream.

“Look, I’ll have to ask you to go now,” said Rozia. “I need to sort her out.”

“No problem,” said Kaleem. “I’ll let myself out.”

“Just wait until I’ve got to her room before you open the shutters,” said Rozia.

“Of course,” said Kaleem.

His hand and face tingled where she had touched them. He rubbed his face with the hand she had touched and breathed in her perfume. She was wearing his favourite.

“Okay,” she called from the bedroom.

“Open shutters, put on lights,” he commanded the dataserve. The room flooded with light.

He left the apartment. The lift was already waiting for him.

Just do the next thing, he thought to himself. He should probably contact Zandra. And think how they could get some more help on Terrestra.

His fingers found the box with the brooch in it in his pocket. Why on Terrestra had he brought that along with him? Madness!

Decisions

Rozia watched Zendra pass the wand over Petri's body. The child whimpered.

Zendra shook her head. "It's taking an age to work this time," she said. "It's the strongest medication we've got. And it's far too strong for her. We shouldn't really be using this on her. She's much too young."

Petri's eyes slowly closed. Her breathing became shallower.

Zendra frowned. "This is all beyond me, now," she said. "I really don't think I can do any more for her."

"Will… will she die?" asked Rozia.

"Not even that," said Zendra. "That would almost be… well… you know what I'm saying."

This was terrible. Rozia swallowed hard. Petri had been so poorly after Kaleem's visit and had then got worse. Had her own confusion disturbed the girl? Had she sensed something wrong in Rozia and that had made her ill?

Petri's face creased up in pain.

"This goes totally against my Hippocratic oath," said Zendra. "I shouldn't be letting her suffer like that. But not even all the elders would know what would happen if I came clean about what I've been doing with Petri. I'd probably get struck off." She laughed. "Then I don't suppose it'll matter about the oath after all."

"Is there nothing we can do?" asked Rozia.

Zendra shook her head. "There's nothing else that we can do here. There really isn't," she said. "She needs some specialist help. I doubt there's anyone on Terrestra who can help her," she said. "If she were an animal she would be put down."

Rozia suddenly thought of switch-off. That might have been appropriate here. But how could she think that? Even with all the pain, Petri's life had value. Or was it just selfish of her to think like that?

"I'm going to have to go," said Zendra. "Look, I'll come back tomorrow. The sedative should keep her calm for the night. Mainly. I'll go and look for something else to do but I don't hold out much hope."

"Please don't go," Rozia begged.

Zendra sighed. "I probably should have stopped a long time ago. Confessed to the authorities."

"Please help me." Rozia took hold of Zendra's arm. "You've got to help me."

Zendra pushed Rozia away gently. "I've tried my best," she said. "Really I have. I really can't think what else to do."

"I know. I'm sorry," said Rozia.

Zendra put her hands on Rozia's shoulders. "She'll be out of pain for a long time now," she said. She sighed. "It could even be… that the wand treatment slows her breathing so much… that…"

"No," whispered Rozia. "No, please, no."

"I'm sorry. I'm really sorry," said Zendra. "Call me if…"

Rozia nodded.

"I'll let myself out, then," said Zendra. "I'll be back. I promise."

Rozia closed her eyes as the young medic left. What could she do now? She looked at the sleeping child. She did seem peaceful. At least with the strong sedative that Zendra had given her she would have several hours free from the pain that tortured her.

Rozia curled herself round Petri. "Sleep, little one," she whispered, stroking the little girl's hair. "Sleep and dream."

She must have fallen asleep herself. She dreamed of Razjosh. He seemed so clear and alive.

"I knew it," he said. "I knew it all along. You were hiding somebody. This secret is too big for you to bear alone, child. You must share it. You must. You know who can help." He'd seemed so real. Yet she knew she was dreaming. She remembered even in her sleep that he had died.

Then it was Louish. "You've been so brave, sweetie," she said. "And so has your little girl. But enough. She must have no more pain. You just speak to him. Speak to Kaleem."

Then there had been others, but they'd been shadowy figures and a little mixed up. Narisja, telling her that she would have healthy child one day, and Kevik, even, telling her she was brave and Saratina, just loving Petri. She would, of course. Oh, Saratina, if only she could help her to look after Petri.

Then she woke up. It was daylight. Her heart thudded. The child had not stirred once in the night. Did that mean…?

Rozia felt for a pulse. There was a strong one there. She was just fast asleep. She had survived and she seemed to be pain free. For the moment. But what about when it came back?

The girl's eyelids fluttered open. She smiled up at Rozia.

"Hello, sweetheart," said Rozia. "Are you feeling better today?"

"Yes," said Petri, smiling sweetly. "Rozia, can Kaleem take me to Zandra and can they make me better there? Forever?"

"Oh, sweetheart, I don't know," said Rozia. She kissed her forehead. How could she tell this child that the authorities might not like the fact that she existed at all?

The dataserve buzzed to indicate that she had a message. It was Zendra.

"I've worked all night," the medic said. "There is definitely nothing more I can do. Really, your only chance is to get her to Zandra. How is she now?"

"She seems a lot better," replied Rozia.

"That will only last another twelve hours or so. Then the pains will come back. Possibly even worse than before."

"No!" whispered Rozia.

"Get her to Zandra. Tell them about me if you have to. I don't mind. I really don't. But do it. Now."

Zendra's face disappeared from the screen.

Rozia sat for half an hour with Petri in her arms.

"I'm hungry," the little girl said.

"I'll get you something soon," said Rozia. "But there is something I must do first," she added. Hardly trusting herself to breathe, she turned to the dataserve. "Get me Kaleem Malkendy, Peace Child," she commanded.

Almost at once Kaleem's face appeared on the screen. "Rozia!" he said, and blushed deeply.

She felt herself blush as well.

"What can I do for you?" he asked.

The Tower

They were all there, watching him. Rozia, Razjosh, Saratina, even Narisja, Kevik and the Adulkis. Petri was there as well, somehow tolerating the sunlight. Maybe they had already been to Zandra and perhaps they'd cured her?

Kaleem knew he was dreaming. Anything was possible, then.

A young woman stood a few metres away from him. She was wearing old-fashioned clothing and had a scarf tied round her head. Kaleem sensed the scarf was there to hide her unsatisfactory hair rather than for any religious reason. She started to walk towards him. She was smiling. Kaleem knew at once that she was Davina Patterson.

She was followed by a young man. Kaleem recognised Calver Toms. Calver nodded.

Then the others came up the steps – Abel, Menjit, Ben Alki, Ben Mariah, Pierre, Stuart, Alistare, Charlek, Ella, yes, even Ella who smiled shyly at him and then looked away, Danielle and Sandi. Finally, Louish, Frazier, Marijam and Nazaret.

The circle was complete.

A cloud that had been hiding the sun moved and Kaleem was dazzled. He glanced towards Rozia and Petri. The child smiled at him. She still seemed unaffected by the strong light.

The view from the tower was even clearer now. They could see across the desert towards the mountains in one direction and towards the sea in another. Kaleem was not sure where he was. It didn't look quite like Terrestra, nor Zandra, not even Zenoto, but it did seem familiar. The tower cast a finely-edged shadow across the dry land.

The master builder bowed and handed Kaleem a trowel full of mortar and another smaller, silver trowel. Kaleem bent and smoothed the mortar over the last but one brick. The master builder handed him the final brick. Kaleem carefully placed it so that it lined up with the others. He tapped it into place just as Enmerkar had shown him. He forced some more mortar into the gap between the bricks. The master builder helped him to smooth off the excess. Then he tapped Kaleem on the shoulder and nodded.

Kaleem stood up and stroked the dust from his tunic.

Everyone started to clap and cheer. The sun seemed to shine even brighter now.

The choir started to sing. Kaleem didn't want to speak to anyone, so he was glad that they offered him an excuse not to. Everyone started to move down the tower. It was going to take some time. There were hundreds of people here and they were higher up than in any other building Kaleem had ever been in. There was no lift.

They all seemed to walk to a soft lilting rhythm. The music dictated it and the thin air slowed everyone's movements. Kaleem could see Rozia and Petri a few metres in front of him. The child was walking apparently without pain. Even so, after a while Rozia bent down and picked her up. Kaleem wished he could help carry her. But Rozia had made it clear that although she would accept his help in getting Petri to the medics on Zandra, she wanted to manage Julien's child by herself. She wanted to be on her own.

Every so often, the choir paused and then he could hear the murmuring voices. After a while, he could hear the mumbling even while the choir was singing. None of it made any sense. Yet as they carried on going down, as they came to where the air was more normal, Kaleem began to understand the words of the song, and he began to understand what people were saying to each other. In fact, the most unlikely people understood each other, and not just the words. The Zandrians were talking to the Terrestrans as if they had been friends for years.

It's because the air is getting more normal, Kaleem told himself. *Or it's because this walk is so long that we've had time to decode the words and we've had time to get to know each other.* Or could it be because they'd got the tower right now? Did he dare think that?

It all became clearer the further down the tower he got.

At one point Razjosh was walking with him. The elder didn't say a word but it felt to Kaleem as if he was talking to him.

"They need your stories," the old man seemed to say. "And you can tell them by living them. Just be. Be yourself."

The Adulkis were there too, and the girl with the almond eyes. Two of the Adulkis slipped their hands into his.

Rozia was waiting at the bottom. She was still carrying Petri. Petri kissed her fingers and blew the kiss to Kaleem. Rozia held her closer. She smiled and waved at Kaleem. "I knew you could do it," she called. "I knew you could rebuild the tower and truly become the Peace Child."

But then she turned and started to walk slowly away from him. It felt like a wrench.

"Remember, just the next thing," he heard Rogin's voice. "Always the next thing."

And he knew he would understand what he needed to do.

Kaleem drifted softly out of the dream. It had been bitter-sweet this time. Soft and gentle and not at all like the nightmare it used to be, but Rozia had walked away from him.

He should get up now and start getting ready. It was a big day. Today he became an elder. Possibly the youngest ever.

He knew he would never have the dream again.

He would try always to do the next thing. He would try to help people get what they needed. He would be as much a Peace Child as he could be.

And then there would be the next thing. At least Rozia and Petri would be coming to Zandra with him. Petri had blown him a kiss. Rozia had smiled. And she had praised him. Even if it had been just a dream.

He picked up the small box off the table. The brooch was still in there. He would give it to her on the Supercraft. Who knew what might happen? Perhaps? There was always hope.

Kaleem opened his wardrobe and selected his blue dress tunic.

Glossary

Abel Stansted
Abel is a Z Zoner. He and fellow Z Zoner Menjit Crossman drive the supercraft that takes Kaleem to Zandra. Z Zoners are quite resourceful. Menjit and Abel are able to help Kaleem when the supercraft breaks down. They use a form of teletransportation to get Kaleem on to Zandra.

Abel and Menjit also help Kaleem and Rozia a lot when they come to the Z Zone. They help Kaleem in his struggle against Kevik and to persuade the Z Zoners about the Normal Zoners good intentions.

Adulkis
These are old, people who never grow up physically or mentally and remain childlike. They have featured in Kaleem's dreams of the Babel Tower but they actually exist in the Z Zone. Kaleem always feels uncomfortable around them, probably because of the dream. Rozia gets on with them really well and knows exactly how to handle them.

Alistare Rogerin
Alistare is a good friend of Kaleem's and one of his former students. He lives on Zandra. He is a mathematics expert. He has a very similar, easy-going nature to that of Pierre LaFontaine, Kaleem's good friend on Terrestra.

Autoflieg
This is the name of the individual transporter on Polynket. It seats up to four people and moves in such a way that the occupants feel as if they are flying. It needs no driving. Autofliegs do not follow fight paths but always fly in a straight line to their destination. When two Autofliegs meet, they dance around each other until they find another straight line.

Babel Prophecy
This is a prophecy about a special Peace Child. It says that the Peace Child's mother will enter the place where the poorer people live, carrying a copy of The Tower of Babel book. The woman will be pregnant. There are two oddities here: on Terrestra in

3500 babies are grown in test tubes. Few people own books and even fewer can read Wordtext.

Marijam, pregnant and frightened, indeed enters the Z Zone, carrying a copy of The Tower of Babel by Davina Patterson. She calls her son Kaleem.

The prophecy further states that the Peace Child born to this woman will save the universe. Kaleem's strange dreams seem tied up with the tower of Babel.

Kaleem, however, cannot take the prophecy seriously and his mentor, the elder, Razjosh, also seems ambivalent about it.

Ben Alki
Ben Alki used to conduct the switch-off ceremonies. In *Babel* he actually decides that he doesn't like switch-off and fights against it.

Ben Mariah
Ben Mariah is a Z Zoner. He is the same age as Narisja and a good friend of hers. He has the official function of story-teller in the Z Zone. This is a highly respected role there. He is a good friend to Narisja, and also becomes a good friend to Marijam and Kaleem.

He fights with Kaleem to overcome Kevik's rebellion. Then he comes back to Terrestra to help in the negotiations about switch-off. He helps Kaleem fight Razjosh's switch-off.

Black Tulpen
These are gigantic black tulips, grown with considerable difficulty, on Zandra. They are the symbol of lust. If you fancy someone, you send them a bunch of Black Tulpen. Girls can send them to boys – or girls, and boys can send them to girls or boys as well. It can cut out a lot of awkwardness.

However, this is not the case for Kaleem. Tulla Watkins sends him some after their first meeting. Kaleem feels unable to take up the offer, much as he'd like to, as he is new to the planet. He has to return the gift.

This actually causes much awkwardness between them.

He does present Rozia with a bouquet of them and more conventional red roses the first time he makes love to her.

Charlek Smithin
Charlek is Kaleem's one human prison guard on Zandra. He and Kaleem actually become great friends. Charlek is with Kaleem when he meets his father for the first time.

Charlek is quite fond of romantic encounters with young women.

Chief Makisson
Makisson is the chief of the elders.

Citadel of Elders
Elders live in the Citadel. This is a luxurious dwelling place where every comfort is catered for. At the time of the poison cloud, the elders lived in a cave that was full of crystals. This seemed to give them intense energy and allowed their minds to become brighter.

After the poison cloud disappeared and a new Citadel was built on the surface of Terrestra, the crystalline atmosphere was replicated… by using crystals. There are no walls at right angles in the Citadel. Even the shape of the place adds to the energy.

Guests are allowed in the Citadel, even to stay overnight, but only at an elder's invitation.

Comfisessel
This is a technologically advanced chair. It actually moulds itself to the person sitting on it and hovers at exactly the right height so that the occupant's legs may rest at exactly the right angle.

Unusually, the comfisessels on Terrestra are more advanced than those on Zandra.

Council
This is a little like our Parliament. However Members of Council are elected by proportional representation. When a member is switched-off or gets fed up of being a member of Council, anyone

can put themselves up to replace him or her. There is no party culture. After all, Terrestra is a one-world planet. It comes down to personalities.

There are two levels of voting within the Council, however. Some votes are open to all members, and some just to Heads of Service.

Counsel of Elders
This is in effect the "upper house", a little like our House of Lords. It tends to rubber stamp most decisions made by the Council. However, the elders can overrule and they can make executive decisions. If a majority vote has not taken place at Council level they can decide on a course of action.

This has happened once before in Razjosh's life time. The decision to send Kaleem to Zandra is also an example.

Danielle Thomas
Danielle is the very young Head of Science. (See Heads of Service). She discovers that the disease that hits Terrestra is a mutation of the old Starlight Racer Fever. She accompanies Razjosh on the failed mission to Zandra.

She is very serious, and terrified of space travel.

Dataserve
A dataserve in 3500 is to Terrestra what a computer is to 21st century Earth. It is, of course, much more sophisticated and interacts with other systems. It is voice controlled and there is rarely any Wordtext on them.

When Kaleem gets a new one he is able to set its voice to sound like his own.

On Zandra the dataserves are so clever that they seem to be able to read their owners' minds.

Davina Patterson
Davina Patterson was a talented artist who produced several books in the 21st Century. Most of them were picture books about Bible stories, and myths and legends from ancient

Terrestran cultures. Her books are characterised by their rich illustrations containing many shades of blue, silver and gold. The books became collectors' items. By 3500 most of them have disappeared.

In *Babel* we meet her and learn how she came to produce the pictures for the Tower of Babel book. She is more or less of our time, living in London a few years into our future.

Detran Malthus
This is the alias that Kaleem uses on Zandra.

Diastics
Every Terrestran household is fitted with a diastics system. Terrestrans monitor themselves on it at least every other day. They simply touch a control pad and the system is able to detect if there is any threat of illness or disease in the body. It then administers a drink that rectifies any potential problem.

An alarm sounds if someone fails to monitor themselves or if the system cannot cope with the problems.

Kaleem manages to make the alarm sound several times.

However, the system works so well that there is a real danger of overpopulation – especially as Terrestrans refuse to communicate with others. Therefore, switch-off has been brought in.

Elder
Elders are elected to the Counsel and are the supreme form of government. They have the power to veto what Heads of Service decide, though they usually just rubber stamp these decisions. They are generally men and women of over 65. Often, they have had a long career as a Head of Service.

The voting system is ritualistic, a little like the way we elect the Pope. Only Heads of Service and other elders may vote for an Elder. The one exception is the Peace Child elder who may only be selected by the current Peace Child. This is because the position is onerous and requires a long apprenticeship.

Elders have access to both Hidden Information and Golden Knowledge.

Erik Svenson
Erik is a close friend of Stuart Davidson. They both bully Kaleem because he looks different.

Executives
These are the ruling forces on Zandra. Zandrian executives have more power than Terrestran Heads of Service, but less power than Terrestran Elders. They are a little like ministers in our own government. Unlike on Terrestra, or even in our own world, there is no Upper House like our House of Lords or the Counsel of Elders on Terrestra. Zandra also has ordinary members of its parliament, so executives are a little like our ministers.

They often have quite quirky areas of responsibility e.g. Marek Ransen is the Executive for Language and Story.

Executive Palace
This is where all the Zandrian Executives have their high-level meetings, celebrations and formal occasions. They do not live there as Terrestran elders live and work at the Citadel.

Figurescript
Although more widely learnt than Wordtext, Figurescript is not understood by most humans. Scientists and mathematicians learn it. It is the language of maths, including the symbols that we know. Most intelligent beings understand mathematics in a visual way – e.g. fractions look like slices of cake.

Franck
Frank is one of the Z Zoners who finds Marijam and puts her in contact with Narisja.

Frazier Kennedy
Frazier Kennedy is the charismatic Head of Education. (See Heads of Service). He has a great sense of humour though is not to be trifled with; he expects the best of everybody, including his family. However, he really cares for everyone around him. He is

an excellent public speaker and very conscientious about his job.

He is angry when Gabrizan disappears and devastated when his daughter Marijam also leaves a short time later. Nevertheless, he continues to be a good Head of Education.

He is naturally delighted to welcome Kaleem back to Terrestra, both as his grandson and as the Peace Child. He and Louish are also overjoyed to be reconciled with Marijam.

Frega
Frega juice is the alcoholic drink available on Zandra. Kaleem finds it much more enjoyable than Terrestra's nectar. Both drinks are sometimes made stronger or weaker by the authorities.

Gabrizan Taylor
Gabrizan is a Zandrian, with the Zandrian name of Nazaret Bagarin, sent to Terrestra to help investigate the poison cloud that plagues the planet. When the cloud lifts spontaneously, the mission is aborted and he is called back to Zandra.

Whilst on Terrestra he meets and falls in love with Marijam Kennedy. He has the impression that his feelings for her are stronger than hers for him; he sees her as someone who is intent on having a very interesting career. In an attempt to impress her, he applies to be part of a very prestigious project. It is whilst he is attending his two day interview that he is called back to Zandra.

He never really gets over Marijam and never has another serious relationship.

He works hard on restoring plant life to Zandra, a planet that will soon be in even more crisis, because of its dying vegetation, than Terrestra was at the time of the poison cloud.

One day, however, he meets Kaleem. He is shocked to find that he has a son. He is reconciled with Marijam and she agrees to become permanently attached to him (see Permanent Attachment).

Golden Knowledge
Only elders have access to this. It is the totality of Hidden

Information and then some. The Babel Prophecy is Golden Knowledge, for instance. Elders are so naturally wise and have access to so much extra wisdom that they are close to knowing the meaning of life, so normal Terrestrans believe.

Heads of Service
These are to Terrestra 3500 what ministers are to UK government. They are elected by other members of Council. And will take on a particular role. So, there are Heads of Transport, Science and Education, for example.

Hidden Information
This is information that is kept from the general public. Heads of Service have access to Hidden Information that pertains to the service they administer. Elders have access to all Hidden Information and also to extra information called Golden Knowledge. For instance, the Head of Transport would have known that in fact a few people did leave the planet, but the Head of Education would not. All elders would know this.

Information is hidden in order to control the population and because a little knowledge can be dangerous. Hidden Information is to Terrestra 3500 what drugs are to earth in the 21st century. Punishments for accessing or attempting to access Hidden Information are severe.

Marijam dabbles in this a little and Kaleem more so. Kaleem also gets involved with Hidden Information Pedlars.

Hidden Information Pedlars
These are the equivalent of our drug pushers. They live underground. They try to pull others into their world. They are a criminal force. Kaleem has quite a brush with them in *The Prophecy*.

Hololesson
As Kaleem is not able to travel to other planets, he spends some time in interactive scenes that are created with sophisticated holograms and extremely clever dataserve programmes. He learns how life on other planets amongst other cultures might be.

Holoscene
The technology for this is good on Terrestra and even better on Zandra. You can go to the gym in your own home, for instance, by calling up a holoscene. A good holoscene will really make you think that you are there.

You can also project yourself somewhere else in a holoscene. Razjosh visits Kaleem several times this way.

Ianus
Ianus is one of the Z Zoners who finds Marijam and puts her in contact with Narisja.

Joshran Kemnat
This is the elder whose switch-off ceremony Kaleem watches at the beginning of *Babel*. He was the Elder of Culture and Education. Frazier Kennedy takes over from him.

Kayla (Aunt)
Kayla is the sister of Louish Kennedy and therefore the aunt of Marijam. She has constantly tried to instil some fashion sense into Marijam – and failed. Marijam still prefers dull grey ripon tunics.

Lana Gylson
Lana is the line-manager of Tulla Watkins. She knows much about the poison cloud on Terrestra. Kaleem is so taken aback by this that he pronounces a word that Zandra and Terrestra share the Terrestran way. Shortly after that, Kaleem is arrested and is charged with being a spy.

Lorretta
Lorretta is the android guide who shows Kaleem around during his hololesson on Tarantet.

Kaleem Malkendy
Also known as the Peace Child, Kaleem Kennedy and Kaleem Bagarin. However, until almost the very end of the book, he is known as Kaleem Malkendy.

We first meet him when he is sixteen years old. He is different from other young people: he is blond and has skin that tans easily at a time when white Terrestrans are pale-skinned and have dark hair, he lives in a cave apartment beneath the surface of Terrestra whilst most other families live on the surface now that the poison cloud has gone, and he has no idea who is father is at a time when family connections are well-documented. He is bullied by some of the young people in his schooling group.

The elder Razjosh, the current Peace Child, has been watching him and sees his potential as the next Peace Child. There is also a suggestion that he might be the Peace Child who is associated with the Babel Prophecy. His mother, Maria Malkendy, also happens to own a copy of the famous picture book The Tower of Babel, written and illustrated by a well-known 21st century artist, Davina Patterson.

Razjosh provides Kaleem with a better dataserve and starts training him up as the new Peace Child. He also uses hololessons and also visits Kaleem in holoscenes.

Kaleem becomes ill with the Starlight Racer Fever. This is extremely worrying as there has been no disease on Terrestra for over 200 years. The diastics system cannot cope with this disease, and soon it is widespread, causing several deaths and Maria to go into a coma. Whilst ill, Kaleem begins to dream about the Babel Tower and some strange children with adult faces. He continues having these dreams throughout the novel.

Kaleem is desperate to find out about his father. Whilst Razjosh is on a Peace Child mission, and whilst all on Terrestra are confined to their homes, Kaleem leaves his apartment and starts looking at some Hidden Information. It brings him no news about his father and he only just manages to get clear of the Hidden Information pedlars.

Razjosh's mission to get help from Zandra with the Starlight Racer Fever fails. The situation on Terrestra becomes even more desperate. Kaleem has to go and live as a spy on Zandra. All is going well until he gives himself away by mispronouncing a word.

He is put into prison. Prisons on Zandra are quite benign, though his situations is slightly uncomfortable as his is kept in isolation. However, the one human prison guard who visits him from time to time, Charlek Smithin, becomes a friend.

Whilst in prison, Kaleem is allowed to carry on with some projects. Ironically, it is whilst he is there that he learns more about the role of the Peace Child. He suddenly has a brilliant idea about how he can persuade Terrestrans to trade with Zandrians. He and Charlek establish that Terrestra can swap Starlight Racer Fever vaccine for acorns, which Zandra desperately needs and which are plentiful on Terrestra. This can be done without any fear of spreading disease and without any need for Terrestrans to leave Terrestra.

Kaleem is allowed to discuss his ideas with the experts at the Planation Centre. He goes there with Charlek. He meets Nazaret Bagarin there. Nazaret looks like an older version of Kaleem. They manage to talk. Nazaret aka Gabrizan Taylor is indeed his father.

Kaleem successfully gets the powers that be on both Terrestra and Zandra to accept his ideas. Nazaret and Maria are reconciled. In a voice file, Marijam Kennedy aka Maria Malkendy explains the circumstances of Kaleem's birth.

Kaleem now feels a little more secure about his identity, though he still worries about his otherness, the burden of being the Peace Child and the aggravating mystery about the Babel Prophecy.

Kevik
He is Narisja's son. When he was born, Narisja thought he might be the Peace Child. Kevik tries to take over from Kaleem, almost killing Kaleem in the process. Towards the end of *Babel* they work together to help overcome switch-off.

Laguna
The Laguna Bar is found deep within the cave system. However, it has a skylight that connects to the surface through a system of mirrors, a little like a periscope. It is such an iconic meeting place

that it stays open even after the poison cloud has shifted.

Marijam and Gabrizan met in this bar the night the poison cloud lifted.

London Harbour
This is the biggest town in the A Zone (see Normal Zones). Most Heads of Services and even most ordinary Council Members opt to live here as they can more easily get to the meets, even though most of the time, of course, they work from home.

It has the name "harbour" because in the days when Terrestrans still travelled, most of the spaceships, including the big supercraft departed from here.

Louish Kennedy
Louis is the permanent attachment of Frazier Kennedy and mother of Marijam. She is full of fun and very glamorous. She stops Frazier from taking life too seriously and is a good contrast to her rather serious daughter.

Now that she has found her grandson she looks after him really well. She becomes very fond of Rozia.

Marek Ransen
Marek Ransen is the Executive for Language and Story (see Executives) on Zandra. He has a lot of respect for Kaleem, even though the latter has become an enemy of the state. He helps Kaleem to find out a little more about the Babel Prophecy and about the Peace Child role.

Maggie Johnstone
Maggie Johnstone is a teacher for Kaleem's schooling group. At a meet when some of the students are teasing Kaleem about his hair and skin colour, she inadvertently lets out some Hidden Information about genetics. She is suspended from duty.

This adds to Kaleem's worry about his otherness and about his identity. It also makes him question society.

Chief Makisson
Makisson is the chief of the elders.

Maria Malkendy
Maria is the same person as Marijam Kennedy. After she returns to the Normal Zones from the Z Zone she lives in a cave apartment as Maria Malkendy. She keeps a low profile as she does not want the authorities to start investigating her false identity. She scrapes a living by doing a few rather boring research projects.

She and her son Kaleem are close, but he occasionally resents their poverty and her secrecy about his father.

Marijam Kennedy
Marijam is the daughter of Head of Education, Frazier Kennedy. She disappears shortly after the lifting of the poison cloud that has forced the Terrestrans to live underground for years. She has become pregnant after a brief romance with Gabrizan Taylor. On the very evening she was going to tell him about the pregnancy, he fails to arrive. Pregnancy as we know it is unknown on Terrestra; babies are generally produced in test-tubes.

Marijam flees to the Z Zones where she gives birth to Kaleem. She suffers from postnatal depression. Once she recovers from this she returns to the Normal Zones where she lives quietly as Maria Malkendy in the old underground apartment that used to belong to her parents.

She keeps the identity of Kaleem's father from him.

When the puzzling Starlight Racer Fever arrives on Terrestra, she becomes very ill and goes into a coma.

Later she is reconciled with Gabrizan aka Nazaret Bagarin and she tells Kaleem the full story of his birth. She and Gabrizan become attached – which is a little like getting married.

In *Babel* she and Nazaret struggle to make people believe her story.

Meet
In 3500 everyone works form home, aided by droids, robots, dataserves and other IT equipment. Occasionally, groups do need to meet face to face. They hire a room in a building and hold a meet. The occasional meet is an important part of the school system, though meets are also held for school students when something important happens e.g. when the poison cloud on Terrestra lifted.

Menjit Crossman
Menjit is a Z Zoner. He and fellow Z Zoner Abel Stansted drive the supercraft that takes Kaleem to Zandra. Z Zoners are quite resourceful. Menjit and Abel are able to help Kaleem when the supercraft breaks down. They use a form of teletransportation to get Kaleem on to Zandra.

Abel and Menjit also help Kaleem and Rozia a lot when they come to the Z Zone. They help Kaleem in his struggle against Kevik and to persuade the Z Zoners about the Normal Zoners good intentions.

Unfortunately, Menjit is killed in a rock fall caused by an explosion Kevik sets off.

Narisja
Narisja is a Z Zoner (see Z Zone). She is a typical "wise woman". She is also the midwife who delivers Kaleem. She takes care of Marijam. She is very respected amongst the Z Zoners. She knows a lot about childbirth and the Babel Prophecy.

In *Babel* she becomes old and demented, eventually dying. She does show Kaleem and Rozia the collection of work she has from Davina Patterson and some strange sound files that seem to be something to do with the Babel Prophecy.

Nazaret Bagarin
Nazaret is a Zandrian, sent to Terrestra to help investigate the poison cloud that plagues the planet. Whilst there he uses the more Terrestran name of Gabrizan Taylor. When the cloud lifts spontaneously, the

mission is aborted and he is called back to Terrestra.

Whilst on Terrestra he meets and falls in love with Marijam Kennedy. He has the impression that his feelings for her are stronger than hers for him; he sees her as someone who is intent on having a very interesting career. In an attempt to impress her, he applies to be part of a very prestigious project. It is whilst he is attending his two day interview that he is called back to Zandra.

He never really gets over Marijam and never has another serious relationship.

He works hard on restoring plant life to Zandra, a planet that will soon be in even more crisis, because of its dying vegetation, than Terrestra was at the time of the poison cloud.

One day, however, he meets Kaleem. He is shocked to find that he has a son. He is reconciled with Marijam and she agrees to become permanently attached to him.

He takes over the project for importing Terrestran acorns in exchange for Zandrian vaccine against the Starlight Racer disease.

Nectar
This is the alcoholic drink served on Terrestra. It comes in a variety of flavours, many of them very sickly and sweet. The authorities often strengthen it or weaken it as a way of controlling the population.

Normal Zoner
An inhabitant of one of the Normal Zones, A-Y.

Normal Zones
Terrestra 3500 is divided pragmatically into 26 zones, each named after a letter of the alphabet. Now that the population has stabilized after the introduction of switch-off some of the Zones are no longer used. The nearer the Zone is to London Harbour the higher the letter of the alphabet.

Zones A-Y are called the Normal Zones.

Oban Metrad
Obran was appointed with Ray Denkin by Narisja to help look after Kaleem when he was in the Z Zone.

One-world planet
These are planets that have one central form of government. They do not have separate states, no matter how big they are nor how long it takes to travel across the planet's surface. They have democratic principles and are inclusive of all people living there. Most planets, including Terrestra and Zandra, like to think of themselves as being one-world planets. However, Terrestra cannot really claim to be a one-world planet because of the Z Zone.

Operation Acorn
Acorns are sent from Terrestra to Zandra in exchange for vaccine against the Starlight Racer Fever. Zandra's trees are dying out. The Terrestran immune system is too weak to tackle the disease without help.

Oxton Mesrip
Oxton is the special carer put in charge of Maria Malkendy when she is in a coma as a result of the Starlight Racer Fever.

Peace Child
Kaleem eventually learns where the idea of a Peace Child comes from towards the end of *The Prophecy*. Millennia ago, warring tribes in Papua New Guinea used to swap a child at the end of a conflict. This child is born to one culture and brought up in the other. The child belongs to neither culture but understands both and can act as a go-between when further disputes arise.

Terrestra, and most other one-world planets, keep a Peace Child. The Peace Child learns the cultures and the languages of other planets and acts as a negotiator between planets.

Even though Terrestra is isolated, it maintains a Peace Child. Razjosh is the current one at the beginning of *The Prophecy* and Kaleem becomes it by the end. This does involve leaving the planet every so often and that that happens is Hidden Information.

The Babel Prophecy states that a very special Peace Child will come that will save the universe.

In *Babel* we get a few more clues about where this prophecy comes from.

Permanent attachment
A couple can opt for permanent attachment. They are then bound to each other by law and go through a ritual that resembles a wedding ceremony. Tulla and Petro become permanently attached as do Marijam and Nazaret. They may opt to have children made from their sperm and eggs or from donor sperm and eggs. (See Stopes programme.)

There is absolutely no stigma attached to gay and lesbian couples becoming permanently attached or creating and raising children.

Petro Ransen
Petro is a Zandrian. He is the son of Marek Ransen, Executive of Language and Story (see Executives). He is a health expert and the lover and later permanent attachment of Tulla Watkins.

Petro becomes a good friend of Kaleem, although Kaleem remains a little jealous of him because of Tulla.

Pierre LaFontaine
Pierre is in Kaleem's school group. He is a good friend. He is easy-going and laid back. He never seems to mind that Kaleem ignores him for much of the time and turns up when it suits him.

Plastiglass
This is a glass-like substance used for windows and doors on Terrestra and Tarantet. It allows quite a lot of light through, though is not as good as veriglass. Plastiglass also includes something that guards people against the elements: the poison cloud on Terrestra and the extreme heat on Tarantet, for example.

The Poison Cloud
This probably began as early as the 21st century or possibly

towards the end of the 20th. Climate change, greenhouse gasses and general pollution did not kill off Terrestra completely. Those who stayed on the sickened planet became pretty wily and found ways of sustaining life despite the fact that the air became unbreathable. The citizens of Terrestra eventually moved to live underground.

The Prophecy begins on the night that the poison cloud begins to disperse of its own accord.

No one is quite sure how it happens. We might assume it has something to do with the activities of a working party that has come from Zandra to investigate the cloud. It may be a case of what is observed being changed because it is observed.

Most Terrestrans do not know about this working party as its existence belongs to Hidden Information. They are told that an object has entered Terrestra's atmosphere and somehow seeded the cloud. Even the reader has to believe that at first, as we do not find out about the Zandrian working party until near the end of *The Prophecy*.

Polynket
Kaleem encounters Polynket in one of his hololessons. The occupants of this planet are trying to use a different sort of logic. For instance, when fuel for their transport is short, they are obliged to buy a minimum amount rather than keep filling up their vehicles.

Kaleem learns a new way of thinking whilst on Polynket.

Ponty Davidson
Ponty Davidson is the Head of Transport (see Heads of Service). He is bitter and cynical. Could this be because he was in love with Marijam when they were younger and she rejected him?

He is very xenophobic and twice tries to sabotage the Peace Child mission to Zandra.

His son, Stuart Davidson, helps the second time round. Once we've met Ponty, we can understand why Stuart is as he is.

Rainer Elbman
Rainer a classmate of Marijam Kennedy

Ray Denkin
Ray was appointed with Oban Metrad by Narisja to help look after Kaleem when he was in the Z Zone.

Razjosh
Razjosh is an elder, who like all elders lives at the Citadel of Elders. Most of the elders' roles reflect those of the Heads of Service. However, Razjosh's is slightly different; he is the current Peace Child.

He tracks down Kaleem as a replacement for himself. He will soon face switch-off and there must be another Peace Child in place before he has to go. He teaches Kaleem everything he needs to know in order to become a Peace Child.

Razjosh has left the planet several times. This is Hidden Information, available only to other elders and Heads of Service.

When Terrestra is suddenly hit with the Starlight Racer Fever and several deaths occur, Razjosh has to go to Zandra to seek help. A stale-mate is reached; Zandra will only offer help if Terrestrans agree to trade. Razjosh knows that this can never happen. His mission fails.

Complications set in when a mercy mission from Zandra is misinterpreted by the Terrestrans as an act of aggression. Razjosh has to complete Kaleem's training quickly and get Kaleem to Zandra. He is the classic mentor to Kaleem and in true mentor-style, leaves Kaleem to cope on his own in the end.

He is saved from switch-off just in time in *Babel.*

Refreshment Park
This is a favourite leisure facility on Zandra. Kaleem proves himself to be a Terrestran spy by imagining a red dog chasing rabbits when the Zandrians are watching his thoughts with a mind-reader. There are no rabbits in the Refreshment Park. The Refreshment Park is one very elaborate holoscene.

Ripon
This is a droid-made material used in most clothes on Terrestra and on several other planets. It is cheap to manufacture, is extremely practical and hardwearing, and protects the wearer from all of the elements. It keeps them cool in the heat and warm in colder temperatures.

It is very practical, but a little boring. Everyone likes occasionally to wear the old materials – silk, satin, wool and cotton.

Rozia Laurence
In *The Prophecy* Rozia is in Kaleem's schooling group. She is quite kind to him and he is quite taken with her. However, from time to time, she seems to be friendly with those that exclude him – which means that she excludes him too.

In *Babel* she becomes Kaleem's partner and goes with him to the Z Zone. She becomes badly injured there and Kaleem decided he has to break up with her as he feels it is all his fault.

Sadie Rojens
She is a classmate of Marijam Kennedy

Sandi Depra
Sandi Depra is the Head of Health. (See Heads of Service.) She is somewhat outspoken and has a wicked sense of humour. Like Kaleem, she has unusual colouring. However, she makes the most of this and constantly changes her hair style to make it as outrageous as possible.

She accompanies Kaleem on his secret mission to Zandra.

Saratina
Saratina helps Narisja and Marijam when Kaleem is born. Marijam suffers from post-natal depression, and it is mainly Saratina who looks after the baby until this depression lifts.

She is deformed because of an accident that happened when Normal Zoners came into the Z Zone. She has a limp and a hunched back. One eye is permanently shut and looks as if it is melted. Partly because she was left to fend for herself as a child and did not have contact with other humans and partly because her face is deformed, she does not speak very clearly. She is quite childlike, so it is difficult to work out her age.

Not many people can understand what she says but Rozia understand her perfectly.

Starlight Racer
Starlight Racers are small interplanetary craft that became popular when space travel became the norm. They were actually very slow compared with supercraft. They had transparent sides, so that passengers could stare at the stars as they travelled.

They were often very crowded because you did not book tickets in advance – you just turned up at the terminal and got on to the next available vehicle.

The crowded conditions aided the spread of a particularly virulent form of 'flu' that gained the name Starlight Racer Fever.

Starlight Racer Fever
This disease becomes a pandemic on Terrestra. Kaleem is the first victim.

It is a 'flu'-like disease but the strain that arrives on Terrestra is extremely strong. Terrestrans' immune systems are weak as they never have to fight disease because of their diastics system.

Starlight Racer Fever had been eradicated before it came to Terrestra. The last outbreak before that had been on Zandra.

It is called the Starlight Racer Fever because it spread widely when many people travelled between planets on crowded Starlight Racers.

Stopes programme
This is the birth control programme used on Terrestra and on all other planets where humans live. Children are sterilized shortly after their eleventh birthday. Just after their sixteenth, the procedure is reversed and sperm and eggs are harvested, frozen and stored.

Later, couples can have babies grown form their stored sperm and eggs. Single parents can also opt for donor sperm or eggs. They can choose whether to know the identity of the donor. Permission to use the sperm or eggs is always asked from the donor. The donor is always allowed to know the identity of any offspring. Children can only know the identity of the donor with the donor's permission. Hence, Kaleem's problems about his identity are escalated. He believes either Marijam or his father, or both of them, are deliberately keeping his identity from him. They are, but of course they have good reason to: the story of his birth is almost unbelievable and Nazaret has no idea.

After the harvest, the children are resterilized. They hardly notice this happening: they are invited to a special celebration meet with other young people. They are sedated at the end of the party by special nectar. They wake up the next morning in their own beds.

Stuart Davidson
He is the son of Ponty Davidson, Head of Transport. (See Heads of Service.) He is in Kaleem's school group and bullies Kaleem.

Supercraft
These are huge interplanetary vessels. They are as big and as luxurious as our ocean liners and have similar facilities, as well as those that belong to 3500, such as holoscenes. They travel at very high speeds, often using wormholes to move rapidly through space. This can be visually very disorienting for passengers, so much of the time shields cover the windows. However, passengers can still enjoy admiring the stars at the beginning and end of their journeys.

There are supercraft and supercraft. Both Kaleem and Razjosh travel by supercraft to Zandra. However, when Razjosh returns, his supercraft is overtaken by a Zandrian super supercraft that is much more powerful.

Super Kanasa
This is the planet where Kaleem learns about spiritual values. The planet has no physical problems and everything seems to work

there in a very logical way. The occupants of this planet spend much of their time trying to improve as people.

Kaleem has an added challenge here. They speak a form of very modified English, which is even more difficult to understand than a language that is totally foreign. It is certainly very difficult for Kaleem to make himself understood in this language.

Switch-off

This is compulsory euthanasia. People of Terrestra are "switched off" when they reach the age of 100. This is to keep population under control. The diastics system ensures complete health. Preparation for switch-off is intense. People receive counselling and are given sedatives as their turn approaches.

Medics administer a form of lethal injection.

Bodies are then sanitized and mulched to be used as fertilizer.

The Z Zone actually came about because of objections to switch-off. In *Babel* Kaleem fights switch-off and persuaded the Z Zoners that it is being dropped.

Tarantet

This is the planet that Kaleem first visits in a hololesson. It has low reserves of energy and is so hot that it has many different names for heat. In the hottest part of the day, when the sand-storms occur, the people sleep. Because of the sandstorms, the shape of the terrain keeps shifting. Buildings are protected by force shields.

This planet is so sparsely populated that their airborne transporters do not have to follow flight paths.

Water is so precious that it is intensely recycled. It is really difficult to sustain plant life.

As evening entertainment, the residents of Tarantet go "sand boarding" and then drink in the local bars.

On this planet, Kaleem learns to respect environments that are physically different form his own.

Terrestra
Terrestra is the planet from which all humanoid life stems.

Terrestra takes 365 days to travel around its sun. It takes 24 hours to spin on its axis. Before the poison cloud and by the end of *The Prophecy* it was possibly the most beautiful planet in the whole universe. It used to be known as The Blue Planet. There is every possibility that it will be known by that name again once people, hopefully including Terrestrans, get used to seeing it without its poison cloud.

Terrestran
Terrestrans are descendants of the inhabitants of the planet Terrestra. 1,000 years before our story begins, Terrestra became overcrowded and Terrestrans started to colonize other planets that could support human life. They chose only empty planets, such as Zandra and planets that had sparse populations of non-human life. On the whole, the non-humans accepted the Terrestrans happily.

A hard-core of the population remained behind on Terrestra. They developed a very good diastics system that kept them disease-free. The Terrestrans decided to become self-sufficient and cut off contact with all other people on all other planets so that they would not confront new types of disease.

They did encounter two other problems, however. They became overcrowded again. Their self-sufficiency put a strain on the ecology of the planet and it eventually became surrounded by a poison cloud. The Terrestrans solved the first problem by inventing switch-off and using the strict Stopes birth control programme, and the second by moving underground. Massive plastiglass tubes came to the surface so that the Terrestrans could observe the night sky and importantly such spectacles as the President's Christmas and Midsummer laser shows.

Thoma
One of the better-known Adulkis. He is actually Narisja's youngest child and brother to Kevik.

Tower of Babel
This story is near the beginning of the Bible. It tells of the people's ambition to build a high tower to reach God and show Him how clever they were. But God was angry about their arrogance and caused the tower to fall. As it fell, people began to speak different languages and could no longer understand each other.

Some historians believe that they may have found evidence of such a tower. Several problems can happen with such a tall building especially when architecture was not as advanced as it is today. If the walls do not taper enough, the building will collapse under its own weight. If it is too tall, people will run out of oxygen as they climb to the top.

Part of Kaleem's mission is to learn languages so that he can negotiate between people. In other words, he has to repair some of the damage done by the tower. In his dreams about the tower he thinks he has to pull it down.

Linguists inform us that most languages come from the same earlier one. Although our languages are now becoming similar again, originally they were even more similar.

The book telling the story is a very important part of the Babel Prophecy. In *Babel* we learn how the book was made by Davina Patterson.

Tulla Watkins
Tulla is a Zandrian. Whilst on Zandra, Kaleem works as a language teacher. Tulla is his first student. Kaleem fancies her like mad. She reminds him of Rozia Laurence, but has blond hair. She obviously fancies him as well as she sends him a consignment of Black Tulpen.

Kaleem cannot afford to have a romantic relationship whilst on Zandra. He reluctantly gives her up and has to watch as she becomes permanently attached to Petro Ransen.

Tunics
These are worn on most planets, with leggings. Men and women

dress alike. The actual cut of the tunics and leggings vary from planet to planet and are affected by local conditions e.g. on Tarantet, they are looser to allow air to circulate. This planet is very hot and does not have a good enough energy supply to have air control everywhere.

Veriglass
This is much more sophisticated than the old plastiglass. It still protects the people inside a building from the elements but it is extremely clear – much clearer in fact than what we have in the 21st century. There is no glare. You can zoom the view in or out. By touching a switch you can easily make it so that you can see out and people cannot see in. You can also make the glass translucent or opaque if you wish. You can point to something you can see and the room dataserve will tell you all about it.

It is droid-made, cheaply and sympathetically.

Wordtext
This is print as we know it on 21st century Earth. Only nerds and scholars bother learning to read it on Terrestra in 3500. It is a little like Latin is to us today.

Kaleem learnt it just for fun when he was twelve. Not because he was a nerd or a scholar but because he was bored senseless living in the cave apartment: he didn't go out much because he tended to get bullied. And, he has a naturally curious mind. He finds it useful as he starts to learn many other languages.

Zandra
Zandra is a planet that, like Terrestra, supports life. It is several days travel by Supercraft from Terrestra. It was colonized by Terrestra 1,000 years before the story begins.

Zandra faces two suns. Each day, twenty-five hours long, contains spring, summer autumn and winter.

Zandrian
Zandrians are the people who now live on the planet Zandra. They now are very outgoing, and they have fantastic advanced

technology compared with Terrestra. This includes fabulous holoscenes that are really convincing. However, their plant-life is dying off and their atmosphere may disappear. The Zandrians are eager to befriend Terrestra as they feel they have much in common.

Z Zone

Terrestra 3500 is divided pragmatically into 26 zones, each named after a letter of the alphabet. Now that the population has stabilized after the introduction of switch-off, some of the Zones are no longer used. The nearer the Zone is to London Harbour the higher the letter of the alphabet.

By default the Z Zone has become the place where all those that are disaffected by society go. They have little contact with the Normal Zones. They have some technology but it is nowhere near as advanced as in the other zones.

Z Zoner

An inhabitant of the Z Zone. The Z Zoners have become tough and inventive. They are to some extent survivors. However, they also age more quickly than Normal Zoners and they die natural deaths. There is still, however, no disease. There is some natural childbirth.

The Z Zoners are a little superstitious. They have knowledge of the Babel Prophecy and have real faith in it. The new Peace Child will save them.

Other novels by *The Red Telephone*

The Prophecy

by Gill James

The Prophecy is the first part of the *Peace Child* trilogy.

Kaleem Malkendy is different – and, on Terrestra, different is no way to be.

Everything about Kaleem marks him out from the rest: the blond hair and dark skin, the humble cave where he lives and the fact that he doesn't know his father. He's used to unwelcome attention, but even so, he'd feel better if some strange old man didn't keep following him around.

Then the man introduces himself and begins to explain the Babel Prophecy – and everything in Kaleem's life changes forever.

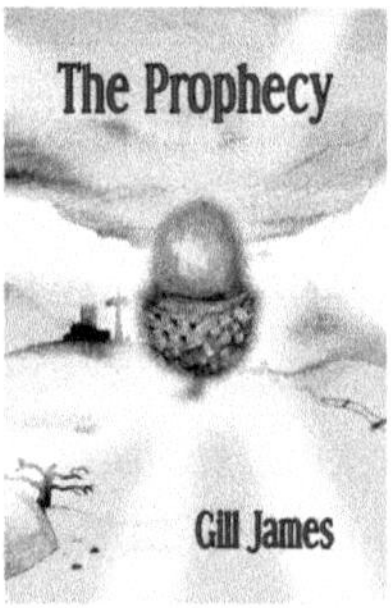

"It's thought-provoking and it's unique. I enjoyed it wholeheartedly, and will be looking forward to visiting Gill James' vision of the future again in the second Peace Child novel. Those who enjoy stories set in the future should definitely consider giving this out-of-the-ordinary tale a look." *(Amazon)*

Order from http://theredtelephone.co.uk

Paperback: ISBN 978-0-955791-08-6
eBook: ISBN 978-1-907335-12-9

The Red Telephone

Babel

by Gill James

Babel is the second part of the *Peace Child* trilogy.

Kaleem has found his father and soon finds the love of his life, Rozia Laurence, but he is still not comfortable with his role as Peace Child. He also has to face some of the less palatable truths about his home planet: it is blighted by the existence of the Z Zone, a place where poorer people live outside of society, and by switch-off, compulsory euthanasia for a healthy but aging population, including his mentor, Razjosh.

The Babel Tower still haunts him, but it begins to make sense as he uncovers more of the truth about his past and how it is connected with the problems in the Z Zone.

Kaleem knows he can and must make a difference, but at what personal cost?

Order from http://theredtelephone.co.uk

Paperback: ISBN 978-1-907335-10-5
eBook: ISBN 978-1-907335-13-6

The Red Telephone

Milton Keynes UK
Ingram Content Group UK Ltd.
UKHW020115190424
441332UK00010B/408

9 781907 335297